Room For a
Single Lady

Room For a Single Lady

CLARE BOYLAN

LITTLE, BROWN AND COMPANY

For my parents, with love

A *Little, Brown* Book

First published in Great Britain in 1997
by Little, Brown and Company

Copyright © Clare Boylan 1997

The moral right of the author has been asserted.

A CIP catalogue record for this book
is available from the British Library.

ISBN 0 316 63986 9

Typeset in Ehrhardt by
Palimpsest Book Production Limited,
Polmont, Stirlingshire
Printed and bound in Great Britain by
Clays Ltd, St Ives plc.

Little, Brown and Company (UK)
Brettenham House
Lancaster Place
London WC2E 7EN

Chapter One

~

On the day I found my mother gazing into the pantry with an awestruck expression, I thought she was having a vision. It was the year of Our Lady and we lived with the possibility of extraordinary occurrences. I crept in beside her but I saw nothing but the Bird's custard and Becker's tea, the yellow and red cocoa box, yellow tins of mustard with a snorting bull, the big bags of flour and sugar and oatmeal, the scarred enamel crock for bread, a vegetable rack with forgotten hundred-year-old vegetables sprouting pale, dainty ferns. 'What is it?' I said, and she came out of her trance to whisper, 'There's nothing for dinner.'

'We'll go to the shops,' I said.

A bleakness gathered over her, like a crust of ice. She settled into this before she spoke again. 'I have no money.' She put her hands on my shoulders and rubbed them lightly. 'Go upstairs to the bedroom. In the wardrobe you will find your father's tweed jacket. Look in the pockets and bring me whatever you find.' She turned away and put her hand over her mouth.

There was a strange, intimate feel to that dampish green cavity. It was as cold as water. I searched in every pocket and brought down what I had found, a tin of Zam-Buk for chilblains and a column torn from a newspaper, headed 'Situations Vacant'. Mother studied them in silence and then said, 'Put them back.' From that day we were poor.

~

My mother could have had any man at the drop of a hat. She often said so but we knew it anyway. Father seemed aware that a freak wind had blown the hat in his direction. He could not take his eye off her in case another gust bore it off at a different angle.

Our father was like a shadow on the wall. Sometimes he was a looming shadow that made us walk on tiptoe. Sometimes he seemed like a ghost, hungry for the living. Early on, we sisters tried to catch his attention, but he knew what we could not understand, that we were his rivals, and he always hurried away, impatient to get back to Mother, to break the magic circle that she made with her girls.

We underestimate our years spent in the company of our mothers. We have stolen a woman in her prime and she has someone on whom to reinvent her history. Tunes are printed on the brain and we hum them all our lives. Patterns of speech and prejudices become tendrils that wind in and out of our character, strengthening and obscuring. We love and are loved, a careless tossing back and forth of a ball that we think can never be lost. We live at the very centre of the universe, held up to the sun, shining, beautiful, all-important. And we get to eavesdrop.

'All the same,' Mother said to a woman in the street, 'you should not let yourself go.'

'Why not?' The woman was rosy and bedraggled. She had a tribe of children, all beautiful, but with green slime running from their noses. I kept out of their way because from time to time they hit out at one another with their fists.

Mother, glossy in a silver-grey suit and red high heels, said, 'Think about your husband.'

The woman laughed a great big open-mouthed smile. Thinking about her husband must have been a happy thing. 'Ah, sure he thinks I'm Scheherazade in a knickers and vest.'

I was three when Mother bought a new handbag. I sat beside her at the dressing table and watched her unwrapping it. First she removed a crunchy, whispery wad of tissue. From secret compartments she fished out little tissue-wrapped gifts – a bevelled mirror in a felt case, a small black comb, a leather purse which snapped shut on overlapping knobs of gilt. She said that buying a new handbag was like making a fresh start in life, so everything that went into it had to be new. There was a glistening new lipstick, a new powder compact, a starched hankie with a basket of flowers embroidered on the corner.

What would become of the old one? The other handbag, which yesterday had been plump and important, now had the sideways, sleeping look of a dead cat on the road. 'Would you like it?' She tossed it over indifferently.

I carried the bag everywhere. I hugged it in bed and dragged it to the shops. Bit by bit I added my own personality. One day at Mass I watched the priest arrange his treasures on the altar. Mother was lost in prayer so I slipped into the aisle and spread out the contents of the bag: a grocery list, some letters (which I could not read), a stub of pencil, a powder compact with a balding centre and the faint smell of roses and lemons and of something decomposing, a comb with two teeth missing, a small brown paper bag containing two Scots Clan toffees. There was even a purse with pennies in it, and a miraculous medal. And then my new acquisitions – a pair of Mother's drawers in a silky pink material, which had been consigned to the polishing press and were smeared with lavender polish; an old

3

grey pillowcase which I sucked on at night for comfort, a hairnet. No one took any notice until the priest held up the host and I held up the powder compact. At once everyone was staring. Mother rushed out of her seat to retrieve me. People looked at her strangely as she gathered up what appeared to be the contents of her handbag.

When Bridie and Kitty went to school I stayed behind with Mother. Until I was four she took me with her when she went for a nap and I lay beneath a lunging green quilt in a sort of suffocated dream, but after that she left me on the front step with a picture book. It was in one of these interludes of timeless boredom that I made my first contact with the outside world. There was a new boy in the neighbourhood. His parents kept having to move house because he was something called a delinquent. He was thirteen, lanky and pale with a slice of dark hair that fell over one eye. He didn't say anything when he walked in the gate. He just put out a hand and I put out mine.

'Give us a song,' Mother coaxed when a neighbour came in to drink tea. I asked them to face the wall and sang the song my friend had taught me. Slowly the women turned around. 'What is that? What is she saying?' The visitor's teacup developed a curious tilt, although she kept smiling, but Mother seemed completely transfixed, not with the urging pride she normally had, but as if someone had come up behind her and put a gun to her head. She laid her hands on me slowly as if to heal me, gripped me very firmly and ran out of the room with me. 'Where did you learn that?'

'From my friend,' I wailed.

'Who is this friend?' She seemed demented. 'Don't ever have anything to do with strangers,' she said when I told her.

The boy's family moved again. I waited on the step until I could no longer remember why I was waiting. One day I was going to the toilet and I saw a crack of light coming from the maid's room. Green light came in from the trees and field outside and green darkness came up from the lino. The room always had an air of expectancy. I went in, closed the door behind me and sang the song he had taught me. But I couldn't remember the words. I could only recall the tune.

A thin woman with thin red hair in a bun came to whisper with my mother. Mother was not sociable, for she had no small talk, but people in trouble sought her out because you could say anything and she would just sit and smoke her cigarettes. The woman had brought her son. Mother put us at the kitchen table with crayons and paper, but no one introduced us. 'Who are you?' I asked. 'I am your prince,' he said, 'and you are my princess.' The same lavish sense of satisfaction I had known with The Delinquent, and which I had forgotten, lapped around me. He drew a prince and a princess on a piece of paper. Every day we sat together while his mother delivered the instalments of her crisis. I can still remember the thick aura of pleasure that surrounded us. We owned a small cloud of tingling air. In due course the woman's crisis ended and we only saw her now and again. The boy was older than me and had found some other life, school or other boys. I don't think I minded. Like a cake it had been there and now it was eaten.

Our house was a women's house. The visiting men were an entertainment and an education. As a mother cat hunts mice to show her kittens how to hunt, Mother wanted to demonstrate to us the skills necessary for enslaving men. I only ever remember one other boy coming into the house. His father had died and he was left to play with me while his mother went to work. Because there were no boys in the family, Father had made us girls leather holsters and bought us toy guns to go with them. We were the only girls on the street with guns and we loved them. When Mother gave one to the orphaned boy, he seemed not to have any idea what it was. I loaded it up with caps and fired it and he burst into tears.

5

'What would you like?' Mother asked him.

'A sheet,' he said.

Every morning he dressed up very carefully in the sheet, covering his head and as much of his clothing as possible. For the rest of the day he played alone with a doll's tea set made of tin and a little green wooden dresser Father had made to go with it. I sat for hours on the red-tiled floor, staring at him in fascination. 'What are you?' I asked him. 'Are you a boy?' There was a brief pause in the faint clanking of crockery. 'I am a nun.'

Chapter Two

∽

The year our money ran out, the whole country was like a carnival. Marian Year, which was to whip up a frenzy of fervour for The Blessed Virgin, clashed with a great national festival called An Tostal. Out of doors people rehearsed for the country's biggest ever May procession, which would have 15,000 people, several bands, fifty flower girls and a decorated statue of the Mother of God borne by forty members of the Legion of Mary. Across the rooftops came the drone of hymns and prayers mangled through a megaphone, while public address systems belted out melodeon music for Irish jigs. Flags and floral garlands embellished lamp standards and public buildings.

It was actually the first anniversary of An Tostal, which had been launched with great fanfare the year before to welcome returned emigrants. The focal point was the Bowl of Light, a triumphal flame which was to burn forever on O'Connell Bridge, but after several days a drunk pitched it into the Liffey, and the monumental plinth which remained was christened The Tomb of the Unknown Gurrier. That might have been the end of the matter, but 1954 was an election year and politicians needed to distract from the dazzle of the Queen of Heaven, so the festival was reinstated with a nine foot

·candle, which was to glimmer outside the Mansion House for three months.

In fact all the emigrants seemed to be going the other way, and life was hard for those who stayed behind. In a Dublin court three children charged with stealing Oxo and Bisto wept as their mother begged for them to be taken into care, for she could not support them. A widowed bus driver, also in tears, told the judge that his children, who had been placed in an industrial school in Kilternan, were starving and covered in lice and boils and would be dead within a month. Small paragraphs daily reported deaths by gassing. Our father read out these items at mealtimes. Perhaps it was to let us feel the climate of misfortune. He never said anything about our money running out. People like us did not talk about money. Even when Mother finally confessed that she had nothing with which to buy the dinner, I kept quiet, although my head swarmed with questions. I just crawled under the shelves of the larder into a recessed space where things were always rolling away and came out with a clutch of old potatoes, wizened and sprouting spindly white legs. Mother found a few eggs and milk and a heel of cheese. These were assembled into a recipe called Swiss Eggs. With the potatoes fried into chips it was eaten by the family without comment and my mother smiled across the table as if the crisis was past.

But the next day, there it was again. Bridie and Kitty went to school but Mother kept me back. We held the guilty secret between us now. 'I have to go,' I told her. 'I have been picked as a flower girl for the May procession.' She ignored this, for she did not like to think of me growing up and having an outside life. 'God will understand. Today we will pray and we will polish the hall.' She put on a pair of old slacks and got out the rags and a tin of Lavendo. She even rolled back the runner of red carpet to shine the tawny lino. 'Look at that,' she said. Bedded into a silt of old polish was a shilling. Its dull silver glinted in the waxy pink like a trout under water. Mother felt sure it was a miracle. 'If you trust in God He will never desert you,' she proclaimed with certainty.

The day after, we searched the back of the sofa and under beds for stray pennies. I investigated the remaining packs in the pantry and came out with some rice, an old onion, tomato ketchup and paprika. I had to go to school then, for this was the day on which we were to rehearse for the procession. The flower girls wore white dresses and scattered petals from little baskets, and everyone knew they were the nuns' chosen pets. Other mothers would be up all night, stitching gowns, ironing ribbons, whitening sandals, baking hair into ringlets, but Mother took no notice of anything that happened outside the home.

At this point, being a flower girl was the most important thing in my life. Mother used to tell me she called me Rose because I looked like a rose, and there were photographs to prove it. But I knew I wasn't really a Rose any more. People said I looked intelligent and whispered at me not to smile for the camera. My skin had turned sallow and my hair was shading down to string. I had grown too tall and my lanky size emphasised Mother's smallness and delicacy. I was a thin girl with mousy plaits and my front teeth were crooked, but I guessed from films and advertisements that glamour came from the outside and had only to be put on. I looked hopefully in the wardrobe but there was nothing except my old Communion frock. I had grown a lot in the last year, so I put a slip under it with the lace coming down underneath. It was too tight under the arms. I covered it with a long pullover belonging to Bridie.

Sister Brigid lined up her four pet girls and Mother Archangel came to inspect them. She walked around us several times, watching me balefully out of the side of her little grey eye, and then she roosted

9

beside Sister Brigid and leaned her head on one side. 'Not her! She's a disgrace.'

'Mexican rice,' Mother said defiantly as she spooned out the slimy pink mess on to our plates. My father ate it all up with a look of misery, but Bridie and Kitty dragged their forks through the rice so that the strands of onion clung like maggots. 'There's nothing in it!' they said. Mother began to cry. 'Eat it!' Father said furiously, and at once the two older girls began to weep as well. I had saved up my shame, but now I too burst into tears and blurted out what the Reverend Mother had said. Everyone looked shocked. I expected sympathy but Mother flew into a rage. 'Why must you make a disgrace of me? There are plenty of clothes if you would take the trouble to put them on. I spend half my life washing and ironing.'

I went upstairs to try and find something to wear that would not disgrace my mother, but each thing I tried on looked worse than the last. From the window I watched my sisters leave for school. A creak and a sigh from the next room said that my mother had gone to bed. She went to bed a lot now. She wore a hairnet and sometimes did not bother with make-up. I hadn't noticed until now, but our beautiful mother was no longer glamorous. The lack of money, even the withdrawal of my role in the May procession, suddenly seemed less alarming than the loss of the only person we knew who could pass on the secrets of female allure.

The street was thickly wrapped in silence. The red-brick houses were like ships sunk to the bottom of the sea and forgotten there. Although we had lived in the same street all our lives, we knew nothing of the real lives of people inside those houses. I stayed where I was, reading an old copy of the *Evening Mail*. At the bottom of the letters page was a column called 'About Dogs', with a small box giving details of dogs lost and found. The people who wrote in did not only describe their colour and breed, but little aspects of their personality, how they were loyal or hungry or fretting. When I read it it always made me cry. There were birds lost too. People who lived in single rooms kept budgerigars. Two thousand escaped every year from their cages and flew out of open windows. Most starved to death, although a few were found, but they were in the 'Lost and Found' column. No one ever mentioned cats.

Chapter Three

~

We woke to the sound of stampeding hooves and crashing glass, as Max the milk horse thundered down the street, hurrying to those houses where he got a treat. As our supplies ran out, Father forbade us to feed the horse, so we listened guiltily until the swaying crates and clashing bottles passed on. Then one day he would not leave, so we sneaked out with bread and sugar and found our cheerful Milkie on the step in tears. 'The dairy's going electric,' he blurted out. 'They want to give me a van.'

It took a few seconds for the significance of this to sink in. 'What about Max?'

He heaved a great sigh and his shoulders shook. 'Max is for the knacker's yard.'

We ran out to the horse. Max accepted the delicacy and gazed ahead with a dreamer's eye on the next handout, and Mother brought Milkie in for tea.

'That horse and I have been together for fourteen years,' he said. 'I've handed in my notice. I won't hang around for this so-called progress.'

'Nor will we,' Mother said indignantly, 'for we are emigrating to New Zealand.'

Clare Boylan

We were still stunned by the news about Max. Mother noticed our new astonishment, so she repeated her announcement very calmly, as if it was a perfectly normal thing. 'We are going to New Zealand. For a fresh start.'

What became of our money? It must have gone somewhere. No one ever said. For a long time we had been better dressed than other people and owned the only car on the street, and then we grew shabby like everyone else.

But we weren't like everyone else, because we had Father. It was a part of his nature that as soon as he got over a disappointment, he began to see it as an opportunity. The disaster that had made us poor had turned into a stroke of fortune that would lead us to a new land with decent prospects. Nothing could hold us back except the house and as soon as it was sold we would be transported to this sunlit place where we would have a damn fine future. At school we became celebrities. Children whose parents' died or who were to emigrate were always fussed over by the nuns, and we were given inscribed holy pictures to take with us to our new life. When a man came and hammered a 'For Sale' sign into our neat front lawn, a moment of terror was replaced by jubilant relief, as if he had plunged a stake through the heart of a vampire.

We lived between the mountains and the city in a terrace that faced another terrace. Around the corner were more red-brick houses and the next corner proved that the whole world was made of red brick. Terrace ran into terrace, still and silent as rusting trains. Half a mile away a lively village suddenly appeared, with shops, a cinema, a chipper, a school, a church, a synagogue. The fronts of our houses were modestly decorative, with pointed brick, mosaic porches and bay windows. The backs showed grey concrete, snaking waste pipes and string clotheslines where limp underwear dripped. There were occasional signs of life in the street, a little dog that barked and

14

barked, a cherry tree billowing over black railings. Lace curtains masked the eye of neighbour watching neighbour. Because of the neighbours we were never allowed to do anything. We could not stand on our heads or play in the street or fight with each other. When Bridie was small she was chased by a dog. 'What was it like?' Mother asked, and Bridie, lost for comparison, exclaimed with dread, 'It had a face like a neighbour!' Most of our neighbours were bachelors and spinsters. They had lived in the houses all their lives and no one had found their way through the maze of terraces to rescue them.

We got a fright when we looked at a map and found out how far away New Zealand was. What was it like? As we drove to an expensive shop in the city to buy clothes for our new life we suddenly grew anxious and began to pester father with questions.

'Hush!' Father cautioned. 'We are approaching traffic lights.' He was wary of this new invention. But Mother had a brochure which she produced as calmly as if it was for a holiday by the sea. There were round thatched houses and barrier reefs, exotic birds and modern business developments. If it wasn't for the traffic lights we would have pointed out that the people in the pictures wore little or no clothing, but Father wanted us to make a good impression in our new life. He had borrowed money to take us to the Silk Mills in Dorset Street. I got a yellow dress in American poplin. We were brought to Clarks for gleaming new sandals. Disappointingly, Father whipped us off the machine where the saleswoman placed us to test the fit of the shoes, for he did not trust anything that showed up the green skeleton of your feet. Mother shopped as if she was going on a cruise – a boldly striped jersey top, smart linen slacks and a cream beret, little gold slippers, a silk dress with a pattern of roses.

Father said that there would be no shortage of takers for our house, as it was a good address. He was partly right, for plenty of people showed an interest. The shortage was of money. When the first purchaser failed to come up with the price of the house, it was offered for a lower sum. Again it was snapped up but no payment appeared.

'There is a shop for sale in the village,' Mother said. 'We could set up our own business and live overhead.'

'People like us do not go into trade,' he stated with finality.

He told his parents that we had nothing to eat. Granny Rafferty sent home the little grey skeleton of a chicken. 'The children can pick on it and the bones will make a good soup,' she promised.

Bridie knocked on the house of our next-door neighbours, the Misses Cornelia, and said we were hungry. Miss Queenie asked us in and gave us glasses of very sour home-made lemonade and a plate of plain biscuits called 'Nice' with grains of sugar on the surface. When she invited us to have a 'Nees' biscuit, we thought this was a polite, Protestant pronunciation of 'nice'. Miss Jude entered with a mottled silver dish of pancakes. They were thick and burnt and they were cold. There was nothing to put on them but lumpy sugar which would not come out of its glass shaker. Hungry as we were, none of us could eat more than one of them. The old ladies watched us guiltily as they gobbled their way through the big pile of pancakes. Something struck me about the manner in which they ate, but it wasn't until I was lying hungry in bed that night that I realised what it was. They were as poor and hungry as we were.

'Go and talk to George Bates,' Mother pleaded. 'George will find you something.'

George and Alma Bates were the richest people we knew. They owned an advertising agency and had no children of their own, so they always brought free samples from clients when they came to visit. George was in love with Mother and we girls loved Alma, who was kind and smart, but Father had mixed feelings. 'You cannot ask me to go cap in hand to the sort of people who take afternoon tea in the Gresham,' he complained bitterly.

But he did go and George nodded in gloomy sympathy as we girls explored a big round tin of English sweets called Quality Street. 'Bit of promotional work – how does that sound?'

Father conceded that it sounded fine, until he discovered that the work of illustrating publicity leaflets was being offered to Mother. 'We will all be in the gutter before any wife of mine goes out to work,' he promised.

A parcel was sent by rich cousins, dresses with smocking, pleated skirts, woollen twin sets, a green coat with velvet buttons and a hood lined with velvet. Mother knelt to button me into this coat. 'You look like a little woodland fairy,' she said, and then, clutching the lapels as if she felt faint, she said, 'Oh, I hate these clothes. They were bought for another little girl.'

~

When food ran out again, Mother went to bed. It was what she always did when she could not face life. Father pawned his camera and declared that it was the last straw, but it was not. The last straw was when Dusty had kittens. Every so often our black cat would dump a mousy brood on some haphazard perch like a chair or a shelf, from which they plopped off on to the floor. At once she deserted them, scurrying off with her sagging nipples while they screwed up their blind eyes and showed fishlike teeth in irritation, but she always galloped back and fell exhausted into her bed in a cardboard box in time to feed them. For a while we played with them and then they disappeared. We never thought about it. This time the sight of so many mouths to feed was too much for Father. He gathered up the kittens and crammed them into a wooden box. While they

17

were adjusting to this new environment on wobbling, worried legs, he seized the lid, slammed it down and held it with his knee, as if the box contained a panther. From inside came little baffled, muffled, irksome squeaks and small squiffly sounds as he commenced to nail down the lid. At first Dusty squirmed around our legs, wailing, and then she sat on the blue dresser, with her ears slightly flattened and her face like a wise old woman, hunched with knowledge. 'Mother!' Bridie cried. 'Mother!' She thundered upstairs to the bedroom. She came down slowly, reluctantly. 'Mother is resting,' she said, although it seemed unlikely that anyone could rest with such a noise going on. We stood around, quite silent, with jumping hearts, convinced that the terrifying trick would have some reassuring ending. At one point he lowered the hammer very gently and looked around and said, 'You girls know nothing of life. I pray God it will always be so.' He raised the weapon again and struck the box such a blow that the wood began to splinter. Then he put the box full of tiny, rising wails beneath his arm and went off in the car and came back an hour later without it.

'A small dog is being cared for at present. It followed boys. It is a type with hair falling down over its eyes. It seems to be fretting.'

Chapter Four

Our milk now came in a three-wheeled electric float which sighed slowly down the road. The new milkman had a sad face and oily black hair. We called him Norman Wisdom, but we hardly ever saw him because Max had been our alarm clock. We were used to waking to the thunder of hooves. Now we slept in and were late for school.

'He has gone!' Mother shook us gently awake as the milk van wistfully exhaled down the road.

'Max!' I sat up, imagining there might have been a notice of his death in the paper.

'No, your father.'

'He left without us!' Bridie accused. She was thinking of New Zealand.

'Your father has taken the boat to England to look for work.'

We struggled into our clothes, but Mother detained us. 'There is no need to go to school. Let's make a big pot of tea and go back to bed.'

'Why didn't he say goodbye?' we asked.

'He would not have liked you to see him cry.'

We were relieved not to have to go to school. As the plan of emigration faded, our fame subsided and we had sunk into a sort of quiet disgrace, as if we had been caught cheating. Mother turned the clocks to the wall. The ordinary routine of housework was abandoned and she marshalled us for grand tasks – scrubbing the kitchen tiles and polishing them with Cardinal Red, black-leading the stove. After a few days she got bored with cleaning. 'Leave the rest of the little insects in their corners,' she instructed. 'When Padre Pio was building his church he ordered the workers not to harm a single living creature, no matter how small.' She disappeared into the drawing room to paint a picture.

'What are we to do?' Without the normal routine of meals, the days seemed the wrong shape for school.

'You girls come from a long line of very gifted people, artists and musicians,' Mother instructed. 'You will be creative.'

Bridie went off and played the piano. She had not played before, but after a day or two the house was full of her stirring renditions of ragtime jazz. The music seemed not to have been learnt, but stored up inside her. Kitty and I lay on the floor and made cramped drawings in our jotters. After five minutes we used the results to disturb Mother.

A letter arrived from Father with a pound inside. Mother put it in her bag and led us out to the hardware shop.

'Black emulsion?' the assistant queried.

'Why do men always think that women are incapable of knowing their own minds?' she said.

We watched in admiration mixed with trepidation as she dipped her brush into the black paint and swept an arc of pitch across Father's sedate colour arrangement of cream and green on the kitchen wall. 'Me! Let me!' Bridie took the brush, and standing on tiptoe, and with great concentration, sketched a huge black cat, leaving holes for his eyes, so that the cream shone through.

'Me! Me!' Now Kitty and I jumped up and down. Mother stood

back and breathed in our vandalism and talent. She did not interfere until the wall was covered in scribbles, and then she took the brush and painted on very calmly in measured strokes, standing on a chair for the high bits, until the entire surface was smoothly black. The sun was setting as we sat to eat. Our great bout of spring-cleaning had run out before we reached the windows. Creatures still wove and scuttled safely in corners and the light of heaven was poured softly through a gauze of dust. It leaked in amber patches on to the big black wall. We could not take our eyes off the wall, which was slowly sucking in its patches of wet. These seemed to shimmer and trickle like dark patches of blood before vanishing into the dull surface. As the paint dried, the light died. We had painted out the light, and by our very act of defiance, we had painted out our father. Guilty and worn out, we went to bed.

In the morning, Mother was up early, sketching a huge sun on the wall. 'Women have such little lives,' she slapped her hands together to disperse the chalky dust, 'expected to do the small, unrewarding chores that must be done again tomorrow, to turn their talents to niggling skills like embroidery. No wonder there are so few great women artists. You girls are to express yourselves without restraint. We will have our own school here in the kitchen.'

'What will we learn?' Bridie took a potato cake from the pan and ate it from a fork.

'You will learn to be unconfined.'

Every day we drew huge houses and girls and dogs and some- times whole towns. At night we slept in Mother's bed and in the morning she told us stories. All of her stories concerned beautiful girls who had been locked away, or married against their will, and how they managed to escape. As we snuggled under the green quilt, like a single piece of requited flesh, we did not know that a part of us had flown away. The stories implanted in us a

21

longing for a world outside and for some magic that would take us there.

In our house the post was usually bad news and it was a surprise when Mother came into the kitchen in great excitement, waving an envelope. 'A cheque,' she said.

'From Father?'

'No. I sold some illustrations to a magazine. Let's go and celebrate. We could go and see Alicia Markova dance at the Theatre Royal. Would you like that?'

'I'd like to go to school,' Bridie said treacherously.

'School?' Mother was hurt and amazed.

'You said we would learn to be unconfined. We *are* confined,' she protested. 'You want to keep us with you and shut out the rest of the world.' Kitty and I ignored her and went on scratching at the wall with our chalks, but I knew by the way Kitty ignored her that she would follow Bridie.

'You stay with me,' Mother begged as I watched the older girls go off without me.

'Can I have a dog?' I bargained, but Mother said that Father would not like it and offered instead to open up the maid's room for me to play in.

To relieve the boredom I made sandwiches of bread and golden syrup, broke them up and threw them on the sloping roof outside the maid's room window. Flocks of gulls swooped down. They watched me sideways out of doleful yellow eyes and their beaks worked back and forth in silent perplexity as the syrup glued them together. A fat tabby chased them off and rolled about, eyed by a solitary tom. He stalked towards her and slowly began stroking her with a paw. I was completely mesmerised but I felt I should not be watching. There was a tension between the cats but a tenderness too. The tabby rolled on her back and made little mews. After a long time she got on to her feet and crouched and the tom crept up behind her. 'Dirty cats! Dirty cats!' came a frenzied shriek from Miss Marmion next door, who had also been watching.

We were in bed one morning when we heard the front door opening all by itself and then someone came in. We froze, thinking it must be a burglar, but it was Father. Mother's jaw dropped in surprise and he burst into tears. He looked very tired and shabby. He had been gone a month. 'Could you get no work?' she asked in fright.

'Yes, there was work,' he said. 'But I could not exist without you.'

The 'For Sale' sign came down from the house. As if the house really was a vampire, Mother soon grew pale and weary again and took to bed. Father padded around guiltily, bringing her cups of tea. He occupied himself in painting the kitchen wall back to its original colour and pottered in the maid's room. For a time he was subdued and then he began to whistle. 'I've had a thought,' he mentioned mildly. He showed Mother a notice he had drafted in his beautiful copperplate handwriting: 'Room for a single lady. Twelve shillings per week. (Only 3d fare to the Pillar.)'

'What has this room to do with us?' Mother queried.

'We have a perfectly good room which is not used. Twelve shillings would go a long way towards paying the grocery bills.'

'Which room?' Mother wondered uneasily. She did not mention the money she had earned in his absence.

A rustling sort of silence followed when he said it was to be the maid's room, for the room was too small for any real person to live in, and it had bars on the window, and it belonged to Josephine.

'People we have never met in our lives before. We could be harbouring criminals. What about the children?' Mother looked to us for support, but we began to be excited at the thought of the maid's room coming to life again, with an interesting person in it.

'A lady,' father coaxed. 'Some refined person. These are hard times. Some very nice women have to make their way in the world.'

'I do not like the thought of strangers under my roof.' Mother was still reluctant but Father's tone had changed. 'We could go to the pictures on our own. There would be someone to keep an eye on the girls. It will be like the golden era before the children were born.'

Chapter Five

~

'I once moved out of your father's bedroom for a whole week.' From the time I was born my mother talked to me as if I was another woman. She had a slightly racy and bitter air when talking about men, and from an early age I could taste this other side of life, sharp and exciting, like a stolen apple. 'We had a tiff, so I took you and went off to the maid's room. That soon brought him to his senses.'

Even at two or three I could imagine the sense of shock. Mothers and fathers belonged together like knives and forks. But it wasn't the row that impressed me. It was the sense of adventure. Mother talked of this episode as if she had sailed over Niagara in a barrel. And the maid's room! That belonged to Josephine. The vague, uneasy excitement that brewed up whenever Josephine was mentioned was now only an aftershock, like a dog twitching in its dreams. 'What happened to Josephine?' I pestered my sisters. Josephine had taken care of Bridie and Kitty when they were small. She sang to them and bathed them in the kitchen sink.

'*You* were born.'

As far back as I can recall everyone in the house seemed to start each sentence with 'Remember . . . ?' 'Remember the rose garden?'

When Bridie was a baby she fell into the roses and crawled into the kitchen covered in blood. It had been a shock to Father to have a girl. In fact Bridie was as good as any boy, strong and handsome, with radiant blue eyes and cinnamon curls. In spite of himself, Father adored her. The pride he had saved up for his son became a vengeful, protective ardour for Bridie. A son was an achievement but girls were like money, they had to be saved. When the roses hurt her he advanced with his shears and hacked away until there was nothing but bare earth. He filled in the borders with the white limestone chips used to keep weeds away from neglected graves.

Kitty came along and Father, peering into the parcel of his family life, was disappointed to find that there were no boys. Kitty was frail and fey, with plaits thin and pale as woven stalks of corn. If Bridie wanted to be a boy, Kitty wanted to be an Amazon. She practised body-building exercises and attempted judo. She saw herself as an avenger of the weak. By the time she started school she was a champion of justice and stony-faced opponent of brutal teachers, but at two she was tiny and unworldly and had a spirit companion in the garden. 'Remember the Little Man?' It was the Little Man I missed the most, although I never met him. No one did. Kitty would come in from the grave chippings in the garden with one fist tightly closed. 'What have you there?' Mother would prise open her fist and find a tiny car, a marshmallow fish. 'Where did you get that?' 'The Little Man gave it to me,' she always said. Mother, fiercely sheltering, peered out over the neighbouring walls, ran into the back lane. He gave her presents, tiny metal cows or sweets, sometimes wicked things, a needle or scissors. My mother could not bear it and questioned the neighbours, gentle single ladies on either side. No one could have entered from the lane, for the gate was locked at all times and the wall was fanged with lumps of glass.

It seemed to me that the other family members had arrived early and got the best seats. When they said the rosary, I sat in a corner and sucked mud from the soles of my pink boots. Before I understood the words I felt as if we were on a little raft sailing on an endless sea with no land in sight. Glorious mysteries. Joyful mysteries. Sorrowful mysteries. But there were no new mysteries.

For a time, Gram Lambert had lived in the maid's room, with her black bag which she would not let out of her sight. 'What's in there?' Bridie and Kitty said when they saw her gobbling from the bag. 'Skins,' she said. 'Potato skins.' From then on they would follow her everywhere, begging mournfully, 'Skins, Mama Lambert.' After she wet the bed she was sent away to live with Auntie Brenda.

There was even a dog once, but she died before I got there. Mavis didn't like male dogs but they liked her so much that one sprang over the six-foot garden wall. Father filled a sack with bottles and attacked the contents with a hammer. He iced the wall with wet cement and then selected the most juicily jagged morsels of glass from his sack. Mother and the girls watched from behind the apple tree. Mother, already pregnant with me, said she wondered peacefully if he was mad and might some day take the hammer to herself. When I was born, Father reacted like a dog to the family cat. Mother, with no diplomacy at all, fell in love with me the day I was born and everyone was scandalised by the lip-smacking that went on under their noses. She forgot about Kitty. 'What have you got there?' she said months later, seeing Kitty with white face and clenched fist. 'Did the Little Man give it to you?'

'What little man?' Kitty said coldly. When Mother went to get my bottle, Kitty leaned over the pram and opened her fist, emptying white limestone chips into my open mouth.

My sisters made it their business to dispose of me. Tea leaves, buttons, fruit stones were forced down my throat, knitting needles

were poked at me. I beamed worshipfully at the big girls and shat
bric-à-brac.

~

One day on the street, I discovered the mystery of Josephine. Mother
and a neighbour were talking about a terrible thing: a girl gone on
the boat to England to have a baby.

'That happened to our Josephine,' Mother whispered. 'And I have
been left without a girl ever since.'

'Wouldn't you wonder at unmarried women?' Their voices dropped and my hearing sharpened. 'It's not a thing you would do
for fun.'

'Some of these country girls are built like canals. They could take
a barge.'

Chapter Six

~

As the last of our food ran out, our first lodger appeared. It was a fine April and the air sat like Turkish delight over our solid houses. There was a vague powdery dustiness where midges twanged and the damp air was sucked up into cloud. The dark brick was fired with a desert glow as hymns to Our Lady rose above the rooftops. Jealously, the politicians struck back with the nation's biggest ever pageant of St Patrick, with a cast of 1,700 and a massed choir of four hundred voices. In the distance, in some less respectable suburb than ours, an ice-cream van played 'Greensleeves' over and over. The notes plopped like water over stones and there was the feeling that in another part of that pink light people were out of doors, dancing. We weren't allowed to go anywhere. Our house was a harem but the stillness was now charged with waiting. We had lured some part of the outside world to ourselves.

Our tenant was Selena Taylor. Father had picked her for her name, which sounded smart but stern. He loved Mother but his ideal woman was a more severe sort of beauty. For years he had worshipped Ingrid Bergman from afar, until she cheapened herself with a married man and gave birth to twin girls. It would be another, untouched Miss Bergman who would come under our roof.

We girls kept watch on the landing, which got a faint, volcanic glow from the pebbled amber glass in the hall door. *The Black Museum* drifted up from the wireless so that the first shrill of the doorbell struck us like the thrust of a dagger. Father left off playing Chopin on the piano and went to answer the door to the woman who was to change our lives, whose train we would step on to pick up stardust. There was a lady in a felt pillbox and barathea coat in princess line with a Peter Pan collar. On her arm was an imitation ostrich handbag.

'Miss Taylor!' he greeted courteously, but she gave a little rueful smile and said she feared not, but hoped she could count on his vote for Fine Gael. He took her leaflet and crept back to the piano. Then, after a pause, there was a little hesitant, dribbling ring, and this time we clattered down the stairs.

'Lovely yevening,' Miss Taylor said. She laughed anxiously. Her arms in a donkey-brown suit looked like bent metal pipes.

'Yevening,' I explored, under my breath.

'Meanie,' she laughed.

'Miss Selena Taylor?' Father had emerged once more from the drawing room. He looked over the cheap suit, her worn, timid face and curly hair pressed like limp Persian lamb close to her face. Cardboard showed through the frayed edges of her suitcase.

She laughed apologetically when he told her to come in. We wanted to know the weight of her case and hoped to see the contents later, so we offered to carry it, but she said 'No' in a shocked but timid way which suggested that she considered us children to be her social superiors. She put down her case and began to rummage in a big brown bag like a nun's carry-all. She pulled out a note and a fistful of change. 'I'll pay in advance,' she tried, to give herself some advantage, but Father felt that she was putting one over on him, securing the room before he had offered it. 'In an envelope on the hall table.' He pointed stiffly.

'An envyelope,' she echoed forlornly, and put the money back in her bag. Mother didn't even appear from the kitchen. She had been waiting for some fanfare that hadn't come. Father showed Miss Taylor the room, which had been livened up with haphazard curtains in a pattern of leaves, green and grey on black. A cupboard was set in a corner for utensils and on top of this was a tiny gas ring cooker. Into the fireplace was fitted a hissing gas fire. Through the bars on the window you could see the tops of apple trees and a green field, other people's lines of washing and rooftops thistled with tom cats. Father's voice had an oddly hectoring tone as he told her when she could use the bathroom and the change required for the gas meter. 'Thank you,' she said. 'Thank you.'

'Should I take her a cup of tea?' Mother wondered when he came downstairs. 'I was going to ask her down.'

'There is no need to trouble yourself,' he said. Clearly he felt deceived. He had forgotten that it was our tenant's rent money that was going to redeem us and had come to believe that it was her presence that would uplift us. Miss Taylor must have heard him, for she stood a long time with the door open and then closed it softly. We waited on the landing. We wanted to sniff the bathroom after her visit, to smell her soap or bath cubes, or, most rewarding of all, to see her corset pegged on to the little line that had been hung over the bath for her convenience. Sooner or later she must come out to fill the kettle. At night, a devil lived on the landing. It occupied a thick sphere about three feet in diameter, and when you entered it, you could not breathe. If a drunk old man spat on the ground and an insect was trapped in it, it might feel like that. We thought that in the day the devil lived in the bureau, a large wardrobe which Father kept on the landing and where he kept private papers. We waited

31

until it grew dark and we felt the devil's breath. No seam of light leaked out beneath her door to save us. I imagined her inspecting the yellow teacups and pulling open the wardrobe with its slightly battered hangers. She might try the bed and look out of the window through the bars, watching the green leaves of the apple tree turn black and silver. She would pull the curtains then, and light the gas fire, pull up a chair and mottle her knees. But our ears were attuned to sounds and we would have known if any of this had taken place. She seemed too large for the silence, like a ship inside a bottle, and at last it was broken with a burning cry: 'Oh, Mammy!'

We thundered down the stairs, heedless that she might hear, and into the dimly lit paradise of the kitchen. Mother poured tea but before we were allowed to drink it Father warned us gravely: 'Girls, if you wish to make an impression on the world, never go without a hat. A woman without a hat is not a lady.'

~

Within a month we had almost forgotten about Miss Taylor. All we saw of her was the brown envelope which she placed on the hall table every Friday. The twelve shillings rent did not go very far with eggs at two shillings a dozen, and rashers three and fourpence a pound, but it renewed Father's self-esteem, and he resolved to get his camera back from the pawn and start a photographic service for communions, weddings and fixtures.

With my ninth birthday came a warning from Father that there would be no more birthday parties. Secretly, I was relieved. I didn't like having to share my birthday cake with strange children. Then came the exciting news that I could have a solo treat of my own choosing, so long as it did not cost more than two and sixpence. 'Afternoon tea in the Gresham Hotel,' I decided at once.

'We must wear a hat,' I told Mother. Mother hated hats but she produced from the top of her wardrobe a strange, shiny nest made from black feathers which swept down over her forehead. I was allowed to borrow the solemn Panama hat that had been bought for Kitty's confirmation.

The gold-framed doors were swept aside by a uniformed porter and we sat in soft armchairs at a circular table covered in snowy linen. Our food was brought on tiered plates which the waitress carried with a kind of swing: the tiny crustless sandwiches with different fillings, scones the size of fruit drops and silver spoons for dotting them with jam and whipped cream, complicated little doll-sized cakes, pastry boats filled with fluted cream, fairy cakes with winged tips nesting in jam, eclairs, cakes that were topped with icing or rolled in nuts. Ladies plump and soft as goosedown smiled at me indulgently, and a wattled pianist made astonishing ripples on a huge, gleaming piano like a cruise ship. My parents often warned me not to stare at other people, but how could one not stare when a hole appeared in the dull landscape of one's world and a foreign country showed through.

The weather turned wet and the flags of An Tostal sagged and dripped. Then summer came, and with it a summons from old Aunt Midge, who was really Father's aunt. She instructed us to bring buckets and basins. We assumed she needed the house cleaned and dressed in our oldest clothes. When we arrived she complained to Mother, 'Your children look like tinkers.' None of the women on Father's side of the family liked Mother. They were plain women and believed that pretty women were no good. Then she broke the joyful news that she needed someone to pick the fruit in the orchard as her brother was away playing desperadoes.

Uncle Bernard was an inspector for the post office. Upset by a series of unsolved robberies on the mail train, he had himself tied

33

into a mailbag with holes for his eyes and his summer was spent crouched inside it, travelling up and down each day, waiting for the thief. We liked Uncle Bernard. He was easily recognisable, like a character in a story book, from his sagging jowls and trousers to the marbled pinkness of his head, from his gravel voice to the way he turned aside to squirt soda into his brandy, as if it was an activity akin to peeing. Aunt Midge, however, did not like him. The unmarried brother and sister had not spoken to one another for many years. In spite of their ill-humour, their garden was the very opposite of ours, bursting with colour. Shocking scents reeled out of dark corners and border flowers presented themselves in succulent bouquets. It was as if the maladjusted pair had directed all their natural human emotions towards the garden and fed the plants with them.

We spent the afternoon in a prickly underworld of bugs and slugs as we filled ourselves and our containers with raspberries, strawberries, gooseberries, redcurrants. We looked like the survivors of a massacre as we travelled home on the bus, dazed and spattered with red. In the days that followed, jam was made and fruit was preserved and we even tried a recipe for raspberry vinegar. Our favourite thing was a big bowl of raspberries mashed with sugar to preserve them and left in the cool larder, and we ate dishes of this for breakfast. We gorged until our faces and bodies came up in big red bumps which made us itchy and lethargic, and we staggered around like sun-stunned insects with faces daubed in red and bodies daubed in calamine lotion. Mother began to relax and look in the mirror again. She decided to give herself a beauty treatment and made a vinegar chin mask, which was a sheet of brown paper soaked in vinegar and honey, and held beneath the chin by means of elastic bands hooked over the ears. It attracted a bewildered following of wasps and bees. She found a sunny spot in the drawing room and crouched with her sketch book in a still column of light, the bees exclaiming on the air like notes of music.

Our house absorbed Miss Taylor like dust or cobwebs in a corner. She was so quiet that she had even perfected a manner of flushing the lavatory that made it sound as if it came from the house next door, and we scarcely thought about her until the evening when the mouse's scratch of her key in the door had a more frantic sound, as if someone was chasing her, and instead of the lonely footfall on the stair she ran right down to the kitchen. She stood like someone on the stage, her stiff fingers clasped before her breast and her feet apart. 'I've got a job!' It was in that moment we noticed that she had beautiful eyes. They were nearly always downcast or darting nervously, but when she was happy they lit up to a brilliant moist hazel full of wildness and light. Mother, who could always catch joy if it was thrown, invited her to sit down, poured tea from the battered enamel teapot, lavished jam on a slice of Hovis. 'A shop in Camden Street,' Miss Taylor boasted. She sat back to eat her bread and relaxed her legs, one on top of the other, the flat navy shoes and thick stockings seeming mocked by her attitude of relish. She particularised the items sold in the shop, the drawers and buttons and lace and baby frocks, the cylinder of cash that sailed overhead on busy cables. She noted its convenience to the bus and to the Stella Cinema. She had earmarked a branch of the Kylemore Bakery, where she would buy cream buns or iced eclairs for lunch. It seemed as if a life of feasting and society had opened up through her connection with the drapery shop. When she was drunk on tea she reeled off to bed to dream of this idyll.

She continued to come home at half six each evening, a paper bag in hand, splitting from the dampness of rashers and sausages. The gas fire hissed and then the frying pan. When the cooking smell died down there was only the gas fire, and it sometimes seemed as if she were something in a box kept alive by the glow. On Fridays the brown envelope appeared on the hall table. Her childish knickers hung above the bath and we heard her stifled sobs from the landing.

The way she drew us into her life was much in the manner of enticing a stray cat. She would sing a snatch of song and Kitty, who was able to harmonise, would absent-mindedly pick up the tune. There would be little smacks of applause and a plate of biscuits was brought to the door. After a week the biscuits remained on the table with the door open. 'Take one yeerselves,' she would call out, offhand.

She took us to the pictures, paid for our seats and bought a bag of caramels in patterned silver paper, with soft chocolate inside. On the way home she held our hands, urging the disconnected sister to take anyone's free hand. 'Imagine!' She remembered the story on the screen. 'Wouldn't it be lovely having someone of your own?' She laughed. The notion was pure fantasy to her. 'I'd love cooking a tart for someone and them coming up behind you when you took it out of the oven. I'd love the close feeling.' From the way she said it, she didn't seem to know there was any other kind of closeness. We knew there was something else, although we didn't know what, but the undertone of scorn in women when they complained about men, the tension when my father kissed my mother as she put her lipstick on before tea, removing himself gingerly as though his lips might remain stuck to that carmine fudge, led us to believe that men had some kind of weakness when they got too close to women.

The outings to the cinema became a regular event. We saw an Italian farce called *The Miller's Beautiful Wife* which was full of ladies' bosoms popping out of blouses and men and women rolling in haystacks. We loved bosoms and laughed drunkenly all the way through. Miss Taylor rustled in the dark like an animal in a strange house. Afterwards we teased her slyly. 'Did you like that?' 'No,' she said. 'But if they loved each other then I am happy for them.'

In May the weather turned wet and cold and we emerged from the cinema into a thunderstorm. Kitty was nervous and Miss Taylor put an arm around her. '''Tis only the giants foostering about in the mountains.'

'It's clouds meeting cold air,' Bridie clarified. 'That's a scientific fact.'

'That may well be so in the city,' Miss Taylor said gently. 'Country people have respect for the elements.' She bent down and squeezed my hand. 'What do you think happens when it snows?'

'Rain freezes in the clouds,' Bridie said.

'Someone above does be plucking a goose,' she said to me, 'and the feathers fall down.'

'When our mother was a child, this was the country,' Kitty said.

'Do ye ever stop to think where the Little People went when they built the houses?'

'Remember the Little Man?' I said to Kitty, but she shook her head. Miss Taylor wrapped her raincoat around us. 'We had a goose. When his mate was killed he got so lonesome he crept into the kitchen and spent his time with his head stuck in a shiny saucepan, looking at his own reflection for company.'

'Tell us more,' we begged, but we had reached the house and she clammed up coyly. 'Let me in out of that. I'm as cold as a holy trout.'

After that we stuck to Selena Taylor, for she held the key to a strange new world without any brick walls. Even her school days were like a story. She had gone to a school by a river with only one classroom for all the children. Some of the children had to come by boat. 'Sometimes we couldn't get to school at all, for the river would be in flood or else there'd be a fairy asleep on the bridge and no one would pass. We'd go through the fields and search for mushrooms or berries or wild flowers. There was always something to look at or gather, depending on the seasons. Speedwell, figwort, plantain, silverweed, foxgloves, yellowflags.'

'Foxglove,' I said, liking the name.

She spoke of animals and flowers as if they were people. 'Do you know foxglove at all? She has a long mauve skirt, bell-shaped and kind of silky, and long skinny legs inside with fluffy yellow slippers of pollen.'

'You were lucky,' we said. 'There's nothing to see in the city.'

'Them big city buildings is only perched on the surface like a top hat on a toff. You'll always find something if you keep your eyes peeled.'

We began to look for lupin growing out of builders' rubble, wild roses winding out of the park railings, buttercups, honeysuckle. She took our offerings and buried her face in them as if they were from an admirer. Once we brought her hawthorn, but she made us throw it out in the yard. 'Nice fool you'd be, Selena Taylor, inviting in bad fortune just when you've struck it lucky,' she said.

'Are you happy with us?' Bridie demanded, and she said, 'For sure.'

'But we sometimes hear you crying in the night. Are you home-sick?'

'Homesick for my mammy,' Miss Taylor admitted. 'She died, but I have ye all now.' She loved us and we loved her too, but we never saw her as an equal and we made fun of her accent behind her back. She liked to hear us singing and always called out: 'Come in where I can hear you,' the plate of confectionery temptingly in view. There was a popular song called 'Poppa Piccolina' and we rehearsed a version of this in imitation of her accent, where every 'i' or 'e' was preceded by a 'y'. She sat on the bed and put her face in her hands. 'Oh, children,' she said, 'that is very cruel.'

We assumed it was because of this that she stopped asking us out. But she did not go out either. On Friday the envelope was left on the hall table and apart from that there was silence. Mother went up and asked was everything all right? 'Yes. Grand.' And then she set up a great yowl. She had lost her job. 'They said I did not suit the image.' Mother backed away slightly as she murmured sympathy, for although Miss Taylor washed herself, her jumpers and blouses were only sponged and she carried with her the stale aura of an old and shuttered room. She rarely did anything with her brown curly hair.

'Have you tried the Swastika Laundry?' Mother wondered. 'They are looking for sorters and packers.'

'I tried them but they said they had sorters enough.'

'How long have you been out of work?' Mother said sharply.

'A month.'

She had only been with us three months.

It was Mother's contention that country people always had money, and surprisingly in this instance she turned out to be right. Miss Taylor had five hundred pounds that had been left to her by her mother. 'You should set up your own business,' Mother advised. 'Outside the city you could get a small premises very cheaply with living accommodation.' She held Miss Taylor's hands while she talked and Miss Taylor shook her head from side to side, not in protest, but in grief, for she knew she was being thrown out. In the end she flung her arms around Mother. She couldn't help herself. 'I have been so happy here,' she sobbed.

Mother's enthusiasm was genuine, for she had always wanted a little business of her own and was offering the advice she would have given to Father, but he thought that trade was common. She located a public house in County Meath which was for sale with living quarters for £1,000. 'It is the perfect business for a sober person,' Mother said, 'and you will have a queue of country men wanting to marry you.'

It was only after she left that we realised how much we would miss her. For my parents, it was the loss of the small rent that hit them hardest. In July, wartime ration books were abolished in England and in the north of Ireland, and Mother once more started to worry about the price of bread and tea. We girls searched Miss Taylor's room to see if there was anything for us to keep, but we only found a halfpenny and a hair clip in the dust beneath the bed, and the faint smell of clay and ferns that seemed to come from her clothing. 'She left nothing,' we said in disappointment, but we were wrong. For a long time afterwards, whenever we entered the green room we could shut our eyes and see once more the primrose hedges, the bridge of fairies, the skies that stretched all the way to America.

In due course a plain, clever, bad-humoured girl took her place. When we opened Ruth Kandinsky's case it was full of books – nothing else except her underwear and wash cloth. Because that was all there was to see, we examined them but they weren't even stories. The names on the spines had a crackling sound, like eating dry toast: Marx, Engels. 'Be careful!' she said. 'Those works are precious. They are the future of the world.' When she had settled in we hung around to see if she would give us cakes or biscuits, but she barely seemed to notice us, and spent her time writing or muttering with her head close to a page, while we gazed in disappointment at the cupboard, which was bare of all but tea and tins of soup.

We were surprised when she announced that she was getting married. Who would marry Ruth, with her round face and spectacles, her large mouth which was slightly cracked from lack of lipstick? 'Daniel Fine,' she said. A week went by while she looked for somewhere for them to live, and then she said they couldn't find anywhere that they could afford. Could she and Daniel share the room until he qualified?

My parents said no. There wasn't room for two people. What if there were children? 'There is no question of anything like that,' Ruth said. 'It's not that kind of relationship. We are comrades united in a common purpose. We are Communists.'

Father was shocked, but Mother liked Ruth, for she admired clever women. When she left she advised her not to say that they were Communists when they looked for a room. 'One cannot change the world by stealth,' Ruth said.

Miss Taylor went to the auctioneer's to put a down-payment on the pub. She was met by a nice gentleman who told her that she was too much of a lady to run a public house, where she would be serving the dregs of humanity. He invited her out to his house in Blackrock and showed her his newly erected shrine to Our Lady. He suggested that they pray together. After they had knelt, he remembered that he had just the thing for her – a café in North Earl Street where the girls from Madame Nora's took their lunch and which had a turnover of £50 a week.

We went once to see her in the café. It was a dismal place, and she confided that although a couple of girls from Madame Nora's came in for a cup of tea, they brought their own sandwiches. The turnover of £3 was not enough for her to make her repayments. Within a month the café had to close and she lost nearly all her money. 'What will I do now?' Mother suggested a novena of nine holy hours. 'What would I pray for?' she whispered. 'What would you like?' Mother said. 'A husband,' she said, and she squirmed in her chair and screwed up her hands and laughed at this nonsense.

About a month after this there was a letter from her to say that she had met a beau. 'All will be well DV, but as the old saying goes, the course of true love never runs smooth.' She enclosed the advertisement she had placed in the *Evening Mail*: 'Would gentleman to whom young lady entrusted purse containing £25 at Macushla Ballroom on the 13th inst. please contact Box Number . . .'

Chapter Seven

~

Miss Taylor was almost forgotten when our family became famous. We opened the paper one day and there was a familiar face, pink and jowly and disapproving. 'It's Uncle Bernard!' we cried in amazement.

After two months sealed into a dusty sack, he had finally caught the mystery mail train robber. He was pictured in the paper and awarded a plaque by the post office. Mother said the stubborn Rafferty nature was an awful thing, that a man would allow himself to be tied up in a sack like a poacher's ferret, but he told her he had grown used to his dark world, and spent most of his time asleep. 'It was so peaceful that I sometimes forgot the purpose of my confinement,' he admitted. 'I got an appalling fright on the day when I opened my eyes to see the gleam of a blade through the holes in my sack.' But the knife moved away to sever a different sack and he sprang forth and apprehended the villain.

He turned away to squirt soda into brandy as he gloomily confessed that the thief turned out to be a very decent packer called Roche, who had a harelip and always called him sir.

For a while he was the centre of attention. Then the headlines were claimed by a baby stolen from Holles Street hospital. When he descended from that peak, he said he knew there would be no other great event in his life. Aunt Midge broke her silence to taunt him, telling him he was an old fool who thought he was Gary Cooper in *High Noon* when he should have been thinking of his prayers and his pension. Uncle Bernard knew she would not leave him alone now that she had found her voice, so he took to bed with a bottle of brandy and locked the door. For three days he remained undisturbed. Once, she heard him singing in a startling deep voice, 'Do not forsake me, O my darling, on this our wedding day.' After that he gave a deep chuckle and then he died.

We were sorry about Uncle Bernard. He was our only uncle. Aunt Midge was furious. 'In this household, it has never been ladies before gentlemen. I am more than ready for my reward but it is he who is comfortable in a coffin while I have the wallflowers to lift.'

Father tried to cheer her up. 'You will live to be a hundred, Midge.'

'Don't wish for it,' she said. 'Who do you think will benefit from my passing?'

'I have never thought about it,' Father blustered. 'I am sure you are not a wealthy woman.'

'Bernard left me ten thousand pounds.'

I looked at Father, and his face was like someone in the pictures when they first encounter the woman they will love forever. 'Aunt Midge!' he said. 'I never thought . . .'

'The men in this family rarely think.' One peak of her upper lip rose in distaste.

'You must allow me to look after you.' He grappled for the cloth with which she wiped the table, but she hung on to her rag, for she did not like to lose control. 'As you are the only one of my relatives with whom I am on speaking terms, I would expect that.'

She wanted a lift to Mass every morning and to the shops in the afternoons. 'On those days when I don't feel up to it, I'll give you a list.' She also made out a catalogue of heavy gardening chores. Father, who had silenced the demands of our garden with several sacks of limestone chips, now had to bend his knees to weeding. 'She is making a boy of me,' he complained to Mother, but Mother reminded him that sooner or later Aunt Midge must go to her reward, and then his would come to him, and so he did what he was told.

I think Aunt Midge expected Father to put up a good fight. When he didn't, she told him he was a weakling like her brother. She said she was not surprised all his children had turned out girls. Father and Aunt Midge both had the same bright-blue eyes, the colour of blue paraffin, and a stubborn nature. If she was determined to rile him he was resolved not to respond. Aunt Midge flourished on adversity. She began to pine for her brother. Within two months she was dead.

Father sat quite still while tears gathered in his eyes and a corner of his jaw worked.

'She was a good age,' the priest comforted. 'She has gone to her rest.'

Father whispered something and a tear fell.

'I did not hear you, my son,' the priest said gently.

'Ten thousand pounds,' Father said, and he wept without control.

Mother urged him not to spend the money until it was ours, but Father assured her he had no thought of spending it, only of making more. Having learnt about tenants the hard way, he said, he would buy a whole house full of them and be a landlord. He finally settled on a brownstone terrace in Rathgar, which was already tenanted so all he had to do was to collect money once a week. 'This will be as easy as picking apples from a tree,' he promised. 'It is not like having to share your house with strangers. We will have an income and still retain the property as capital.'

Mother always got worn out by Father's enthusiasms and when the time came to view the property she needed to lie down. 'I'll go,' I said, because I loved other people's houses.

He had been given a set of keys. I think he was disappointed that the owner was not there to meet him. He wanted to see what a landlord looked like. There was a faint smell of gas in the house and different sounds from rooms along the hall, of babies, and a hysterical sports commentary from Michael O Hehir on the wireless. Father listened at each door, a look of caution on his face. A door opened suddenly, and a woman watched him in fury before scuttling back into her rented space. Father led the way upstairs. It was cool on the landing and yellow light came from a big gaunt bathroom. I touched a door handle and Father shook his head and then rapped faintly. Silence rushed in around this pawprint of sound. He scowled at me for what I had made him do and then pushed back the door.

The first impression was of a room on fire. The room was engulfed in a fierce orange light. My heart pounded with excitement. When the door was opened it was revealed that the light was the effect of sunlight streaming through half-closed curtains, brightly patterned in orange and gold. We were in a dining room and kitchen combined. This was obvious from the table, still littered with the remnants of a dinner. The setting seemed not so much abandoned as preserved, savouring its essences and memories. Father and I, still as mice, took in every single thing; the bright-orange cast-iron casserole dish with its congealed content which singed the nose with its smell and was the colour of a baby's nappy. A scorched salad in a wooden bowl. Plates smeared with sauce and littered with lumps of bread and even cigarette ash. Candles burnt down to the stub, their long white tresses of wax spilling over the table. Big glasses with dregs of purple wine. A sweaty-looking piece of Cheddar on a board and two green apples. I took long draughts of the curious breath of that room, of wine and curry and ash and wax, of perfume and coffee and something voluptuous and repellant that I tried to block out and inhale at the same time. Life, life.

When I moved forward, Father stretched out an arm to defend me. 'Stay,' he ordered so I wandered over to a gramophone and dropped the needle on the turntable. 'Softly, softly turn the key . . .' Ruby Murray's throbbing, choking tone implored. Father was in an open doorway. He seemed weakened by what he saw and had to lean against the doorpost. I followed him into the bedroom. Clothes spilled from the wardrobe, dance clothes, stiff slips, long scarves. There was underwear on the floor, black and shiny with a doggy smell overlaid with scent. The cheap dressing table was covered in dust and powder and dirty tissues. Jars and tubes of make-up were left open all over it and there was a cocktail glass, still with a golden dreg at its bottom and a bright-scarlet half-grin on its rim. Father hated untidiness. Although Mother did not care for housework she always did a mad run-round to erase all evidence of any activity – even our chalk drawings on the wall – before he came home. I looked at him to see what he was thinking. He seemed in a daze. On his face was a look of desolation and wistfulness. He appeared not even to see the bursting wardrobe or the dressing table. It was the bed he watched, the unmade bed with its tortured sheets and battered pillows, its look as if some terrible struggle had taken place there. And in the middle lay some small pink thing with lace, which, like the meal on the table, looked half eaten. He took my hand and stormed out.

~

Whenever Father talked of the past he always defined it with the phrase, 'before the children were born'. He would glance at each of us as he said this, not in an accusing way, but as if begging our understanding for the landslide that had buried his life. His emotions were too soaring for the foggy, mauling attachment of family. He was only happy when he had a new scheme. His plans always went wrong, although sometimes we had money for a little while. His photography business folded after he declared that all his subjects were plain and common. It was only the pure ideas and the pursuit of them that delighted him. For a long time I thought that was just Father, but as I grew older I began to see that nearly everyone had a strategy for getting through life, or getting around it.

Bridie got what she wanted by means of hypochondria. When she was small and powerless and couldn't bend others to her will, she used her control over her own body. If she didn't immediately get her own way, she would rise up in boils or fevers or rashes. Once she dragged a leg behind her for a month and told everyone that she had polio. On another occasion, she leaned out of the bed and vomited up a great deal of blood, mixed with clots that looked like currants. Kitty suggested that they might be currants, that she might have swallowed a whole pot of blackcurrant jam, but where would she have obtained a pot of blackcurrant jam? She got violent headaches, which could be cured only by the removal of obstacles to her desires. I can still remember an occasion when my parents held out against her and a small, grim voice drifted down the stairs: 'The blood is leaking out of my head.' When she took a hatred to a nun in school, she solemnly announced that she had tuberculosis. We all got a shock when lumps came up on her neck which were actually confirmed as primary TB, and she was removed from school for a year.

Kitty spent long and patient hours trying to teach me how to lie. It was a labour of love, for I was a hopeless liar. Kitty said she had learnt on her first day at school that the questions asked by teachers were not for information but to see if there could possibly be any excuse for hitting you.

'A lie is always sinful and nothing can excuse it,' I recited from the catechism.

'All right. Suppose a murderer appears at the door with a big knife and says he has come to murder your mother. He asks if she is at home and you know she's in the kitchen. What do you say?' She offered this dilemma in a calm and practical way and while she spoke she knitted with a thread spool, winding pink wool onto nails hammered into the top, and looping them off.

The cruelty of this made my blood run cold. 'What has she done?' I watched as a horrible little pink tongue of knitting poked through the bottom of the spool.

Kitty was always a good story-teller. 'She has disappointed him in love,' she said without hesitation. 'It was a very long time ago but he has found it impossible to forgive her.'

I had no idea what to say to the murderer. I supposed I would have to block his way and let him murder me instead, while calling out to Mother to flee for her life.

'But then poor Mother would be broken-hearted and you would be responsible for the sin of murder on the man's soul. All that because of the stupid catechism,' she said with contempt.

It wasn't just the catechism. Father was equally passionate about the truth. He said that without it, no exchange, whether between lovers, or parents and children, or shopkeeper and customer, had any value. Mother said that all men talked about integrity and all men were liars, but she never said this in front of Father.

Kitty not only tried to teach me why I should lie, but also how. 'Stick to the real facts as closely as possible.' She claimed that she had trained herself like a Spartan, even forcing herself to do some really terrible things. One time she had stolen a shilling.

'I took it from the collection plate in church. I had a penny and I put it on the plate and took the shilling that was underneath.'

She had only partially passed this test. She couldn't spend the money and she couldn't put it back in case anyone saw her. She lay awake at nights and worried until her hair started to fall out and she was treated for worms. She was too young for confession, so she decided to give herself a penance. Every Saturday she knelt on the cold hall lino to smear on the brownish-pink Mansion polish and then she rubbed it with rags until her arms ached. The idea then came to her that she could polish the stolen shilling into the floor. It took six weeks for the coin to settle and then it was only a glimmering shadow, like a fish in a stream. It stayed there for several years until the day when Mother ran out of money and found it and thought it was a miracle.

I never learned how to lie, and anyway my problem was different. I needed a bridge between home, where I was cherished, and the outside, which was my calling. My only worldly images came from the cinema, where women with glossy hair and rippling gowns looked haughty as love and spies and whooping Indians passed their way. But the cinema audience was more like Miss Taylor. They smelled of sweets and raincoats. I began to look out for models from whom I could learn. Learn what? The thing Father had warned us against, had sworn we knew nothing about, and prayed it would always be so: the ways of the world.

Chapter Eight

~

Sissy Sullivan said that the most sensitive part of a woman's body was the crook of the arm. We held out our arms and she scraped them with the glistening mauve ovals of her nails. 'Close your eyes,' she instructed. ''Tis pure bliss.' We closed our eyes and tried to imagine pure bliss. The fleece of a very white sheep came to mind.

The soles of the feet, the hollow of the leg behind the knee, the inside curve of the ear – these as well as all the 'routine places' were the sources of bliss. Best of all was to run the tip of the tongue from the crook of the arm to the pit. 'We can't reach all the way,' we complained after we had trailed our tongues, snail-like, up our arms. 'Ah! 'Tis not a thing you would do for yourselves.' She knelt down, took us each by the hand and ran her tongue up our arms. Her tongue was wetter than ours and like a dog's tongue, it had a questing eagerness. When she got to the armpit she rolled her tongue around like a dog trying to lick the cream out of the top of the bottle, and we were startled by a faint electric tingle that ran down the backs of our necks. From this moment Miss Taylor's world began to fade like an old photograph.

~

We got Sissy in the spring of 1956 shortly after The Calamity. Father had been morose since viewing the flats, and Mother suggested some less challenging investment, such as the bank.

'You know nothing of money,' he mourned. 'There has been no inflation since the War. Interest rates are worse than useless.' A few weeks later his mood improved again as he came across an advertisement for Shanahan Stamps, a new investment business which bought valuable stamps on the international market and sold them at auction for profit. 'Profit from stamps without risks,' he read out. 'The probability of outstandingly large profits within four months.'

'We have not seen a penny of Aunt Midge's money and yet already you are prepared to gamble it all away,' Mother objected.

This accusation stung him into a reproachful silence, and I began to wonder if Aunt Midge had left them her nature along with her fortune. The silence ended on the exciting day when they were summoned to a solicitor's office to hear a reading of her will. Afterwards they commented on how shabby his premises had been, dust silted up in the gaps of the lino, bentwood chairs craving a coat of paint.

'But the fortune?'

'A calamity!' Father winced as if remembering the disappointing setting.

Kitty and I jumped up and down impatiently. 'How much? Did we get the house?'

'She left us a silver teapot,' Father said.

We laughed out loud until we saw Mother's warning look.

'But the money . . . ?'

'All of her estate including the proceeds from the sale of the house has gone to the missions in Brazil.'

The room was advertised once again and he took up a new

scheme, the sale of small three-wheeled trolleys for transporting large industrial packages. The advantage of this scheme was that there was very little capital outlay. He need only purchase a dozen or so trolleys and show them as demonstration models before taking orders. The house filled with these red metal-wheeled rectangles and Kitty and I skated up and down the hall on them on our stomach. After several months they were piled up in the shed.

~

'She's too young,' Father had said when he first saw Sissy. She was a round-faced, round-chested country girl with mousy hair and small grey eyes. Mrs Sullivan appealed to my mother: 'I want the best for Sissy. She is not suited to rural life. She is a refined and gifted girl.' Sissy appeared to be asleep on her feet. Her little eyes took in some things, but only on a low level, as if she was looking for lost money. Once or twice she caught our eyes and her plump mouth rolled down on one side in a kind of smile.

My parents agreed to take her. I think they were reassured by her lack of personality. They imagined we would never have to think about her. Sissy's mother burst into tears and clung to her daughter, and Sissy remained speechless, expressionless until the country woman had gone in a taxi to the railway station, and then she followed my father up the stairs.

'Well, she won't set the world on fire,' Mother said. 'I suppose we should give her something to eat on her first evening.' I ran upstairs at once. Sissy was lying on the bed smoking a cigarette. She was wreathed in smoke, as if she had been smoking there all day. Something about the way she smoked made it seem that she might very well set the world on fire. I stood by the side of the bed and stared at her, and she rose up on an elbow and blew smoke in

53

my face. In this manner I made the delightful discovery that Sissy Sullivan was not shy. Her inertness came from composure.

'My mother says come down to tea.'

She put out her cigarette, smoothed her childish pleated skirt and followed me downstairs. There were boiled eggs for tea, and Mikado biscuits. Sissy said she didn't fancy an egg, having seen where they came out of, but could she have two Mikados? 'Have ye a telephone?' she asked. 'A television?'

Mother asked her if she would like the loan of a book or a magazine to read in bed. 'A book?' Her plump pink mouth hung open in astonishment. 'Gawny mackerel, yis are living in the dark ages.'

What happened to Sissy Sullivan then was like a fairy story. Every day she went to work at Maison Prost, where she was apprenticed to a hairdresser. Each evening when she came home, some feature had been dramatically altered. Her mousy hair went pale gold, her doughy skin bloomed peach pink, the slab of her chest became two peaks pointing in slightly opposite directions. The little grey eyes turned large and luminous under wedges of blue shadow. Wherever she went there followed in her wake a shock of scent, sweet as fudge but with a sting of spice and lemon. Even her short, nibbled nails were quite suddenly transformed into long, painted, pearly moons. We soon discovered that those little oval masks came in a packet and were glued on over bitten stumps. Her bosoms too we located, peaks of white rubber foam like uncooked meringue. 'They're falsies,' I accused. 'All you have to do is catch a guy's fancy.' Sissy pushed the rubber cones into her bra. 'Reality is immemorial to men.'

We were intrigued by the way Sissy occupied her room. It had grown almost as cluttered again as it was in the years of neglect, but it was Sissy's space, and she moved around it as if it was a palace. She never sat on a chair, preferring to stretch at full length on the bed, reading film magazines or painting her artificial nails. There were clothes heaped everywhere. The table became a buffet and a beauty parlour,. Lipstick, powder, rouge, eye shadow, mascara, nail polish, hair curlers, tissues and cotton wool shared space with a half-eaten Battenburg cake, a box of cocktail biscuits and some slices of cooked ham on a torn paper bag. Over everything was a fine silt of face powder. It was one of Sissy's attractions that she never ate proper meals. Cooked meat was eaten from its bag, milk gulped from a bottle, the cake plucked in pieces from the box. The nearest thing she got to a real dinner was to heat up a tin of beans on the gas ring and then fork in a tin of corned beef. The dish, she said, was called corned beans and was her own personal invention. She allowed us to share tiny morsels from her spoon. It was the most delicious thing we had ever eaten.

Her mother had been right when she said Sissy was gifted. She had a gift of sex, which is as irresistible to women as it is to men. Sissy's sleepy personality had about it an air of ferment that drew men as money does. Almost from the first day she had boyfriends, sometimes strangers who followed her home from the bus. They brought her out and paid for her. She had been taken to see Pier Angeli in *Tomorrow is Too Late* at the Astor, and to the Theatre Royal, where teenagers shrieked and screamed at Nat King Cole. She was invited to *Sweet Rosie O'Grady* with Betty Grable but said she would as soon go to Father Peyton's Rosary Crusade. At night when she returned from the pictures with a date we girls would cluster at the bedroom window. Under a sticky veil of violet sky with a sparkle of star chips she laughed in little trills, and when the man kissed her he seemed at once to strangle and struggle like a murderer and his victim. In the morning there would be a half-eaten box of chocolates in her room, or a limp bunch of flowers which she had not bothered to put in water. 'What do you talk about with a man?' we pestered her. 'What does he say to you?' 'Sweetheart, darling, love – all that flabbergasting,' she shrugged.

Apart from Sissy our only contact with the outside world was school. I got on well in class but the dull diet of sums and verses seemed far less real than Sissy's rubber bosoms. There were other girls, like Francey Murnahan, who paid no attention to lessons, but moved in relaxed and intimate gangs. Francey always had sweets and money in her pocket. Already she knew how to select only those parts of life that she liked. I tried to be friends with her, but she passed me over like a dull toffee in a box of chocolates. I got on with my lessons and hurried home to Sissy.

That summer we followed Sissy Sullivan everywhere, consumed her leftovers and looted her waste for souvenirs. When she ate an apple she slowly carved off the skin with a penknife, paring small separate strips, offering them to us on the knife, and we took them with reverence. Then she would examine the apple for imperfections and gouge out any wormy bits or bruises, and we would eat those as well. She made use of us too. While we hung around her room she would have us boil the kettle, make her a cup of tea, rinse her nylons, run to the shop for a pack of biscuits or cigarettes. All of this we regarded as a privilege, and we fought with one another to do things for her. While she talked we examined her wardrobe, which was no longer an empty coffin with a few battered hangers, but a hothouse blooming with brightly coloured net skirts, Swiss cotton blouses, swagger jackets, all with the slightly suffocating fragrance of her perspiration and perfume. Sometimes we even rooted in her rubbish basket for clues to her personality. Once it was overflowing with bloody wads of cotton. 'What happened, Sissy?' we asked in concern. 'Did you hurt yourself?' She only laughed. 'Don't fret yourselves. 'Tis a messy business being a woman.'

Even the messiness seemed a kind of licence. She was the only grown-up we had ever met who had the sort of life we envisaged for ourselves, eating sweets and biscuits, doing whatever she wanted or nothing at all. The most exciting thing about her was that when she arrived she had been ordinary like us, and now she appeared rich and beautiful. It seemed as if all the other adults we knew had failed some examination early on and been disqualified from participation in real life.

If she had taken the trouble Sissy could have charmed our parents as she did us, but she did not know how to defer to men, only how to provoke them. 'That oul' fella hasn't the yard in him for the women any more,' she dismissed Father. He felt her rejection and responded with bitter criticism. 'That female seems to spend half her life in the bath. She uses hot water as if it grows on trees.' 'That female was behaving like a tramp with some man outside the house last night.' My mother speculated less dramatically, 'I wonder where she gets all her money for clothes? She is supposed to be living on thirty shillings a week but she has a new outfit for every day of the week.'

Unwisely, I carried this back to Sissy. She was wearing a beautiful black umbrella skirt, with bright patches of felt sewn on in a pattern, and a wide scarlet patent belt. 'Jay's Pay-as-you-wear,' she said, and then she laughed. 'All right, for your information only, miss!' She hit me on the head with a matted hairbrush, and beneath their startling blue ceiling her little grey eyes narrowed in excitement. 'I fecked 'em.' I felt as if my whole inside had been scooped out like a spoon of ice-cream. I knew what she meant. Fecked meant stole. Then I thought, maybe it had some other meaning in the country. 'But you did pay for them . . . ?'

She fell back on the bed with laughter. 'Aren't you the right gooseberry! Amn't I after telling you? I fecked 'em. There's nothing like it for kicks. Your heart does be going like the clappers. Tell your mammy and I'll cut your ears off.'

57

For a few weeks after that I stayed away from Sissy's room. It wasn't that I disapproved of her. Her character was so much larger than mine. It was as if she had revealed that she was somebody famous, an actress in the films.

We were listening to *Emergency Ward Ten* on the wireless when the police arrived. 'It's about your lodger,' they said. Father's normally bright complexion deserted him and his skin went waxy white. Nothing could be worse than being visited at your home by the gardai. My dismay was mixed with relief, for Sissy was getting to be too much for me. Since her confession about the clothes she had taken to waylaying me and pinching me on the arms. 'Did you tell anyone? Did you ever hear about an accessory after the fact? For your information that's you, miss. You and I will be locked up in irons in tandem.' I believed her. The mere possession of her guilty secret weighed me down like iron chains.

'The young lady appears to have a spot of bother,' the policeman said.

'I do not doubt it!' Father shot Mother a look of grim triumph, as if it was all her fault. 'Any fool could see that she would go to the dogs.'

'Ah, now,' the garda soothed. 'It's hardly a case of dogs.'

'Sissy Sullivan has not the morals of a monkey,' Father rejoined with spirit.

The huge officer looked uneasy. 'She says her name is Selena Taylor.'

~

Some time later Sissy gave me a present of a cracked mirror compact and a shilling. 'What's that for?' she quizzed. I assumed it was for not saying anything to my parents or the police, but I was not sure.

'For information. Easy money.'

By now I realised that Sissy's glorious, uncomplicated life was won at the expense of other people's peace of mind. 'What information?'

'What night do your parents go to the pictures?'

'Wednesday.'

'There now, that was easy, wasn't it?' She scooped a pinch of cake crumbs from a plate on the table and fed them into my mouth. As always, I was touched by her lack of squeamishness, the way she thrust her pearly nails right past my lips into the wetness of my mouth.

When my parents had gone out, Sissy came downstairs. 'What do yis think?' She wore a green dress, cut low at the front, tan nylons, pink pearls and in her hair, a green artificial flower and a little green comb. The effect of the green against her pale skin and vivid make-up was electrifying. We could not hold ourselves back and ran to her. 'Oh, Sissy, you look fab. Where did you get that dress? Where are you going?'

'Going nowhere. I have a visitor. I'd say he'll probably bring me a box of sweets. Mind your business and I'll save you some.' She went out of the room with a swish. We at once left our homework on the dining room table and went into the drawing room so that we could spy on her visitor behind the window and see what kind of sweets he brought.

Hours later we heard her cry. We had finished our homework and were listening to Radio Luxembourg and talking about the man. We thought he looked too young for her, which was strange since he was about twenty-five and she was only seventeen, but the eager way in which he had glanced up at the house before unlatching the creaky gate made us think of her knowing eyes and how easily she could make him feel inferior. We turned down the wireless and sat very still. There was another cry.

'It sounds as if she is being strangled. Her voice is all muffled.'

I left the room and crept upstairs. The door was not properly closed and I pushed it and went in. I knew I should not be there and I knew I should stay quiet, but I couldn't help myself. 'Sissy!' I whispered. She half turned her head towards me, half opened little slitty eyes. She was lying underneath the corpse of a man. She touched his hair and he grunted. She smiled at me. Pure bliss.

I did not go back downstairs but went to the bedroom. I took a doll and pressed it to my stomach as hard as I could until the strange, wintry, solitary excitement died away.

~

When the police mentioned Miss Taylor, silence filled the room like a fog. The young man finally forced his way through this with a cough. 'Taylor, she says.'

'What has she done?' Father now looked utterly damned and wretched. He had let the room to relieve his worries. Instead he had added to his string of responsibilities by taking on more females.

The policeman took off his cap. 'She did nothing, sir, only threw herself in the Liffey.'

'Oh, the poor girl!' Mother cried, but Father looked bitterly aside as if her sinking corpse would drag us down.

She was not dead. We went to visit her in hospital. She lay in the bed as limp and passive as Sissy had lain with her visitor, but Miss Taylor's look was pure misery. Mother took her hand. 'Oh, Selena, why did you do it? Why did you come back to the city when you knew there was nothing here for you?'

Miss Taylor's luminous hazel eyes filled with tears. 'I missed the bright lights.'

~

I tried to avoid Sissy, but she lay in wait for me on the stairs. 'Well – now you know!'

'I don't know,' I cried. 'What was he doing?'

She laughed. 'It's a private thing between a man and a woman.' She watched my struggling face and sighed in pity. 'Ah, you poor city kids are pig ignorant. Try to imagine, now, that the man is the key and the lady is the keyhole. Do you get me? Think if you had this little box and it was locked and then along came someone with the perfect little key. You can get a baby that way too, if you're misfortunate. The man sprinkles seeds inside the lady.'

'Does it hurt?' I remembered her cries.

Sissy had to consider this. 'You'd need the niceties,' she decided. 'That's why I came to the city. City guys have a bit of an oul' coort in them. Farmers is all out for themselves. Gawny mackerel, they'd stick it in a cow or a keyhole.'

I carried around, like stones in my shoes, the gappy information she had given me. I often thought about the box and the key. I had no idea what she was talking about and yet I felt, contrary to what she had said, that I now held the key and would someday find the little box. My imagination had been caught and it ruined my concentration. I no longer paid attention to my lessons, exasperating the nun whose pet I had been, until she was driven to hit me with a ruler. Francey Murnahan smiled her languid smile at me, a wide grin that spread across her brown monkey face and brought her prominent front teeth to lap moistly over her lower lip. From that day I was a part of her gang.

At night I still belonged to my sisters. We took turns in telling stories. Our beds were houses or ships and we made carriages by pulling one another round the shiny lino floor on a blanket. Kitty told

61

the best tales, featuring a powerful heroine called Hawna Maroyle. They were nail-biters with plenty of daggers and blood. None of us could sleep afterwards, so we passed the time spitting on our torches and shining them on the ceiling to see who could make the most interesting pattern.

'Mountains of the moon,' Bridie said.

'Intestines of a pachyderm,' said Kitty.

'Miss Cornelia's pancakes,' I decided.

I thought Mother would be pleased with my social success, so I invited Francey to tea. Instead she greeted her in a very formal way and said stiffly: 'This little girl must go to her own house for tea. Her mother will wonder where she is.'

'My mother never wonders where I am.' Francey smiled and rested her teeth on the slightly flattened ledge of her lower lip. Mother made her wait in the hall while she pulled me down to the kitchen. 'Who is that girl?' she said. When I told her where my friend lived, she said with genuine pity, 'Oh, the poor child!' For the family was very poor. They lived in a terrace of tiny, tumbledown hovels close to the convent, known as the poor cottages. There were ten children and most of them grew up on the street because there was no room inside the house. But Francey wore her cast-off clothes as if they had been specially made for her. Sometimes she adopted a woman's straw hat with shrivelled roses, and gold sling-backed high heels, several sizes too large, which flapped from her heels as she walked.

Mother said it was not really kind to ask her to a house like ours, where she would be ill at ease.

I had never met anyone who was less ill at ease than Francey. 'Can she come to tea another day?'

'No.' Mother looked uncomfortable. 'Your father would not like it.'

'Did your ma not take to me?' Francey smiled when I took back my invitation.

'Of course she did.' I was mortified. 'My father doesn't like visitors.'

'Never mind! You're my friend – not them.' We went to the shops and Francey handed over sixpence for two marshmallow mice, two liquorice whips and two sherbet lollipops. Before she shared them out she said, 'Which would you rather do – run a mile, suck a boil or eat a basin of scabs?'

~

To my delight she called for me for school the following morning.

'Rose is not ready.' I heard Mother's chill voice as I scrambled for my clothes.

'I'll wait,' Francey offered calmly.

'Wait in the hall,' Mother said. She was quiet as she wound strips of my hair into the knotty plaits she called Indian braids. I was flattered since Francey almost lived beside the school and had to go out of her way to collect me, but time and distance meant nothing to her. 'Let's go to the shops,' she said.

'Who is this stupid, idle child who cannot be bothered to turn up in time for her lessons?' Sister Cecilia spoke directly to me, taking no notice of Francey.

'I'm Rose,' I said in a shaky voice.

'Not the Rose who I know;' and she turned away.

All morning my lessons were seen through a blur of tears. I was mostly bored with learning but there were occasional words and phrases that delighted me, such as 'a rose-red city half as old as time' and 'Himalayas'. That morning she read out a poem about a squirrel which was likened to a silver coffee pot. 'This poem deals in simile,' she said. 'A simile is the likening of one object to another for the purpose of stimulating the imagination.' I don't know what had taken hold of Sister Cecilia that morning, for she normally only read out whatever was on the page and asked us to repeat it. Now she did a strange thing, planting one little hand on her hip and waving the other one away from her body, like an actress on the stage. 'I want you to picture now, the squirrel and the coffee pot – paws and curled tail, spout and curved handle.'

I saw it – not the squirrel, but a coffee pot, elegant as the silver tea service in the Gresham. I had never seen either a squirrel or a coffee pot. Coffee came in a cup and was made from Irel essence; but I knew what squirrels looked like and I could imagine them posing as a coffee pot. It was the most interesting thing that had happened so far at school. I added it to my own squirrel's store and from that moment I developed a secret double vision which gave all sorts of unlikely objects an unrelated twin. I also liked the word 'simile', which had an exotic, faraway sound, like Himalayas.

'Let's go and buy midge gums,' Francey said. I was surprised that someone so poor always had money, and she was very generous. She did not head for The Honeybee where we usually bought our sweets, but crossed the road to The Gem. We were not allowed to go there because it involved crossing a main road. Crossing main roads was a taboo in our life, along with riding bicycles, using roller skates and talking to strange men. She emerged from the shop with a newspaper cone filled with little scented gluey nibs, shaped like miniature puddings. 'Take as many as you like.' My hand was still cramming as she wheeled away.

'Where are you going?' Several midge gums dropped on the pavement and I bent to pick them up.

'Bushy Park. Coming?'

'I'm not allowed.'

'No one's allowed.' Francey's green eyes looked amused.

'You could be murdered in there,' I said doubtfully. 'There's dirty men.'

She stopped and grinned at me. 'Dirty men don't murder you. They only show you their thing.'

'Oh, is that all?' I said, embarrassed by my own confusion, and when she held out her arm I linked it.

The park was a disappointing, scrubby little place, and as soon as I got there I wanted to be home with my mother having tea and toast. Jackie and Rita Mulvey were already there, and we joined them, heading into a gloomy thicket where they squatted down to share the sweets. There was a sort of competition going on between them: who had gone to which film, who had a boyfriend, who was going away on holidays. I was surprised to see that Francey, whose family never had any money, was very well able to compete. She said she had a boyfriend who had given her a box of chocolates. I said that we were going to Sandymount on holidays, where my grandparents lived. Everyone, including Francey, laughed. They said you couldn't go on holidays to a place that was only five miles away. After this I passed a quiet and boring hour until we left.

When we got to my house Mother darted out. 'Where were you until this hour?'

I gazed at her miserably. I still had no idea how to lie. Francey tugged at Mother's jumper. 'We are sorry, Mrs Rafferty, but we were followed by a dirty man and had to run away and hide. We were afraid to come out.' I watched her in amazement. What made her think my mother would be fooled? 'Where did you hide?' Mother demanded.

'Behind a hedge.'

'You should have knocked on a door,' Mother said. 'Any woman would have taken you in.'

'It might have been a man in the house,' Francey reasoned, and Mother at once nodded. 'Did the dirty man do anything?'

'We closed our eyes.' Francey squeezed her eyes shut to demonstrate. 'He was still there when we ran away. I could see his bicycle peeping out around a corner.'

'In that case,' Mother herded us into the drawing room, 'he will have to pass this way.'

Angry flies stumbled like drunks against the closed windows and we were shrouded in the dust of the curtains. Francey was perfectly composed. Her face had its usual amused, impassive look. All very well for her. When we had to confess the truth she could run off home and I would be blamed. After a congealing half-hour an old man entered the street on his bicycle. He pedalled slowly, well insulated against the heat of the day by a gaberdine raincoat. 'Is that him?' Mother whispered. Francey nodded. Mother ran out into the street. 'Pervert!' she shouted at him. The man turned in terror and his bicycle wobbled. 'I know what you have been at,' Mother cried in a passion. For a moment he seemed suspended by fear and Francey began to laugh, thinking his bicycle was going to fall over, but then he fled on his pedals and disappeared off down the road, showing only the soles of his little stamping feet and the hunched back draped in dingy cloth. 'I am warning you!' Mother exulted. 'You will go to prison for the rest of your days.'

Chapter Nine

~

My grandparents' house was a small, dank, ivy-covered villa by the sea. Each summer we spent a fortnight there, while they, with as much fuss as an entire tribe transporting its caravan, moved themselves ten miles away to Bray. Mother complained that the sheets were damp and the cooker did not work, but my sisters and I were completely happy there. We loved the house because every inch had been filled with interesting things, gilded mirrors, marble sideboards, *chaises-longues*, stuffed birds, plaster blackamoors bearing vases of dried flowers. At the bottom of the garden a wall divided us from a field with a house where a man kept rabbits. If we hung over the wall he would bring them out and hold them up for us to stroke. It was true about the sheets. In fact the whole house was so damp it seemed to have soaked up the salty ocean which ran parallel to the long terrace of villas, but after the sheets had filled with sand we failed to notice the clamminess.

We plucked furry caterpillars from leaves and lined them up on the wet grass to run races. The finishing point was a raspberry, placed on a leaf. We watched the rain turn to mercury in the leaves of nasturtiums, ate apples, pears, plums and raspberries, the peas of sweetpeas and the succulent petals of gladioli, walked for miles along the dank grey strand, went to the tiny cinema, wandered in and out of the shops that were threaded around a pretty village green. In The Monument Creamery they sold bread rolls that were shaped like a miniature loaf of Hovis, right down to the writing on the side. Each tiny slice would be spread with a delicious preparation called Honey Cream, which was also sold in The Monument Creamery, and served on a doll's plate along with tea from a doll's teapot. In another shop was a man called Dan and he was fond of children. Granda Rafferty had given each of us two and sixpence to spend, and a good hour each day was spent in Dan's shop, trying to decide how best to budget it. There was a barrel marked 'Mystery Parcels' and these intrigued us more than anything else. 'What's in them?' we asked, but he said it was no good if you knew, because then they weren't a mystery. They cost sixpence each and we didn't want to be disappointed. As the week drew to an end he relented and held the parcels up to the light. They were wrapped in thin yellow or pink paper, and with the sun behind you could vaguely discern the shape of the contents. We made wild predictions, growing more and more excited – a yo-yo, a hair band, a skipping rope, delighted if we found we had guessed right, even more thrilled to discover something different.

When we returned home the house had been baked into dusty silence. We would have liked to fling open all the windows but our parents felt insecure with windows open, so instead we ran through the rooms, shouting. At Sissy's room, we stopped and fell silent. It was like a room the morning after a party. Webs of her festive existence clung to everything – the apricot dust of her face powder, crumbs of cake and biscuit, which Father said would bring mice, and everywhere, in the bed, in the wardrobe, on the dingy curtains, her sharp, exotic smell.

But the room was empty.

'Sissy!' We peered hopefully into the wardrobe, where the battered hangers made skeleton music in the empty space.

'She has run off!' Mother sounded as startled as if it was one of her own children.

'Not quite,' Father uttered with quiet satisfaction. 'I sent her packing.'

'Why on earth . . . ?' Mother trailed off, for we could all think of reasons why she might be sent packing.

'She is a thief!' Father announced.

My face went red as if I was the thief, but everyone's attention was on Father. 'How do you know?' Mother said.

'Money went missing from my pocket.' He was enjoying his audience. 'At first it was only pennies, but I laid a trap. I left out a shilling. It was missing the following day.'

'Did you speak to her?' said Mother. 'Why didn't you say anything to me?'

'I had no wish to speak with her,' he said. 'Nor did I wish to involve you in the unpleasantness. I wrote directly to her parents, requesting them to remove her before our return from holidays.'

Looking around the abandoned room, it occurred to me that she did not exist any longer, that she had simply materialised and then vanished like a rainbow. But for my father, her presence was still all too real. He did a thing he never did. He flung open the window and took in a lungful of air. 'Now all her secrets are out.'

But I knew another secret. Sissy was going to leave us anyway. About a week before we went she told me, 'I have to go home. I'm after gettin' caught.'

'The police caught you?' I said, wide-eyed.

She rubbed her eyes and laughed. 'No, not the police. Some oul' whoremaster. I suppose he could have been a copper too.'

She pulled me on to the bed beside her. 'Come here till I tell you.

69

Don't ever listen to a word any guy says. They don't mean anything. Men are hard and women are soft – soft on the outside and soft on the inside, and above all, soft in the head. I'll have to go to the nuns now for the nine months and then afterwards take any oul' fella I can get. Not that it makes any odds. Heap of maggots, the lot of them. I should have been a nun myself.'

While I was considering this odd notion, she got up and began examining her possessions. Into one pile she put the dull, childish items with which she had travelled to Dublin, and the other pile was full of beautiful, garish things. When she came to the false bosoms she held them up and then, surprisingly, pushed them up inside my cardigan, pressing them into place in her usual unprudish way. She laughed delightedly and then got pink lipstick and the flower she had worn in her hair and coloured in my lips and decorated my hair. 'There you go, now. That's how you'll look when you're a grown-up lady.' I ran to the wardrobe mirror to see, but the rubber breasts looked like mountains between my narrow shoulders, and beneath the vivid lipstick my teeth were still crooked. I sighed. That's how I would look when I was a lady. 'Write to me, Sissy?' I begged.

She tweaked the points of my falsies between her thumbs and forefingers. 'Some men do that to your real natural nipples,' she remarked. 'Horrible it is. If I wrote to you, kiddo, it'd only be lies, so I'll tell you the truth now. I'm not much for writing and there won't be much to say. I'm a fallen angel. I'm hanging up my harp.'

'How will I find out about things?' I said sullenly.

She concentrated on this for a minute and then said, 'When it comes to money, keep your eyes open and your mouth shut. When it comes to men, keep your mouth open and your eyes shut. Now you know as much as I do.'

Sissy left under a cloud, but we would always feel she walked on one. Before she returned to the country, she dumped her whole

glorious persona in the bin and returned as the sullen, mousy girl we
had met three months earlier. After her departure we girls descended
on the bin and raided it in a silent frenzy, making off with matted
combs, half-full bottles of scent, film magazines, broken strings of
pearls and even bits of underwear. Long after these had been lost
or forgotten we each still retained the habit of licking our arms from
the crook as far as you could manage on your own, whenever we were
feeling lonely.

~

When he offered the room again, Father altered the wording of the
advertisement. 'Girls are too unsteady,' he decided. 'Next time we
will take someone older.' Mother urged him not to advertise for an
older lady in case it drew a procession of old women in search of
somewhere to die. In the end the word 'settled' was agreed upon.

As Mother had feared, the advertisement attracted elderly widows
or spinsters with alcohol-tinged breath. Their voices creaked with
unuse. The lonely luggage of their lives followed them into the hall,
clanking like tins on a string, and Father said, 'Out, out, the room is
taken.' The apples in the garden turned russet and thumped on to the
grass. I twisted hard, juicy knobs from the tree but Mother said the
good apples must be stored and we should eat those on the ground
first. Each one I turned over was home to a dangerously revving
wasp. At night the air was heavy as paste. We could not sleep and
stretched out on the lino to cool ourselves, tracing coins with pencils
through pages of school jotters and discussing ways to cool ourselves
down or fill ourselves up. The actress Jayne Mansfield, who was soon
to marry the famous strong man Mickey Hargitay, bathed in chilled
champagne every day. We imagined a bath of iced Cidona, followed
by the three-course, two-shilling lunch at Woolworth's. We all agreed

that Woolworth's stew and chips was the most delicious thing in the
world. To take our minds off food we wrestled fiercely and painfully.
We had never got used to hugging and kissing like sisters, but fought
in order to be close to one another. Our diet was dominated by apples.
We had them in pies, fritters, sauce. They were baked, stuffed with
sausage meat, layered with cheese and potato. The meticulous misery
with which Father ate up every scrap, encouraging us to do the same,
made us feel that we were anchored to a sinking ship. Mother grew
sleepier and sleepier, staying in bed late in the morning, napping
in the afternoon, drowsing under our overburdened tree with her
sketch pad in her hand in the evening sun.

Only Bridie remained rebellious, refusing to eat the fruit in any
form except apple crumble, which even she could not resist. Mother
worried about her, for she ate almost nothing but voraciously gulped
cups of water, but anyone who knew her could have told that she was
hatching something. 'I have a plan,' she revealed one night as we lay
on the lino. Kitty and I were immediately alert and apprehensive, but
glad to be shaken out of our torpor. 'We're going to have a sale,' she
said. 'We will open the back door to the lane and set up stalls in the
back yard.'

'But we haven't got anything,' Kitty protested. 'What will we
sell?'

Bridie smiled, one of her rare, angelic smiles. 'Mystery parcels.'

'What will we put in them?'

She leaped in the air and spread her arms, exultant in her own
brilliance. 'Mysteries!' she cried.

It was Bridie's idea that we would spend the rest of the summer
writing mysteries like the ones we told each other in bed at night.
Every parcel would contain a story, along with a piece of fruit to
give bulk and promise. There were to be fifty parcels, each to sell
at sixpence, which would make twenty-five shillings.

'What shall we do with the money?' Kitty said.

'Invest it,' Bridie said.

'Invest it in what?' we wondered.

'Books!' Bridie said, 'We'll have a sale of books. There are books all over the house and people give you them for almost nothing. We'll collect old comics and magazines free and sell them at twopence each. As for the books, we will charge a shilling for interesting books and give a dull book away free with every purchase. We will easily clear five pounds.'

The profit from the book sale would be invested in antiques. Everything Bridie said seemed so simple and practical that we could not now imagine why everyone was not rich. 'But what do you know about antiques?' Kitty said cautiously.

'They're old!' replied Bridie with authority. She told us that grown-ups bought broken clocks, old chipped plates, china statues. 'We'll make a fortune,' she promised.

'What will we do with a fortune?' we wondered.

'It's a surprise,' Bridie said primly. 'I can say no more than that it will change all our lives.'

Mother made no objection to our sale. She did not really mind what we did so long as it did not involve friendship with strangers. She even promised to make a large apple crumble in the roasting tin, to be sold in portions, and iced biscuits each with a silver ball in the middle. We set to work writing tales, stretched out on our beds or on the floor, or crouched in the drawing room armchairs. Bridie had said we had only to remember the stories we had told each other, but those plots came and went like dreams in the night. Although they remained vivid in our heads, we could not remember them except in fragments.

'It's because we've never written them down before,' Bridie said. 'Kitty can tell the stories and Rose can type them.'

73

Still they would not emerge. After a week there was only one story, and it wasn't any good.

'Everyone doesn't have to get a story,' Bridie decided. 'We can put drawings and coin tracings as well.' In the end all sorts of things went in – cartoons cut from magazines, old menus and cocktail parasols which our parents had brought back from parties of the past, a few faded souvenirs of Sissy.

Like my father, Kitty had beautiful writing, so she made a poster. 'Monster sale of mystery parcels, this Saturday at 3 p.m.' And to lend virtue she added, 'In aid of lepers.' This notice was put on the outside of the small door that led to the lane. The kitchen table was carried out to the yard and covered with a cloth and set up beneath an apple tree. On it were arranged the mystery parcels, mother's little iced biscuits, the giant apple crumble and a stack of plates and spoons. The parcels were priced at sixpence each, the biscuits at a penny and the pudding at twopence a serving. It was a warm, silver day. Wasps rose from their rotting caves in fallen apples and floated noisily over the fruit crumble. For an hour we sat, quite happy to preside over our arrangement. Children who had been playing ball in the lane came in to peer and jeer. When they went away they told other children. Soon the garden was packed and we had only to find some way to turn the curious onlookers into customers.

'Amazing, unmissable mysteries.' Bridie began a sales pitch on the parcels. 'One of these contains a genuine masterpiece. Each parcel is guaranteed worth two shillings.' One child handed over her sixpence and began to poke a hole in the parcel and peer inside. 'Don't open it until you get home,' Bridie commanded.

'Why not?' asked the customer.

'There could be a major cash prize inside,' Bridie improvised. 'You could be prosecuted for winning an illegal lottery.'

By half past five everything had been sold. The sale had been a great success, with only one small setback. A girl called Dora Curran handed over twopence and ate the whole tin of apple crumble. We tried to stop her and said she could only have a bowlful, but she said it was hers, she had paid for it, and she held on to it until she had eaten it all. All the same we made thirteen and sixpence. As we sat down to tea we each had a shivery, shimmery feeling of success, as if we had performed to an audience and had applause.

At seven o'clock the children came back. Some were in tears. Most of them were with their parents. They held up the scraps of paper with drawings or stories, the apples with a worm hole, and demanded their money back. Bridie refused a refund. She said they had handed over their money of their own free will. Father declared that we had brought shame on the family and he would never forgive us as long as he lived. Kitty sidled past him and fled up to the bedroom where she fetched the money box.

'Traitor!' Bridie hissed.

'We only had to give back six shillings,' we soothed. 'We have more than half the money left.'

'And what do you think will happen now?' She rounded on us furiously. 'Word will get round and everyone will want their money back. All our efforts will have been for nothing.'

Of course she was right. There was not an evening in which some angry parent did not come banging on the door. Mother begged Father to leave her to deal with them, for he did not merely reproach us, he also berated the callers. It was a week before the commotion died down, and we had only three shillings left. Everyone was depressed and exhausted. Even Bridie seemed to have lost faith. She handed us each a shilling. 'There's no point in trying to do anything for anyone,' she said. 'We might as well spend it.'

Kitty and I resolved that we would renew Bridie's faith in us by investing our money. We went to the Iveagh Market to look for something we could sell again for profit. This vast red-brick building in the centre city area known as The Liberties sold second-hand items of every description. The stalls were heaped up with old clothes, wrestling and sinking – fur and lace, drawers, jumpers, trousers, the odd boot or shoe poking through. We meant to buy sensible things but were captivated by two women's nighties, moth-eaten and camphor-reeking. One was in mint-green silk with smocking on the front and a print of pink rosebuds. The other was apricot-pink crêpe de Chine with tiny silk buds on a cream lace panel. We brought these home and wore them for days. I was Liz Taylor and Kitty was Debbie Reynolds, and I offered her the advice which had been quoted by Miss Taylor in one of Sissy's film magazines: 'Never leave one husband, honey, until you have another one lined up.'

Every so often we would examine ourselves in the wardrobe mirror, admiring the way the rouleau straps slipped down our narrow white shoulders to show a plank of pearly chest. The nightwear had been made for tall women with tempting hips and melted around us in pastel folds, waiving all our imperfections. We passed the end of the summer in a hazy torpor until the doorbell rang.

'Who is it?' Kitty said.

'I think it's another parent.' I peeked out of the window and saw the squat figure of a child or woman.

'What will we do? The money's all gone.'

'We'll hide.'

At that moment she looked up. 'I can see you,' she shouted out. 'It's not a view I would pay to see.'

'We'd better answer it,' I said reluctantly.

'We can't go down like this,' Kitty protested, but we heard Father's footstep coming from the kitchen and we raced down together, falling over our hems. We opened the door to find ourselves on a level with the smallest adult we had ever seen. She had a sallow complexion and a searching sort of nose and a little button mouth. Her head was like a dandelion gone to seed. In spite of her low height she had a stoop and came into the hall head first, with her chin jutting over her shelf of a bosom, which was like a rolled-up blanket. She didn't take much notice of Kitty or me except to finger the fabric of our nighties. 'Nice stuff. Pity about the figure.' She clicked her tongue. 'Hope your father has some spondulicks.'

'These are not our normal nighties,' Kitty explained very formally. 'These are our dressing-up nighties.'

'They're not nighties,' she said with disdain. 'They're négligés!'

'Niggly*what?*'

'Négligés. It's continental. It's like negligent. It's what loose women wear.'

At this point Father appeared and stood stiff and silent waiting to command respect. 'Minnie Mankievitz,' she said. She had a faintly foreign accent. 'I don't suppose you take Jews.'

He had no idea what she was talking about but he had to defend himself. 'I have nothing whatever against Jews.'

She began moving from room to room, bending as if she was very tall so that we were presented with the cloth bundle of her bottom. 'Can I help you?' Father said. Having satisfied herself with the ground floor, she proceeded up the stairs, lifting her feet like a duck to negotiate the steps.

'Shame about young couples now.' She ducked into the lavatory and sniffed.

'What about them?' Father pursued her uneasily.

'No respect for decent values. Can't be bothered to get married.'

'I cannot say I am acquainted with such people,' he said.

'Yes, well, it is easy to turn a blind eye.' She now did a quick tour of the bathroom. 'You have nothing, I suppose, against marriage?'

77

'Certainly not! What is it that you want?'

'Mo will be pleased to hear it,' she mused slowly, and then she rounded on him. 'I have to remind you why I come? Some businessman! I am here for the room. You have forgotten you have a room for rent? Now, where is this room? We have almost run out of house.'

Kitty and I had followed them upstairs and were mouthing frantically at Father to tell her that the room was taken, but he felt a need to justify himself. 'Certainly, I have not forgotten. It is right here.'

The small room grew large around her. She inspected everything with an equal measure of criticism and satisfaction, and when she came to the bed she pressed her two hands down on it and then spread them out to caress the counterpane.

'Who is Mo?' Father said helplessly.

'My husband,' she smiled.

For a moment Father wrestled with this information, and then relief swept over his features before he made them grim again. 'You are married?'

'You would prefer we were living in sin?'

He made a sweeping movement with his arm as if ordering out a dog. 'No marrieds! You saw the advertisement. It is a room for a single lady.'

She sat on the bed. 'I saw the advertisement. That is not what it said.'

'I wrote it myself,' he protested.

'You don't even know what you wrote,' she cried in triumph. 'Nowhere it says single. It says, a room for a settled lady. See!' From her bag she produced a torn sheet of newspaper. 'What am I if not settled?'

Father groaned. 'I'll take it,' Mrs Mankievitz decided.

'You cannot have it. It is an error,' he said. 'I will not take a married couple.'

'That's not fair,' she said.

'No,' he agreed.

She remained seated on the bed. She was clamped to it, her two hands grasping the edges. 'I'll take it anyway.'

'What do you mean?' he said feebly.

'I'll live in it alone, stay here until I can find a place for us both. Mo can stay with his father.' She sighed. 'No one expected for us to be happy anyway. I married Mo because no one else would have him. No one would have me either. I suppose you have no objection if he comes to visit me? I'll leave the door open.'

Father tiptoed out of the room, both guilty and resentful. 'She's ugly, she's loony! You should have told her the room was taken,' we whispered bitterly.

Without warning he turned on us. 'Why are you two dressed like trollops? This house has gone to the dogs since Sissy Sullivan set foot in it.'

Mother came home from the shops and put the frying pan on at once, without taking off her hat, in order to reassure us. 'There is no need to make a fuss,' she said, when we had described our new lodger. 'If she is a married woman then she will want to be with her husband as soon as possible, so she won't stay long. In the meantime, we have a rent.'

We became curious about Mo and were all waiting when he came to visit. He too was very small and resembled, more than anything, a mushroom. His head was large and almost bald. His face was pale and slightly wrinkled and his eyes were pale, pale blue and mild as a fish's. Mother answered the door to him. 'Ma?' he said. Minnie flew out of her room and ran down the steps so fast that she almost tumbled over herself. 'Mo!' she cried.

They clung to each other in the hall. Both of them cried. 'I missed you, Ma,' he sobbed, while she patted his back.

They went up the stairs together, wrapped around one another, stopping on every second step to kiss each other on the mouth as if they were very thirsty and each was water. At the top of the steps he cried again, 'Don't send me away, Ma. I'll be good.'

Minnie struggled to say something but she just looked sorrowfully down at my mother. 'Don't send him away,' Mother said quietly. We were all quiet. We had never before seen people who were happily in love.

Chapter Ten

~

September came and Francey was on the doorstep. She wore a boy's cap and trousers. The trousers were too big for her and she had hitched them up and snapped a waspee belt around her middle. From her pocket she took a tarnished silver cigarette case. She flicked it open with her thumb and offered me a sweet cigarette. The achingly sweet white cylinders, made from some chewy, putty-like stuff and stained red at the tip to imitate a glowing cigarette end, offered the brief pleasure of practising at being grown-up, before we ate them. 'Greetings from gangland,' she grinned.

Our new nun, Sister William, began the day by lining the children up against the wall and whispering at us timidly to put out our hands. She then produced a short, thick stick and dealt each girl a savage blow. Occasionally she would sigh regretfully and gently probe a particular girl with the stick and say, 'I think you are a good child but it does not do to make exceptions.' Whack! went the stick. When she came to Francey she asked in a whisper, 'Why are you dressed in male attire?'

'I'm not,' Francey said. 'I'm wearing trousers. They're comfortable.'

As she finished beating the class, she said in her sad and gentle whisper, 'Girls, I am going to tell you a true story. There was a girl who borrowed her brother's trousers to go to a fancy dress party on Hallowe'en. The following day she died and her poor parents saw her ghost flapping on the moon, still wearing the trousers, and crying, "Mother, Father, help me, save me."' She was mild and withdrawn for the rest of the day.

~

After school it was natural for us to go to Minnie's room. Half the neighbourhood children congregated there. She did not care for children but she was more on a level with them and she talked to them as if they were adults, giving advice about money or making scathing comments about their appearance. 'You want to make money, you got to know the market. You got to go where the money is. When I first come to Ireland, I think there's no money at all. People look so poor, so downtrod. Then I see where the money goes. It goes on Jesus.'

She was making cheese straws on her little table. First she mixed the pastry in a bowl with a lot of grated cheese. 'Where do the people spend their spondulicks?' When she had squeezed it into a piece she gave me that bowl to hold and spread a white linen cloth on the table. Then she sprinkled it with flour. She emptied the pastry out of the bowl on to the tablecloth. 'First Communion, Christmas, weddings, that's when the goys get out the wallets. And what do they get for their money? A lot of relations fighting, if you ask me.'

We watched in surprise as she fetched a rolling pin and began to flatten her pastry on the good white cloth. 'That's not where you roll out pastry,' I muttered unwisely. She put her hands on her hips, the rolling pin slung from one hand like a weapon. 'Who says?'

'Nobody rolls pastry on the tablecloth,' said an onlooking child.

'Who's nobody?' jeered Minnie.

'Our mothers,' we all chorused confidently.

'Exactly!' Minnie sliced the pastry into perfect long fingers like piano keys, using the sharp knife so purposefully that we wondered if the cloth would afterwards dangle in shreds. The outside bits were rolled again and fresh fingers were made. 'So Mo and me decide that what people need is a little memento to bring back special memories of their happy day, something they will treasure forever.' She wiped her hands on her apron and went to a drawer, where she removed something wrapped in tissue paper. Carefully she unfolded a prayer book with a pearlised cover and an iridescent Sacred Heart set in its centre. With her eyes on us she lifted the cover and the tinkling tune of 'Faith of our Fathers' flew out. We were all rapt. We thought it utterly gorgeous. 'Musical missals, musical cribs. We thought maybe musical funeral wreaths, playing, "We'll Meet Again".'

'How will you pay for them?' I asked, remembering our own financial problems.

The prayer book went back in the drawer and the biscuits went into the oven. Minnie lifted the floury cloth and shook it out of the window. 'Mostly Mo gets a down-payment with the orders. He also takes my baking door-to-door so he brings home some money every evening.'

'What if people want their money back?' I said.

'No one will want their money back,' she scoffed. 'Such beautiful items! Anyway, everything we sell comes with a money-back guarantee.'

'Father will go mad if people come banging on the door looking for their money back,' I warned.

'You think I am slow upstairs?' She thumped herself on the side of the head. 'Naturally I do not give my real address.'

When the cheese straws came out of the oven she gave us one each and they were the best we had ever eaten. The rest would be sold door-to-door. We took them into the back garden to eat them and noticed that the whole garden was powdered with white, as if it was winter, from where Minnie shook out her baking cloth every day.

~

Minnie and Mo had nothing, but she ran her room like a large household and treated Mo with great respect, as if he was intelligent and intimidating and important. They had three possessions – a small gas oven which they were purchasing on instalments, and two damask linen tablecloths which her uncle had given her as a wedding present. When she wasn't baking, Minnie was forever washing or turning or airing her tablecloths. In the day the small table was temptingly spread with neat batches of tarts or cakes or loaves. At six o'clock these were put into boxes beneath the bed and she spread a white cloth on the table as if for a feast and set up little napkins and dishes and a tea cosy, although they only had a boiled egg like anyone else.

Mother said they were like children or like the mice that played behind the hearth in the dining room, but this was not quite true. I had seen Minnie put away her takings for the day. Now there were notes underneath the piles of coppers and florins. Sometimes she set the box on her knee and opened it just for the pleasure of looking inside. 'You should have a musical money box,' I suggested. She thought about this. 'No. When a poor person makes some money each coin plays its own tune. You want to know why I don't spend my money? You think I am mean? I think I am like a good farmer. Some day his animals have to go to market, but in the meantime, each one has a name and a bell around the neck.'

It was as natural as breathing for Minnie to interfere in everyone's affairs. 'Look at you!' She shook her head in exasperation at Mother.

'Pretty girl like you, rattling round this great big gloomy place like peas at a wake. You look like someone is holding you prisoner against your will. You ought to show some pride in your house, show some respect to your husband.'

'If I showed my husband more respect your husband would not be with you now,' Mother reminded her.

Minnie smote her breast to show remorse, but she went on: 'When you go into your church you put on a scarf to show respect. To show respect to your husband, you put on a scarf. A man has to be set up, made to feel something. That way he is out from under your feet and you can get on with your life. A woman's got to have a husband, but you girls nowadays got this dumb idea that a husband is there to give you everything. A husband is there to give you marriage. For this you give him respect.'

'Don't you miss having children?' Mother tried to gain some advantage.

'What's to miss? I myself was a child. I wouldn't want to look at another one like that in a hurry.'

She had a kind of vanity we had never come across before. Sometimes, with her hands and apron covered in flour, she would swagger in front of the wardrobe mirror and say, 'Look at me! The worst-looking woman that ever lived. And guess what? I got the best husband in the world.' She would tell us about the moment when they met, how her uncle said he wasn't going to look after her no more and he gave her fifty pounds. 'Now you go look after your cousin Mo. You go and marry him and give his parents a break.'

'I made up my mind I would marry him if he was like Bela Lugosi. A woman is nothing without a husband. A woman needs a house to run. They sat me in the parlour and made me wait while they got Mo ready. There was I saying my prayers, expecting some big ape with fangs and a drool out of his mouth, and they bring in the sweetest little guy I ever saw. When I put my arms around him he looked so happy. If he had a tail he would have wagged it. My parents were dead. I never had anyone of my own. I knew in that moment that heaven had made him for me.'

Every morning Mo went out with his case containing the musical prayer book and around his neck a covered tray on strings with samples of Minnie's baking. For the first time, people in dull brick houses, used to dull food, tasted almond macaroons, chocolate pyramids, coconut pyramids, wine biscuits, spiced biscuits, vanilla biscuits, or Minnie's Purim cake, which was a pastry triangle filled with cream cheese, raisins and sugar. Minnie's baking had a particular crispness. No one could resist it. And Mo looked so enchanted when the prayer book opened and spouted harmonies that he often sold a missal too.

'Wouldn't it be better to give Mo shillings and pence instead of pound notes?' I watched as she took out a neat slice of pound notes from the cash box and laid them on top of a black notebook and put both into the suitcase with the musical missal. 'If people want change a big note of money won't be much use.'

'If your muscles were as big as your eyes, you'd be Tarzan,' Minnie observed. 'Well, it's never too soon to learn, since your parents have as much sense as a boiled hen. When Mo shows people the missal, they want it and can't afford it, the first thing they do is give him a tale of hardship – how much it costs, the wedding, the funeral, the First Communion. So now I offer a little extra service – small loans at low interest. You see, a business is like a little tree. It doesn't grow straight up like a stick. It grows branches.'

If Mother refused to take Minnie's blunt counsel there were others who noted her rapid progress and she traded also in advice. Often we saw her emerge from a house bearing her fee – a brass ornament, a brocade cushion, a glass sweet dish. It was by this means that the room was furnished. Her favourite exchange was a framed photograph of some stern and noble man or a good-looking woman. She was building up a family. Next to a husband, she said, one needed forebears. 'Four bears.' She emphasised both syllables as if she had memorised the word a long time ago, but even she seemed surprised when Bridie appeared clutching a photograph of our beautiful dead grandfather in a military uniform. 'You have to help us,' she said. 'Our parents are hopeless and we are poor and unhappy.'

'Unhappy?' Minnie inspected the photograph as if for forgery. 'You want to know what happiness is? Happiness is to own a space in the world that was prepared for you by people who love you. You think your parents are holding you back. I think they have given you a nice red carpet you will walk on all your life.'

'That's just family life,' Bridie said. 'Everyone has that.'

'Do they now? I was brought up by an uncle. When I was a child he said I was so ugly he hoped I was useful. I looked after him until he was old and then he found a young wife and threw me out with nothing except fifty pounds to set me up with a man he said was backward and needed looking after. But Mo's not backward. He's just not forward. I hardly remember my parents. We lived in a slum and they died of typhoid poisoning when I was five.'

'I'm sorry,' Bridie said.

'Don't you feel sorry for me,' Minnie snapped. 'Sorry for you I feel. I take one look at your parents – dyed-in-the-wool babes the both of them.' Her anger subsided and she sighed. 'I know. It's not easy to be a child, expected only to pray or play all the time.'

'I don't do either one,' Bridie said.

'Well, what do you do?'

Bridie said that she could draw and play the piano.

'Very ladylike,' Minnie sniffed. 'Can you make spells?'

'What sort of spells?' Bridie was cautious now.

Minnie shrugged. 'You wish for what you want.'

'But I do,' Bridie protested. 'I wish all the time.'

'No you don't. Your life is too soft. You don't know what it is to wish. You got to wish with all your might. You have to wish so hard you become the wish. A girl's first menstrual blood is also useful.'

'What?' Bridie said.

'You don't know about the curse?'

'No.' But even Bridie was impressed. Curses and spells.

~

Shortly after this Minnie invited us to her room. She had an announcement to make. 'Mo has acquired a position in the public domain.' Mo's eye was on a plate of teiglech. We were becoming familiar with Jewish baking and particularly liked these sticky pastries made from ginger pastry cooked in ginger syrup. 'My husband is now the principal usher at the Princess Cinema.' She handed round the plate and allowed us each to take a pastry, and then she gave the plate to Mo, who counted the remaining pieces and ate them one by one.

With Mo in the public domain Minnie did not want him worn out with walking the pavements all day, so she asked us to help sell her baking. Bridie made us carry trays of biscuits to school, as Mother would not let us knock on strange doors. At the end of the week, when Minnie paid our commission, I watched sadly as Bridie dropped my profits into her money box. 'Can't I have anything for myself?' I begged. 'No,' she said. 'You will only spend it on sweets. Every penny must go towards the surprise.'

~

Minnie began to prosper. On the outside nothing had changed, for she would never consider spending money on herself. 'Mutton dressed as Lady Muck,' she would say scornfully. She did not grow noticeably fatter or sleeker. The change was in her expression. It was as if her eye had been fed. She no longer stooped to peer around corners but walked with her head up, sending the roll of her bust ahead, proudly, as if she had baked it herself. It was in this new carriage that she went to ask Mother if she could use her oven.

'You have a very good little oven up there,' Mother said. 'I hardly think that mine is better.'

'Better is not the issue. Bigger, the point is. I need a bigger oven. I cannot keep up with orders.'

Mother looked uncomfortable. 'I'd like to help, but you have rented a room, not the whole house.'

Minnie shook a fist at her, but then she opened it and inside were two shiny half-crowns. 'Five shillings – only to use your oven. Only when you yourself do not require it. I give you five extra shillings a week.'

Mother looked longingly at the money, but then she covered Minnie's hand with her own to put it out of sight. 'My oven is clapped out – no better than a candle sometimes. I wouldn't be doing you any favours.'

When she had got rid of Minnie, she confided to us in a whisper, 'I don't like the idea of sharing my kitchen with another woman.'

To her embarrassment, Minnie poked her head back around the door. 'You do not share. I do my baking at night, when you are all fast asleep like sheep.' Triumphantly she slapped the two half-crowns on the kitchen table, where Mother could not ignore them.

We slept with the smell of cheese, vanilla, cinnamon, almonds, chocolate rising in our dreams. When we came down in the morning, the kitchen, which had always been dank and cold, was warm and still scented with baking, and the yard outside was frosted with flour. There was always a plate of fresh biscuits on the table, or a fresh sponge cake, which she called a plava. 'Damaged!' Minnie shrugged off our thanks. 'It is a crime to waste good food.' But the biscuits were the most perfect we had ever eaten and we knew Minnie scattered them like good-luck charms to ward off any change in her fortunes.

Mother didn't like the arrangement. True to her word, Minnie stayed out of her way and only crept downstairs with her bowls and pans and boxes of ingredients when the rest of the house was in bed. And she always tidied up after her. That was the problem. Our gloomy, homely kitchen was now spotless and shining. Mother liked the relaxed air of her own space, where she could do some ironing, or toast bread on the fire, darn socks while she listened to the wireless, cook and eat a meal. She no longer felt at home in this sterile environment. One morning she came down to find that Minnie had scrubbed out the pantry, and that the shadowy recesses were now lined with bright oilcloth and the top shelves, where old lumpy glucose and out-of-date medicines were kept, had tins of biscuits and boxes of cakes. 'She is taking over my house,' she complained to Father.

But Father admired Minnie's devotional housekeeping and he also had a very sweet tooth. 'I cannot see that there is any harm in thorough cleaning, and I have not tasted such pastries since I was a boy,' he said.

'I will never take another woman lodger,' Mother swore. 'Men are less trouble.'

'The toilet floor would be awash,' Father said in disgust, and we wondered about this in silence.

~

Bridie had become obsessed with making money. Kitty and I used to lift the money box and try to guess how much was in it. It grew heavier and heavier. Picking it up was like lifting a drowned man from the river. 'How much is there?' we asked Bridie.

'Not enough,' she said. 'When I'm old enough to leave school, I'll go into partnership with Minnie.'

'Can you bake?' Minnie asked when she put forward this proposal. It was Friday, so she took from the oven a freshly baked Challah loaf, with its twisted shiny surface and the mouthwatering smell of poppy seeds.

'I can do other things.'

'You do not put your heart in them. Everything you do is a means to an end.' Minnie rapped the loaf with a knuckle as if summoning up spirits, and then set the table with her good white cloth and candles. 'Always in a hurry. Selling is work, but making is art. Into everything you make, you put a little bit of your soul. Then when that thing goes out into the world, your spirit is set free.'

Bridie muttered, 'All that fuss over a loaf of bread.'

'So?' Minnie said. 'You have better to offer? You are a clever girl, but if you are not true to your talents you could turn out to be a pain in the tail.'

'Pain in the tail yourself,' Bridie said, and she stamped out of the room. At the door she turned back. 'I can draw,' she said.

'Well then, stick to drawing, and I hope you can draw good.'

Kitty and I got bored with selling. Bridie's plans were too remote and we weren't allowed to spend any of the money we made. Then I lost a whole week's earnings. I was sure I had left the money in my coat pocket. Bridie was convinced I had spent it. At this point I decided to give up.

'There isn't enough money yet.' Our big sister was furious.

'For what?'

'A surprise has to be a surprise. You'll find out soon enough.'

'When?'

'Christmas,' she muttered as she pulled on her nightie. I was startled by the sight of a dandelion fuzz of golden hair under her arms, but Kitty's glance signalled a different sort of awe, and it only then sank in just what Bridie had said. At last she was about to reveal the plan that would change all our lives.

Chapter Eleven

~

Before that there was another surprise. It was Dora MacAlorum, who turned up on a freezing day demanding to see Mo.

'What do you want with him?' Mother felt impelled to protect Mo from the sharp-looking blonde in a thin red coat that matched her peeling chin and gloveless red hands.

'Matrimony,' Dora said in a slightly mocking way. 'Seeing as I am to be the mother of his child.'

Mother's first thought was to get her inside quickly before this proclamation would bounce off the high walls of the red-brick houses and in the windows, into the ears of the neighbours. 'This must be some mistake.' She hurried down to the kitchen, pursued by the tattle of Dora's heels. 'Mr Mankievitz is a very happily married man.'

'It's a mistake right enough.' Dora shook off her coat. She was so thin that the hard little bump of her stomach was visible at once. She went to the gas cooker, where she stood warming her hands. Then she leaned down as if to warm her cheek. Her frail blonde hair shrivelled as she lit a cigarette on the ring.

'What do you plan to do?' Mother said.

'If it's all the same to youse,' Dora sat down and crossed her legs, 'I'll stop here the minute.' She had a Belfast accent that made each word sound as if it had been sliced off sharply at an angle.

Mother looked doubtful and Dora said, 'I could always wait next door. The thing is, I'm in a jam and I don't really care who knows.'

This became evident when Bridie and Kitty and I got home from school. 'You don't believe me, so you don't.' Mother had put up a wall of indifference, which was the nearest she could get to disapproval, and Dora was hammering on this wall. 'You're going to ask me what opportunity we had, where we done it.'

'No I'm not.' Mother cast a cautionary look our way.

'We done it in the toilet. Before the patrons was admitted. I work in the Princess with Mo.'

We stared at her, longing for enlightenment, knowing it would not come. She stared back at us, her bright, lively eyes without expression or feeling, like a bird or a cat. She wore a lot of lipstick and mascara and powder, but with one curious feature. She seemed to have taken literally the expression to powder your nose, for her nose was a bright, dusty island of rose and the rest of her face was greasy and wan, except for her red, peeling chin.

Minnie came in, laden with bags for Christmas baking. She dived into the pantry, where she had taken to storing her dry goods. 'I won't stay, Edie,' she panted. 'I've got something in my oven.'

'This is Mrs Mankievitz,' Mother said to Dora.

'I've got something in mine.' Dora slapped her middle. 'And guess who put it there?'

Minnie gave her a long, hard look. 'Your husband, I hope.'

'No, yours!' Dora said in triumph.

'Oh, poor Minnie!' Mother flapped. 'Don't upset yourself.'

Minnie planted her own hands on her hips and stared at the girl. After a while she gave a yelp. 'Hah! Some other Mo you may have had, but not my Mo. Eeny, Meeny and Miney also, you may have had.' She laughed and left the kitchen. She waved at Mother to reassure her. 'Take no notice. She got herself in trouble with some other guy. She's just looking for a pansy.'

'I think you mean a patsy,' Mother said.

'Whatever she can get.'

Minnie put raisins soaking in brandy, dusted cherries with flour, sliced up angelica and candied orange peel and crystallised ginger. 'This should have been done months ago but how was I to know everyone was going to want a cake for Christmas? Growing up Jewish, Christmas kind of passed me by.' She did not mention Dora at all, but the rest of us were dying of curiosity. Mo came home and Minnie plumped his cushions, took off his jacket, gave him tea and a hot jam pastry. 'Put up your feet, Mo. You look wore out.' She listened while he told her how sales were going on the new musical crib, and later helped him to read out some items from the paper. After he had had a rest she buttoned him into his usher's jacket and sent him off to the Princess. Then she told us to scram. 'Tell your mother to come up here.' Carefully she tucked greaseproof paper around one of the beautiful cakes she had made. 'Tell her I got a nice little present for her.'

~

'Of course Mo is not responsible. We never thought so for a minute.' Mother's whispered conversation came like strands of mist through the keyhole. 'But why on earth would she pick on him?'

'Mo's nice,' Minnie said defensively.

'Yes, but he's married. Even if he believed her, he would be in no position to do anything about it. There is no divorce in Ireland. Why not find some single man?'

There was a pause while Minnie thought about it. 'Between you and me and the postman,' she decided, 'I don't think she's picking on Mo at all. I think it's me.'

'What could she possibly have against you?'

'Nothing personal. Just I've got something she hasn't.'

'You mean Mo?'

'I don't mean Mo. I mean money. I think she's trying to blackmail me. I do business with a lot of good and respectable people. I sell religious artefacts as well as cakes and biscuits. If word got out that Mo was a fancy man, you think these people would wish to take holy things from his hands?'

'Where would she get the idea you have money?' Mother wondered.

'It's my own fault,' Minnie admitted. 'I've done a lot of foolish things in my time, but the most foolish thing is to give Mo large lumps of money to carry around. Sometimes Mo ain't got much sense. Maybe he got to showing off his money. Oh, missus, what are we going to do?'

'I think we should leave it until after Christmas,' Mother advised. 'If she comes back then we will all confront her together – you and me and Eugene and Mo. When she sees that none of us believe her story, I am sure she will back off.'

'Edie, you're a saint! I work so hard just so Mo will be safe if anything happens to me. I want nothing for myself. It just doesn't seem fair that some termite-faced little tramp should get her hands on my money.'

'No one's going to get their hands on your money,' Mother promised her.

There was a pause and a sigh. 'I think maybe they already have. Several times when I count the money in the day there is a little bit missing – not a great big lot – a pound or a ten-shilling note.'

'Well, they won't any more,' Mother promised.

~

A few days after that we heard a piercing cry of 'Thief!'

Who could it be? We were all in the kitchen and there was nobody else in the house except Minnie and Mo upstairs and Francey waiting for me in the hall. Francey! I raced from the room, tearing my half-knotted plait from Mother's grasp. Francey came thundering down the stairs, her gold slingbacks flapping, her bare toes blue with cold from the freezing December weather. Hot in pursuit was Minnie, waving her rolling pin. 'Filthy little swindler!' She caught Francey and held her up by her hair as if she had beheaded her. 'I catch her red-fingered. When I went to the toilet, she sneaked in my room and stole a pound from my purse.'

'I wasn't taking it.' Francey tried to squirm away. 'I only wanted to see how much you had.'

'A lot less since you've been round. This isn't the first time.' She tweaked Francey's ear. 'That's where my pounds and ten-shilling notes been going. One day she tell me it's raining and to get my washing from the line. Another day she says there is a letter for me in the hall. Each time, she is lying. Each time she is thieving.'

'It's not true,' I cried.

'Save your breath,' Minnie snapped. 'Better you use your eyes for watching the coat pockets in the hall. I'm willing to bet some of you's been finding holes in your pockets lately.'

I knew then that it was true. I remembered the biscuit money that had gone missing from my pocket. Then an awful thought struck me. I had to ask Francey, but not with all the others standing round.

Father commenced a tug-of-war with Minnie, who was busy searching Francey's clothing. 'Two pounds one and sixpence – a lot of money for a little ruffian. I would like to see her rot in prison, but failing that I would settle for never to see her at all.'

97

Father, too, would have liked to see Francey rot in jail, but she was too young to go to prison and he would have hated the shame of having policemen at his house. When Minnie let go, he led her to the door and thrust her out.

'Schnorrer!' Minnie yelled after her. 'Scrubber!'

'I knew that child was not a suitable companion,' Mother said to me. 'You are never to see her again.'

She seemed to forget I sat next to that child every day in school. 'Sorry, pal!' She slid grinning into the desk beside me.

'How long have you been stealing?' I said.

Francey laughed. She had very white teeth in spite of all the sweets she ate, and she was growing up faster than the rest of us. With her grimy brown skin and her little gold earrings and her figure that was already getting a grown-up appearance, she looked so smart my heart ached with admiration. 'As long as my fingers could hold on,' she said. 'If I didn't I'd have starved to death long ago.'

'Yes, but how long have you been doing it in my house?'

'Quiet!' Sister William said meekly. 'Are you going to make me slap you both again?'

Francey eyed her in a slow, amused way and then turned back to me. 'I made a mistake with you. You always look so neat with your plaits and your bows that I thought your folks would be loaded. I never met such bare pockets in my life. A penny here, thruppence there. Once I got a bob. That must have been six months ago.'

'Last summer?'

'Just before the holliers.'

I felt as if I had gone on fire. I sat there blazing while Sister William timidly tiptoed down the aisle and administered two whacks, but the whole of me burned so badly I hardly felt the slap. Francey had been responsible for the theft that had sent Sissy Sullivan back to the country. All morning I sat in silent shock.

When lunchtime came, Francey called, 'Coming?' in her usual unconcerned way.

I shook my head. 'Snob!' she said.

'Scrubber!' I brazenly echoed Minnie's insult.

I felt awful after that. Francey wouldn't have taken any notice of Minnie, but she wanted me to admire her just as I wanted her to admire me. When we parted for the Christmas holidays I knew we would never be friends again.

~

Minnie gave Mother a turkey. It lay like a great reclining nude in the pantry. Too big for any of our dishes, it had been hoisted into a roasting tin where its limbs lolled over the rim. The cat's face jerked with longing. My sisters and I could not catch sight of it without thinking of it crisped and fleshy on the tongue. And there was so much of it. This thought upset our mother. 'How will we get through it? It will still be looking at us in January.'

The fowl had a different effect on Father. It made him sentimental. 'I haven't seen a bird like that since I was a child. Mother used to cook dinner for twelve. She had to set a second table up by the window.'

'I daresay she ate it whole and gave the guests the bones to pick,' Mother muttered.

'Ma and Pa don't even have a turkey any more,' he said. 'Why don't we ask them? As you say, there is far too much for the five of us, and I feel I should repay their hospitality.'

Mother gave him a bleak look. 'Ask Minnie and Mo too, why don't you, since it is they who have provided it.'

He went at once to do so, feeling too expansive to sense the irony.

'Nine for dinner!' Mother lamented. 'He has forgotten that everyone will have to have sherry and wine as well as turkey. He has

99

forgotten that someone has to do the washing-up. It sometimes seems that I am the only grown-up around here, and yet I have no authority.'

'I'm grown-up,' Bridie said indignantly, but this only upset Mother more, and she hugged Bridie in an agitated way. 'No, little Bridie – don't grow up yet.'

Although Mother and Minnie had grown close after Dora MacAlorum, there was competition between them. Mother believed the world of the mind to be the superior one and felt that intelligent women were wasted on housework. Minnie could not understand Mother, with a whole good house at her disposal and nothing to show for it but a few shillings in rent. She did not believe in the life of the mind, considering it a superficial thing, like prettiness, but thought the brain should be bent to practical matters. Now Mother felt under siege, as if Minnie had sent the giant turkey down to act as watchdog. 'Sometimes I wish she had never come to the house. Jews are very sociable. They do not understand that the thing I value most in all the world is privacy. I know that she has a kind heart, but we would have been better off on our own with a boiled egg and a biscuit.' We agreed with her out of loyalty, but we loved the bustle and excitement in our quiet house. More visitors meant more presents. Suddenly the house was full of people. It was as if the turkey summoned them. George and Alma Bates, our wealthy friends who owned the advertising agency, arrived with a large box of chocolates and a bottle of whiskey. Father had forgiven George for the time he had offered work to Mother and was anxious to show off our temporary plenty. 'Come and have Christmas with us,' he said. Mother moaned and went off to count the good plates.

A few days before the feast, Kitty and I went to the wardrobe to feel the weight of the money box and found that it weighed nothing at all. 'Where's the money gone?' we asked Bridie.

'Where do you think?'

'The surprise!' we cried out delightedly. 'Let's see.'

'Since I had to manage all on my own in the end, it is really none of your business,' she replied.

This stung, since so much of our money and effort had gone into it. We decided to buy Mother something from ourselves. There was a novelty shop in the village owned by a hunchbacked shoemaker, and we spent several hours poring over its enticing treasures, turning them upside down to see the price pencilled on the bottom. We both loved a set of smiling pink china cats with gold eyes and whiskers made out of tufts of real white rabbit fur, but they cost a shilling. 'Could we have one of them?' we asked, but he said they came as a pair. 'How much have you got?' he asked, and we told him sixpence. 'You could order them now and place a deposit,' he said. 'Or you could buy them on the HP: sixpence now and tuppence a week.' 'We'd like to place an order,' we decided. 'But we would like to take it with us now.' As he wrapped the cats in white tissue and then in Christmas paper, decorated with robins and holly, we could imagine Mother's happiness as she performed this ceremony in reverse, and we owned this happiness with the added excitement of having conducted successful business.

Christmas was unlike any other day, for it began in the middle of the night. From the moment we woke to Santa's muffled curses as he deposited our parcels, we lay in a rigid pretence of sleep until the first wan leavening of dark had us up and tearing at our presents. We came down to find Mother already sitting at the kitchen table drinking tea and smoking a cigarette and staring wearily at the great big turkey which had been laid out on the kitchen table beside a basin of stuffing. She smiled as we told her excitedly about our surprises. 'You stuff the turkey, girls,' she said. 'I can't bear to look at the damn thing. I will go and get dressed for Mass. I want you all to be very good girls

101

today. I am feeling weary. Christmas is not the same for adults as it is for children. Nothing really nice ever happens when you are fully grown up.' We presented Mother with the china cats. She unwrapped the tissue and gazed at the cats and she laughed. She was as pleased as we had imagined. We felt delirious with happiness. 'In all your lives,' she said, 'no one will ever love you as much as I do.' She put the cats on the drawing room mantelpiece along with some Victorian ornaments. Then she glanced around the room, at the lighted tree and the cards, and the paper-chain ornaments which had been hung by Father with as much grim tension as if he had been hanging a felon. She gave a small shudder and said to herself, 'Oh, the price one has to pay to get children.'

The turkey went into the oven and we went to Mass. Then the fire was lit in the icy dining and drawing rooms. Father inserted a handle into the end of the mahogany table and cranked it apart, showing bare metal spines in the centre. Two more slices of wood, known as leaves, were rested in the space and the table now nearly filled the whole room. When the good tablecloth was taken from the press it was limp and cold as chilled pastry. China plates were brought from the outside pantry and left on the hearth to warm, while Kitty and I squatted on the floor to polish the cutlery. Chairs were carried from the kitchen, which was full of rattle and steam from the pudding and ham which simmered on the stove. The guests were due at one and we were to eat at two. It was about half past twelve when Mother gave a yelp from the kitchen. We ran down to find her standing at the open oven door, staring at the turkey, which had lost its creamy nudist look and had now acquired a bruised and lacklustre appearance like a peeled potato left out of water.

'What's wrong with the turkey?' we cried.

'It's the gas supply,' she moaned. 'The oven is no more than a glimmer.'

'Temporary overload!' Father diagnosed. 'We may be half an hour late with lunch, but that will just give us time for a drink beforehand.' He was usually in a bad humour at Christmas, but this year he was excited.

'If the temperature rises it will toughen the bird,' Mother said gloomily.

'I'll sharpen the knives,' he promised.

He went in the car to fetch his parents. Mother's humour improved with the arrival of George and Alma Bates. Alma, who had brought us all selection boxes as well as a bottle of vermouth and one of gin, commanded George to make some drinks. 'And put on some music. Let's get a bit of cheer into the bloody day. No Christmas carols!' she warned. 'Find something we can dance to. Put some more coal on the fire. The place is like an ice-box.'

'"Mountain Greenery"?' George rummaged agreeably through the selection of records.

'Eugene doesn't like the fires too high,' Mother said. 'He says it damages the furniture.'

'Oh, Edie, stop parroting the blasted man. He is stingy.'

'Don't eat those bars before lunch,' Mother said, as we began opening our selection boxes.

'Don't nag, dear,' Alma said.

To everyone's dismay, Mother then sort of crumpled up as if she was going to faint, but in fact she only slid into a chair and tears slipped down her face. George ran to wrap his arms around her, but Alma got there first. 'The drinks!' she hissed at him. She mopped Mother's face with her hankie and patted her back. 'What is it, dear? Is it because Eugene has been out of work?'

'Hush!' Mother eyed us sadly. 'I have said nothing to the children.'

'Oh, why not, Edie?' Alma was impatient. 'You feel you must carry everything on your own shoulders, and then when you can't, you suffer from guilt. What is there that is so shameful about Eugene being out of work, except for the fact that he could find some sort of work if he was not so proud?'

'Don't, Alma. Don't criticise him,' Mother begged.

'No, all right. Is it money? How stupid of me. Of course it's money. George!' she ordered. 'Write out a cheque.'

George, in the middle of mixing cocktails, looked bewildered, but he went for his chequebook.

'No!' Mother pulled herself together. 'Actually, we're all right for money at the moment. We have a married couple in the maid's room paying a good rent.'

'What is it, dear? What is the matter?'

'It's the damn turkey.' Mother put her head down again and wept. 'The oven is down and it will never cook.'

Alma went and opened the oven in a discreet way, as if peering into a room with a dying patient. She twiddled the oven's knobs and came away sighing. 'Who wants a turkey anyway? Awful bloody bird. Have you got any celery and cheese? I'll make some cocktail things. Children!' She turned to us. 'Eat up your selection boxes.' George ambled over with giant drinks. 'Here, darling!' Alma held it to Mother's mouth as if she was a baby. 'Drink up! That's better. Now, put on your lipstick before Eugene gets back.'

~

When Granny arrived she was upset to find Mother dancing with another woman. Alma was leading and Mother drooped on her shoulder. George conducted from an armchair with a stick of celery. We girls sat on the sofa laughing as we peeled a bowl of potatoes.

'The Queen's speech will be in an hour,' Granny hissed at Father.

'We're back, Edie!' Father called loudly and hopefully. Mother waved sleepily. 'Dinner may be a little late!' he shouted at the new visitors, as if they were deaf. 'The oven is down.'

'Why did you bring us here?' Granny grumbled. 'I did not come all this way to stand famished while your wife makes an exhibition of herself.'

As always, when Father felt under attack, he took it out on Mother. 'What has got into you?' He had to follow her in a circle as Alma whirled her around. 'You look as if you have been drinking.'

'Leave her alone!' Alma clutched Mother, who made a slight noise of protest. 'Why should she not have some fun on Christmas Day?'

'There are visitors!'

Alma reminded him sharply that she too was a visitor. She handed him Mother and pushed Granny into a chair, ordering George to give the bloody woman a drink.

'I never touch anything but sweet white wine,' Granny said bitterly. We always had sweet wine with the dinner, and this was Granny's way of bringing the subject back to her meal. Bridie fetched the bottle labelled Spanish Sauterne that was to accompany the turkey. 'One of these days,' Alma splashed wine into a glass, 'Edie and I will just take off.'

Granda wondered mildly if the men might get anything to wet their whistle, and Alma promised she would give him a stiff one.

'I'll give you a stiff one!' He winked at Granny.

'Shut up, you old fool,' Granny said.

He drank thirstily from Alma's generous measure and then did what he always did when he was a bit drunk. He began to sing. He had a good voice, although he was old. George accompanied at the piano and Alma sank on to the sofa with Mother. Lured by song, Minnie and Mo came down. Father watched them in panic. 'How is the turkey doing?' he whispered to Mother.

105

'Oh, the turkey!' Mother roused herself guiltily and Alma snapped at him to stop upsetting the poor girl.

'What is to be done?' Father begged.

'Announce the surprise!' Kitty urged Bridie.

'Have we come too early?' Minnie, holding on to Mo, could sense the unstable air, but Kitty told them that they had come just in time for the surprise.

'I want my dinner.' Granny stood up, a little unsteadily. 'I have always been seated at the table for the Queen's speech.'

To Mother's dismay, Father began to lead a deputation to the dining room.

'This is ridiculous,' she worried. 'I haven't put on the sprouts yet.'

'We won't go,' Alma said. 'We are quite happy where we are. Why should we obey, just because a man says so?'

'Because the man is a husband,' Minnie said automatically.

'Don't cause trouble,' Mother begged them both. 'Let us just try and get through the day.' She looked at us beseechingly. 'Girls, maybe you can help out.'

I think she meant that we should put on the vegetables, but Kitty leaped into action. 'Ladies and gentlemen,' she said, 'now that we are all here, I wish to announce the surprise. This is a surprise that is going to change all our lives. We have saved for it with our own money.'

I interrupted her to point out that we weren't all there, for Father was missing.

Mother rose reluctantly to look for him, but Alma held her back. 'I'll go. Eugene!' We heard her heels on the steps down to the kitchen, and then a yelp. This time Mother left the room at a run and Kitty and I followed. Alma leaned on the door frame, limp with mirth. Father was in the kitchen, crouched at the open oven door. He held a small lit electric fire inside the oven.

'He is trying to cook the blasted bird by scorching it,' Alma said.

Mother took the fire from him and led him away. When he returned to the drawing room he seemed weak. 'Lunch may be a little while,' he said faintly.

'They are making a fool of you, Eugene,' Granny said. 'You have no control in this house. The women drink and dance. The children ride bicycles in the hall.'

'None of my children has bicycles,' he protested. 'They are forbidden to ride them. Bicycles are dangerous. You could knock your front teeth out in a fall.'

'She has a bicycle.' Granda pointed to Bridie, who cycled into the drawing room.

'What are you playing at? Where did you get that bloody thing? Whose is it?' Father found a welcome focus for his pent-up anger.

'Mine!' Bridie dismounted calmly in the doorway.

'Where's the surprise, Bridie?' Kitty and I said nervously.

'This is the surprise,' Bridie said. 'I have bought myself a bicycle.'

'But it can't be!' I protested. The surprise was going to change all our lives.

'Can I have a go?' Kitty fingered it eagerly but Bridie snatched it away with a look of menace.

'As I am the eldest I mean to change your lives by example,' Bridie said. 'No one in this household ever does what they want, except me. I will show you that no one can stop you doing what you want. We do not have to do what Father says or be poor because he is poor. I have set myself free. I will set you all free.'

'You will take it back to the shop next week. You are forbidden to ride it. Good God, to think that your mother and I have gone without so that you could squander money on this. Where did you get the money?'

'I earned it.' Bridie squared up to him. 'And if I can earn money, you could earn money.' She mounted her bicycle and rode serenely down the hall.

'I will burn the blasted thing,' Father shouted after her, but you could see from the way he stopped then and gritted his teeth that it was a futile threat and he was caught between anger and admiration.

'The Queen . . . !' Granny moaned.

'What is going on, Edie?' Minnie whispered to Mother. 'Is something the matter?'

Mother whispered about the dinner and Minnie nodded. 'I'll fix it for you.'

Granny stood up. 'I am going to the table now. Perhaps someone will give me a drop to toast the Queen.'

Father marched after her as if they meant to lead a revolution, and then Mother began ushering in the Bateses as if it was a perfectly normal situation. 'Come along, Minnie,' she said. 'Where is Mo?'

Mo was staring out of the window. He looked small and wistful, as if he was on the lookout for Santa.

'Mo, come along. We have to roast the Queen,' Minnie called.

'In a minute,' he said, like a child.

'Poor Mo,' Mother sighed. 'He thinks there should be more to Christmas. I expect he is right.'

Minnie went and jogged his elbow. 'Come along. We are all here.'

'Unless he has asked someone else,' Mother joked edgily.

'Mo!' Minnie scoffed. 'Who does he know?'

'Dora.' He smiled as the front gate squealed, and our gaze was startled by the bright glow of her chin and overcoat against the leaden winter day.

Chapter Twelve

~

For a week Minnie stayed in her room. When Mother brought up a cup of turkey soup, it seemed as if all the nights of staying up had caught up with her at once. She wore an old dressing gown. The curtains were drawn and the room looked jumbled.

'He broke my heart,' she said. 'I got no heart left for nothing no more.'

Mother put a hand on her arm and spoke carefully. 'A broken heart is not the same as broken legs. You can still get around.'

'I used to pretend to be hard on the outside, so people don't take advantage of me,' Minnie said. 'Now I got to pretend to be human on the outside.'

Mother sighed. 'Lots of people do. Half the women in the world are composed of paint and peroxide. Think of Dora MacAlorum. Without the help of the Walpamur Paint Company she would not look half as good as a Woolworth's teacup.'

Minnie shook Mother off. 'Last thing I want to do is think of Dora MacAlorum.'

~

But it was all any of us had done since her arrival on Christmas Day. 'No room at the inn, eh?' Dora had only laughed when Mother told her she could not come in. 'Plenty of drink, though, by the looks of youse lot. I wouldn't say no.'

'I'm so sorry, Minnie,' Mother said. 'I'll get rid of her.'

'No!' Minnie's voice was very quiet. 'Let her stay. You said we would face this all together. Well, we are together now. Ladies and gentlemen,' she addressed the room very solemnly, 'this young lady claims that my husband has got her in the family way.'

'Who's her husband?' Alma whispered eagerly, as if we were in a theatre. 'The little fellow? Oh, how sweet.'

'What is going on, Eugene?' Granny said. 'Has your wife been renting out rooms in this house for immoral purposes?'

'Oh, shut up,' Mother said.

'Yes, shut up,' said Granda.

'Everyone be quiet,' Minnie said. 'Only Mo has to speak. Mo, you hear what the young lady says against you. What do you wish to say about her?'

We all turned to Mo expectantly. It was only then that we saw how he watched Dora. 'She's my girl,' he said.

There was total silence in the room. Even our faces had been robbed of expression, until Minnie forced a laugh. 'Listen to him! Always the ladies' man! So chivalrous, my Mo. Come on, Mo, you can say what you want. We'll send her packing.'

'No!' Mo cried in distress. Dora gave her small, wintry smile. 'There's my wee man,' she said in her mocking way.

Minnie no longer laughed. 'Mo, she's trying to take you away from me. She's only after our savings. You know you don't really like a dirty little liar like her. We only need for you to say it.'

'Mo won't say nothing against me,' Dora said. 'He thinks I'm the cat's pyjamas.'

'Mo, say it!' Minnie pleaded.

Mo thought before pronouncing slowly and carefully, 'Mo loves Dora.' He smiled proudly.

Granny shot out of her seat as if she had sat on a thistle. 'It is time!' she said.

'Oh, what is she on about?' Alma groaned, but Granny merely rushed across the room and wrestled with the wireless. Within moments, the room was filled with the high, floral notes of young Queen Elizabeth's voice. Granny cast around the room a withering look. 'Whatever the personal standards of you people, I assume you can still stand for the Queen's speech.'

And everyone did. It was what we always did at Christmas. Mother and Father stood, and then we girls. It was natural for Alma to do so, being English, and then Mo imitated everyone else. All the adults were drunk, except Minnie and Mo, and we felt drunk too. It was the unfamiliar heat of the room and the lack of proper food. It was also the fact that for the first time all day, the smell of Christmas dinner had begun to permeate the house.

When the speech was finished we all sat down again. 'Where's Minnie?' Mo said. 'Where's Ma?'

'Oh, poor Minnie,' Mother said. 'I'll go to her.'

She went up to the room and knocked on the door. 'Minnie,' she called.

'Here, missus!' Minnie called from the kitchen, where she was finishing the dinner. The heat had come up and the turkey was done. Minnie was pouring cream into mashed potatoes and scraping the turkey tin to make gravy. She worked as if nothing had happened, heating the sauce boat, tasting this and testing that. 'Get the plates,' she said to Mother. Mother put a hand on her shoulder. At this she bent her head and began to cry. 'In front of everybody,' she whispered. Her voice was full of grief and shame.

111

'Minnie, don't fret,' Mother said. 'Mo doesn't know what he's saying.'

In spite of its odd process, the dinner was delicious. Everyone was starving and fell on it silently. Of course Minnie's finishing touches were partly responsible. We ate and ate in silence until we could eat no more. Only Minnie did not touch her food. All through the meal she gazed soulfully at Mo.

'Don't you love me, Mo?' Minnie begged. 'Don't you love Ma?' His mouth was full so he nodded. She held out her arms and he came to her and buried his head on her breast. It looked for a moment as if everything was going to be all right again, but then Mo wrestled free. 'But you're my ma,' he explained. 'Dora's young. She's pretty. You're old.'

~

The thing that nobody could get over was that Mo Mankievitz now had two women fighting over him. 'Men are like dogs,' Minnie sighed. 'It don't much matter how they look. If they are loved, they get kind of lovable.'

Mother advised her to move away and get a fresh start with Mo where Dora MacAlorum would not find him.

Minnie shrugged as if nothing mattered any longer. 'Mo don't love me no more. He says I'm old.'

'Of course you're not old,' Mother said, 'any more than Mo is.'

She rocked back and forth. Her face was grey as ash. 'I am fifty years of age. Mo is thirty-two.'

We were shocked. Because she was so small, we had never thought of her in terms of age.

'It doesn't matter,' Mother said quickly. 'That woman is only after your money.'

Minnie blew her nose. 'She can have all my money if only she leaves my Mo. But I see how she looks at him. I don't think it's only money. I think she wants my man.'

'Well, then,' Mother said. 'You must use your money to fight her. Get yourself some new clothes and a hairdo.'

'Mutton dressed as Lady Muck!' Minnie laughed unhappily. She heaved herself off the bed and went to draw the curtains. Daylight poured in cold as water. When Minnie turned back into the room she paused in dismay at her reflection in the wardrobe mirror. 'An old woman making a fool of herself over a younger man,' she said. Her hand went to the door of the wardrobe as if to support herself, but she grappled with the catch and swung it open. Bending down she reached inside and touched her cash box, like a lucky charm. 'But you're right, missus. I've still got my money.'

~

Nobody believed what Dora had said of Mo, but the accusation changed him. He became more like an ordinary man. Mother watched crossly as he strutted out, 'As if he was Heathcliff!' but her anger melted when she saw that he was still carrying the black box that contained the musical crib. 'Christmas is over, Mo,' she explained to him.

'Over?' he said in wonder.

'Over,' she said firmly, and then seizing her opportunity she added, 'It is over between you and Dora MacAlorum too. You are a married man. You belong to Minnie and Minnie belongs to you.'

'Yes, but Minnie's my ma,' he said. 'Dora's my sweetheart.' He said the word carefully, as if it had recently been taught to him.

'Minnie is not your ma. She is your wife. What you are doing is wrong.'

'I did nothing wrong.' He looked bewildered.

'No, but she said you did. She said the baby is yours.'

He nodded eagerly. 'Dora says I can have it.'

Mother was losing patience. 'It's a scandal,' she said. 'It makes no difference that you don't understand. If you continue to see that woman you can't go on living in this house.'

Mo gave a long sigh and then hoisted the box under one arm and held out the other one to shake hands. 'Goodbye,' he said.

Around midnight we were woken by Minnie's wails. 'Mo has not come home. Something has happened to Mo.'

'Oh my God,' Mother said. 'Oh, Minnie! He can't have taken to heart what I said.'

'What? What did you say?'

'I told him he could not live in this house if he went on seeing her. I only meant to bring him to his senses.'

Minnie gasped. 'What will happen to him?'

This mystery was resolved by Dora MacAlorum, who turned up alone the following day. 'So yis threw the poor wee man out!'

'Where is he?' Minnie said.

'He's with me. Youse needn't worry. I'll look after him now. I've only come for his clothes.' She laughed and patted her belly. 'Two kids, I'll have. I don't mind. Mo's a good cuddle and I've had enough of big bastards.'

'You send my husband back here,' Minnie said. 'What do you think you are going to live on? Not one penny of my money, that's for sure!'

'Don't fret yourself. We're well away. Mo's loaded,' Dora sneered.

'I know how much a cinema usher earns,' Minnie said.

'Look in your wardrobe, you mean oul' cow,' Dora tittered.

Minnie's hand flew to her face. She fled upstairs and there was a cry. 'Police!' She ran downstairs again. 'My cash box is gone. She stole my money.'

'I've stole nothing,' Dora said calmly.

'Was it a black box? Oh, Minnie!' Mother said. 'It was Mo who took it. I saw him walking out with it. I thought it was the musical crib.'

Minnie ran at Dora, as if to strangle her. 'She made him steal my money. I want the police.'

Dora butted back with her handbag. 'Youse better mind your language. All this talk about stole! That's Mo's money, so it is. He's your husband, so anything that's yours is his in law.' Minnie just gaped. 'Och, I can't stand here all night. Forget the oul' clothes,' Dora said. 'Yis had him dressed up like a wee boy, any road. I'll get him done up like a proper wee man.'

We brought Minnie down to the kitchen. 'It's so unfair,' Mother sympathised. 'Mo is entitled to everything you own just because you married him. What will you do now? All your money gone.'

She stayed hunched over her tea for a time and then she said vaguely, 'Oh, no. There's a whole lot more. It wouldn't fit in the box so I put it in the bank. Maybe I'll go and pay it a visit now. Maybe it's all I got left.'

'Poor Minnie,' Mother tutted after she had gone upstairs. 'She had such spirit. This will finish her.'

What happened next taught me an interesting lesson. Sadness does not kill people so that they stop breathing. It merely finishes off the person that they were and then a different person appears in their place. A cold, wet January came in and stripped every last leaf from the trees, and Minnie entered a strange, tropical summer. She went out one day, a sad old woman. All the following day she was gone too. She came back late on the second night with a tight golden-brown perm like a toffee nut cluster. She wore a purple suit and a new fox fur knotted around her neck. Make-up tinted her complexion to a bright orange tan and her lips were a taut orange-red wave, slightly off-centre, as if someone had kissed her smack on the lips. She did not look glamorous but she did not look at all ridiculous. She looked remarkable. She looked self-confident and wealthy.

'Minnie!' Mother said in amazement.

'Madame Mankievitz,' Minnie pronounced solemnly.

'Oh!' Mother was slightly taken aback. 'You've changed your name.'

'No, Edie. That is the name of my new business. I bought a small bakery in the village. Madame Mankievitz – Viennese Pisserie.'

'You mean Patisserie?'

'Yeah, whatever. My own business, Edie!'

Mother was delighted. 'Minnie is her old self again,' she said with satisfaction. 'No woman should be dependent on a man. All she really needs is to prove herself.'

But Minnie was a different self. While she was waiting for her new premises, she resumed baking at home. We sniffed in happy anticipation of the familiar perfumes, but they were not the same. 'Why should I waste butter on fools who know no better?' We no longer helped her squeeze wet almonds out of their skins before grinding them down for marzipan. 'Okay, so ready-ground almonds got no taste – add some almond essence, who's to know?'

Who was to know? Only those who did their own baking, and they did not buy cakes anyway. When Minnie left us to open her bakery we would have bought our cakes there too, out of loyalty, but the episode of Mo and MacAlorum had upset Father, and the maid's room was shut up and we entered 1957 with no money once again. We used to peer in the window of her new premises. The cakes looked magnificent, iced and layered for birthdays and bar mitzvahs. She was very successful, and people remembering her legendary confectionery still spoke of her cakes as if they burst on the mouth like a song. But it was rumoured that the beautiful cakes were a bit dry and the pastries had the high, chemical note of bottled essences. They were still good cakes. But they were no longer peerless.

Chapter Thirteen

~

Something was happening to Bridie. From the time I had started school we three sisters had existed almost as a single person, but now she was drifting away from us. 'I am becoming a woman,' she told us, but she looked as if she was turning into a boy. Since starting at secondary school she had cut her hair short and wore ski pants and sloppy joes and was always cycling off somewhere at high speed. For most of our lives we had shared everything. Now she became secretive and superior. 'I have a secret,' she taunted us. 'And I can't tell you, because you're only kids.'

Enraged, we went to Mother. 'Bridie says she has a secret.' 'Oh, it's no secret,' Mother sighed. 'You'll find out soon enough. Enjoy your innocence while you can.'

We ganged up on her in the bedroom to try and wrestle her secret out of her, but it was also a way to get close to her. For the first time in her life she would not join in but nipped us viciously with her nails and then folded her arms on her chest. 'If you wring my bosoms I may die,' she said. She seemed tall and bossy, and we were unable to tackle her. 'Brute bully, brute bully,' we murmured as we backed away.

Kitty and I dealt with this by retreating into childhood. We took our dolls and held tea parties in the maid's room. Much of our conversation concerned Dr Southall's sanitary towels, which Bridie kept hidden in her drawer and which must be connected to her mystery. We tried them as a cold compress, soaked in water. Bridie was enraged to find the sodden sanitary towel replaced in her pack. 'Brats! Imbeciles!' she bellowed. 'Now they're all soaking. What am I supposed to use?'

'Use for *what*?' we begged, but she turned away abruptly, rustling her womanly property in the drawer as if it was a bridal trousseau. 'Brute bully, brute bully,' we mumbled in futile envy.

We watched her wheel away like a bird on her beautiful silver bike. She now seemed to us all-powerful. She could do anything. Father had not, in the end, forbidden her to ride her bicycle. The truth was, she was the only one he admired. Kitty and I did not know whether to respect her or resent her. We stuck together, dressed in our négligés from the Iveagh Market, but Kitty's mind was no longer on play. It yearned after Bridie. Every day she stared out of the window as Bridie rode away, and one day she flung open the window and squealed after her, 'Wait for me!' Bridie slowed down and Kitty ran downstairs and out on to the road, her sandalled feet ripping through the lacy hem of her négligé.

'Can I have a go?' she said shyly. Bridie shook her head. 'A new bike is like new clothes,' she said. 'It belongs to the owner until they get something else, and then it can be a hand-me-down.'

Kitty fingered the handlebars with awe. 'Give me a carry, then.'

Bridie flicked her head in assent and Kitty hitched up her négligé and leaped on to the carrier, and I watched the two big girls wheel away out of my life.

~

Bit by bit the scent of Minnie's baking died from the room – her real baking, into which she had put a part of her soul. The room went cold from unuse and there was nothing but a faint odour of gas from the tiny oven. How had she produced such quantities of delicacies in that small oven? How had she lived with such bustle and flourish as to make us feel that she was the mistress of the house and we were the tenants in the dim downstairs? She had even managed to make a man out of Mo, enough for some other woman to want him. We missed Minnie. It was Mother who missed her most. Even though they would never see eye to eye on domestic matters, they were alike in one important way. They couldn't be bothered to say anything they didn't mean.

'I wish I had someone to talk to.' Mother despondently sorted a large pile of socks with holes in them.

'Talk to me.' I knew she missed Minnie, but I had always been her ally.

She hugged me so close that I felt our bones folding over like needles knitting. 'You are my best little pal. I would be lost without you to talk to, but it is unfair to weigh children down with adult problems. I meant, I have no one to unburden my heart to.'

'What about Auntie Brenda?' Kitty suggested. Auntie Brenda was single and lived with her mother, Gram Lambert. We could not understand why she and Mother saw so little of each other when they were sisters.

'Yes,' Mother said uncertainly. 'One can never be sure with Brenda. She has a jealous nature.' That evening she sat down and wrote a long letter.

'Are you writing to Auntie Brenda?' I hung over her shoulder.

'No. Sometimes it helps to consider someone who is worse off than yourself. I sent a line to poor Selena.'

'Miss Taylor? Did you tell her the room is empty?' I said eagerly.

She shook her head. 'I didn't mention the room. It would only upset her.' Her face took on a brittle look that showed she too was upset by the thought of our only source of income going to waste. 'Maybe I should drop Brenda a line while I'm at it.' I remained latched to her shoulder as she scrawled away, her loopy handwriting covering the page with her usual total absorption, as if all the words were packed inside the pen and she just shook them out. *'I feel so futile. Here we are with no money and a good room going to waste.'* At the end she added, 'Love to Mama. I miss you both.'

'There!' She put down her pen and picked up her darning basket. She stretched a sock over a red wooden darning mushroom and began to close the raggy crater with a delicate black web. 'I feel better now. I had forgotten how good it feels to get your problems off your chest.'

~

Several neighbours were drawn to their windows by the sight of a taxi pulling up at our gate. Gram Lambert clambered out and stood on the pavement, beaming serenely, and we knew Auntie Brenda must still be in the car, flustered and rooting for the right change.

'Oh, Lord,' Mother groaned from the kitchen. 'She should have let me know. I am in the middle of getting the tea.' She came up smiling and kissed her mother. We had gone to greet our auntie, but there was no one in the car except the driver, waiting to be paid.

'Where's Auntie Brenda?' Mother said loudly. Gram Lambert beamed. 'She ran off with a fella.' We laughed, and Mother looked at us crossly and stroked her own mother's hair. 'Oh, poor Mama. You're confused. Did you run away? Look at the state of you.' Gram wore a navy cardigan and a navy floral print skirt down to her feet, and white runners with no laces. Her salt and pepper hair was wound in untidy plaits over her head and she carried a huge black handbag.

'The driver wants money,' we said to Mother.

'Now what am I to do?' Mother frowned. 'I haven't got any money.'

'I've got money,' Gram said. She rummaged in her big black bag, the oddly assorted contents of which reminded me of the bag my mother had given me when I was small and which I had emptied out in the aisle at church. She thrust an envelope at Mother. 'Brenda sent you this.' Inside was a sheet of paper and a ten-pound note. Written on the paper was, 'It's your turn now – Brenda.'

'Oh, Lord!' Mother said.

'Lord of all, we bow before Thee . . .' Gram Lambert began to sing in a raucous voice. The taxi driver came to the gate with a large suitcase.

Mother handed him the note of money. 'This is a mistake. You must take her back.'

The driver offered his arm to Gram. 'Don't you want to go home?' Mother coaxed. 'What do you want?'

'Skins,' Gram said.

The driver gave a groan and let go of her arm. 'You can keep her.'

'What is the matter with you?' Mother rebuked. 'She is perfectly harmless. She is just confused. Are you afraid of a harmless old lady?'

'Afraid for my motor.' He pointed to the floor, where a large puddle was growing around her feet and soaking into her runners.

'Oh my God!' Mother gasped. 'Father will have a canary. Brenda can't do this to me. She must understand that I have a husband and family to look after.'

Gram's face suddenly seemed clear and full of pain. She threw her arms around Mother. 'Edie! Don't throw me out,' she begged.

~

'It's very nice to have you, Gram.' Father handed her a small measure of whiskey. 'We don't see enough of you.'

She watched him suspiciously as she gulped down her drink.

'Edie will make you a nice tea and then I will drive you home.'

In the doorway, Mother was silently in tears.

'Why did you put her to bed?' Father turned to her querulously. 'Now we have the bother of getting her dressed again.'

'I can't,' Mother said.

'Get the girls to help you,' he said shortly.

'I can't throw her out. She's my mother.'

'For God's sake, Edie, she doesn't know where the hell she is.'

'Let her stay a while.'

'How long? She has not been here an hour and already the hall carpet is destroyed and you are a wreck.'

'I'll send her back in a little while. A week or so. Brenda will change her mind when she has had a rest.'

'And how are we supposed to feed her? Answer me that. We have no money to feed ourselves.'

Gram reached for her bag and dug into it. She took out a two-shilling piece. Beaming, she handed it to Father.

'What is this for? Is this meant to pay for your keep?'

'Go down to the shops and buy me some skins.' She caught Mother's eye. 'He's very loud. I've sent him for sweets.'

Mother took from her apron pocket the change the taxi driver had given her from the ten-pound note. 'Brenda sent it.'

The money took the wind out of his sails. 'Are you sure you're up to it, Edie? Only for a little while, mind.'

'Of course I am up to it. She is my own mother. Now, leave us alone so I can get her settled.' While Mother tucked her in, Gram's shoulders began to shake. Her toothless lips crumpled over her gums. 'Your man's peculiar,' she confided loudly.

In the middle of the night there was a thump and a groan. We heard Mother's light, careful step as she ran from her bedroom. 'Oh, no!' she gasped. 'Oh, Mama!' After a series of grunts from Mother and groans from Gram, Mother said, 'Hush! You'll wake Eugene. Oh, God help me. I cannot do this on my own.'

Mother said Gram had been very beautiful when she was young and had known much unhappiness, and as a result of this she had lost her mind. I didn't believe it because she looked like a witch with her long straggly hair and wrinkled brown face, and I didn't believe she was crazy. She wouldn't wear her teeth. She had put them away somewhere because they were uncomfortable. I thought it was the same with her mind. She had put it away somewhere because it was uncomfortable. One thing was certain. Mother was getting more and more worn down and Gram was growing fitter. She ate everything, making noises of contentment as she munched toothlessly. She smiled as she counted her sweets or the change in her purse, smiled as she wet the floor, peering down with a slightly mischievous surprise as a lake spread out between her shoes. She smiled as she insulted my father, whom she treated as if he was a small boy and she a small girl.

Father wrote angrily to Aunt Brenda. The letter came back, marked 'Return to Sender'. He told Gram she must contribute to the cost of her keep. 'Help yourself, you highwayman!' She threw him her black bag. As his hand went in, he let out a howl. 'I've been bitten! There's something in there! Something bit me.' He flung the bag away in horror but his hand remained fastened in the grip of Gram's false teeth.

Every night Gram fell out of bed with a thump and Mother ran to her and wrestled despairingly with the larger woman's weight, afraid of Father's bad humour and his accusation that she could not cope. She could have asked us girls for help but she did not believe that children should be burdened with adult troubles. We could have helped anyway, but we did not. A sour, yellow, old woman's smell had spread around the room. It sometimes seemed like a sticky web, where you could go in and never come out.

Soon the pattern of the nights, like Minnie's night-time baking, became a part of our dreams and we had mild nightmares in which we cried, 'Mama, you must help me,' although it was our mother begging Gram to make an effort to get up off the floor. We struggled mildly in our sleep, like a cat being stroked the wrong way, on the night when there was a slight change in this pattern, when we heard Gram's voice, sounding sane and concerned: 'Edie! Edie! Get up. I cannot lift you.' Father woke to an empty bed. We heard the dread in his bare feet as they skimmed the stairs. 'Edie!' he called.

She lay on the lino floor in her nightie. She looked too pale, and a pool of blood had spread out around her nightie. Gram bent over her, stroking her hair. It was the first time I really believed that she could be my mother's mother. 'She won't get up,' she said to Father.

Father roughly pushed her aside and equally roughly he shook Mother. 'Edie, Edie! Wake up, now.'

Bridie had done a first-aid course and she knelt down and took Mother's pulse. 'She's all right. She's fainted,' she said in a way that was very subdued for her. 'Put her to bed and I'll go on my bike for the doctor.'

Kitty and I glanced at each other in relief. Three cheers for grown-up Bridie. Mother had woken by the time we got her to bed, and wanted to get up and see to Gram, but we made her stay. The doctor came and made his awful pronouncement. She would have to go to hospital.

'Where's Mother?' Gram said meekly after the ambulance had taken her.

'She's not your mother,' I said. 'She's my mother.'

'Oh,' she said sadly.

Father looked frightened and bewildered when he returned. 'She was expecting a baby,' he said. 'She told no one. She had not even told me. The baby is dead.' He turned back to Gram with a bitter and accusing look. 'Get dressed.'

'Where is she going?' I held up her dress and she docilely stuck out her arms. As I dropped it over her head she clamped them to her bony chest. 'Am I being sent to prison?'

'You're going home, Gram,' I guessed. 'Back to Auntie Brenda.'

'Brenda's gone.' Inside the tent of her dress she was weeping. 'No one wants me.'

Somehow we got her dressed and Father bundled her into the car. When I saw her anxious face at the window, I ran out and got in beside her.

'I don't want you. I want Edie,' she said.

'I don't want you either. I want my mother too,' I said, but all the same we held each other's hands.

~

'What is this place?' Gram said.

The gaunt, red-brick building had no flowers, nothing but a statue of Our Lady in a niche with a woeful expression on her face and one hand held up as if in a warning to keep out.

127

'It's a convent,' Father said in a respectful whisper. 'We're going to see the nuns.'

Gram said nothing until we had been let in by an old sister with a face like an owl, and then she ventured, 'I had a notion to be a nun myself once. Will they give us tea?'

'Would you like a cup of tea?' the nun said. 'Come to the parlour and I'll send for some.'

'I haven't had a cup of tea all day.'

This was true. We had gone to great trouble to get her to the lavatory before coming out, and were afraid to give her anything to drink. 'We won't put you to the bother.' Father winked at the nun, who looked surprised. 'A little problem with the bladder,' he whispered.

'He has a little problem with his bladder,' Gram said loudly to the nun. She showed no interest in the wards we were shown, full of old ladies, most of them bed-ridden, but when we got to the small candle-lit chapel she did a twirl. 'Is this a ballroom?'

'It's a chapel,' Father said. 'Would you like to say a prayer?'

'Can I sing a hymn?' She did not wait for an answer, but roared out a tuneless verse of 'Sweet Sacrament Divine'. We tried to shush her but she was delighted with herself. 'That was great. There's great echoes in here. Do you know,' she seized the nun's arm, 'I have not been inside a church in three years.'

This was probably true too. No one had brought her to church since she had been living with us, although Mother told us she used to be very religious when she was young. 'Well, then,' the nun said, 'the Lord will be very glad to see you. You must kneel down and have a quiet word with Him.'

'Sorry!' Father mouthed at the sister when Gram had been pressed into a pew. The nun shook her head to dismiss the apology and we knelt to pray. I wondered what was going through Gram's head. Her hands were joined and her eyes closed and she seemed completely absorbed. Then I let out a gasp. A small lake of water had gathered around her shoes. Father heard me and turned to look. 'Good God!' he said, and then the nun looked around too.

We bundled Gram out of the chapel, mumbling apologies. Only she and the sister remained serene. 'It is quite all right,' the nun said to Father. 'Old age is the country in which we serve and we are well acquainted with its customs.' We were mortified but the sister shook hands with Gram and to our surprise she said, 'If you decide to join us, you will be very welcome.'

'You'll take her?' Father said. 'Of course she'll join you. Only too delighted.'

'She must make up her own mind. No one is here unless they wish to be.'

'Can I be a nun?' Gram said. 'I'd like to be a Little Sister of the Poor. I don't want to be a kitchen nun.'

'In this house, it is we who serve our little sisters,' the holy woman said. 'Won't you come with me? You will be wanting your tea.'

Afterwards, we drove around the Phoenix Park, slowly circling the curved and tree-lined paths in our sealed car like goldfish in a bowl. I watched deer grazing and dogs jumping and children running in bright sunshine, supervised by Father's stern eye in the driver's mirror. 'There is no need to say anything to your mother. When she comes home she will be very grateful that I have taken the decision out of her hands.' For the rest of the drive, the car was as hushed as if it drifted in outer space.

~

At home, we searched the pantry for food, remembering when it had been filled with Minnie's baking. We found porridge and raisins, left over from Minnie's time, some paprika-coloured cubes of dried tomato soup, a bag of lentils. We made a big pot of tomato and lentil soup, but no one liked it and it stayed on top of the stove until it developed scummy bubbles, and then Bridie threw it, saucepan and all, out in the yard. It stayed there for a long time until a large, hairy red spider clambered out of it, as if this slimy red concoction had started a whole new cycle of evolution.

The gas ran out and there weren't any shillings to put in the meter. When the doorbell rang I was sure it must be the grocer, wanting his bill paid. Bridie and Kitty had gone off on the bike to see if they could find some other house where they would be fed, and Father was at the hospital with Mother. I crept downstairs and saw a sort of rustling shape behind the glass panels of the door, and even before I thought about it I ran to the door and opened it and flung myself into the arms of Miss Taylor.

Chapter Fourteen

~

'I heard from your mammy.' Selena swung me around. 'She told me her news!'

'What news?'

'About the baby! I was that pleased I couldn't stay away. I brought eggs and scones from home and country butter and jam and a lovely bunch of wild flowers. Glory be! What ails you?' she said as I threw my arms around her neck and began to cry. Between sobs I told her everything, about Gram, and Mother, and even about Minnie and Mo.

'Put on the kettle, now,' she said gently. 'We'd need some tea.'

'There's no gas,' I said. 'We haven't a shilling for the gas.'

She clucked her tongue in awe and took a shilling from her bag. 'I have money. I've been doing a bit of cleaning for the nuns. They're very good to me.'

She was like a nun herself and she seemed so lost in the world that I wondered why she did not join an order and enter a convent. 'I can't.' She whispered the shameful truth into my ear. 'I'm a black Protestant,' and she laughed nervously.

'But you had a crucifix in your room.'

'I won it for a prize. They were all Catholics in our little school.'

131

I was very surprised to think of Miss Taylor as a Protestant. All the Protestants we knew were well educated, and although in one way we felt sorry for them because they would not go to heaven, in another way we were respectful to them because we believed them to be more refined. 'Since you left us we had a Jew and a Communist and a girl who fecked things,' I told her.

After tea we went on the bus to visit Mother. 'And how is my lovely lady?' Selena greeted her.

'Idle as a cat.' Mother was delighted to see our first lodger. 'I should go home.'

'You will not!' Selena was indignant. 'Aren't you grand and cosy where you are? Don't set foot out of that bed until the doctor says.'

Mother patted her hand. 'Who will look after my children?'

'I will!' Selena said, and then she looked abashed. 'The nerve of me! I only meant, I could look in and throw together a meal or something.'

'Don't apologise,' Mother said. 'You are a good and kind girl.' For a moment she looked hopeful, but then she shook her head. 'How would we pay you? And there's nowhere for you to sleep.'

'I'd sleep in any nook or cranny. As for cash, I have a small bit put by. I've been in a little job.'

Mother pulled herself up and took both Selena's hands. I could see from the effort she had to make to support herself that she was still weak. 'You must use whatever you have for yourself. Get your hair done, Selena. Buy yourself some lipstick. With the proper care you would have a very good appearance. You are such a pleasant and honest person that you might find work in one of the big shops – Pim's or Clerys.'

Selena held on happily to Mother's hands but she looked scornful at the suggestion, as if a part in the pictures had been suggested.

'Scarecrow I am. Frighten off the fashionable ladies. I'm a weed, Edie, built for the fields. I was never a prize blossom. I'd always be out of place in a fancy setting.'

'No, not a weed – a wild flower.' Mother probably only said it to be nice, but when she turned to us with her huge smile and her hazel eyes shining with pleasure, we could both see that she was right.

'There's nothing fancy about our house,' Mother said with a frown. 'It's just Eugene. He would never agree.'

'I'm like a mouse. You'd never notice me,' she said quickly and quietly.

~

Early next morning she arrived to announce that we were going on an excursion.

'Where would we go?' Nobody in our house liked exercise. Mother always said that sensitive people only needed to exercise the imagination.

'To the mountains. We'll take a picnic.'

'We haven't the bus fare,' we moped.

'Fat lot of fresh air you'd get on the bus. Go on bikes.'

'They've got no bikes,' Bridie said in triumph. 'I'm the only one with a bike.'

'So you can give Kitty a carry. Hasn't your father an oul' boneshaker in the shed? I'll put a bit of air in the tyres and set Rose on the crossbar. Put on your woollies, and I'll go and slap together some sandwiches and pour cocoa in a flask.'

It's *raining*,' they tried at last.

'No, the rain's stopped. There'll be mushrooms.'

It was this last magical assertion that put a stop to the moans and got Bridie and Kitty into their clothes. But for me it was Miss

Taylor's offer, to take me on the crossbar of the bicycle. I felt we had crossed some barrier. I would be with the big girls now.

As we pushed uphill past the village, I clung to Miss Taylor. I smelt her familiar smell of stale wool and soap and half dozed for a long time. 'Wakey, wakey.' When I opened my eyes the red-brick terraces had disappeared, the skies had widened and there were hedges full of primroses, lamb's tails that dangled from hazel trees, sending puffs of pollen into the air, larks rising out of fields full of silver dew. 'We'll leave the bikes here and we'll walk, now,' she said.

As we tramped through fields she named each tree and flower, identified the different birds we saw and told us stories about them and about many other things. The wren builds a lot of nests and the lady wren picks the best. In cold weather they'll all huddle together in the one nest to keep warm. To kill a robin was bad luck. A lump would come up on your hand that would stop you from working. A morsel of wood burnt in a May-eve fire and tied around your neck with a piece of rag would save you from The Plots. A red-headed stranger at the door was bad luck. When someone died you had a great party and it was called a wake. There would be drinking and dancing. The corpse had sixpence put in their pocket to pay their fare to the next world. When someone went to America you had a sad party and that was called a live wake. Everyone waited on the letters from America. A letter with no money in it was an empty letter. If you found a snail at dawn on May Day and it was tight in its shell, you were sure to marry a rich husband, and if it was out of its house you would be poor and homeless. The hand of a dead baby would cure anything from a bald head to a sick cow. You got the hand from the keel, which was a little cemetery for unbaptised babies.

We came to a wooded area that was full of mushrooms, pale as soap, velvety as moles. 'Only pick the ones I pick,' she instructed, and we crouched together to twist the soft stems out of crumbly brown earth. The earth smelled dank and mouldy but when you lifted a new mushroom to your nose, it only had a scent of newness. We emerged from the wood to weak, bright sunlight and she laid her coat on the ground for us. We ate our sandwiches lying down, squinting into the glaring blue sky.

'Isn't the sky lovely and big?' Kitty marvelled.

'Where I come from, it goes all the way to America,' Selena boasted.

That evening we had the mushrooms cooked in cream, but for Father she cooked steak and served it with mushrooms fried in butter. Meals had been haphazard with Mother away, and he ate this with the stunned expression with which he used to listen to music. Afterwards he could hardly speak. 'Very nice,' he said to Miss Taylor.

'It was nothing,' she said, delighted. 'Homely country fare.'

He was an emotional man, and this phrase affected him so that his eyes glistened. 'Very wholesome,' he whispered.

'Miss Taylor is going to stay and look after us until Mother comes home,' I boasted.

His expression changed and he began to bluster. 'And just where does she plan to stay?'

'My little room . . .' She laughed uneasily and then stopped. 'I meant well.'

'The path to hell is paved with good intentions,' Father muttered, before going out and banging the door.

'Don't mind him,' Bridie said. 'He's awful.'

'No, he's not,' she said quickly. 'My father's awful. Your father's not a mean man. He's only windy.'

She was probably right. Father was afraid that as long as there was someone else to look after us, Mother would never come home.

Miss Taylor sighed. 'I was going to make ye eggs. It will be Easter on Sunday.'

'Chocolate eggs?'

'No. Proper country ones, boiled up in an old scarf or sock to dye them, with wild flowers pressed on the side, to leave their pattern. You'd have your initial on the side, dripped off a wax candle.'

'Make them now,' we begged.

She shook her head. 'I'll go up to my room for one last night.'

I found her sitting by the gas fire in the dark. 'Don't turn on the light,' she said.

'Why not?' I whispered.

'When the electric came in, the fairies went out,' she replied in her timid, melancholy way.

~

The first thing Mother did when she got home was to look for Gram. 'Mama?' She went into the empty room, the bed peeled back to air. We explained that Gram was well and happy, that she was in the hospice and thought she was a nun. 'I had sweets saved,' she said accusingly. 'Someone brought me sweets and I saved them for her.'

After tea, she said she wanted to rest, but when I looked for her I found her on the stripped bed of the spare room in tears.

'We can go and see her whenever you like,' I said.

She dried her eyes. 'I suppose I am really crying for my little lost baby. When something really terrible happens, it's always your mother you want. Why did no one tell me?'

'Why didn't you tell us about the baby?'

'We had so little money.'

I sat down cautiously beside her. 'But you told Miss Taylor. Why didn't you tell me?'

136

She pulled me into a hug. 'The truth is, I thought you would be jealous.'

'I wouldn't,' I protested. 'I would have loved a baby to mind. I'm tired of being the youngest.'

'There'll come a time when you'll be glad to be the youngest,' she said. 'You'll be the one who'll get the compliments longest.' She rocked me as she hugged me and I realised with surprise that I would have been fiercely jealous to see her in such an embrace with a younger child. I had never really had to share her with my sisters.

It was different for Mother. 'Children grow up so fast,' she murmured sadly. 'You girls have been my only concern. Now that I have lost my poor baby, I don't know what it would take to interest me in life again.'

Chapter Fifteen

~

In the end, it only took a postcard. 'You are invited to a warming of the house.' Mother's face lit up as she read out this mysterious message. 'It's from Minnie! She has invited us to see her new house, which she saved for with pennies and shillings in a box. Look at the signature!' She passed the card around. 'Mrs Mo Mankievitz! Do you suppose she is back with Mo again?'

The house was a small Victorian villa in a run-down neighbourhood called Kimmage. It wasn't really a rich woman's house but it had been lovingly cared for, with new paint and polished brasses and the stiff lace at the windows. As a maid took our coats and showed us around, Mother kept looking for Minnie. 'Where is she?' she said. 'Where is Mrs Mankievitz?'

'Madame is resting,' the girl said.

'I'm early,' Mother apologised. 'I'll wait.' But then she called out, 'Minnie!' and went upstairs without waiting for an answer.

'I'm getting lazy,' Minnie greeted from her bed. There were dark shadows under her eyes and her colour was high.

'You've been working too hard,' Mother worried. 'The house is lovely, but all that on top of your business . . .'

'I'm fine. A bit too much excitement at my age.'

'You don't look well.'

'Ha!' Minnie laughed. 'You just forget what I look like without my war paint. Help me up. It's a big night for me. Mo is coming.'

'You've been in touch with Mo?'

'I have my spies. I hear that blonde bottle's been treating him bad. I tell him, come on his own.' She paused as she struggled out of bed, her hand across her chest.

'Stay there,' Mother said. 'I'll look after the guests. If Mo comes I'll send him straight up.'

'No, Edie. Let me be. My heart beats too fast, is all. It's because Mo's coming back. I feel it in my bones.' With slow determination she got into a bright-green brocade dress. Her hair had been dyed to the colour of gold chrysanthemums.

'Dora MacAlorum will never let Mo out on his own,' Mother whispered as Minnie put on her lipstick.

All the important people from the village were there. They praised Minnie's house, her cooking, her green brocade. Cards piled up on a silver dish in the hall – people who wanted her baking for weddings or bar mitzvahs or business functions. Minnie's dress sparkled and her gilded hair flexed under the lights as she smiled and chatted and negotiated business. We were the only ones who noticed that each time the maid went to answer the door, Minnie would stand on tiptoe to watch, and as each new person entered and she came back on her heels, she seemed to sink down lower and lower.

'He might not have got the message,' Mother warned her. 'I wouldn't put it past that woman to open his post.'

'I think probably she'll try to stop him, but he will come.'

The food was eaten and the guests had begun to go home. Empty glasses piled up. Mother asked us to start tidying so that Minnie and the maid would not be left to deal with it afterwards. In the

140

kitchen we ate any leftovers and marvelled at her great big gleaming refrigerator. When we came back to the drawing room there was only Minnie with Mother and Father.

'I feel wore out,' Minnie said. 'I think I'll lie down.'

We helped her upstairs and she sat on the edge of the bed. 'I'm getting to be an old woman. I'm all alone in a strange house. I haven't even got myself any more. When I look in the mirror, some bottle redhead looks back.'

'Would you like to come and stay with us for a little while?' Mother said. 'The room is empty now.'

Minnie shook her head. 'I've got to have the place nice for when Mo comes back. But I missed you, Edie. I feel better now I see you. I'll come and see you again soon.'

'Take off your dress now,' Mother coaxed. 'Get between the sheets and have a good rest. In the morning you will remember the evening as a great success.'

'No, leave the dress.' She lay back on the pillow. 'Just in case.'

'In case what?' Mother said. 'Mo will not come at this hour.'

'Just in case.' Minnie folded into sleep.

~

It was shortly after this that Kitty gave me the gift of a grown-up secret.

'I know something,' she whispered. 'After she got back from hospital Mother had a talk with me.'

'About what?'

'About being a woman. Listen . . .'

'Ugh,' we said together, when she repeated what Mother had told her. I had thought of the womb as a saintly property, like sanctifying grace because it was a part of the Hail Mary. We inspected our older

141

sister's private package with new interest. 'Bridie says it makes you feel like a Marmite sandwich,' she revealed.

'Has it happened to you yet?' I asked. She shook her head, and when I caught her eye I could tell that neither of us believed it would happen to us.

'These yokes Bridie uses are back in the ark,' she said to regain her authority. 'There's a new invention you can't even see.'

'It's invisible?'

'No,' she said uncertainly. 'Internal. I suppose that means you swallow something.' She showed me a cutting she had taken from a newspaper. '*Tampax – internal sanitary protection. For free sample send 5d in loose stamps to The Nurse, Greenford, Middlesex.*'

The package came on a day when Mother went to visit Minnie. When Bridie and Father went out she tore open the narrow carton. Inside were two white cylinders made of cardboard, and we took out the fold of crinkly paper that accompanied them and read the instructions with astonishment. 'It says there's a place!' I said.

'We're about to find out.'

'What if someone comes in?'

'We'll go to the room,' she said. 'Then if anyone comes in the door we'll hear them. Bring up the Ludo and we can pretend to be playing.'

We were shaky with excitement and a kind of shame as we squatted on the floor and tried to locate somewhere to lodge our discovery.

'I can't find anywhere,' Kitty admitted at last.

'Neither can I. Maybe we should get the torches.'

'And look at ourselves?'

'Oh, no!' we both cried in unison.

Suddenly we got a fit of giggles.

'Maybe there isn't anywhere. Maybe it's a swizz.'

'Maybe The Nurse is a stamp collector.'

We laughed and laughed until we rolled around the floor.

'Maybe you have to have a baby first, and it makes a hole coming out,' Kitty said. At the thought of that we both stopped laughing.

We dressed quickly when we heard Mother coming in, but she didn't look for us. We found her at the kitchen table, stroking the saucer of an untouched cup of tea. 'Minnie's gone,' she said. 'She had a heart attack.'

I sat down, the pleasurable heat of my secret afternoon with Kitty turned cold. 'Is she dead?'

She shook her head. 'She's in hospital. I found her little house deserted. A neighbour told me what had happened.'

'Will she live?'

Mother wiped her face as an angry tear fell. 'I think she has lost the will to live.'

Father was even more upset. 'Everything she worked for will now fall into the hands of that MacAlorum woman. If Minnie dies, you may be sure she will rush Mo up to a side altar and marry him at full speed.'

'It's worse than that,' Mother sighed. 'Minnie is handing everything over to them now. She made me write a letter for her to Mo and Dora, inviting them to come and live in the house while she is in hospital. Dora is to run the bakery.'

'You didn't write it?' we said in horror.

'I had to. You can't fool Minnie and you can't go against a dying woman's wishes.'

'It is abominable,' Father said. 'She has as good as handed everything over to that pair of wretches.'

Mother lit a cigarette. 'I suppose that in the long run it will all seem unremarkable. By autumn Mo will be rocking a pram on the small front lawn of Minnie's villa. Dora will run the bakery, producing cheap, tasteless products, which will be bought and eaten anyway.

She will eat too many of her own products and put on weight and those who don't know the whole story will only see a fat bossy woman and a bald little henpecked husband with a baby which is not his but which he will adore.'

'When you put it like that,' I said, 'it sounds a bit like a fairy story.'

'I no longer believe in fairy stories,' Mother said.

Chapter Sixteen

~

The gold knives and forks were the size of pins, perfect, gleaming. They caught a shaft of light which entered my heart and made a sunlit window there. They were set alongside flower-patterned porcelain plates, the size of a shilling. Mouse-sized sofas had satin pillows which looked as if you could suck them like sweets.

'Where is Titania?' I asked my Father.

'She only makes an appearance on state occasions.'

'You can see all the rooms. She must be somewhere.'

'They are not rooms. They are chambers. Royal chambers.'

Titania's Palace was housed in a series of glass cases in a big room with red walls. In different cases were the ballroom, the bedrooms, the bathroom, the kitchen with perfect little pots in which you could boil a single pea. If my mother had been telling me this there would have been between us a conspiracy of amusement, but Father did not smile. He liked his fantasy neat. In fact we kept our voices down in case Mother would hear. She had grown weary of Titania's Palace and had gone outside for a smoke with George and Alma Bates. 'Oh, Lord, what will we do now?' Alma's theatrical voice rang out from the doorway of the small theatre where the world's most baroque doll's house was exhibited.

'I could use a spot of lunch,' said Mr Bates.

'Lunch!' Alma scorned. 'We could have that at home. Let's do something different. Let's take a boat out.'

'Looks like rain,' he tried.

'You look like rain yourself,' she teased.

'The child will be hungry,' he said kindly.

'I'll buy something. There's a shop. I'll get some fruit. You go and see about the boat.'

George and Alma Bates had arrived in their big car at ten that morning. 'We have a plan,' they told my parents. 'There's an idea we'd like to throw at you.' My parents looked startled at the notion of having something thrown at them at this early hour. Mr Bates had sat down and was about to divulge his scheme but Alma saw Mother's fretting eye on the unhoovered floor. 'Never mind all that,' she said. 'Let's go out. It's a lovely day.'

'Oh, we couldn't,' both my parents said at once.

It was in fact a dull and chilly day. 'Come on, you two,' Alma said. 'You need taking out of yourselves.'

'There's Rose,' my mother said. The older girls were off somewhere on Bridie's bike.

Alma Bates was one of those few adults who really liked children. She told us we could call her Alma and on an occasion when we visited her house she took us to the kitchen and gave us interesting things to taste – anchovies, pickled walnuts. 'How would you like to go and see Titania's Palace?' she said to me. 'A miniature palace where everything is for people the size of your thumb. Little mirrors, gowns and crowns, little gold knives and forks.'

'I expect they're made from silver paper,' Father said, but he could not hide his eager look any more than I could. 'That's settled,' Alma said, and then, to mollify Mother: 'We'll stop somewhere for a nip on the way home.'

~

By the time Mr Bates had arranged the boat, Alma was back with a brown paper bag, carelessly clutched so that already it was stained with pink. 'Lunch.' She held up the crumpled bag indifferently. Apart from Alma, the grown-ups looked disgruntled. None of them was comfortable out of doors. She lifted me into the boat and then she followed and the others clambered after her. 'Gloop, gloop,' went the water. The boat rocked and the men groaned faintly. It was obvious that neither of them knew anything about boats. 'Alma, have you ever done this before?' Mr Bates querulously enquired. Alma lit a cigarette and sat back, looking at the sky. 'I've never known a man who couldn't row,' she said. At once Father and Mr Bates took turns with the oars, and then they hunched together, taking a paddle each, but it was hopeless. The boat kept turning round and bumping into the shore. Alma finished her cigarette and threw it into the water, where it hissed angrily. She pulled her cardigan up over her shoulders and stood up, making the boat tip, and handed me the brown paper bag. She squeezed her bottom down between the two men. 'Scoot,' she said. They looked baleful and moved out of her way.

I opened the scrunched-up mouth of the bag. I was looking into a bag of jewels, ruby red and softly gleaming. The plump, bursting crimson perfection was like women's lips when they have just put on their lipstick. 'What are they?' I said. She smiled her hard-bitten smile. One more idiot. 'Cherries, honey. Watch the stones.'

The boat glided into a tunnel of branches. Leaves splattered over our heads. The water splayed out in soft, greenish ribbons and gurgled over stones. I held a cherry by its stem and bit into the flesh. It burst softly and the dense sweetness cut with tartness made me feel like a bee diving into the centre of a flower. Wine-red juice ran through my fingers. I took a handful and passed the bag around. The grown-ups were silent now, lost in admiration of Alma's handling of the little boat, the graceful reach of her arms and the way her wrists seemed to coax the oars, rather than wield them. We came out into the light again, but it was not light. The sky was taut and silvery grey like a fish, and the water blotted up its slatey sheen so that we sailed through a hall of mirrors. The only colour came from Alma's yellow cardigan and fans of lime green fern that spouted out of slimy rock and the ruby cherries that seemed to turn black like blood under the sunless sky. If we had seen Titania perched on a rock I would not have been amazed.

Alma grew bored and threw down the oars. She stood up, rocking the boat again, and came to sit beside my mother. Both men scrabbled for the oars and the little boat shuddered and twirled. 'Edie!' Alma put her arms around my mother. 'You've got to get yourself a life. Eugene's a good man but they're all the same in the end. They either leave you or die on you or hang around your neck. You're like me, I can tell. You need to be fulfilled.'

Mother was silent for a moment, and then she said, 'Yes, I . . .' and Father gave a wretched groan: 'Christ!' Mr Bates said dolefully, guiltily, 'We've lost an oarlock.' Father rowed furiously on one oar and the boat went round. 'What's a warlock?' I asked. 'It's a male witch,' Alma said, and she stamped over to where the men were, making the boat lean to one side. 'Don't be a fool, Alma,' George begged. 'I don't need to be, I married one,' she snapped, and Father begged, 'In God's name, what are we supposed to do now?' Mother clutched me and for the first time I was nervous. 'Are we going to drown?' Alma just laughed. 'Honey, if this boat turned over, we could wade ashore.' This notion depressed everyone into silence.

'Why do men make such heavy weather of everything,' Alma sighed as she expertly manoeuvred the boat to shore, and at once it began to rain, huge, rattling drops that made the branches shudder.

In the pub George Bates apologetically bought large brandies for the adults. I had a Taylor Keith and a packet of Tayto Crisps. Like a cat, Father hated being wet. And he hated to fail in front of women. In the end it was Alma who brought him round. 'Eugene, you look like a kid, with your hair wet and your face all pink.' When everyone was happy, George and Alma eyed one another and said: 'Eugene, Edie! We've got a surprise!'

'You're pregnant,' Mother said at once, for Alma had wanted a baby for years. 'Ah, no,' Alma said, and she patted Mother's wrist for her own disappointment. 'It's for you. It's for both of you.' My parents looked embarrassed and hopeful. 'We have a girl for you,' Alma said.

Father grimaced in disappointment. 'Wait, Eugene,' Alma urged. 'Hear George out. Gladys is a special person.'

'Gladys,' Mother mused, liking the name, and at once Mr Bates turned to her. 'The moment we met her we thought of you and your special gifts, Edie.'

'Gifts?' she repeated in a daze.

'The way you cared for your mother and then poor Miss Taylor.'

'It was the other way round,' she said, but she was curious now. 'You want me to look after Gladys?'

'No, Edie, all Gladys wants is to make her way in the world.'

'No more hard cases.' Father put down his glass too vehemently and it made a bang.

'Money is not her principal problem,' Alma said. 'She needs to forget.'

'Forget what?' Mother said with interest.

'Her concern is to help others now – to save them from the suffering she has known.'

'What suffering?' Mother pursued.

'We thought your little room would be a haven.'

I pictured the little room with its barred window and smothering wallpaper, its haphazard furnishing already battered by people who were only passing through. Already, after two weeks without Gram, it was growing in on itself, as a garden reverts to forest in an empty house.

'Miss Partridge is a lovely girl,' Alma coaxed. 'You really would like her.'

'Gladys Partridge,' Mother said.

Tatters of rain wrestled on the pub window. The sky outside was as densely grey as putty. The pub, which had seemed cosy when we first arrived, was now only dull and boring, and I settled in for one of those long afternoons of stillness while Alma murmured on about Miss Partridge.

'Where is she?' Father said suddenly, as if he expected her to spring up behind the bar.

'With us,' Alma said gently. 'We have been looking after her. She is ready to move on now.'

'You're trying to get rid of her,' Father snarled, and Mother looked crestfallen.

Alma lit a cigarette and shook the match in a gesture that was like winking. 'It might be to your advantage,' she hinted. 'We're thinking of setting her up in a small way of business. Maybe you'd consider helping her out.'

'I have no capital,' Father bleakly established, before he wondered, 'What sort of business would a woman do?'

'Oh, it's not so much business . . .' The patient way Alma coaxed him reminded me of the way a woman would iron the gathers on a skirt. 'More a bureau.'

I thought of Father's bureau on the landing where the devil lived at night, and immediately I had an urge to warn him, but they were looking at my mother. 'Actually, we thought . . . Edie?'

'What has this got to do with Edie?' he said. 'No wife of mine is going to work.'

'Now, Eugene, this isn't really work – more a sort of social service. Think of it, Edie,' Alma begged. 'Helping poor lonely souls to find a bit of happiness.'

'You would make a fortune,' said Mr Bates.

Both of my parents had seemed to be slinking into separate alleys – Mother into her dreamlike state to avoid disappointment, and Father in a kind of protective huff, but now they were shaken awake. 'What sort of bureau?' Mother whispered.

'A marriage bureau,' they said.

~

'What on earth possessed you?' Mother whispered to Alma as we drove home in pouring rain. 'You know how he is about these things.'

'What do I care how he is?' Alma smoked rapidly and the car was filling up with gusts of grey, as if the stormy sky had seeped in through the window. 'Eugene is disaster-prone, but look at you! If you had your chance there would be no holding you back. I was only thinking of you.'

'It is I who have to live with him,' Mother said miserably.

'You speak of him as if he is a lion to be held at bay with a chair and a pitchfork of raw meat.' Alma's voice rose in unwary indignation, and Father's head swivelled around, the pipe clenched between his teeth as if to bite down on his anger.

'The marriage rate is the lowest in Europe,' Mr Bates offered with caution.

151

'I am not surprised.' Alma knotted the sleeves of her cardigan across her throat.

At home we used to joke that Father did not go into high dudgeon but low dudgeon. His anger wore out quickly and then he grew sad and silent as if unable to understand why we were all against him.

'All the men gone to America.' Mr Bates now spoke to himself. 'Country girls are given huge dowries to get them married – a thousand pounds. So many of the men have emigrated that the women cannot find husbands. Mrs Brewster of Westmoreland Street is taking the cream of these dowries in order to arrange introductions. She is living, literally, off the fat of the land.'

'I have had enough of country girls,' Father said. 'I suppose this Gladys of yours is another country girl.'

'No,' said Mr Bates. 'She is English. In fact she is an old school friend of Alma's.'

'Oh!' said Mother with unsuppressed yearning.

~

Kitty was too old for dolls so we played at ladies in the empty room, using lemonade crystals which we mixed with water and poured from a doll's teapot into liqueur glasses. 'Good husbands are so hard to find. I paid a thousand pounds for mine and he is only a red-headed farmer with one leg.' I tried to entertain Kitty with adult conversation but her attention kept wandering.

Our two apple trees were in fruit and were once more cooked into endless variations – stewed apple, fried, apple sponge, turnover, apple and bacon pasty. Mother had said that with no rent coming into the house she could not afford to shop and we must make do with what was to hand. Father brought home a pig's cheek. We stared in disbelief at the bristling head, cloven down the middle with an axe, so that its skull and brains, its half-nose and teeth were exposed. 'I shall cook it myself,' he announced. He boiled it up and brought it to the table as it was, fanged and whiskered in its slimy half-snarl. He carved off a few pieces and tried to encourage us to eat it by showing his own appreciation, but then his knife and fork went down gently. 'I seem to remember a tenderer meat,' he admitted. The whole thing was given to the cat on the kitchen floor. She wrestled with it for an hour and then ran to a corner and vomited with reproachful cries.

Sheep's heart, pig's feet and tripe. We entered a world of nightmare food. The sight of it raw, the smell of it cooking, the gelid look of it on the table, and then the faint reek of it through layers of newspaper in the bin, made us feel slightly ill all the time. 'Do something,' we urged Mother as we crouched over the fire, listless and grey, toasting slice after slice of Hovis on the long brass toasting fork.

'What can I do?' she shrugged, but that evening she approached Father. 'We must let the room. I can't wait until my children starve to death.'

'There is nothing whatever the matter with your children.' He fingered the knob of the wireless as if to keep his place in Hughie Green's *Double Your Money*. 'I am doing this for everyone's good. I do not like to see perfectly wholesome food go to waste.'

'And I do not like to see a perfectly good room go to waste.' She took her nightdress, her cold cream, her paints and her novel and moved into the maid's room. 'Edie!' Father's frantic whisper was like the gasp of someone falling into water. Most of the time Mother was made helpless by Father's moods but on the rare occasions when she took any positive action it was he who was made vulnerable and powerless.

Naturally, he took this out on us. 'There is a pair of knickers in the laundry press.' He burst into the dining room where we were

153

listening to our new record of 'The Three Bells'. 'They are bloody and stinking! Decent women keep these matters private.'

'Not mine!' Bridie said, without looking up.

'Not mine!' Kitty cried indignantly.

I blushed deeply and Father glared at me. 'Not mine!' I protested in a little choky voice.

I ran up to Mother and knocked on the door. There was no reply although I knew she must be there. The room had claimed her. There was a feeling that it had grown used to occupation, had developed a craving for interesting new company and would seize on whoever happened to enter to satisfy its appetite.

As when there was a new lodger, we became attuned to the sounds. We heard her filling the kettle, humming snatches of song, sometimes a jaunty creak from the bed, as if she had flung herself down in high spirits rather than from tiredness, but the door was never left ajar. She did not ask us in. She came down to meals, which Bridie had taken over. She was an indifferent and uninterested cook and made burnt and greasy chips or scorched sausages or mashed potatoes with tinned sardines, but we ate them and Mother ate hers with relish, enjoying a cigarette and a cup of tea afterwards before returning to the room. In the course of a week she began to change. For the first time, she wore the clothes that had been bought for our move to New Zealand, the soft slacks and little silky sweaters, the gold slip-ons. She used a different lipstick now, one we had not seen before, a purplish red that made her eyes look very vivid. 'I'm working on a new painting,' she announced.

'I'm glad you've taken up painting again.' Father forced a smile. 'I'm very proud of you, you know.'

'Thank you,' she said. He looked despondent. He had been seeking a way to win her round. 'Come out with me?' he begged.

'Out where?' She looked reluctant.

'We'll go into town. A drink in the Gresham, tea in The Capital, take in a film. A pork chop and a grilled tomato,' he mused, having already, in his mind, scanned the menu in the crowded tea room above the cinema and impressed the waitress with his order. We girls had a longing to gnaw on the crisp and salty fat.

'We have no money,' Mother reminded him.

He stroked some crumbs on the table into an orderly pile and smiled. 'I have a little put by.'

Mother seemed bored by this information. She sat with her elbows on the table, her chin cupped in her hands, gazing past him out of the window to the yard. 'The cat has got a bird,' she said softly. We were all drawn to the spectacle of Dusty pawing diligently at the thrush, whose wings still battered frantically, as if the larger creature was trying to read a book in a high wind. Appalled, we did not notice that Mother had begun to cry. There was no change in her attitude and her face was without expression but large drops of water rolled between her fingers and ran over her wrists and were soaked up by her sleeves. She gave a sigh then and sniffed hard, took her hands away from her face and inspected them. 'You have made a fool of me,' she said.

This time it was Father's turn to look stunned. 'Edie!'

'All this time I have been scraping pennies, my nerves worn away to nothing with worry, and you had a little put by.'

'Edie, I had to. It is a man's duty to protect his family. Suppose one of the children got sick. No man tells his wife the whole truth about money. My dear love, everything I do is for you.'

She stood up from the table. 'You think that I am one of the children. I became a servant for you but you leave me in the dark so that I am eaten by worry and can never be happy.' She ran to the door and he ran after her. We heard her gulping sobs from the

155

passage and Father's pleading tones, trying to make her understand. 'Edie, Edie! No one is happy.'

The cat had gone away but the bird still struggled, its wings flapping more feebly now like a wasp stuck in jam. We crowded at the window, watching it bitterly. Father had come back into the kitchen. He told us to come away and wash the dishes but then he stood and gazed out for a long time. 'I'll have to finish it off,' he murmured. He went to the shed and got the spade. He leaned on it and peered down miserably at the tiny creature. We saw him raise the spade at a golfing angle, swing it in the air and then let it fall. The bird struggled harder now in terror and Father watched it in consternation. Clenching the spade in both hands, he lifted it high above his head. He eyed the dying bird with resentment and pity, then clenched his eyes shut and brought the spade down with all his might. He remained, exhausted, eyes closed, leaning on the spade.

For the next few days Mother did not come down to meals. Occasionally she went out and we guessed it was to return a library book or go to church but we couldn't be sure because we only heard the front door closing softly.

A portion of the money that had been put by was given to Bridie to buy a Sunday dinner. We girls were to cook the meal and lure Mother downstairs with our effort. When we went up we got the most astonishing surprise. She had dyed her hair blonde. She seemed about ten years younger. Inside the room she was transforming, as Sissy Sullivan had done. Furtively we glanced around, expecting to see the litter of cakes and cosmetics on the table, the half-eaten box of chocolates, but the room itself was almost untouched by her. Her sketch books and paints were on the table. Her nightie was folded on the bed.

When she came down she was like a visitor. She made no comment on the luxurious food we had prepared but asked what was happening in the world, as she had not seen any newspapers or listened to the wireless.

'It is not,' Father said, 'that I have anything against Miss Partridge.'

She took a piece of bread and cut it into quarters on her side plate.

'If George Bates had had the decency to discuss the whole damn business with me privately instead of trying to make a fool of me in front of my wife . . .' He recovered himself as Bridie took the carving knife out of his hand and set his meal before him. 'I am sure she is as good as any other girl.'

Mother ate her meal slowly, accepting a second roast potato.

'We need the money,' he pleaded. 'We cannot afford to let a good room go to waste.'

'It is not going to waste,' she assured him, 'any more than this delicious food will go to waste.'

'You were right,' he said very quietly. 'We have to let the room.'

'I don't know,' Mother said. 'I have had time to gather my thoughts. I could go out and get a job tomorrow. The girls are managing very nicely.'

'None of that, now, Edie!' Father warned, but when she picked up her cardigan to return upstairs, he called after her: 'Why would you go looking for a job when there is one waiting for you?'

'What job?'

'If this damn bureau business is to be decently run, there really should be a married woman involved.' His voice was so low that she had to come back into the room to hear him.

'You would let me go out to work? Eugene, are you sure?'

'I would prefer to think of it as a social service. And you would not actually have to go out. With Gladys in the house you could work from home.'

157

'Gladys Partridge is to take the room and I am to work with her in the marriage bureau?' Mother had to sit down again to take in this astonishing news. 'Shouldn't we have a look at her first?'

'She'll be a decent girl, Edie.' Father took Mother's hand and squeezed it. 'All she cares about is other people's happiness.'

Chapter Seventeen

~

A sign went up on the door of a small office in Harcourt Street. 'St Anne's Christian Marriage Bureau – discreet introductions by caring experts.' The name of the bureau was Miss Partridge's idea and contained a small joke, for there was a favourite saying among country girls, 'Holy Saint Anne, send me a man.'

We waited for father to go mad and blame everyone, but he remained serene, for Gladys Partridge had done what he had hoped. She had brought happiness. In fact it was having something useful to do that pleased Mother, but Father could only feel the warmth of her gratitude, her new energy that gave the house a festive feel. It never occurred to him that having work gave a woman pleasure.

Mother helped Miss Partridge devise a questionnaire for prospective clients. She saw it as a way of giving girls a clear picture of what they were getting, although Miss Partridge preferred to think of every union as one of potential joy. 'My mission in life is to bring people happiness.' Her eyes blurred when she said the word. 'I don't think of myself. I've known the pitfalls, never the prizes.'

We had all been on edge when our new lodger arrived, awaiting Father's reaction, but he scarcely seemed to look at her. 'I am sure she is very nice,' he declared firmly.

'Of course she is a nice girl.' Mother smiled in relief. 'She was at school with Alma.'

And Gladys was nice. We had watched with interest as she swayed up the stairs in her many folds of gypsy clothing, her gold curls bobbing, her gold earrings clanking and her two eyes inspecting separate views, for one of them was slightly turned. From within the folds of her garments she had produced a bottle of gin. 'Mother's ruin, old maid's reward!' She gave her metallic laugh. 'You must join me for a drinkie in my little den.'

When she came downstairs, she leaned on Father. 'Imagine . . . !' Her voice dropped to the kind of murmur that pared our eavesdropping ears into pencil points. 'If a single lady were to confide to me that she had had marital experience, do you think I would have to tell that to a man who wanted an introduction?'

'You would not have to tell him!' Father stoutly declared. 'For you would already have informed that lady that she had no place in your books.' And she nodded sadly.

There was only one small disagreement. Gladys wanted a party to launch the bureau. She had bought balloons and a cake with a horseshoe on the top. Father went into one of his silences and had to be cajoled by Mother before he would express his view that marriage was sacred and ought not to be dragged down to the level of a speakeasy. He had asked a priest to make a speech and planned to offer the guests tea and USA assorted biscuits.

'Never mind. We'll have our own party afterwards,' Gladys soothed. 'I've a bottle of champagne! Come on, Rose. You can come up and put things on little biscuits.' And she swayed up to her room pursued by the balloons on their string leads.

I was surprised by the change in the room. The bedside light was draped in a red silk scarf and there were beaded curtains on the window. Over the bed was a large picture of a naked lady. 'What do you think?' Gladys refreshed her lipstick and I pulled back the beaded curtains to make them tinkle. 'Do you think your father will approve?'

'Do you like living alone?' I avoided her question, knowing Father would not approve, for the room had an air of celebration which would not fit in with his picture of a respectable lady.

'Nobody likes to be alone, sweetheart.'

'Why aren't you married?'

The light from the window showed up circles of rouge on her cheeks and her two eyes stared sorrowfully into separate distances. 'I've always been a magnet for the wrong types. It's my soft heart. But I do draw the line at married men.' She smiled then. 'Of course I'm not alone. I have all of you.' She sat down on the bed and made a rueful face. 'I miss Scottie.'

'Who's Scottie?' A very faint beat of hope had started up under my ribs. I had always wanted a dog.

She picked up one of the cushions and rattled it in a regretful way. 'You can't have everything. I know that. It's human nature, though, to want something to cuddle.'

'Where is he?'

'The Bateses are looking after him.'

'Why don't you bring him with you?' I said. 'We wouldn't mind. I could take him for walks.'

She laughed then, a very merry laugh that showed her gappy teeth. 'That would be good for him.'

'She has a dog,' I told my parents excitedly. 'His name is Scottie. She had tears in her eyes when she talked about him,' I added, getting carried away.

'Oh, that's too bad,' Mother said. 'Poor Gladys.'

'Can't we tell her to bring him here?'

161

'She would have understood when she rented the room that she could not bring an animal,' Father reasoned.

'Why?' Mother said. 'We had a dog for years. Remember Mavis?'

'All too well,' said Father, as if that finished the matter.

But that evening when they were in the drawing room I heard Mother say, 'Rose told us about Scottie.'

'He's no trouble,' Miss Partridge said. 'I worry about him. He doesn't eat when I'm not around.'

~

When Gladys went to fetch Scottie in a taxi I ran to the butcher for a bone. I presented this to her, wrapped in newspaper. 'Oh, darling, I'm afraid poor Scottie's teeth are not up to bones,' she laughed.

'Dogs like bones,' I said. 'Even old dogs like them.'

She laughed again until she was almost speechless. 'Not this old dog.'

Father heard her rattling laugh, as if a tin can was rolling on some hard surface deep in her throat. He was on his way from the bedroom with Mother to collect her for the grand opening. 'What's the joke?' He smiled, but his eye showed alarm at her brightly patterned kimono. Both my parents were dressed in their sombre best.

'I've brought a bone for Miss Partridge's dog,' I explained. 'But she says he doesn't like bones.'

'Kiddies and their little jokes!' Miss Partridge wiped tears from her eyes. 'Well, now that you're all here I suppose you'd better meet him. Scottie, come and meet my dear friends, the Raffertys. This is Scottie, an old dog for the hard road.'

Scottie did not move from his comfortable perch on Miss Freeman's silk-covered bed. He was old and balding but I liked him at once because he looked so gentle and sad. I was confused though, and continued to look around after I had taken hold of the grizzled paw he extended.

'Where's the dog?' I said.

Chapter Eighteen

~

Life was beginning to settle down when the werewolf appeared. Every evening he was in the paper, the small, hairy, fanged face framed in an advertisement for a film called *The Werewolf* which was showing at the Adelphi. 'Prepare for terror!' was written in crazed letters above the werewolf's ragged skull, but you could not prepare for terror. It was a hot breath on your neck, a jagged leap inside your chest. I tried to avoid the paper but my sisters would spring it open at the page. I could not sleep but lay awake, clenched with panic, waiting for the slightly snorting breath that I imagined, the first, cold, tentative touch of talons on my face.

For the month of September the summer came and went. There were days full of heavy golden sun like syrup, and late roses and bewildered bees, and then irritable spells with a futile, nervous wind and little nibs of rain. One day I awoke to a hard, cold smell in my nose, flinty air, a pinched look over the gardens. The year had grown old. We went to Benediction and when we came out of the church, dusk was falling so thick and heavy it was like a blackout. The mist of incense gave way to tents of smog, chimneys of suburban houses making sulphurous scribbles on the sea of murk. There was a change of scenery too. The pavements had vanished under leaves and when you bent down, buried underneath the crispy silt were lost mittens, beech nuts and sometimes hazel nuts. Even our voices sounded different. 'Bridie! Kitty!' I called out, hearing a strange tinny sound with an edge of fear. They had vanished into the fog. Silence lapped in around me like a tide until it bore with it the very faint sound of breathing – raspy, snorty. I began to run, my feet making the crazed, scattery sound of the pursued female, until I bumped into the schoolbagged backs of my sisters. 'Come on, slowcoach,' they grumbled. Then a startling thing happened. It snowed, and the tops of the mountains were veiled in white lace. This unseasonal apparition was followed by the free gift of a flu epidemic, which closed twenty-four schools within a week, and we loafed around the empty room, sniffling and whispering about the exciting scandal that had taken place there.

~

At first Gladys had been bewildered by Father's fury. 'Where's the harm? Scottie is not a married man. I would never sleep with a married man.'

She backed away when she saw his look of anger and loathing, as if he might spit in her face. 'You have been living in sin.'

He would not even let them stay the night. After they left, he stormed off to bed, full of self-pity, and Mother dutifully followed, leaving the marriage bureau to open by itself. We sneaked back to the spare room to eat the party that Gladys had prepared. When Kitty cut the cake the icing had the texture of snow, soft, but crisp and squeaky on its surface. Bridie opened the bottle of champagne and we gulped it voraciously down.

Because of the champagne we burst into loud giggles and then froze when we heard footsteps on the stairs. It was Mother. 'What do you girls think you are doing out of bed at this hour?' she reprimanded mildly.

'We were hungry,' Bridie said. 'We didn't get a proper tea.'

Mother could not be unreasonable and felt sympathetic towards hungry Bridie. 'Well, don't make a noise,' she said. 'Don't wake your father.' She sat beside us on the bed. 'Bring me some champagne.' She drank down a glass with a shudder as if it was medicine and poured herself some more. 'Your father is right, of course. We could not have allowed them to set such an example before you girls. But I can't help thinking we could have sorted things out if only he had not taken it so personally. We could have had a bit of money,' she mused. 'I could have done something useful with my life.' She began to cry. She sank on the bed and her body writhed and twisted like a sheet that is being wrung out, and we girls had to fall on her and make her quiet in case Father would wake.

~

Hallowe'en brought small, ghoulish figures who prowled the streets wearing sheets with holes for their eyes or blacked-out faces or fearsome face shields of hags or horned devils. We were not allowed to roam about at night like other children, which was a relief as the werewolf might be under any sheet or mask. Mother consoled the older girls by saying we would have our own outing, and we shopped for cheap fruit in Moore Street and then went to a rickety store in Kevin Street that sold nothing but second-hand magazines and comics, and then we went to an expensive shop and bought a pomegranate. Every year we bought one piece of exotic fruit just to acquaint ourselves with it. The roundness of the pomegranate, with its hide-like skin of gold and russet and its crowned top, made me think it might be filled with frankincense and myrrh, but when it

167

was peeled it broke into segments that were like a chrysalis full of red glass beads, and these burst like raindrops on the tongue.

Father was coming out of his period of resentment and had advertised for a new lodger. He poured a small drink for himself and Mother and she left her tea and sipped whiskey and smoked her cigarette, her legs crossed, one foot dangling a red high heel, the other foot bare with the neglected shoe lying on its side. Pipe smoke signalled peace from behind the newspaper and Mother crumbled a little bit of brack and sprinkled it on the floor. We peered beneath the table and started to giggle. Father put down his paper. 'What is it?' he said in perplexity. 'It is nothing,' she said with a straight face. 'It is nothing except Marmaduke.' He thought she was making a joke and smiled obligingly and went back to his reading.

Marmaduke was our mouse. When the coast was clear it darted out of its hole behind the bookshelves to feast on the brack that she dropped into her empty shoe. The tiny mouse was one we had recently wrested from the jaws of the cat and it feared nothing now, having humans on its side. We named it Marmaduke and Mother regularly fed it morsels of cheese or bread from her tea.

At one point there was a knock on the door from the trick-or-treating children. I looked at our lovely party on the kitchen table and thought that in a minute it would all be eaten by strange children. In a panic, I ran to the table and filled my skirt with nuts and fled into the pantry. Then I raced back, filled my skirt with fruit, and ran back to the pantry. Mother laughed so much she could not speak. When the terrifying gnomes presented themselves and the masks were ripped away it was only our cousins, and we played games of bobbing for apples and Father showed a cartoon film of Felix the Cat with his projector. When the cousins had gone, my mother gave me a half-hearted lecture, telling me I ought not to be selfish but should be prepared to share whenever we had enough to go around.

It was almost nine o'clock when another knock came. We had eaten nearly everything and were sleepy. Mother quickly gathered the remaining nuts and sweets on to a plate. 'You answer the door,' she said. 'Don't ask them in, it's too late, but give them these. You must learn to be generous.' I went sleepily to the door. And there stood the werewolf. After the first shock there was an interlude when I was merely acquainting myself with my fate, the hairy face, the squat, thickly furred body, the tiny eyes full of malevolence. For some reason the werewolf wore a black rain hat. I held out the plate and the beast took a fistful. Only after I had shut the door did I begin to tremble. 'You look as if you've seen a ghost,' everyone teased. My stomach contracted with fear but I said nothing.

The knocking began again. This time it was louder. Nobody moved until Father, looking as reluctant as the rest of us, went to the hall. All the festive air fled with him when he opened the kitchen door, and we waited stiffly until I heard his unwilling voice saying, 'Come in.'

We heard a clumping sound like a wooden leg. When he came back his eyes were silently saying 'Help.' The whiskery thing followed, dragging a case, which was what had made the noise in the hall. The hairy body was now seen to be a fur coat, passed down through generations, but the hair on her face was all her own. 'This is Miss Heaslip,' Father said. 'She has come about the room.'

It is almost certain that he would not have accepted Miss Heaslip had he not been placed at a disadvantage by my slamming the door in her face. Actually, I had closed it gently, but when Father went to the door the second time, that is what she said: 'I am not used to having the door slammed in my face.' And she stepped straight past him, humping her case into the house. She was a school teacher and very strange. Her bristly face and square figure made her look not so much like a man dressed as a woman, as like a sort of patchwork of man and beast and woman. From the

169

very start we were bound together by my dread of her and her resentment of me.

Every week her rent was paid on time. She was very devout and when not teaching in school, spent a great deal of time in the church. We all disliked the angry slam that announced her entrance, the grinding sigh she made before ascending the stairs to her room and the stagnant smell she left in the lavatory, but these were not reasons to dismiss her. One Sunday she came in after Mass to find a copy of *The People* on the hall table. She stormed down to the kitchen where she flagged my parents with it. 'Do ye not know that the Bishop of Cork, the Most Reverend Doctor Cornelius Lucey, has warned the faithful against the dangers of reading imported Sunday newspapers!' On another occasion she asked us where she ought to go on her holidays. 'To Butlin's,' we said at once, for we all longed to go to Butlin's. Miss Heaslip growled with rage. 'That place has been condemned by the holy Catholic Church!' she said. 'That is a hole of the devil. It is the whore of the devil!'

Sometimes in the morning she was in the lavatory for half an hour while we jiggled outside, waiting to go to school. Father had a word with her, pointing out that there were other people in the household. She told him that no gentleman would broach such a subject with a woman, but the problem was resolved. She did not have much to do with us except, occasionally, to ask for jam jars. We wondered what kind of jam she made that permeated first the landing and gradually the whole house with its strange, familiar smell.

The weather grew cold. In school, the pipes froze and the toilets broke. I ran all the way home, desperate for the bathroom. Mother was not in. It would have been unthinkable to knock on the doors of neighbours to ask for the use of the toilet, for our neighbours were elderly ladies. On our street there were never any ordinary women with shopping bags or children. It was like living in a desert, or, in this weather, in the North Pole. Dirty puddles clacked with shards of ice and the sky looked as if it had been written over in pencil and then rubbed out. Cold seeped into me. It leaked up my sleeves and my skirt, plastered my bare legs, but inside, I was all boiling water, a blister, waiting to burst. A small dog scuttled along the street, lifted its leg and released a stream of yellow on to a railing. Around the corner, by the postbox, a woman appeared. It was Miss Heaslip. 'Let me in, let me in!' I begged as she lumbered down the street. She smiled as she opened the gate, rooted in her great big bag as if selecting from a whole bag full of keys, and at length flicked the key into the lock. As the door opened she sidled in and with a cackle of laughter slammed it behind her. From inside, she opened the letter slot to call out, 'Now you know what it's like to be shut out in the cold, you bold little brat.'

I lifted the knocker and banged on the door. I heard her clumping up the stairs. For a moment I felt so desolate that my immediate need was almost forgotten. Then Mother came around the corner. As she did so, on to this desert landscape drifted another neighbour. They stopped to talk. Their bodies grew slack as if it was summer. They nodded and smiled. They gazed off into separate distances. They frowned and murmured secrets. Then they shuddered and shrugged as if they had just noticed the cold. They strolled away, relaxed by the encounter. Mother saw me and she waved. Something about the wave suggested farewell instead of a greeting, and in that moment I lost hope. A torrent appeared between my legs. I gazed at her accusingly as it gushed out on the tiled mosaic, dissolving fragments of ice. Still she did not hurry, for when she saw what had happened she paused and clutched the railings, bent almost double with laughter.

I had wet the floor. My knickers were wet, my shoes were wet and my mother had laughed. I was like Gram Lambert. No one would take me seriously now. But Father did. He had begun to look on the room as the source of all our troubles, and my shameful accident decided him that Miss Heaslip was one more bad influence and that she should go.

'Eugene, all our tenants leave,' Mother protested. 'You forget that they owe us nothing but seventeen shillings a week. She is far from ideal, but she is harmless.'

'We shall see.' He did a thing he had never done before. While she was out he took the spare key and went into her room. After a while we heard him racing from the room to the lavatory. A splash and a flush, and then back again and again. A brief pause, frantic footsteps, splash and flush. We wondered if he was ill. 'Keep away! Keep away!' He charged from the room with several jars held stiffly away from him. Splash! Flush!

'What is it?'

'It's filth! It's piss!' he said through gritted teeth.

We had not heard him use such language before. 'What's wrong?'

'Beneath the bed!' he roared, and it was unclear if we should look there or hide there. While he made another dash we went into the room to peer under the bed. There seemed to be hundreds of jars in there, filled with dark-yellow fluid, and the smell was awful.

'What is it?' we said, but we knew. We gazed at the spectacle and then glanced at one another and began to laugh. Mother tried to look severe but she bit down on a smile. 'She's too mean to spend a penny,' she laughed. But we had to be serious when Father returned, for he thought the event was catastrophic.

'No!' Miss Heaslip said when he ordered her to leave.

'This is my house. My room!' Father said. 'I will rent it to whom I please.'

'As it is furnished you will need an eviction order. What grounds will you cite? I have broken no written rule. My rent is paid on time. You, on the other hand, have broken into my lodgings.'

Mother would have been willing to admit that she had a point and we had a problem. 'She may be mad,' she said, 'but she's not stupid.' Father could never admit to being in the wrong. He offered his ultimatum: 'You will leave by the end of the week or I will have the locks changed.'

The weekend came and our tenant remained. While she was at Mass, father packed her possessions and put her suitcase on the step. Then he changed the hall lock. For hours we cringed inside while she battered the door. Father turned up the wireless. 'Sooner or later she will have to go away. Then we will be rid of her forever.' As darkness descended, peace also came. We breathed an uneasy sigh of relief. It was well after tea when there was another knock. This one was timid and refined. Father went into the drawing room to look out of the bay window, and there was gentle Miss Queenie Cornelia, peering in perplexity at the house to see if there was anyone in. He liked Miss Cornelia's genuine goodness and gentility and her old-fashioned veneration of anyone male. He opened the door and faced Miss Heaslip.

'Oh, thank goodness you're home.' Miss Cornelia spoke from behind her. 'Poor Miss Heaslip has been knocking all day.'

'Stay out of here!' Father tried to bar the lodger's way.

'Mr Rafferty, what is the matter? Can I help in some way?' Miss Cornelia advanced timidly but stoically. 'This good lady says you locked her out of her lodgings. She came to me for a drink of water. She said you would not give her water.'

'Water?' Father looked as if he was going to have a fit. 'I'll give her water. She gave me her water!'

'Mr Rafferty,' Miss Cornelia pleaded, 'don't upset yourself. This good lady assures me that she has done nothing wrong.'

'And I assure you . . . !' Father tried to control his anger but the effort of subduing it almost choked him.

173

Miss Heaslip regarded him slyly. 'What have I done, Mr Rafferty?' She knew he could never explain her behaviour to a refined person like Miss Cornelia.

'Stay out of this!' he said. 'Stay out of my house.' He put up his arms again, but she was bigger than him and she heaved him aside and stamped up the stairs to the room. He swore silently, for he had neglected to change the lock on her room.

'Come in,' he said to Miss Cornelia then. 'I am so sorry about this. You know I have the highest regard for you, but you really cannot interfere in matters you do not understand.'

Miss Cornelia looked stricken but she stood her ground. 'It is my Christian duty to intervene when a poor soul is denied even a drop of water. I thank you, Mr Rafferty, but I think I won't come in.'

Father's humiliation was increased by his admiration for Miss Cornelia's integrity. He crept away to the drawing room and for a long time we waited to hear some mournful sound from the piano, but the keys were silent. After a long time he emerged with two envelopes. 'I have written a letter to each of the ladies.'

'What did you say?' Mother wondered anxiously.

'I have informed Miss Heaslip that I do not intend to resort to rough-arm tactics but whenever she emerges from the house, as eventually she must, she will find no familiar keyholes on her return.'

'What did you say to Miss Cornelia?'

'Merely that her 'good lady' has yet to discover that the lavatory has been invented.'

'Oh, Eugene, don't say that,' Mother begged. 'I will explain to Miss Cornelia some other time. I will say that Miss Heaslip has had a nervous breakdown and has been frightening the children.'

He agreed to this but slid Miss Heaslip's warning under her door. For four days we waited for her to emerge. Mother began to worry that she would starve to death. 'Perhaps I should just leave a pint of milk and some bread outside her door.' Father never gave any quarter to his enemies. 'Why not leave some empty jam jars while you are at it.'

'Since you mention it,' Mother said, 'she hasn't even been out to visit the bathroom. What will she do when she runs out of jam jars?'

Miss Heaslip had thought of this. When Father went out to call the cat, she opened her window and began emptying the jam jars on to his head. As the foul content trickled over his skull he unwisely looked up.

On Sunday, as usual, she went to Mass, leaving the rent on the hall table. Father would not take the money but could not help reading what she had written on the outside of the envelope, in jagged letters like the banner above *The Werewolf*. Miss Heaslip's message said, 'Prepare for battle.' It was so like the werewolf's message that I began to believe she would sneak in at night and tear us all to pieces and then vanish without trace.

Father studied it with a set jaw and walked heavily upstairs. We listened for splash and flush but none came. There was silence and then the noises began.

'Go up and see what he is doing,' Mother said.

He was dragging the wardrobe up on to the landing. He was a small man but drew strength from his purpose. Next the bed went, hauled up to his bedroom and propped against the wall. He appeared with an armload of cups and saucers, pots and pans and towels. 'Get a tray,' he panted. 'Bring these to the kitchen. Get them out of sight.' I was carrying down the tray when we heard the window squealing on its sash and then there was a tremendous crash. Looking out of the kitchen window we saw that a chair had landed in the garden. A rug sailing past our vision was followed by a small table, then

175

the bedside lamp. Mother went on basting the Sunday roast as if nothing was happening. Two badly hemmed curtains drifted on to the lawn and an alarm clock was shattered on a splintered chair leg. She looked up then, calmly and vaguely. 'Girls,' she said, 'you are young but I will tell you something. The very act of marriage which men are compelled to perform is so peculiar that I believe it influences all of their behaviour. Whenever they behave strangely, it is as well to think of something else.'

He came downstairs looking haggard and exhausted. Mother merely commented that he might like to tidy up before dinner. He went away to put on his Sunday clothes and comb his hair. As we sat to eat, the clamour started up again, but this time it was Miss Heaslip at the door. 'Bless us, oh Lord, for these Thy gifts . . .' Father's drone was like a priest giving a sermon on a stormy sea. We could think of nothing except the banging at the door. His hand shook slightly but he carved in his usual measured way, so that each slice was wafer-thin, and cold before it was eaten. The crashing on the door sounded as if Miss Heaslip was flinging her whole bulk against it. It stopped. There was an interlude of peace, and then a different sort of knock, a sharpish but unemotive rat-tat-tat. 'Miss Cornelia!' Mother said.

Father held up the steel knife, blackened by use and whittled to an hourglass waist from years of sharpening. 'That is not her knock.'

'Miss Marmion, then,' she guessed as the knock was repeated.

'Maybe Miss Heaslip is trying a different kind of knock to take us by surprise,' Kitty said.

'There will be no more surprises,' Father grimly promised, and was about to resume his carving when a stern male voice boomed in the letter box: 'Open in the name of the law.'

With the knife in his hand he looked at if he had been caught red-handed in a crime. Mother disarmed him before he went in a daze to answer the door. Miss Heaslip clutched the garda's arm triumphantly. 'There he is! The villain that took my money and locked me out of my room.'

Father was at the door, his slight frame shaking, the edge of his jaw as chilled and white as if slivers of porcelain had been pushed under his skin. 'Your money is where you left it.' He addressed Miss Heaslip. 'I did not touch a penny.'

'It's not as simple as that, sir,' the garda said. 'This may be a matter for the courts but I cannot see the woman put out on the streets if she is within her rights.'

'I think I know the law.' Father's voice came out forced and dry.

'Will you let this lady back to her room?' the garda enquired.

'I will not.'

'Would you let me take a look at the room in question?'

Without a word Father turned on his heel and marched up the stairs, and Miss Heaslip followed, still clutching her guard.

'Oh, wait!' Mother scuttled after them, perhaps fearing that Father would tip them both out the window. Father opened the room and stood back. Miss Heaslip gasped. So did Mother. The room had been stripped. Not one scrap of furniture remained, not one fork or hanger, not even a light bulb. All there was to furnish the room was about twenty jam jars of reeking fluid.

'Is this your room?' the garda asked Miss Heaslip.

'It is, but . . .' she said.

'But it is not furnished,' he said.

She gazed around her in astonishment. 'But it was when I left here this morning,' She made a lunge at Father. 'I'll do ye for this, you bastard.'

'Anything that is in this room has been furnished by this good lady,' Father said.

The garda pointed at the jars. 'Is this your property, miss?'

177

'Do you think I would share a lavatory with such people?' she demanded. 'They read imported Sunday newspapers.'

He cautiously lifted one of the containers and inspected it. He sniffed and scowled. He looked bewildered and embarrassed. 'Get your things together like a good girl, now.' He nodded to Father. 'I'll see her off your premises. I am very sorry to have troubled you.'

'I hope you are sorry for having destroyed my Sunday dinner.' Father managed to sound indignant.

He need not have worried, for Dusty the cat had taken advantage of our crisis and nothing remained but a ragged bone.

Chapter Nineteen

~

I think Father might have enjoyed being poor if only we could have put our hearts into it. As he sat at the table paring the soles of his shoes with a penknife, he spoke of the generations of Irish people who had flourished on a diet of porridge, potatoes and buttermilk. He had resurrected his oldest footwear, the thick crêpe soles of which had oozed out around the uppers, and lovingly trimmed them back to shape, boasting that they were fifteen years old and good as new. He taught us to make paper covers for our books so that they would remain unmarked and instructed us to use no more than two squares of toilet paper, two inches of bath water and one eighth of an inch of toothpaste. He found a cheap brand of lavatory paper which was grey and squeaky and was called Elephant Brand. He came home bearing an enormous, lardy cake of home-made soap which had been given to him as a present.

Mother failed to enter into the spirit. When he told her how his mother could transform the house with a sixpenny pack of Drummer Dye, she pushed sheets and towels through the mangle and his voice was drowned by the splatter of water into the basin below. She said the woman who donated the soap ran a rescue home for cats and had made this soap from the rendered-down fat of her deceased animals, and we had a feeling it was true, for the soap had a dense, carnal smell and the occasional black hair sticking out of it.

It rained for weeks and the furniture stayed in the garden. Once when I went out to retrieve some washing I saw Miss Cornelia peering in distress over the wall at the wreckage. She gave me a long, wounded look but I could think of nothing to say so I filled my arms with vests and sheets and went back indoors.

Mother urged us not to mention Christmas. 'You are big girls now.' She hid any cards that arrived behind the clock. 'We must all pull together as a family.'

'We don't all pull together,' Bridie grumbled. 'Father pulls in one direction and we all topple in a heap.'

Father watched the hairy soap grow grey and dry. He talked of selling his car and his eyes filled with tears. Mother said that the car was like a horse to him, he would sooner shoot it than sell it.

~

In spite of what Mother had said, Christmas kept advancing like a big, lighted cruise liner. First of all there was a card from Minnie who was home from hospital. 'Come and see the baby,' she wrote. Snow fell again, and we thought the festive season would be white, but it was quickly followed by more rain. Then George and Alma Bates arrived. They always came at Christmas, but Father had not thought they would have the nerve to show their faces again. 'It's Christmas, Eugene,' George boomed. 'Forgive and forget.'

'There will be no Christmas in this house,' Father said curtly. 'It will be shanks's mare rather than Rudolph's reindeer, for I am going to have to sell my car.'

'Ah, Eugene.' George was all concern. 'Things aren't going well? You should have let me know.'

'What would you have done?' Insecurity always made Father rude. 'Sent me another floozie?' He sucked on his pipe and crossed his legs and rocked himself for comfort.

'What about that Ruton company?' Alma said. 'They were keen to promote, weren't they?'

Father continued to rock and suck.

'How about it, Eugene?' George said. 'Nationwide distribution. There would be an allowance for a car.'

After a few moments he stopped rocking, sucked on his pipe as if to extract some bitter marrow, then abruptly took it out of his mouth. 'Did you hear that, Edie?' His glance bobbed up, naked with hope. 'George has a job for me. There's an allowance. We could keep the car.'

Mother wondered why there had to be any such inducement, since there were so few jobs.

'There's a bit of travel,' George explained.

'Nationwide distribution,' Father enlightened. 'Visiting branches around the country.'

'Yes, that sort of thing,' George said, 'although in fact the calls would be to private individuals – private houses.' He shifted on his haunches and added more quietly, 'House to house.'

'Door to door,' Father echoed supportively. A puzzled silence fell. He sucked more slowly on his pipe, as if its taste had gone off, and then he looked accusingly at Mother. 'Door to door! He means to turn me into a blasted door-to-door salesman.'

'Sales representative,' George soothed. 'Don't you want to hear about the product?'

'Get out of here, George Bates!'

George stroked his hat on his lap as if the scene were likely to upset it. 'It's a start,' he persisted. 'You could work your way up the ladder.'

'I am forty-five.' Father was almost in tears. 'I am too old to work my way up the ladder.'

George stood up to go. 'Miss Partridge sends her regards. The poor girl is cut up about what happened. She is talking of packing up the whole thing and heading off with Scottie.'

'Going away?' Mother said in dismay. 'What about the clients?'

George Bates wagged his head regretfully. 'Three couples have been fixed up. There are dozens more on the books. I tried to persuade her to sell the business as a going concern but she says she would not entrust it to a stranger. You could have it.' His lugubrious eye lit hopefully on Father. 'You and Edie.'

Mother looked away. Father pursed his mouth and shook his head rapidly, as if he was being tempted to sin.

'Won't you stay to tea?' Mother said, but she remained slumped on her chair in a completely boneless way. George Bates touched her hair as if it was a talisman and she looked up at him, showing her unhappiness. 'No, Edie,' he said. 'I'm too old for tea.'

Chapter Twenty

~

It took a long time for the smell to fade from the spare room, that vague tang of cats and lemons that emanated more temptingly from the Chinese restaurant in Wicklow Street. When there was a knock on the door, we would say half jokingly, 'It's the werewolf!'

It was a shock all the same when a country priest came to the door to announce: 'I bring greetings from your erstwhile lodger.'

'You need not waste your time or mine.' Father tried to close the door in his face. Mother was mortified and ushered in the bewildered clergyman, and we all looked uneasily at the big brown paper bag he carried, which was slippery with blood.

'I bring Christmas greetings from Miss Taylor,' he began again as Mother tried to soothe him while Kitty made tea and I opened the biscuits brought by Mr Bates.

'Miss Taylor!' we chorused in relief.

'How is Miss Taylor?' Mother said eagerly.

'Oh, fine, fine,' he said unhappily. 'She sent you a present.' From the bag he took out the most beautiful bird we had ever seen. It had iridescent plumage in shades of blue and rust and gold. We children cried out in rage because it was dead. 'It's a pheasant,' he said, and we thought that this was a mispronunciation

183

of 'present'. Mother stroked its feathers in dismay. 'Do I have to pull them out?'

'Would ye not take her back? The nuns she works for asked me to put in a word. She is badly treated in her own house.'

'What's the matter?' Mother said. 'Doesn't she get enough to eat?'

'She's well fed. People eat well on a farm. It's a family matter. You can't interfere.'

'Tell her that if she is well fed, she is better off than any of us,' Father rejoined. The priest left us with a look of reproach, which Father insisted was because we had offered him tea instead of whiskey. 'You think I am heartless.' He saw Mother's disconsolate look. 'You think I am a failure.'

'We think you're mad,' Bridie grumbled.

'Selena was good to us.' Mother began to gather up the teacups, peering into each one as if she might read her future there.

'She has a job and a home,' he reasoned. 'She couldn't find work in the city. The woman is not looking for a room to rent. She is trying to find a family to adopt her. This business of the room has been a disaster from start to finish. We have had nothing but lame dogs, degenerates and the deranged.'

'I'll have the room,' Bridie said. 'I'm sick of sharing with two kids who pry into everything.'

'I thought you felt sorry for women having to make their own way in the world.' Mother took no notice of Bridie.

'I had not known they would be so wilful.'

'Selena's not wilful.'

'Perhaps her more than anyone. She would not accept her station in life. She wanted excitement, happiness, even love.'

~

184

When Mother wanted to do something that disturbed her conscience, she enlisted me as an ally. From the time I was born it was understood that we were a pair, but as life got harder and she grew resigned and religious, I became a sort of *alter ego*. Now that I was eleven, it was as if I was a slightly older, devil-may-care version of herself, by whom she might be innocently led astray. 'You will understand why I am doing this.' She buttoned me into the velvet-hooded coat that had been donated by richer relations. 'There is no need to say anything to your sisters or to Father.'

Afterwards we had coffee and almond buns in Bewley's. At home she had a slightly fevered air, and once or twice I saw Father looking at her suspiciously, but it was a whole week before he found out and went completely mad.

~

We watched from the gate as he urged his vehicle down the street. He was always a slight man, but now he seemed to be made of pipe cleaners.

'Mother! Mother!' We ran into the house. 'Father has come home on a bicycle. He has sold the car.'

Father was the sort of man you could not imagine without a car or a tie. We waited anxiously while he put away his bike. He came in and ate his meal in silence and then took from his wallet a five-pound note. He glanced briefly at Mother before putting it on the table. She noted it nervously but said nothing, just cleared away his dinner plate and replaced it with a bowl of tapioca.

He took up the note and crumpled it in his fist. 'Take it! I hope you all have a bloody good Christmas.'

'Where did it come from?' she said, and then: 'What is the matter?'

185

'You have deceived me!' He bunched his hands into fists as if his anger caused him pain. 'You have betrayed me. God knows I do not ask for much, but have you not the smallest shred of loyalty?'

'I have done nothing wrong,' she said faintly.

'You went to see Gladys Partridge. Against all my wishes you took yourself off to that two-faced woman. You and she have been hatching some plot behind my back. You think I cannot earn money so you were going to try and get the business going without me.'

'I wasn't . . .'

'Don't lie to me!'

'She's not lying,' I said.

'What do you know about this?'

'She knows nothing.' Mother gave me a warning glance. 'How do you know?' she said then.

'She wrote to me. She said that since you had buried the hatchet perhaps I would do the same. She neglected to mention that you had buried the hatchet in my heart.'

'I can explain everything,' she said.

'I have no wish to listen. Why should I believe a single word you say?'

Mother and I exchanged miserable glances. When we agreed to secrecy we had forgotten to bind Miss Partridge to confidence too.

'Why didn't you tell him?' I asked afterwards.

'He would not have listened. Anyway, it would have done no good. He would have found some way to interfere. All this will blow over and perhaps there will be a happy ending for someone.'

~

It was Miss Taylor who was to have had a happy ending. We had gone to Miss Partridge to see if she could find her a husband but it looked as if we had got there too late.

'I'm folding up the business,' Gladys sighed.

'I'm sorry.' Mother felt responsible.

'Don't be.' Miss Partridge took down a large file and dropped it in the waste basket. 'I came into the agency to bring people happiness, but Irishmen don't want romance. Most of my clients are poor farmers in search of women with money. The only decent men are Protestants who cannot find any of their own kind.'

'There's a girl I would like to see settled.' Mother planted herself on the chair that had been placed there for those in search of happiness.

Gladys shook her head with a jangle of earrings. 'I'm heading into a completely new line – theatrical and film promotions. Look at this!' She read out a newspaper item about a party in New York which had been thrown by the film director Mike Todd to publicise *Around the World in Eighty Days*. 'His wife, Elizabeth Taylor, was hoisted by mechanical lift on to a cake, thirty feet by forty feet, which cost thirteen thousand dollars. They ate fried grasshoppers and imported cheeses.' Mother continued to watch her with stubborn hope.

'Oh, what age is she? What is she like?'

'She is twenty-four years of age.' Mother surprised me, for I had imagined Miss Taylor to be much older. 'She is very plain and she has not a penny in the world. But she is a sweet-natured girl and she lights up when she is happy.'

'Don't we all,' Gladys grinned.

'Haven't you men on your books with a bit of money?' Mother coaxed. 'Some widower with a lot of children who need to be looked after? She is very good with children.'

Miss Partridge pointed out that most women were fond of children and quite a few of those had a thousand pounds.

'Maybe some poor man with an additional disadvantage – someone you would not normally consider taking on your books. Almost anybody would do if he was kind.'

'Oh, Edie!' Gladys exclaimed. 'Almost any woman would take any man so long as he was kind.'

'Have you letters from men you turned down? Let me take a look at them.'

'Here you are.' Miss Partridge handed her a folder. 'I have an even bigger one of women – my no-hopers file.'

'That is the best and the worst of human nature.' Mother received the folder as if it was filled with money, and Miss Partridge watched her with a lopsided, ironic gaze. 'We are all hopers.'

~

'Hide this in your room.' Mother gave me the folder. Afterwards, an air of suspense persisted, as Mother waited for Father to find out, or else for him to go out so that she could read the letters. A few days later we were having tea and an argument. Bridie had been invited to a party. Mother did not want her to go as it would mean her coming home alone late at night. 'All the other girls will be driven home by their fathers,' Bridie complained.

'Tell that to your father,' Mother said, but when Father came down there was something about his face that made us fall quiet. His clenched jaw was the colour of bones and his voice was hoarse with passion. 'I went looking for my *Radio Review* and what do you think I found?'

Mother looked completely at bay. In that moment I think she would have been genuinely grateful if the ground had opened and swallowed her up.

From behind his back he withdrew a small box, rather like a pencil box. Mother's dread drained away as she studied with interest the container, which Kitty had hidden for fear of its discovery in the bin. 'These objects have been condemned by the holy Catholic Church!' He brandished the empty Tampax package. 'The Archbishop himself has pronounced that they are liable to lead to excitement in females and to contraception.'

Bridie gave an unwise snort of laughter.

'You, miss!' He boxed her on the jaw with the flimsy carton. 'You are a bad example to the younger girls. I have tried to bring you up to be decent women. I am aware that you are subject to appalling influences in the modern world.' He cited influences, from Elvis Presley, whose striptease-style movements had driven ten thousand teenagers into a frenzy; to the bookseller, Frank Reid of O'Connell Street, who had been fined thirty-five pounds for selling the banned publication *Bodies in Bedlam*.

'They don't use Tampax,' Bridie reasoned.

Father withdrew in an aggrieved and disappointed manner. 'It is as I feared.' He laid the box accusingly on the table. 'You have grown coarse and forward.'

Bridie glared at the box with exaggerated scorn, but it was only to stop herself from crying. As soon as Father left the room she flew into a rage.

'Why didn't you say anything?' she demanded of Mother.

Relief had made Mother weak. 'Perhaps your father is right. Young girls are curious and might be tempted to experiment.'

'Experiment?' Bridie almost breathed fire. 'Whose were they anyway?' Kitty cast her a mute look of appeal.

Mother tried to pacify by saying Bridie could go to the party if Kitty went with her. Bridie grew even more furious. 'I'm not bringing a *kid*. The thing all the girls hate most in the world is younger sisters. You can't even *talk* with kids around.' Bridie was

189

not yet interested in boys but liked to talk intensely to girls her own age. But the thought of a party had kindled hope in Kitty. Having seized it she could not let it go. 'Take me,' she begged. 'No one will know what age I am. I'll make you a dress.' 'My friends don't wear dresses,' Bridie snarled. 'They wear slacks.' When we went to bed I had to listen to Kitty weeping and pleading and Bridie cursing, like a weak wife and her scornful husband.

In the middle of the night Bridie wordlessly decamped to the spare room. Her stealth was ruined by a howl of anger when she found that there was no furniture. She ran back upstairs and tore the blankets and pillows from her bed. The following day, with a great deal of noise, she dragged the bed and the wardrobe from the top of the house. The house then shook with hammer blows as she banged a shelf into the wall with nails. She investigated the furniture in the garden but decided most of it was sodden beyond repair. By evening she was calmer and invited us to come and look.

We were bathed in a strange red glow from the strips of crêpe paper she had pinned to the window in place of curtains. Her books were piled on to the makeshift shelf and she had brought in her bicycle in case Father decided he needed to sell it. On to the walls she had tacked pictures of motorcycles as well as some of her drawings of cats.

'We'll leave it until after Christmas,' Mother said. 'Then we'll see.'

Bridie spread her arms out to protect her possessions. 'It is furnished accommodation. You will need an eviction order.'

'It is our only source of income,' Mother reminded her.

Father, who had been remarkably quiet, considering the walls were now inexpertly punctured with nails, murmured: 'No!'

We all turned to gaze at him.

'You are wrong there. It is not our only source of income.' He pretended to test Bridie's bookshelf, which wobbled like an old tooth. 'I have taken the job. George Bates's job. I start in the new year.'

'But you sold the car!' Surprise made Mother sound accusing.

He found a screwdriver which Bridie had abandoned on the mantelpiece. He concentrated for some moments on securing the nails in her shelf. 'Who says?'

'You did,' Bridie said, but we realised now that he had said nothing at all.

'But . . . !' Kitty spoke now in high-pitched apprehension. 'You came home on a bicycle. You went out that morning in the car.'

'As the car will be needed for long journeys I decided to have it serviced. Someone has to think of these things.' He whistled under his breath as he finished working on the nails.

'What about the money you gave me?' Mother said.

'An advance on salary. Bates insisted on it because of what I had said about Christmas.'

'You should not have kept us in suspense,' Mother rebuked. 'We felt sorry thinking of you without your car, imagining you had made a huge sacrifice.'

'And now you think I haven't? Do you realise I am going to have to go on the road like a tramp for five days in the week? I would have expected some show of enthusiasm, some thanks or congratulations, however insincere.' He walked out of the room.

'Why would he not have said about the car?' Mother was utterly at a loss.

'Don't you see?' Bridie said. 'He was punishing you because you went to see Miss Partridge. He's enjoying himself. He even threatened to take me out of school. Come on, Kit,' she said. 'Get your glad rags on. We're going to a party.'

She and Bridie raced to the bathroom, giggling, and for hours there were thumps and shrieks as they fought and bathed and tried

191

on clothes. Mother was pleased that Kitty was to go to the party but when the two girls came down an hour later, I got a shock. Bridie looked much the same but Kitty was completely different. Her long hair had been combed up into a high pony tail. Bridie had loaned her a bra, which she had stuffed with socks, and now she had little peaks showing through a long, loose sweater called a sloppy joe. She wore Bridie's slacks with the bottoms rolled up and white socks with a pair of Mother's high heels. I thought she looked sixteen. I was sure Mother would be upset to see her two girls looking like women but she was only amused. 'Put on some lipstick,' she urged. She did not believe women ever looked attractive unless they were wearing lipstick. Bridie refused but Kitty eagerly pursed her lips while Mother swirled the scarlet stalk out of its gold tube and made her thin mouth into a decorative bow. She dabbed her nose with powder and then pencilled in her eyebrows. Kitty's pale face now had an eager and lively look, like a fairy-tale princess. When Mother held up a mirror for her to see, she seized it and stared into it avidly.

'What's the matter?' Mother spied my woebegone face after they left.

'They're too far ahead of me now. I'll never catch up.'

She lit a cigarette and for a moment I thought she would offer me one too, but she had leaned across to confide: 'In many ways you are more grown up than they are. You are very grown up for your age.'

'In what way?' I said eagerly.

'You are more practical,' she said, and my heart sank.

'Let's go into town tomorrow.'

We took the bus to the pillar and went straight to Clery's, where one whole window was taken up by a Peschaniki fur coat at twenty-five guineas. I thought she meant to take me to Clery's

Santa, but after she had gazed in silence at the coat she shivered and turned away. 'Where are we going?' I asked.

'To Hector Gray's.' Hector Gray's was a cut-price shop that sold cheap toys and souvenirs. 'I need you to help me pick out presents for the girls.'

'They are nearly fourteen and fifteen,' I reminded her.

'These are not their real presents.' She looked away from me. 'They are from Santa.' She suddenly looked both cross and ashamed. 'You are much more sensible than they are. They still pretend to believe in Santa.'

It was a bitter day. With cold fingers and a crabbed heart I picked out the mechanical mice, small fireworks, tennis balls, chocolate animals, so shabby in themselves but imbued with magic each year when they appeared mysteriously wrapped in crêpe paper outside our bedroom door.

Chapter Twenty-One

~

We hadn't much luck with Miss Partridge's no-hopers: '"RAF sergeant (29), pensioned due to disability, wishes to meet stout, homely girl, RC spinster or widow, with means." "Country working man, RC, small, 40, seeks domestic working girl with own house,"' Mother read out. 'These men have nothing to offer and yet they are all looking for girls with money! "Barman, good family, desirous of acquaintance with young lady (TT), with her own business, cash or capital; view to marriage."' She threw down the correspondence dejectedly. 'It is as if they are advertising for laundry workers or maids.'

'This one sounds nice.' I picked out what looked like an illiterate scrawl but it was an educated man who was a stroke victim. He needed someone to help out with his two children, as his wife had died, but he had a house of his own and a business. Mother glanced at the letter. 'Oh.' She sounded disappointed. 'That would never do.'

'Maybe Miss Partridge was right to think there was nothing to be done for Miss Taylor.'

'No!' Mother said fervently. 'Miss Partridge does not believe in God. If God intends Miss Taylor to have a husband then he may well be here in this batch. He may have put them in my hands to deliver to her. I am sure of it.'

'What if God does not mean her to have a husband?' I said.

'Then He does not know her as I do.'

~

When most of the work of Christmas was out of the way, she rewarded herself with a visit to Minnie. Minnie had made a cake. It was a real cake for which she had beaten up eggs and butter and cracked fresh nuts from their shells. It had been sandwiched with butter icing when not quite cold and had an exquisite ooziness that ran into the sponge and met the cake's crunchy edges. I wondered if I could possibly eat the whole cake while the adults were talking.

'So, Edie, all that time in the hospital bed, stretched out like a bug on a rug, I got to thinking.'

'About what?' Mother said eagerly.

'All my life I work like a dog, and for what? For an early grave is all. I think to myself, if I ever get out of here, things will be different.' Her hair was now a silvery grey and set in nice waves. She wore a plain wool dress which Mother later pronounced to be a good item. She now shared her little villa with Mo and Dora and Dora's baby, and Mother said that all the fight had gone out of her. But there was an air of ferment about Minnie, as when she had first started saving pennies in her black box.

'I decided to get some help at the bakery.'

'What about MacAlorum?' Mother lit a cigarette and blew out a long stream of smoke. There was something about women when they got together and smoked a cigarette as they luxuriously spread out their troubles for display that was like romance between a man and a woman. There was exhilaration and intimacy and a kind of preening, as if their troubles were a crowning glory instead of something that got them down.

'Dora's got to rest. She's feeding the baby.'

'I don't see why you should concern yourself with her health – or the baby's,' Mother said.

Minnie shook her head as if it pained her that Mother couldn't understand even simple things. 'Mo is my concern. I got to take good care of Dora and her baby for his sake.' She laughed, a reminiscent sort of chuckle. 'You want to see him the last month, watching out for that baby like it was your Santa Claus coming down the chimney.'

The cigarette, which a moment ago had been used like a baton to conduct the music of their talk, was now stubbed out angrily. 'I wish you would think of yourself for a change,' Mother said. 'Between them, those two have nearly killed you.'

Minnie patted Mother on the arm to soothe her. 'Sure, I think of myself.' She took the knife from me as I was about to cut myself a third piece of cake. 'Leave a little bit for Dora. So, how are things with you, Edie? Who's in the room?'

'Bridie's in the room. She's fifteen – time she had a room of her own.'

'Bridie of the big ideas! She's going to pay you a rent so you got something to eat?'

'No, but Eugene's got a job. It starts in the new year.'

'That's good news, Edie. Why don't you sound happy?'

'He's going to be a salesman,' Mother admitted flatly. 'Door to door.'

'That's how Mo and me got started,' Minnie reminded her.

Mother sighed. 'He thinks it's beneath his dignity.'

'Pity the ground isn't beneath his feet,' Minnie snorted. 'What's he going to sell?'

'The Amazing Ruton Robot.' Mother looked embarrassed.

'A robot?'

'It's a sort of all-purpose household appliance. It polishes floors, mixes food and drinks, dries hair, cleans carpets and sprays paint.'

Minnie scratched her head. 'I'm not so sure I'd want to mix food with something that had been polishing the floor.' Mother nodded in a worried way. 'Hey, I'll buy one of these new inventions,' Minnie offered. 'How much?'

When she heard they cost eleven guineas she whistled. 'You could buy a fur coat for that. There's a lot more women want a fur coat than a carpet-cleaner that mixes cocktails. You need a payment plan. Thirty-five shillings down and weekly repayments over twenty-four months sounds better than eleven guineas. Tell him, don't be afraid to knock on dirt-poor farmhouses. They always have a stash. Country people never can resist a gadget. Oh, Edie, makes me want to start up again. I always liked business.'

'Thank you, Minnie,' Mother said fervently. 'I'm going straight home to pass your advice on to Eugene.'

'Don't rush off, Edie. First you got to see my treasures.'

'Jewellery?'

'Gilding the scarecrow! No, you have to see the baby. And I want you to meet Stefan.'

'Who is Stefan?'

'I got myself a baker – a real continental one. Dora's no cook.'

'A foreigner!' Mother was impressed. 'Is he French? The French are wonderful bakers.'

'He's not French. He is Hungarian.'

'Oh! A refugee?'

That year the city was flooded with Hungarian refugees. I thought the word 'Hungary' was the same as the word 'hungry', for all the refugees had dark, sad, hungry eyes. They frequently knocked at our house looking for work or trying to sell bits of sewing or woodwork.

Only a week ago I had answered the door to a thin, melancholy young man offering a little wooden house, hand-carved and painted. It had a door that opened on a latch and inside was a slot for a photograph, so that you could keep your favourite person snug in this Hansel and Gretel house. I had wanted the wooden house and it was only a shilling, but I hadn't any money. To my surprise, Mother said that she would buy it.

'Yes, Edie, a refugee.'

'What do you know of this man?' We followed Minnie upstairs. 'Has he references? What experience has he of the baking trade?'

'Did I have a reference?' Minnie shrugged. 'I look at his hands. Baker's hands! That's all the reference I need.'

'Does he speak good English?' Mother's voice sank to a whisper as Minnie hushed her. We had gone into a small bedroom. Mo was there, waving a fluffy white rabbit over a frilled crib. We peered inside.

'Ain't she a picture?' Minnie said. 'Her name's Betty.'

'She's a lovely child,' Mother agreed. 'But Minnie, this baby is not your responsibility.'

'Don't fuss, Edie. Come and meet Stefan.'

Stefan was at the kitchen table, rolling pastry. His shirt sleeves were rolled up, showing well-muscled arms thickly covered in black hair. He turned to us with a slightly amused look, a half-burnt cigarette hanging from his mouth.

'Why is he here?' Mother said. 'He should be at the bakery.'

'I've got to train him first.' Minnie spoke in a whisper as if he was a stage performer who must not be disturbed. 'Watch his hands. A genius with pastry.'

'He's working too slowly,' Mother criticised. 'All the air will go out of it. Minnie, he is smoking a cigarette. The ash is going to fall in the dough.'

Minnie nodded fondly. 'When I saw him rolling his cigarette I

noticed those hands. The way his fingers work the tobacco. A genius!'
She went and patted Stefan on the back. 'You want some tea?'

He shook his head. 'Coffee.'

'Sure, sure. He don't like Irel,' she said to Mother. 'Only fresh.
Such a puritan!'

'I smell coffee.' Dora arrived downstairs in a slinky pink dressing
gown. 'Any chance of a sup?' She looked sleepy, half drugged.

'You like her dressing gown?' Minnie called gaily to Mother. 'I
buy her it for Christmas.'

By now Mother was speechless. She looked as if she was wit-
nessing a burglary in which the house owner was urging the
thief to help himself. Dora's eyes were on Stefan's hands as he
slowly squeezed the pastry. 'I'd kill for a fag.' She perched on
the edge of the table so that the front of her dressing gown
gaped. Stefan shook his hands to free them of flour. He took
the half-smoked cigarette from his mouth and placed it between
Dora's lips.

'Don't you think you should be upstairs seeing to your child?'
Mother could contain herself no longer.

Dora seemed surprised to see us standing there. 'Och, Mo's more
of a mother than I am.'

'Minnie, can't you see what's going on under your eyes?' Mother
said.

'Sure I can. A poor girl in trouble and no one to turn to.'

Mother handed Minnie her Christmas present. As we left, I
turned back to see Dora and Stefan pushing the cigarette into
one another's partly open mouths. Minnie was occupied with her
gift. It was the little wooden house made by the refugee. Inside it,
Mother had placed one of Father's Christmas photographs, all of us
close together, beaming with happiness. Minnie smiled fondly as she
placed it on the mantelpiece with all her other framed photographs

of adopted ancestors. 'Such nice people,' she murmured fondly. 'So little sense.'

~

'Make a wish,' Mother said as we stirred the pudding on Christmas Eve. It should have been done months before but she could never get around to cooking in advance. I dipped a finger into the sweet, wet gravel and silently wished for a bicycle, or failing that, a dog. 'You make a wish.'

'I wish Minnie would see sense. She thinks she can cure everything with kindness but I can't bear to see those people taking advantage of her.'

I thought that it wasn't like Minnie to imagine she could cure everything with kindness. It was Mother who saw goodwill as a universal remedy. 'I wish things would work out for Miss Taylor,' she said then. 'I don't like to think of her unhappy at Christmas. If only that nice man who had a stroke had been a Catholic.'

'Why?'

'Miss Taylor would never marry a Protestant.'

'But she is a Protestant.'

'Miss Taylor?' Mother was astonished. 'She can't be. She looks like a Catholic. She had a crucifix hanging in her room.'

'She won that as a prize in school.' I explained how she had grown up surrounded by poor Catholics and had gone to a one-roomed school where all the other children were Catholic.

'Are you absolutely sure?' It was as if she had won the Sweep. 'Now I wish we had a telephone so that we could let her know at once that she need not worry about her future. I think we should have a drink to celebrate. Get the Christmas sherry. Fetch two glasses. You have a sip as well.'

'Miss Taylor doesn't know about your plan to find her a husband,' I said. 'We should ask her first.'

'She won't turn down the offer of a loving home.' Mother was all confidence now. 'We must remember this Christmas, when we turned the tide of fortune for poor Miss Taylor.'

Chapter Twenty-Two

~

Why did Mother pick on Miss Taylor? There was a whole house full of females waiting for the tide to turn. Why not Bridie with her greasy hair and scowling face and slacks? Or Kitty and me, who yearned for glamour? To us, Mother merely said that we need not concern ourselves with our bodies, which were beautiful and healthy, but should concentrate on developing our minds. Kitty now had her own pack of Dr Southall's. She was self-conscious and suspicious of this new inside-out side of herself and whispered to Mother as she went out, 'Do I *smell*?'

Mother inhaled the silky hair and tense, marble-skinned face. 'You smell of child,' she said, 'and that's the nicest smell there is.'

This made Kitty more thin-lipped than ever, and Mother didn't even notice that she had hexed her with an imaginary aura of schoolbags and liquorice.

Drying me after my bath, Mother found that tiny filaments of hair had appeared on the lower half of my body. 'Oh!' she murmured in a faintly dismayed way.

'Oh, what?' Men got baldy and women got hairy as they grew older, but I was unclear about where the process ended. In the paper there was an advertisement for Mr Christy of Talbot Street who cured baldness in men and another for Mrs Martin of O'Connell Street who freed women of facial hair. Mr Christy's notice showed a depressed-looking man with a head like an egg while Mrs Martin depicted a startled lady with wavy hair and a bristling growth on her chin, like Desperate Dan.

'Nothing. It's perfectly normal.' She scrubbed me briskly with the towel. 'Perfectly normal' grew to be a worrying and depressing phrase.

After Christmas, Father went on the road for five days a week. He travelled from town to town, visiting homes with the Ruton Robot and staying in commercial hotels, where he would patiently wait for the bathroom so that he could clean all the cumbersome attachments of the device. The robot sold well, although he told of householders who had him spray a whole shed with paint, or clean a carpet, before declaring they would not take the yoke for nothing. There were other stories: in a commercial hotel, a salesman with whom he had taken dinner was later seen through the pebbled glass of the bathroom door, wrestling with a woman. In Limerick, a friendly householder had invited him through the house to the yard. 'Would you like to see an execution?' he enquired before seizing a slash hook and hacking the throat of a dog. He meant these tales to evoke a chorus of pity and horror, but we were enthralled and begged for more.

As soon as the weight of marriage was off her shoulders, Mother wrote to the Protestant gentleman, saying that Miss Taylor (24, C of I, fond of children) was in her charge and desired to meet him, view to matrimony. Then she sent a letter to Miss Taylor. At first Selena seemed taken aback when she heard of the plan, but when she saw Mother's hopeful look she rallied: 'Sure, where's the harm? Who'd have me anyhow? Could I have my old room back?' she bargained.

Mother tried to negotiate with Bridie but our big sister would not budge. The small space was no longer a room, nor even a furnished apartment. It was her fortress. She had begun to accumulate furniture. Some warped pieces had been rescued from the garden. She had bought a piano from the junk yard of an auction room. She used the pieces as a barricade, piling them on top of one another to keep intruders at bay.

Selena entered into Mother's scheme as if it was a game. She even wore bright-red lipstick to please her.

'It doesn't suit her,' I whispered. 'It just shows up her false teeth.'

'You may think that,' Mother said. 'You and I are used to Selena and we like her as she is. No man would look at her without a good coat of paint. It is the same even for a pretty girl. When I was going out with your father he said I wore too much lipstick. I told him he had only noticed me in the first place because of my make-up, and if he did not like it, then I would prefer to keep my paint in place to catch the eye of some other man.'

She had begun telling stories again but these were parables of womanhood, centred around herself. Did she mean us to extract advice about growing up or had she begun, unconsciously, to compete with Bridie and Kitty as women? If the tales were intended as maps of the world then vital bits had been left out so that as we scurried eagerly after her, we soon found ourselves stranded on some crag or in some ravine, blinking up at the sun.

'A whole crowd of us got a lift home from a dance one night. I had to sit on a boy's knee and after a while I felt this lump. I was disgusted. Of course, I realise now, he couldn't help it. It was my own fault, but I hadn't a clue. I was wearing a red satin dress and no bra underneath. I can't believe my own mother would have let me walk out practically in my skin for every man in town to gape at me. Poor Ma never even noticed things like that.'

Poor mad Gram, eating her skins, letting her daughter, *our mother*, walk out in her skin. But the *lump*! Did boys come out in lumps when women wore satin dresses? Bridie wasn't interested and the story can scarcely have been intended as a warning for her, since she wouldn't be caught dead in any kind of dress. Kitty and I were very curious but we knew that if we asked questions, the stories would stop.

She told us about a bad man she had known ('a real cad – he used women and then threw them on the scrap heap!') and when he kissed her it had been the most exciting kiss of her life. We could almost smell the scorching lips as she stood dreamy-eyed at the stove. 'That's a thing to remember.' She came out of her reverie. 'Bad men can be exciting. It's because they have a lot of experience.'

She had given us sugar to lick off her finger and then told us it would rot our teeth. We were left bewildered and dazed and disadvantaged and dumb. How had she met a bad man? How would you *know* a bad man? Where would we ever find one?

Kitty did her best to drag me along in her own blundering wake. 'Men have a thing on the outside. I think there's something on the inside of women and there is a connection between them.'

'Something on the *inside*. What kind of thing? Do you mean like a baby?'

'No, not a solid thing, more a feeling.'

'I can't feel anything.'

'I didn't feel it when I was your age either. It must be a grown-up sort of thing.'

'What does it feel like?'

'Sort of hollow and sad and sweet – like a mermaid singing.'

Kitty looked so unworldly that it was easy to imagine a mermaid singing inside her, but when I looked at other adults I decided that, like the Little Man, the mermaid came only to Kitty. I couldn't see Bridie with a mermaid and certainly not Miss Taylor. Yet Thursday came, and we had to accept that she was a real woman, for we were seated round the kitchen table awaiting her bridegroom. She looked quite nice in Mother's sweater of duck-egg blue and with just a trace of mascara and powder and lipstick on her face, but it was spoiled by her look of fright. 'Would we start so?' It was only a quarter past six. This meant that she had abandoned hope completely, for she wouldn't dream of starting a meal without the man.

'We'll say grace,' Mother stalled. 'He might be embarrassed, being of a different faith.' She still couldn't quite take it to heart that Miss Taylor was not a Catholic. 'Bless us, oh Lord,' she begged, 'for these Thy gifts, which of Thy bounty we are about to receive.' And the doorbell rang.

The Protestant turned out a disappointment. He was quite old and shabby and had a walking stick. One side of his face had been frozen into a mask of disgust and the other side was restless and uneasy as if anxious to escape from the damaged half. He had brought no flowers or sweets. He did not wink at us girls or make flattering talk to Miss Taylor. He ate his tea in a finicky way, cutting up everything into small squares. In a voice that sounded as if he had just been to the dentist, he asked Miss Taylor could she do plain cooking and had she experience in coping with an invalid? Had she patience with children? He nodded drily in response to her answers and enquired if there were any questions she wished to put to him.

'Have you a picture of the children?' That was all she wanted to know. He produced a photograph of a dark, unsmiling boy and a girl. When she had admired it and handed it back, neither of them said anything, but he continued to stare at her with his disgusted face. She smiled until she could smile no longer and jumped up and acted as waitress, forcing fresh tea and cake on everyone. We all felt relieved when, after only an hour, his taxi returned and took him away.

'What a dismal old half-dead stick,' Bridie said. 'I don't think he was looking for a wife. I think he must have been looking for The Mummy.'

'Hush, Bridie!' Mother said, but the lifting of tension made her laugh. 'Oh, Selena!' She tried to look serious. 'I am so sorry. I thought he said his name was Boris Carson but it must have been Boris Karloff.'

We shrieked with mirth and Miss Taylor giggled, her powdery face bright pink. She laughed until tears came to her eyes and she had to cover her face. We watched as the tears seeped through her fingers, stained with black from her mascara. Black, powdery drops clinked minutely on to her plate. Mother feared that the excitement had been too much for her. She gently pulled her hands from her face, showing lipstick all mashed with tears. 'Oh, the poor man.' Selena sobbed as if her heart would break. 'Oh, the poor sad man. Oh, I love him.'

~

Our next visitor was a big, unsmiling woman, who I could not remember, although she addressed me by name: 'Rose, tell your mother I have to see her.'

The woman seemed to curse or plead as Mother whispered that we hadn't a room any more and anyway, three people wouldn't fit into such a small space. 'I hope things will work out,' she added. 'I'll say a prayer.'

'What use are prayers?' The visitor left in a rattle of rainwear. 'What is needed is a just society where people will have a roof over their heads and food in their mouths.'

'That was Ruth Kandinsky,' Mother said with a frown. 'Do you remember? She rented a room from us years ago. She left to get married. They are expecting a baby now and cannot stay in their present lodgings. Poor things! I think they must be very poor. She had no proper overcoat. I am sure she felt angry at me for walking back into my comfortable house where there is a fire lit. I wonder if she would feel better if she knew that we sometimes don't have enough money for food?'

We only vaguely remembered Miss Kandinsky and the fact that she had nothing in her suitcase but dry-looking books which she described as the future of the world.

'Plenty of people are poor,' Kitty reminded her.

'Yes, but Ruth is homeless. Since letting a room I have come to realise that there are a lot of homeless people.'

'They'll find somewhere.' Bridie spoke indifferently through a mouthful of date bread.

'I am talking about a proper home – not a dingy room in a house full of strangers where no one knows their name or cares if they live or die.'

You couldn't argue with Mother on matters like this, but none of us thought Ruth Kandinsky cared about a proper home. When she lived with us she never cooked and she didn't own a single hat or necklace. 'Can't we get Miss Taylor married to Boris Karloff before we start worrying about the homeless?' Bridie said.

'I think we can forget about Boris Karloff. Even he thinks he is too good for her. Selena may fool herself but it was all too clear to me that he was giving her the bum's rush.'

~

A week later, a letter came for Miss Taylor. We at once identified the spidery scrawl of Boris Karloff.

'Dear Selena.' Mother devised a coded message, for Selena had warned that her father would kill her if she had an admirer. 'It was lovely to see you when you came to Dublin but you left your umbrella behind. I shall keep it safely for when you next come to the city.'

Chapter Twenty-Three

~

Selena's hands shook as she opened the letter. 'Read it to me.' She passed it to Mother, who scanned the lines of wobbly script. 'Dear Miss Taylor . . .' She looked a bit nonplussed but she went on: '"If you would be agreeable, I would like to arrange another interview. Yours, Boris Carson."'

'An *interview*?' Mother could not conceal her exasperation. 'Does he think you were applying for a job?'

'Maybe so,' Selena said defensively. 'Maybe he wants me to care for the children. He must have liked me.' She smiled, and then amended this vanity. 'He must have approved of me.' She touched Mother shyly. 'Can he come here again?'

'He can come any time he likes, but I think it would be better this time if you two were to meet alone.'

'Alone?' The younger woman sounded terrified.

'In a hotel lounge,' Mother quickly clarified. 'It will give you a chance to get to know each other better. Wynn's Hotel is very respectable.'

What would they talk about in Wynn's Hotel? Would she tell him about the one-roomed school and the bridge with a fairy asleep on it and snow that fell when someone in heaven plucked feathers from a goose? She went to her assignation armed only with this advice from Mother: 'Before meeting a man you must wash from top to bottom, including your hair, and change all your clothes from the inside out. Men like to believe that women are supernatural creatures and smell of nothing, unless it is perfume.' She pressed on her a de luxe spray of Odo-Ro-No.

That weekend Father arrived home as if pursued by the hounds of hell. 'My money was taken. There was no lock on my hotel door. A man crept in in the middle of the night while I was asleep. He tried to take advantage of me.' He lowered his voice to an enticing whisper. 'He got into my bed.'

We began to giggle at this comic notion, but Mother shushed us. She let go of him and sighed: 'All your money?'

'This is no kind of job for a man!' He was close to tears. 'When I call on houses I am left standing on the step like a dog. I have to mix with low types in hotels. Sometimes they don't trouble to change the sheets in these places. I would not like to describe the kinds of filth I find on my sheets.'

'Don't think about it.' Mother put him to bed with a tray like an invalid, and then she sat through tea in worried silence.

'He's going to give up his job,' Bridie warned.

Mother looked vague and anxious. 'He didn't say anything about that.'

'But he will. He'll never stick it. He's like a small child being sent out to school every Monday.'

'He hated school,' Mother agreed.

'He feels trapped because the job is going well. He is relying on you to tell him to come home.'

Mother shifted as if her chair had grown prickly and uncomfortable.

'Men are meant to go to work,' Bridie bossed. 'They're not supposed to like it. They're just supposed to do it.'

'Your father is a good man,' Mother said. 'Everything he does is for us.'

'We are expected to swallow every mad story he tells us,' Bridie protested. 'Next time he will say that he has been poisoned or has crashed his car. Ask for the name of this hotel where he was attacked and robbed. Ask for the number of the room. Tell him we will sue the hotel for the loss of his money since they failed to put a lock on the door.'

'Whatever about the stories,' Mother said gently, 'the truth is that he is miserable. Would I send you away from home each week, to where you would be lonely and unhappy?'

'That's different. He's not a child.'

'I suppose not.' Mother sounded unsure. 'But you should try to understand him, Bridie. Of all of us, you are the one who is most like him. When you were small, you took a dislike to school. I kept you at home for a whole year.'

'I was sick. Anyway, I went back in the end, didn't I?'

'Of course you did.' Mother smiled in relief.

~

Two weeks after this, Miss Taylor wrote to say she was getting married.

When next we saw her she had a rarefied air, not like someone who has fallen in love, but as if she had been chosen for a noble mission.

'Has he discussed his feelings for you?' Mother queried.

Selena was shocked. 'Oh, no! Nothing like that.'

'When you marry a man you belong to him,' Mother cautioned. 'Has he kissed you?'

213

'Mrs Rafferty, no!'

Mother waded on. 'Married life is full of difficulties. Sometimes it is only the small affections that make it bearable.'

'I know all about difficulties,' Selena said in a subdued and stubborn voice.

'Poor Selena. I know you do. But there are a lot of things you don't know.'

'I love him. He likes me well enough. What else is there to know?'

Mother asked if she might invite him to tea again. 'I'd like a little chat with him.'

'You do like him, don't you?' Selena smiled. 'I knew you'd get to like him in the end.'

~

The soft white sandwiches were slippery with butter, the pink wafer biscuits crisp as snow. A Swiss roll was languorously limp, powdered white like a skating rink. It was the kind of food we children loved – the junk food of the fifties. When you lifted the handkerchief point of a crustless sandwich, a delicate pink sliver of ham poked out, smeared with yellow mustard. 'Drunk man's tongue,' Bridie murmured with relish before stapling it with her sharp teeth.

There had been stiff conversation about how many spoons of sugar and how cold the weather was and the price of coal. And then Mother gave a little artificial shiver and asked Miss Taylor if she would be so kind as to fetch her brown cardigan from the chest of drawers in her bedroom.

As Miss Taylor's footfall faded up the stairs, Mother placed a hand on Boris Karloff's stiff wrist. 'She is a dear, sensitive girl. I care a great deal about her happiness. I would like to know how you feel about her.'

214

His frozen stare fell on her hand. 'You need imagine no wrong motives on my part.'

'That's not enough for a girl like Selena. Do you care for her?'

He got a defeated look, as if he had given up trying to menace her hand from his arm. 'I am not in a position to consider love. I know very well no one could possibly care for a wreck like me. I will give her a good home.'

'Miss Taylor loves you. Miss Taylor is head over heels in love with you.' She gave his wrist a final, urgent shake and then let it go just as Selena came back to confess that she could find no trace of the cardie.

~

Raw winter days grew mellow in our sleepy female house with its bridal focus. While we were at school, Selena shopped with Mother for her new life. Money was scarce so the clothes had to be chosen with care, to last. The new colours were fawn, donkey, kingfisher, royal. They hankered after a marmot fur but chose a swagger jacket in kingfisher. Mother urged her to try high heels, but she hadn't the knack of walking in them and settled for the new Louis heels. The jacket would be worn for her wedding, with a tailored beret of rose aramanth fur felt.

In the evenings, we went to the pictures, drowsy in the submarine gloom which transported us to the assorted worlds of Lilli Palmer in *Oh! My Papa*, Doris Day in *The Pajama Game* and Joanne Woodward in *The Three Faces of Eve*. On the way home she chattered about the Protestant's children. She had been taken to meet them and was full of their beautiful manners, their poor, pale little faces that needed a dose of fresh air. We felt hostile towards these competitors who would inherit her secret world. She left, as usual, before Father came home.

215

Father reminded me of a boxer, who keeps getting sent back into the ring after he is beaten. Beneath the pressed suit and bleached shirt, he had a grey and wasted look. 'I'm done for, Edie,' he said.

'Things will improve,' Mother promised. 'One of these days a proper job will turn up and everything will be back to normal.'

He ate a large bun in a mechanical way, hoovering up every last crumb, as if he was The Ruton Robot. 'By the time a proper job turns up, I will be like some poor tramp that nobody wants and it will be handed on a plate to some other man.'

'It is a proper job. He earns good money,' Bridie tried to convince Mother. Harassed by Bridie, Mother let him face the world once more. Besides, when Monday morning came, there was the excitement of a fresh letter. 'For me?' Miss Taylor set down her small case and feigned surprise.

'From your boyfriend,' we teased.

'Oh, now!' She blushed scarlet and waited for us to go away. 'Actually, he is my fiancé.' When she couldn't wait any longer, she tore at the envelope. As she drew in the words that were flung on the page like rusty nails, she gave a sharp gasp. The letter began to shake in her hands.

'Get Mother!' Kitty whispered as the page dropped to the floor and she burst into tears.

'He has changed his mind.' Grimly, Mother dried her hands on her apron. 'I should have known any talk of love would send him running.'

'Don't mind him, dear,' she soothed Selena. 'Plenty more fish in the sea.'

'No!' Selena shouted in a way that was almost petulant.

'What has he said to hurt you?' Mother dabbed at her face with her apron.

'Read it, read it,' Selena demanded in the same tone of outburst.

Mother picked up the letter and frowned. 'This is very private.'

'Nothing's private!' Selena cried in a crippled sort of voice.

Mother patted her shoulder and read on. Her expression now was puzzled and intent. When she had finished reading, she folded the letter. 'I don't quite understand . . . Are you afraid?'

Selena nodded.

'I don't think you need to be.'

'You think I'm the fool – the innocent one.' Her expression was both brazen and fearful. 'I am not innocent. You are the innocent one. For years I have been afraid.'

'Sex . . .' Mother sighed. She glanced vaguely at our eager faces but pressed on anyway. 'Sex is something that every married woman gets used to. I suppose you had imagined he would not be interested in that sort of thing. I should have told you. All men are interested in that.'

'Why did you have to interfere? Everything was all right the way it was.' Selena turned away and bolted up the stairs.

Mother hurried after her and the letter drifted from her grasp. From upstairs we could hear Selena crying and Mother soothing. Mother had been placating for so long that the sound made you want to put your thumb in your mouth. 'Tell me!' Mother urged. Selena's voice came out grazed and raw: 'I *can't*!' We watched the letter in silence and then Bridie snatched it up as if it was in flames, and read the scrawl that was a prescription for mayhem.

Darling girl,

I would not have spoken like this before but I have been given reason to believe that you may care for me. I have loved you from the moment I set eyes on you (and I pray I did not distress you with my gazing) for you represent all the things that I hold most dear – goodness, modesty and innocence. I can scarcely believe

217

that I do not repel you with my age and infirmity, but if not, then I will cherish you with all my heart and soul and body. Yes, my body too, if you don't mind my poor damaged frame. In spite of my seizure I am still capable of functioning as a husband, and yearn to do so. I am sure you know little of such matters, but have no fear. I have waited long and lonely years. I will patiently wait as long as it takes to woo you from innocence to the state of a happy married woman – and perhaps even a mother to our own child, if that is what you would wish.

Forgive me, dear heart, if I have seemed cold up to now. I was not cold – only fearful of rejection. Forgive me, precious girl, if I am now too ardent. It is merely the storm after the dry season, and we will have many years of happy calm.

With all my love, Boris.

'Gosh,' Bridie said. Even she couldn't think of anything sarcastic to say. We were mesmerised. We felt moved and rattled and jealous and softened, as if we had been dipped in experience and transported in time. If Miss Taylor really did not want the letter I decided I would keep it and every so often I would take it out and pretend that it had been written to me – although I would make belief it came from Rock Hudson. We said nothing, but we all wanted to know if our mother had had letters like this from Father. We wanted to know if the dull and dowdy and angry men that one saw everywhere every day had a different centre that shone through when they saw in a woman all the things they held most dear. But then we had to go to school.

Chapter Twenty-Four

~

The way Ruth Kandinsky got back into our house was through a series of misfortunes, like a mouse working its way through a tunnel of holes. Mother was still fretting about Miss Taylor when a note came from Minnie. 'Stefan has gone. He stole my money and ran off with Dora.' It was no consolation to her to be right about the refugee baker. She would have gone at once to her old friend but she was stuck at home with Father, who had had an accident with his motor car.

When Ruth turned up looking sick and miserable, Mother just couldn't bear one more unhappy person so she brought her in. Ruth crouched by the fire but she was reluctant to sit down. She didn't feel at ease in the kitchen. She wanted her room.

'Ruth, there is no room.' Mother looked harassed and guilty. 'Besides, I have already told you. There is no space for a baby.'

'There is no baby.' She pulled her raincoat around her.

'But you said you were expecting. Oh, Ruth, I'm so sorry. Sit down. Rose, put on the kettle.'

'I am not sorry,' Ruth said. 'This is no world into which to bring a child. May I have my room?'

'But I told you – the room is no longer for rent.'

'You said we could not have the room because of the baby. No one will let us have a room with a baby. Well, now there is no baby.'

Mother had her very composed look, which meant she was trying to absorb some astounding idea. 'Ruth . . . you didn't do anything?'

'What would I do?' I gave her a cup of tea and she wrapped her hands around it and let the steam warm her face.

'Because that would be . . . murder,' Mother murmured.

'Millions were murdered in the war. Millions more were left as walking ghosts. What is one little mass of cells?'

'The war ended thirteen years ago,' Mother said. 'Many were lost but we gained a free world.'

'We did not get a free world unless you can be freed from memory. All we got was a world torn open. The rest of us survive to shovel out the refuse.'

'Ruth!' Mother had to touch her knee because her eyes had closed and she seemed to be falling asleep. 'Life must go on. There is no point in trying to carry on the war single-handed.'

The hot tea looped into the air as the other woman fell heavily to the floor. Mother felt her forehead and watched her ruefully. 'Rose,' she said, 'do you think that between us we could get her up to bed?'

'Which bed?' I said.

'Oh . . . the room.'

'That's Bridie's room! She'll kill you.' We hauled on the motionless weight, trying to get her into a sitting position.

'I'm hard to kill.'

'How will we get her into the room? There's a piano in the way.'

Mother sighed as if she already felt the weight of the piano on her bones. We propped Ruth at the wall. 'We'll put our backs against the furniture and push it over to the window.'

The noise of this woke Father, or, as is more often the case, it was the hush that followed the commotion, the complete cessation of any sound, after we had heaved the furniture away from the door and got a look at Bridie's room.

'What is going on down there?' Father growled from his sick-bed. 'Can't I have some peace in my own home?'

We didn't answer right away. We were too intent on gazing at Bridie's drawings, which covered every inch of the wall. There were drawings of all of us and our cat, of Miss Taylor and Boris Karloff. There were pictures of horses and houses and cars. Some of the illustrations were cartoons with funny captions. There were studies of herself, which she had obviously done from her wardrobe mirror, not flattering or pretty, but sort of humorous. She had done sketches of her body without any clothes, then separate ones of her arms and legs. Even I could tell that they were good. 'She never said!' Mother seemed shocked more than impressed. 'She didn't want us to know.'

'Edie!' Father called down on a more plaintive note. 'I got no lunch.'

She responded at once to this, sending me to the kitchen. Ruth had woken and was getting to her feet. 'It will be dark soon. I have one or two other rooms to try.'

'Why do you want our room?' I could ask her now, since Mother was upstairs. 'You talk as if one place is the same as another and all you care about is your work.'

'It's not for me,' she said.

Mother came down to fetch Father's tray. 'I've explained to him that the room is to be temporarily let.'

'He agreed?' I was surprised.

'Not at first, but I managed to convince him that he would recover better if his mind was relieved of money worries.'

221

Ruth was now fully alert. 'I thought you said there was no room to let. Who are you letting the room to?'

'Didn't Rose tell you? It's for you.'

She loomed over Mother, but it was just to bestow a comradely kiss. She set off upstairs and then paused. 'I almost forgot. Daniel.'

'Daniel?' mother said.

'Daniel Fine. My husband.'

We too had forgotten about her husband. In truth, I suppose we had dismissed him from our minds because the notion of Ruth's husband had no appeal. What kind of husband could a woman like her get, with her unsmiling mouth and no lipstick? He would be bad-tempered, with small eyes and glasses. I could tell from Mother's face that she hadn't thought to mention a husband to Father either. Besides, there was only Bridie's bed in the room.

'Ruth, it may take a day or two to get the room ready for two people. Your husband will want to make arrangements to move your things.'

'We have no things,' Ruth said.

'I see. Well, in any case he will have to wait until it's ready. Just tell me how we can find him.'

'Open the hall door.'

'Pardon?'

'He is outside. We had nowhere to go.'

We found him, rain-lashed and cold, his waterproofs billowing about him, his glasses streaming water. He pulled out the edges of his coat so that water sluiced off it. We saw wet hair, wet glasses, a shapeless wet raincoat. Mother was about to tell him about the room but Ruth stepped forward to give him the good news. 'Daniel, get out of those wet things,' she barked. 'If you get sick how will you work?'

Mother tried to persuade them to come down to the kitchen and

222

warm themselves at the fire first, and Mr Fine looked to his wife, blinking in confusion behind his wet glasses.

'The room is ours!' For the first time Ruth's eyes softened. 'The little room I used to tell you about.'

'Are you sure?'

She dipped into her bag and snapped open a small purse. She spoke aloud as she emptied out a handful of coins. 'One half-crown, two half-crowns, three half-crowns. Two shillings, one shilling, sixpence, thruppence, thruppence, thruppence, one penny, four halfpennies. Twelve shillings! We have just paid our first week's rent.'

Mr Fine was convinced, and Mother had not the heart to tell Ruth that the rent had gone up to a guinea.

~

It was harder to persuade Bridie. When she got home from school she ran straight to her room and a cry of rage rang out. 'There is a woman in my bed! There is a man looking at my pictures.'

'Come away!' Mother tried to draw her downstairs. 'That is Miss Kandinsky and her husband.' It would be ages before we would be able to think of them as Mr and Mrs Fine. 'They are to rent the room for a while.'

'You never even asked me. You have usurped my privacy!' Bridie cried.

'You've woken me up!' Father snarled from the upper landing.

'Now, aren't you ashamed of yourself?' Mother said. 'Two sick people in the house and you are creating a disturbance.'

'Where am I supposed to sleep?'

'You will be a good girl and go back to your old room. It's only for a while.'

'I won't,' she said. 'I need space to work in.'

223

'You can hang your drawings in our room, Bridie,' I said. 'You can work at the dressing table.'

'*Our* room!' Bridie snarled. 'I'm only going to be let in on sufferance.' She turned to Mother. 'Father did this. It's his way of worming out of work.'

'I did it,' Mother said. 'Your father knew nothing about it.'

'*You* did it? I thought you were on my side.'

'I did not think you would mind,' Mother lied. 'Miss Kandinsky was ill and had nowhere to live, and we need the money.'

'You sold my room for a lousy guinea!' Mother looked abashed. She hadn't the courage to confess that we were only getting twelve shillings. 'It's not the money, is it?' Bridie challenged. 'And it hasn't anything to do with Miss Kandinsky either. It has to do with Miss Taylor. You feel a failure because you didn't manage to get her married, so you have to make it up to another suffering soul. Nobody cares how we suffer.'

~

What was Daniel Fine like? We could not immediately decide as he went dripping obediently upstairs after his wife. 'I am sure they have had nothing to eat,' Mother said. She sent me up with tea and milk and bread and butter, but Ruth answered the door and took them from me. Mother wondered if she should send up two eggs but decided that we should retain some small profit from the rent. After that we had to deal with Bridie.

At first she would not speak to anyone. She stood with arms folded and her back to the wall, trembling with rage. Kitty and I watched her helplessly and she kept darting wounded and furious glances around the room until we realised there was no bed for her. Kitty and I silently and determinedly wrestled the spare bed from our parents' room, where Father had abandoned it. We divided up our own bedding so that the third bed was somewhat covered.

'Miss Heaslip slept on that bed,' Bridie protested. 'She kept her pee underneath it.' To our surprise we saw that she was trying not to cry. Kitty patted the bed as if she was trying to tempt up the cat. 'She didn't actually do it in the bed. Stay a little while. Stay and talk to us.'

'I don't want to talk. Nobody in this house ever does anything but talk.'

'I'll get you a book then.' Kitty went downstairs and came back with an armload of Bridie's favourite novels. Bridie slumped on the bed and Kitty cautiously put the books beside her. After a time she rolled over and glanced at the volumes. She selected one, rested on her elbows and began to flick through the pages. Even though she took no interest in grooming, she was adorned by womanhood. When she lay on her stomach her bottom curved. Her legs, which were raised at the knees and crossed at the ankles, dipped into a little waistline at her feet. The only feminine item she owned was a pair of Wispee shoes, soft, flat-soled slip-ons like ballet pumps, which were very fashionable. These now dangled from her toes, showing another curve at the arch of her foot.

'I'll ask Mother to make cheese potato cakes for tea,' Kitty said.

'I'm not coming down.' Bridie spoke to her book.

'I'll bring you up something.' I kept watch over Bridie while Kitty made a toasted cheese sandwich. She brought this with a glass of milk and an apple. Bridie ate the sandwich and threw down her book. 'What would you like to talk about?' She had forgiven us.

'About Miss Taylor,' I said at once.

∼

225

We had returned from school on the day of Boris Karloff's love letter to find Selena in the hall with her case packed and her wedding clothes back in their bags. She tried to smile at us. 'At least I get to say goodbye to my little girls.'

'She's leaving,' Mother said unnecessarily. 'Selena, where will you go?'

She shut her eyes tightly for a moment. 'I'll go home.'

'I wish you would wait. Whatever is on your mind, I am sure it just boils down to pre-wedding nerves. It is natural for a virgin . . .'

But Miss Taylor had interrupted softly: 'I'm not a virgin.'

~

Because Bridie would not come down to tea, she missed our first viewing of Daniel Fine. A timid knock at the kitchen announced him. 'It is Daniel . . . Mr Fine.' His voice was so quiet it sounded as if he spoke through a paper bag. We didn't even bother to look up at first and then we saw Mother's expression, startled and almost girlish. Kitty followed Mother's gaze and she blinked in a petrified, rabbity way. I just gaped. Nothing that we knew had prepared us for the idea of a beautiful man, but Daniel Fine was beautiful. He had dried his hair and taken off his raincoat and we saw now that he was tall, with soft dark hair and dark skin and huge dark eyes. How had Ruth got such a man? Had she bullied him into marrying her? Did his spectacles mean his sight was so bad that he could not see how plain and cross she looked?

'Ruth is resting,' he said. 'I wanted to thank you.'

Father was also resting. We had him all to ourselves. 'Come in.' Mother was clearly enchanted. 'Sit down. Have something to eat.'

He stayed where he was. 'I don't want to disturb you.'

'You're not disturbing us. I hope the children won't bother you.'

226

She got another cup and poured him tea and patted Father's seat for him to sit down.

He seemed shy. 'I love children. I wanted to be in a house with children.'

She cut bread for him and put ham on his plate and he watched it in a worried way. 'I am very sorry about Ruth's baby,' she said.

'It's my fault. Ruth works too hard and she doesn't eat enough. I should have got a job and looked after her.'

'You have no job?' Mother looked concerned.

He shook his head and dabbed beneath his spectacles with his handkerchief. 'Ruth insists that I finish my studies.'

'You're a student?' We all picked up Mother's faint unease at the thought of a grown-up man who was still a student. 'What do you plan to live on?'

'We are both at Trinity College. We thought that two could live as cheaply as one on our grants, but books are expensive. Most students get help from their families, but neither Ruth nor I has any family. It will be different for these little girls when they go to university. They will have help from their family.'

Mother's smile signalled to us that what he had said should not be taken seriously. Girls like us did not go to university. We would learn shorthand and typing. There were no grants for Irish students and it was expected that we would go out to work and contribute to the expenses of the household.

'Wait till you see him!' We ran straight up after tea to tell Bridie.

'I did see him,' Bridie said.

'Yes, but he was all wet then. Wait till you see him dried out.'

We were a bit disappointed by her reaction and tried to interest her in the fact that he was a grown-up student, like the Student

Prince, and that although they seemed not to have enough money for food, he would not eat his tea.

'What did you have for tea?' she said.

'Ham salad.'

'Of course he wouldn't eat it,' she said with scorn. 'He's a Jew.'

'How do you know?'

'Because Ruth is. Did you bring me a ham sandwich?' she demanded.

We felt throughly deflated. Bridie knew everything. We had never thought of Ruth as anything but a Communist.

For a little while we were all in love with Daniel, but Bridie and Kitty soon lost interest. We weren't used to amiable men. Even in the pictures there was a sense of abrasion, the rasp of sulphur on sandpaper, when a man and woman met. He wore carpet slippers in the house. His underwear on the clothesline was large and durable. He did not dance or even go to the cinema. He had never heard of the top twenty. I stayed in love with him and hung around his room whenever Ruth wasn't around. I was happy just to look at him because he was free of the strong smells and hairiness that were common to most men and that women had to learn to overlook when they fell in love.

Mother wanted to move Bridie's furniture out of the room but Bridie was savage on this subject. The furniture was her territorial marker. Without it, the Fines might claim vacant possession and decide to stay forever. In the end she could only be calmed down by a promise that everything would remain as it was – the furniture piled up, her drawings on the wall. 'The Fines are big people,' Mother worried. 'How will they fit in with all that? It was one thing for Minnie and Mo. They were small.'

The fact was that neither Ruth nor Daniel appeared to notice their surroundings. They scarcely seemed aware of the piled-up sofa and piano which blocked out most of the light at the window. Ruth didn't cook, so she didn't need a kitchen or a table to eat at. The table was permanently covered with books and one or both of them was always seated there, reading or making notes or writing pamphlets. They had put cushions on the narrow bed and used it as a sofa.

Ruth never seemed aware of any world except the ideal one for which she campaigned. Daniel woke to the world when I came to visit. 'Come in!' His face would light up as if I was a long-lost friend. 'I will see if I can find something for a good little girl.' The small cupboard over the stove was even more bare than our pantry on the day that Mother discovered we were poor. There weren't any basic ingredients like flour or Bisto. The top shelf was used for books. He always seemed crestfallen to find nothing but a packet of soup or a bag of rice. 'I would like to give you some small token.' He would pat his empty pockets, hoping to find a penny or a peppermint he had not known was there. 'Anyway, stay and talk.'

'What does he talk about?' Kitty wanted to know.

He liked to discuss family life, not real family life but the kind you might find in a school essay. 'When Ruth and I find work we will have many children. Ruth will sew dresses for the girls and make bread. We will have a swing in the garden. On hot days we will go to the sea.'

'But Ruth doesn't want children!' I remembered her telling Mother so.

'She will change.' He nodded slowly, as if trying to convince himself. 'History can make people hard but motherhood makes women soft.'

'Why did you marry Ruth?' I asked him.

'Ruth is my family.'

'Where is your own family?'

'Dead.'

'All of them?'

229

'Yes, everyone.' His head hung down and his hands drooped between his knees as if he was confessing that he had lost all the money for shopping, and I felt a brief, unworthy moment of scorn, that he wasn't even capable of hanging on to his family. 'Is that why you are still at school at your age?'

'No.' He almost smiled. 'I am studying for my masters.' I didn't ask him what this meant because he was so quiet it seemed natural for him to have masters.

On one occasion he made me a present of his pen, but Mother made me give it back. A week or so later he brought a paper bag to the kitchen. 'A small treat for the young ladies.'

'Join us for tea,' Mother urged.

'No thank you. Already I have used more hospitality than I can ever repay.' He placed a bag on the table and then retreated.

'What a well-bred young man.' Mother spoke with pleasure.

'What did he bring us?' Bridie and Kitty grappled for the bag.

'It is a pity he did not bring you some of his manners.' Mother took charge of the bag and opened it slowly. She peered in with a puzzled look and pulled out three dry cracker biscuits. My disappointment was intense, not with the gift, for we were well fed at the time, but with the fact my idol should be exposed in this way.

'Cream Crackers!' Bridie squealed in disbelief. '*He's* crackers.'

He knew he had let me down. Next time we met he eyed me soulfully. 'When I have money,' he promised, 'I will buy you a banana.'

Chapter Twenty-Five

~

At the time, no one could have guessed that Daniel Fine would one day become rich, that he would be a distinguished writer and lecturer. It looked as if he had got his start in life too late. How would he catch up on dancing, or learn to make cocktails or conversation? Even though Ruth and he were hungry and had no proper clothes and could rarely bring themselves to spend a shilling to light the gas fire, I don't think he even thought about money, except when faced with a hopeful child. But if we could have seen into the future, we would have known how prosperity would suit him. On the day when he came down to the kitchen to announce that Ruth was pregnant again, he had about him the air of a wealthy man.

Ruth and Mother just looked anxious. 'What are you going to do?' Mother wondered. 'What will you live on?'

'I'll get a job. I'm going to look after Ruth.' He sneaked a hand around his wife and stroked her surreptitiously, as if she was made of silk.

Ruth was incensed. 'All that we have worked for and sacrificed, you would throw it over just like that?'

'I'll get a decent job. I have good qualifications. We'll still work for a better future, but our child will be a part of that future.'

'If you give up your studies, I will get rid of this child and then I will leave you.' She broke free of his grasp and glared at him, before running up to the bathroom, where we heard her retching with a sound like a mad dog's bark. Daniel and Mother watched each other helplessly.

'She doesn't mean it.' He tried to smile. 'She's not feeling well.'

'Daniel, I think she does mean it,' Mother said.

'She's afraid after what happened the last time.'

Ruth wasn't afraid of anything. She returned, looking pale but grim. 'This should not have happened. We do not own our own lives. We are soldiers on a mission.'

'Soldiers have families,' he said in a subdued voice.

'Yes, but not with one another.'

'Are we to have nothing for ourselves?' he asked.

'We have each other.' She looked at him in appeal and it was the first time we saw that she cared for him.

'Don't give up your studies,' Mother said. 'I'll look after Ruth. I will make sure she has enough to eat.'

'This means they will be staying. Bridie will go completely berserk.' I tried to make her see sense after the lodgers had gone upstairs.

'I know.' Mother let herself be lulled a moment by the flurry of harp strings that introduced *Mrs Dale's Diary*, and then she stood up briskly to clear the table. 'It can't be helped. I felt sorry for Ruth.'

'Why Ruth?'

'She loves that man too much. He's a lovely man but he is too unworldly. Because she can't reach him, she wants to create a whole new world for him, and she can't see that all he wants is a home and children.'

I tried to imagine Ruth loving Daniel and came to the conclusion that maybe love sometimes didn't get as far as people's faces. This was certainly the case with the grumpy-looking Boris Karloff. His letters piled up behind the clock. Each time one came, Mother dutifully notified Selena, but we heard nothing and the silence was upsetting her, for she was afraid that Miss Taylor might once more have thrown herself in a river.

'Why don't you write to him?' I asked her.

'I don't know what to say. Miss Taylor told me a secret. I couldn't possibly tell him.'

Things might have gone on like that had not Father come downstairs looking for the *Radio Review*. He had grown bored with bed and had begun applying for jobs advertised in the newspapers. In one of these papers he read that an Enniskerry man had won the record sum of £4,000 in the *Radio Review* crossword and was convinced that he too would find his fortune inside the weekly radio guide. Instead he found the letters.

'Miss Taylor answered a matrimonial advertisement.' Bravely, Mother offered a version of the truth. 'She asked to have her letters sent here in case her father found out.'

'And you have chosen to conspire with her against him. You should not interfere in family matters.'

'You would not say that if you knew anything about her family.'

'What do you know about Miss Taylor's family?' He bristled with suspicion.

Mother asked me to leave the room. She pulled her chair close to Father to whisper. When I came back, he looked even more shocked than on the occasion when a commercial traveller had tried to get into his bed. All the same, he blamed Mother. 'You have been meddling in affairs that are none of your business and you have uncovered a nest of hornets.'

'And poor Miss Taylor is in that nest.'

He drew down his mouth in sympathy until a fresh indignation struck him. 'Whatever the difficulties of Miss Taylor's life, it is no excuse for bad manners. You and she have contrived to involve a third party in her affairs and now you have both washed your hands of the business and left him without any idea of what is going on.'

'I know. I am very sorry for Mr Carson,' Mother said. 'But there is no way I can possibly tell a stranger such a dreadful story.'

'It is not your place to do so,' he said. 'Miss Taylor must attend to her own affairs. Here! Get me a pen.' Shock always put him in a temper and he wrote quickly and without thought, stabbing the paper with his nib. 'Dear Miss Taylor, You have involved my wife in a matter which has nothing to do with her, and led on an innocent stranger. I will not have my wife as party to your poor etiquette. Please deal with your post, enc.'

'Oh, no! Don't do that! Don't send on those letters,' Mother begged.

But Father couldn't stand bad manners. Next to lying, he considered them the worst offence. When he had parcelled up the letters, Mother asked me to take the message to the post. She gave me a conspiratorial look and I understood that she did not wish me to post them at all.

'I'll take it.' Father snatched the package and made for the door. 'I feel a sudden need for fresh air.'

'This is dreadful!' Mother paced the tiled floor. 'What will happen to Miss Taylor now? When he reads those letters her father will kill her.'

'Can't we tell someone?' I said. 'What about the police?'

'There is no point in telling the police, but I must do something.' Her eye fell on the notepaper which Father had left behind. 'Put on your coat. I want you to be ready to run to the post.'

She wrote so fast I could scarcely follow the writing. 'Dear Mr Carson, I must urge you to forget all notions of marrying Miss

Taylor. She has confided a circumstance which puts marriage out of the question. If you care for her welfare, perhaps you can offer her a position as housekeeper and minder for your children. She will want no payment, only her keep. I beg you to act as soon as possible. You can contact her at a convent close to where she lives, the address of which I enclose. If you are able to travel, please do not waste time writing, but go there directly.'

Father returned as she signed it. She scribbled the address and slipped the envelope into my coat pocket. 'Rose,' she put a shilling in my hand, 'go down to the butcher and get a nice kidney for your father's tea.'

I was very conscious of the privilege of being sent on an errand alone and in the dark, and was anxious to seem grown up. When I had been confirmed I waited for the Holy Ghost to descend and give me wisdom. I saw this as a process like the switching-on of the Christmas lights, or like pouring water on to a crystal garden. But I still knew hardly anything. For instance, I couldn't understand what Bridie had told us about Miss Taylor. And until you understood things, your face had a look that meant no one took any notice of you, except teachers, who used it as an excuse to hit you. As I posted the letter, I tried to assume an expression of wisdom. I had an urge to go into every one of the shops – not just the butcher, but the Honeybee, the souvenir shop, the shoe shop, Nolan's fish and vegetables, the Capri chip shop, the cake shop, Tully's drapery, to draw on their sophistication and impress them with my independence, but as I peered in the windows, I saw that individually, the shops had a home-made look. They were dimly lit and items stayed on display until their colours faded. Where was the real, exciting world?

I hurried home with my white paper parcel leaking pink. It was a February night, with trees creaking and clouds that galloped over the black sky. The acid-drop light of sodium lamps threw a bleak glare on shifting leaves and rubbish on the pavement. There was no one out but a woman at the bus stop, but then a bus lumbered down the street and settled with a groan and sucked her in and she was gone. Something tugged the corner of my eye and I became aware of a black thing dangling from one of the trees that lined the road. *Bodies in Bedlam*. I tried to run but I froze, first my feet and then the rest of me. It was something small, a child or a dog, and it flailed and pointed. To my dismay my legs, which were heavy as lead, moved towards it. Halfway across the road there was a shriek and a blinding light which almost made me faint, but it was a car and its brakes. I had walked right out in front of a car. In an instant, the fear that I might have been killed by the car was replaced by relief at another living presence, but the driver only blew his horn, making me jump out of the way, and drove straight on. The dark was regained and the black thing dangled. If I had thought to look a moment earlier, I could have seen it clearly in the light of the car, but I had been distracted. Now I continued that endless trudge, right until I could touch the thing with my hand. It was a broken umbrella. Someone's umbrella had blown inside-out in the wind and they had hung it from the tree.

I was hardly relieved to discover that it wasn't a rotting body, for the dread had been inside me all along, like the knowledge which would be set free by the Holy Ghost. My legs, which had been almost too heavy to move, had now grown light and boneless, as in a nightmare. I was only able to reach home by keeping a fixed image in my mind, of the kitchen table, set beneath the yellow flypaper gloom of a low-watt light bulb, with a fresh loaf of Hovis and half a pound of butter, and jam in a pot, and sturdy cups and saucers, banded with brown. All my life since then, I have had dreams of this image, and the sensations of this dream are of comfort and safety and a faint aura of doom.

~

We watched Ruth for signs of softening. It was too early for her figure to change, but we waited for her expression to get misty, and for her to grow voracious for strange food. When these things happened, it was to Daniel and not to Ruth. She stayed exactly as she was, hunched over her books until all hours, dressed in several layers of sweaters against the cold of the room. There was never any food on the table, just a constant cup of tea cooling at her elbow, and her books, which she consumed as if they were loaves of bread. Mother brought her glasses of warm milk and little dishes of eggs scrambled with butter, and rice pudding. Under Mother's eye she would take in a mouthful and slide it suspiciously over her tongue, as if she was a king's taster. Daniel watched her sorrowfully. He held spoonfuls to her chin, but she shook her head impatiently and with an apologetic look he crammed the food into himself. I thought Mother might be bringing her the wrong food, for pregnant women were reputed to develop curious cravings. When Ruth came with the rent I invited her into the dining room or down to the kitchen to see if she would make a lunge at the coal scuttle or dip her fingers in the Robin starch. One night Mother went to see Gram and she asked me to make supper for Ruth. I didn't care all that much about her but I wanted to impress Daniel. I mashed sardines on to buttered triangles of crustless toast. Everyone in our house loved sardines.

Ruth cleared a space on the table for the plate. She picked up a piece of toast. It went as far as her mouth before she put it down. 'Tell your mother I am taking vitamins. I even drink milk now and then. Tell her not to worry.'

'I made these,' I said, 'not Mother.'

'I'm sorry.'

'Are you feeling sick?'

She shook her head.

'Don't you like sardines?'

'I do.' For once she smiled. 'Oily and salty – delicious!'

'Why won't you eat?'

'I eat enough to stay alive.' She picked up a piece of toast and inhaled. 'Good food is habit-forming. Once you get used to it, you cannot do without. You get pampered and soft. In the struggle ahead, there will be much hardship. Too bad if it was lost because some woman wanted sardines.' She pushed the plate away. 'Take them downstairs.'

'Maybe I shouldn't eat them either,' I said. 'Catholics are supposed to make sacrifices too – to free souls from purgatory.'

She smiled. 'So we are trying to do the same thing after all. But you're a growing girl. You need your food. You don't have to make hard decisions yet.'

I left the plate. 'If you don't want them, leave them for Daniel.'

'Yes,' she sighed. 'Daniel will eat them.'

'Ruth,' I paused at the door, 'why did you get married?'

Her head was already back in her books. She looked up irritably, like someone roused from sleep. 'Doesn't every woman get married?'

'They get married to have babies and keep house for a man.'

'Do they, Rose?' She took off her spectacles to consider this. 'Daniel and I married so that we could work more effectively. We wouldn't need other people and could devote all our time to our purpose.'

'What about love?' I had to ask that, for Daniel.

'Yes, that too,' she said impatiently.

Her parched lips moved as she memorised some phrase from a text book and her finger held the place. She was trying to tell me to leave her alone. But I couldn't go. While she gluttonously ingested dull,

dull words she had vital information carelessly tucked out of sight, like Boris Karloff's letters behind the clock. 'How do you know if you're in love?' I pestered.

Her finger kept its place but her lips stopped moving and pursed. 'You just know.' She peered at me over her glasses, like a school teacher.

'That's a stupid answer,' I said.

'I know. It's not really my area. It just happened.'

'Like the baby?'

'Like the baby.'

Chapter Twenty-Six

~

When Boris Karloff came to see us, he really did look like the mad creature of a horror film. The weather continued wild and windy and his dark clothes fluttered like the broken umbrella in the tree. His lively eye rolled feverishly while the dead side seemed to have settled still further, from disgust to despair. 'Where is my fiancée?' he said. 'What is going on? Why won't anyone tell me the truth?'

'Dear sir,' Father said. 'You have my utmost sympathy. I know exactly how you feel. No one in this household tells me a thing.' He went to fetch the dregs of the Christmas whiskey, while Mother chirped and hovered like a bird whose fledgling has been snatched by the cat. She was desperate to talk to Mr Carson but did not want Father to know she had written to him. When the whiskey was poured she looked at Father in appeal and he gave her a reproachful look as he handed her his glass, for the bottle was low and it should have been the natural thing for the woman to do without.

'I got your letter,' Mr Carson said when Father had gone for a fresh glass. 'I went at once to look for her. The nuns in the convent have not seen her since she last came to Dublin.'

'Did you go to her home?'

'I did,' he said, with a distasteful expression.

'You didn't find her?'

'Her father had thrown her out. He had found letters. They were my letters,' he added miserably.

The whiskey, which lulled Mother and Father, lowered Mr Carson almost to tears. 'What has happened to my girl? Why should she not marry? She's a good girl.'

'Yes, Selena is a good girl,' Mother said.

'Whatever it is, I have to know. I would forgive her anything. I am in no position to judge.'

'Selena's life has been damaged.' Mother spoke carefully. 'She thought you only wanted a servant, that you would give her a position of marriage in return. It was my fault. Under the circumstances, I should not have mentioned feelings.'

'I was glad you did. At the time, it brought me great happiness. Now I don't know what is going on or what anyone is talking about.'

'Edie! Look what you have done,' Father said crossly. 'Sir!' He stood up. 'You are a gentleman and it is a vile business. We prefer not to discuss it.'

Mr Carson dejectedly retrieved his hat. 'Do you love your wife?' he asked Father in a casual way.

'Of course I do!' Father was dismayed and offended.

'Then you will understand. I have to know. If no one here will tell me, I must look elsewhere and I must go on looking as long as I live.'

I didn't see how Father and Mother could bear to leave him so miserable. The circumstance, which had petrified Mother in the hall, had only the faint thrill of a new swear word when Bridie told us in the bedroom. And if it really was the worst sin in the world, then Mr Carson could go home in peace and forget all about Miss Taylor.

242

'She is a victim of incest,' I carefully repeated the acquired phrase.

The shock that followed sizzled like a burn. I felt at once the power of the word and the sense of calamity, of having gone too far and lost my place as the pet of the family.

'I think it means you sleep with your father,' I added, to lessen the alarm, and chaos broke out.

'What are you talking about?'

'Who told you such a thing?'

'Bridie,' I said, close to tears, for the sizzle had burst into a blaze.

'Bridie,' Mother muttered, with a look that meant murder.

~

Some conversations print themselves like songs on your brain. When Miss Taylor confessed that she wasn't a virgin, Mother had sent us girls down to the kitchen, and even though I couldn't understand all of what we sifted through the keyhole, I remembered every word. First Mother spoke, trying to sound calm although we knew she must be shocked.

'You are not the first girl to fall for some unsuitable man and have an unhappy episode in her past.'

Selena's voice sounded dead and cried-out. 'I didn't fall. It wasn't an episode.'

Mother's tone sharpened. 'When did it begin?'

'Soon after Mammy died.'

'How long did it go on?'

No answer came and our gentle parent probed, delicate as a dentist. 'You mean . . . even now?'

'Whenever he can lay hold of me.'

243

'Why didn't he marry you?'

'He couldn't marry me.'

'Then . . . he was a married man?'

'He was.'

Mother wondered how the scandal had gone unnoticed and why no one tried to put a stop to it.

'The nuns knew. I never said much but I think they did. They urged me to get away.'

'But they didn't interfere?'

'They couldn't. No one could.'

'Did you love him?'

'God forgive me, I hated him. I hate him.'

'I don't understand, Selena. Why didn't you end it?'

'Didn't I try to, over and over, any way I could. Isn't that why I came to Dublin? Isn't it why I threw myself in the Liffey?'

'Why couldn't you just turn your back on him?'

'Because I live with him.'

'But . . . you live with your father.'

I couldn't figure out just what Selena had said that had turned Mother to stone, but in the silence that followed, she dropped out of our lives. A small clunk told us she had gone out of the door. After a delay, Mother came down to the kitchen and began automatically to ladle out tomato soup. 'Oh my God!' She hesitated, the raised spoon dripping red. 'She has gone home – to that!'

'Where else would she go?' I said. 'Gone home to what?'

~

'Incest,' Bridie had finally revealed. She added dramatically that it was probably the worst sin in the world.

'Miss Taylor committed the worst sin in the world?'

'Not *her*! Would you want to sleep with your father?' Kitty and I made faces at each other. We often felt sorry for Mother having to sleep with Father, who was usually either angry or feeling sorry for himself and who, from time to time, rubbed smelly liniment on his back. But I couldn't see why it would be the worst sin in the world.

'Can't we rescue her?' I wondered. 'Couldn't we write to Boris Karloff and explain that someone incested her against her will?'

'You don't say "incested". You say she has been a victim of incest,' Bridie instructed. 'And it doesn't matter either way. Boris Karloff made it clear that he wants to do his worst to a virgin bride. He wouldn't touch her with a barge pole now. It is unlikely that any man will ever look at her again.'

~

But Bridie was wrong about that. Mr Carson seemed more determined than ever to find Miss Taylor. 'Oh, my poor girl! Where will she go now?'

'She will go back. She will return to her father. She always does,' Mother said in a dejected tone.

'Then I must go back,' Mr Carson said.

'I'll drive you,' Father said, amazing us all.

'Oh, I couldn't ask . . .' Mr Carson protested.

'It will be no trouble. It is time I returned to work and I have not been to the west for some time. Besides, my family has embroiled you in this sorry situation. I will put you on a train afterwards and continue with my business.'

'You are all as kind as Selena said,' Mr Carson exclaimed. 'You must at least allow me to reimburse you for your petrol and your trouble.' At this, Father looked immensely cheered. He had grown

245

restless and bored from his weeks in bed. He had had no luck with the crossword and no favourable response to any of his job applications. He was getting tired of being confined with a house full of females.

Afterwards, Mother tackled Bridie. 'Your youngest sister shocked us with a phrase she should not have known. You have let me down. I give you children information as I see fit.'

'I do the same,' Bridie said. 'Kitty and Rose asked for information. I saw fit to give it to them.'

'I had been warned that children turn against their parents when they grow to be teenagers.' Mother spoke with surprising severity.

'I haven't turned against you.' Bridie's frustration showed as anger. 'You've turned against me because I'm no longer a child and am capable of making decisions of my own.'

'I will decide when you are capable of making decisions of your own.'

'You never decide anything.'

'Your father and I have sheltered you from the harsh winds of life. For years we suffered hardship and you girls have known nothing about it. Don't get notions of independence. You may find you won't get quite so far on your own as you think.'

'You make me sound like a hobbled goat,' Bridie lamented.

'Just how far do you wish to run?' Mother said. 'Women's lives are limited. That is how it is, especially in ordinary families. I have always done my best to give you girls a life of the mind so that whatever the future holds you will not feel trapped or bored.'

'If I was a boy you wouldn't talk to me like this.'

'No, but you are not a boy. You are a girl. That is something you can't run away from.'

'I will run as far as the wind will carry me.' Bridie's temper collapsed in a flood of tears. She unpinned her pictures from the wall. One by one she plucked them down and then rolled them up together and put them in the wardrobe. 'The first person who touches them will die,' she said.

Mother made a cake to woo her down to tea. 'You think I don't want the best for you.' She cut Bridie the largest slice. 'You are wrong. As far as I am concerned, nothing is good enough for you girls. But nothing is what I have. It would be wrong to give you false expectations. Of course I expect great things of you all, but women usually achieve these things in later life, when they have brought up their families.'

'I don't want a family,' Bridie protested.

'Don't be angry,' Mother said sadly. 'All I want is to stop you the pain of banging your head against a brick wall.'

'Bridie isn't angry at you,' Kitty said. 'She's angry at Father. Father wanted a boy and Bridie did her best to be one for him, but she's not a real boy so it doesn't count with him.'

The conversation slowed as we gradually became aware of the music. It had a parched sound, as if it came from a very old gramophone, but it was loud enough for the quiver of cellos to penetrate the ceiling from the room above. 'Listen!' I said. 'It's from the Fines' room.'

'That's strange.' Mother looked up. 'I didn't even know they had a radio.'

We hardly ever listened to music at home. Father loved music, but he turned the volume so loud it always made us laugh, so he played his gramophone alone, with the door shut. Now we were all affected by the huge emotion of the music, which I later learned was by Mahler. It was full of sorrow and passion, and I wondered if this was how shy Daniel and stern Ruth expressed their feelings for each other. But it turned out that only one of them was home, for then we heard the front door open and close, and footsteps on

247

the stairs. The music died on a squeal, and there were voices, low and tense.

'Oh dear,' Mother said. 'They are having an argument.'

The door slammed and moments later Ruth appeared. 'Mrs Rafferty, I am ashamed to have to tell you we cannot pay our rent.'

'Pay it when you can.' Mother was embarrassed to be involved in a family quarrel.

'Daniel has spent the rent money as well as our money for food on an old gramophone.'

'Then you had better have the rest of this cake for your tea.' She held out the plate as a peace offering.

'I don't want cake.' Ruth bunched her hands into fists, but they went limp as if they were too tired for combat. 'I want commitment. I want him to be the same as me.'

'I'm sure he only meant to surprise you.'

'He did not do it for me.'

'Perhaps he can't live without music.'

'It was not for himself either. It was for the baby!' She uttered this as if it was a shameful admission. 'He said there should be beautiful music for the baby in the womb. Who ever heard of such a thing?'

'You're tired. Go to bed and discuss this tomorrow. I'll bring you up some supper on a tray.'

'Yes, I'm tired,' she said. 'Tired of having to struggle alone.'

~

There was no more music from the room. When Daniel came down next evening he looked sad. I could tell Mother felt sorry for him, but she was compelled to side with Ruth. 'I think you should take back the gramophone.'

'Yes, I have put an ad in the paper. It doesn't really matter. It won't be long until we can afford things. We will both be finished with our studies this summer. I have already been offered a position in an English university. Ruth will probably divide her time between teaching and politics.'

This surprised me, and I could see Mother was surprised too, for we had imagined that Ruth and Daniel would always be poor and struggling.

'When that time comes,' he promised, 'I will repay you everything.'

'You can pay the rent when you sell the gramophone,' Mother said. 'There is nothing else due.'

'I owe you more than that,' he said. 'We both do. I know very well that twelve shillings is not an adequate rent. But the truth is, I came to ask another favour.'

'Do you need food? There isn't very much, but you are welcome to cheese and eggs.'

'No, not food. I need to ask a special favour of you – something personal.' He cast an apologetic glance at us. 'It will only take a little while.'

Mother hesitated, then she said gently, 'Girls! Get a start on your homework.' Upstairs, I hissed at my sisters, 'He wants to kiss her!'

Bridie, who had grown subdued, now got an explosive air. Her cheeks seemed to swell and her mouth got a compressed look that signified war.

'Don't you think that's romantic?' I said. 'He and Mother are both lovely, and Ruth and Father are bad-tempered.'

'Twelve shillings!' Bridie snapped. 'What did he mean when he said the rent was twelve shillings? The rent is a guinea.'

'They were short of money,' I explained. 'They had nowhere else to go.'

'They took advantage of her, like everyone else. Now they think

249

it's all right to come down and say they can't even afford twelve shillings. You heard what he said. By summer they will both be earning. They will walk off, leaving us struggling as usual. And on top of everything, we are feeding them.'

'Shush!' I urged. 'Daniel will hear.'

Into the ensuing silence trickled Mother's happy laughter. I thought they must have finished their kiss so I crept back down. From the landing, I heard Daniel laughing: 'Oh, I am hopeless, hopeless! You are an expert! Please be patient.' I stayed on the landing with the devil until I heard him going back to his room. When I went into the kitchen, Mother was smiling to herself in a private and amused way.

'What did he want?' I said.

'Poor Daniel.' She shook her head and tried to tailor her smile. 'I do not think he and Ruth are at all well suited. I wish they could be happy, but I don't think it very likely.'

Chapter Twenty-Seven

~

Father returned in cheerful humour. 'I have good news!' He kissed Mother as he came through the door. 'The very best.'

'Miss Taylor!' Mother said. 'You have found her! Oh, thank God.'

'Miss Taylor?' He seemed surprised and even annoyed by mention of her name. 'I know nothing of Miss Taylor. Her brute of a father said he had not heard from her.'

Mother turned away. 'Poor girl! She must have ended her life. And in this weather!'

Father was irked. His agreeable mood had been ruined, and his surprise too. 'We did everything we could for her. She has all but taken over our lives. Have you no interest in my news?'

'Oh, yes!' Mother tried to look concerned. 'Sit down to your tea and tell me all about it.'

He tackled his poached egg and bacon, giving all of his attention to it until the last of the yolk had been mopped on an edge of toast. 'I have been offered a job,' he said then.

Mother reminded him that he already had a job. Her mind was still on Miss Taylor.

'A decent job, Edie! It is beyond our wildest dreams.'

251

Mother looked wary now, for she had developed a mistrust of Father's wildest dreams. 'Who offered you a job? You haven't opened your post yet.'

He drank his tea and began to massage butter on to bread with a knife, in his thorough and sparing way. 'Guess!'

'I couldn't.' Mother looked beleaguered. 'I don't know anything about the people you meet on your travels. Was it some person you met in a hotel?'

'I have told you about those types. I have nothing to do with them.'

The Goon Show was on the wireless but we didn't dare to laugh for we could feel the evening beginning to curl up and crisp with tension.

'A customer?' Mother's thumb stamped some crumbs on the table. 'Oh, are we going to have to move to the country?'

'Damn it! Can't you just say you're glad? Anyway, I would not have asked you to guess if you did not know the answer. Who did I set out with this week?'

'Poor Mr Carson.'

'Poor Mr Carson!' He smiled now, quite smugly. 'Poor Mr Carson, as it turns out, is not poor after all. He is managing director of his own company and quite well off.'

'But he always looks so shabby.'

'He has no one to look after him since his wife died. The same is true of his business. He has been unable to take charge since he fell ill. Some fellow was managing it for him, but he almost ran it into the ground. Mr Carson had been on the verge of selling up.'

'And he has changed his mind?'

'I changed his mind. I told him that I had many years of management experience. Edie, he is going to give me a try. It's a small business, but the prospects are good and there is a car that goes with the job. A limousine! There's a fair wage and I won't have to travel – except to the cemetery,' he laughed.

'You are a long way away from the cemetery.' Mother looked nervous, as she always did in the face of Father's schemes. Before she could begin to be pleased, she had to face the prospect of his disillusion if things went wrong. 'What is the business?'

He took out his pipe and then excavated it vigorously with a pen knife and a pipe cleaner. He put the stem to his lip and blew on it twice, softly, as if tuning up. 'A funeral parlour.'

~

Mr Carson came to discuss business with Father and we saw that the job was not just one of Father's fancies. We also grew to see him as a caring and kindly man, although not very amusing. He was still determined to find Selena and planned one more expedition to the country to talk to everyone who knew her. Mother was as relieved by this as she was by the prospect of a stable job for Father. 'It is probably his perfect calling,' she decided. 'He will be dealing with the living at their most subdued and he will be unable to fall out with the dead.'

It so happened that he was to bring his first client to his new business within a week. This would have been seen as a piece of luck, but for the fact that it was an old friend. We had not seen Miss Queenie Cornelia since the time of Miss Heaslip's eviction. He held out his arms in greeting and was surprised when she fell into them in an uninhibited way and began to weep. 'Jude's dead,' she said.

As they were not Catholics, it was natural for the funeral arrangements to be made by Carson's. They had no family left and we were glad that there were five of us to make up the numbers. Mother bought a bouquet of flowers and Bridie sped off to the mountains on her bicycle and came back with the basket filled with wild flowers, which she made into three bunches, one for each of us to put on the grave. In with the bluebells and primroses were some stiff new daffodils and stems of winter jasmine which she must have taken from people's gardens. Mother went to a priest to seek a dispensation for us to attend the funeral, as Catholics were forbidden to attend Protestant ceremonies without special permission. She returned very dejected to tell us that permission had not been granted.

'So what? We'll go anyway.' Bridie was defiant.

'We have been forbidden by the Church,' Father reminded her. 'It is a pity, but that is an end to the matter.'

'No it's not,' she announced. 'I'm going. No black-cloaked old blackguard is going to stop me.'

'Bridie!' both my parents called out as if to stifle her.

'I got flowers!' Bridie cried indignantly. 'I cycled all the way to the mountains and spent hours looking for them.'

'I have invited Queenie back here after the funeral and then we can give her our flowers.' Mother tried to make peace. 'Please, Bridie, just let things be.'

'We have known Miss Cornelia all our lives and she has always been kind to us. How can it be right to leave her alone at her sister's funeral?'

'It is a matter of obedience,' Father said. 'Obedience is part of belonging to a faith.'

'Well, I prefer kindness. And good manners too, since you're so keen on them.'

'Don't lecture me, miss. What about obedience to your parents? I forbid you to go!'

Bridie glared at him. 'If I'm not going to obey the Church why should I obey my bloody old pa?'

'Because if you cannot accept my authority then you are no longer a part of this family.'

Bridie looked like a warrior as she set off for the funeral. She wore several layers of clothing, which the act of rebellion must have required, with a knitted hat and Mother's old Persian lamb overcoat on top. To make up for our faint-heartedness, she had gathered more flowers and the basket on her bicycle now brimmed over with blossoms.

'Why don't you give Bridie a lift since she is determined to go and you will be driving the hearse?' Mother made one more try at imposing harmony.

'I can't condone her defiance,' he said. 'The priest is right. People must learn to live by rules. She may well be putting her faith at risk.'

'And what about you?' Bridie flung back a parting shot. 'Are you sure you're not putting your faith at risk, swanking around in a Protestant hearse stuffed with Protestant corpses?'

After the funeral, Father set out for the country for the last time. He would take Mr Carson back to Selena's home and then proceed with his rounds. He claimed he needed a final week of sales to earn a bonus, but Mother said he really needed time on his own to adapt to the change in his fortunes. In fact, we all needed time to adjust.

'Just think!' She lit a cigarette as we sat around the kitchen table. 'After all the difficult years, we'll have enough money and Father will go out to work every day. There will be no more lodgers. We will have new clothes and birthday parties and go to the pictures as a family. Our lives will be back to normal.'

But what was normal? We had outgrown the life we lived before. None of us would want birthday parties and Bridie wouldn't be interested in family outings. I would miss the lodgers.

'What are you looking forward to most?' I asked Mother.

'I would like to be able to do the shopping without looking at the price of everything and then putting back half the things because they cost too much. I would like to throw out the socks with the largest holes and not have to darn them for the third time. I would like to hand over three and fourpence for a pound of sirloin steak. I want to go to the nice shops – Lipton's, the Home and Colonial Stores and the Monument Creamery – and buy cheese from a wheel and butter from a slab and fruit cake and chutney and home-made biscuits. And then I want them delivered to my door.'

'I'd like a bicycle,' I said.

'Oh, no!' She looked appalled. 'You are too young. Bicycles are very dangerous. If you got a fall you could break your front teeth.'

The trouble was, we all wished for different things. Mother wanted to return to the time when we were small and close to her and we wanted things that were out of reach because we were still too young.

'Bridie can have her room back.' She paused and sighed, for Bridie had not spoken to us since the day of the funeral. But she would not let this spoil her enthusiasm. 'We have to get used to a different way of life. No school tomorrow! We are going into town to practise being rich.'

We took the bus to Aungier Street and went first to the Carmelite church, as Mother wanted to say a prayer of thanks to St Therese. We liked this church, which contained the bones of St Valentine and was full of lighted candles. There was a good-looking young priest who always smiled at us and we smiled at him until our faces ached and he tried to avoid our eyes. Afterwards we dawdled along George's Street looking in the window of Pims and Kellett's and Cassidy's, where crisp spring dresses of cotton boussac and poplin defied the cold March weather and the windows were adorned with little streamers which read 'For Easter!'. We went down Wicklow

Street and into Grafton Street. We did not look at Switzer's or Brown Thomas or Newell's, for these shops were only for the very rich, but visited Fuller's for the great treat of tea and chocolate eclairs and then we sauntered on to Stephen's Green to embark on the real purpose of our outing, which was to shop in Smith's of the Green, which everyone in Dublin believed to be the most exclusive grocery shop in the world. 'We will have a look at everything,' Mother instructed, 'but we will just buy one item. We will decide between us what is the most luxurious thing in the shop.'

The produce in the shop was so rich and foreign and pungent as to almost seem rank – whole smoked hams, wheels of gorgonzola, barrels of walnuts and muscatel raisins, exotic birds and fruits inside tins. In spite of the extraordinary choice, in the end, it was very easy for us to decide what we wanted. There was a barrel which contained brown sugar rock; large crystals of brown sugar strung on to a string, and sold in lengths for dipping into coffee. We bought a string of sugar for a shilling. We longed to suck each lump down to its stringy spine but had to wait until we got home, to cut it with scissors. It made our mouths water, so Mother brought us to the Swiss Chalet on Baggot Street, where we were each treated to a Heavenly Hash, a delicious brick of marshmallow coated in chocolate and then covered in multicoloured dots.

This outing seemed to exorcise Mother of the hardship of all the years of doing without. 'I have only spent five shillings,' she said. 'And I have done as well as anyone living in Foxrock.'

No matter how strong the lure of the world, Kitty and I could never resist the childish part of Mother that sparkled in our dull company and was content with a five-shilling shopping expedition or a bag of sweets. When we got home she made cups of Irel coffee and we dipped lengths of sugar rock into this and sucked off the coffee. Afterwards she sketched us as we munched the Heavenly Hashes and it seemed that no riches could bring greater contentment, but before we had dispatched the last pleasurably sickening chocolate-crusted wedge of sugary rubber, the kitchen door opened with a whoosh as if a ghost had come through, and there was Mrs Fine, all bulk and fury. 'I know what you and my husband have been up to!'

'Ruth!' Mother looked guilty and startled.

'Don't deny it! I have the evidence.'

'There was no harm,' Mother said. 'It's a bit unusual, I know.'

'Unusual?' Ruth scoffed. 'It is perverse. It is . . .' She paused to think of a suitably insulting adjective. 'It is trivial!' she flung out in triumph.

'Oh, Ruth,' Mother sighed.

Kitty and I cast glances at one another. What evidence? we wondered. And what would Ruth do to poor Mother, who was as much at sea as we were when confronted by bad-tempered grown-ups?

'Ruth, I have no wish to interfere, but it is a mistake to curtail a man's freedom.' Mother spoke bravely.

'Freedom!' she said with contempt. 'Is this what you call freedom?' From behind her back she produced the evidence. It was something small and pink and ragged. It looked like the uneaten remains of our Heavenly Hash. I was mystified, but Kitty recognised it at once and went to inspect it. 'It's a piece of knitting,' she pronounced.

'Barely recognisable as such, but yes, it is a piece of knitting,' Ruth said grimly. 'Your mother has been teaching my husband to knit.'

Kitty threw me a wild look of mirth. I didn't know whether to laugh or cry. I felt as let down as Ruth did. Any woman would be ashamed of a man knitting.

'Don't be hard on him, Ruth,' Mother begged. 'Try to understand how much the baby means to your husband, with all his family lost.'

258

'What happened to his family?' I said.

Ruth turned to me, still with the same look of fury, as if I might have done away with them. 'You don't know?' She gave a kind of growl, which terrified me. 'Such ignorance, in a big girl your age! All of you people, safe and smug, behaving still as if the War meant nothing more than a shortage of butter and eggs.'

'The War was over when I was born,' I defended myself.

'Over.' The word seemed a signal for the end of her own outburst. She sat down, studying the small piece of knitting with tears in her eyes. 'Over. Yes. As if it had never happened. All of Daniel's family, they did nothing, except to be born Jewish.'

'Were they murdered for their faith?'

'If they denied it they were murdered anyway.'

'Was there a trial?' I asked.

'No trial. All over Europe they were rounded up in the streets like stray cats, starved to death, beaten, choked with poison gas.'

I felt haunted by the things Ruth had said. It was only when *The Diary of Anne Frank* was filmed that people here really believed the stories of Nazi atrocities, which had been suppressed by the Irish government after the War. It still seemed remote and foreign and we never expected it to affect anyone we knew. In school, history ended at 1916.

'Mother . . . ?' I expected some sort of reassurance but she only seemed annoyed by Ruth's outburst. 'That young woman will have to learn that the secret of a successful marriage is compromise, and it is always the woman who compromises,' she declared.

~

'I am sorry.' Daniel came down to apologise. 'I got us both into trouble. A pity. I liked knitting. I can see now why women are so sensible. The brain grows more ordered when the hands are so pleasantly engaged.'

'Kitty will knit clothes for the baby,' Mother promised. 'Kitty is a great knitter.'

'Thank you. Just one small garment would suffice. You know what I want for this child? I want it to have the most normal childhood any child has ever had. In a normal family, the mother knits.'

'Your child won't worry about knitting,' Mother promised. 'It will feel secure and wanted. It is Ruth who is insecure.'

'Ruth?'

'She feels you are no longer fully dedicated. I think she confuses commitment to politics with commitment to her. She is afraid you no longer love her.'

Daniel looked troubled and unhappy. He ate a large slice of bread without even noticing he had done so. 'It's true,' he said.

'You don't love Ruth?'

'Oh, I love Ruth. But you are right about Communism. When we met we were very young and full of ideals and we both truly believed that Communism would mean an end to poverty and oppression. I don't think so any more. I have come to believe that individual kindness is the way to save the world.'

'How long have you felt this way?'

'Since the Russians invaded Hungary. That one Communist nation should do that to another! It meant a loss of faith for a lot of committed Communists. Many of our friends left the party. Ruth says that they are weak-spirited, that it is more important than ever for the rest of us to retain the true spirit of Marxism.'

'What did Mr Marx say?' I asked.

'He said, "From each according to his abilities, to each according to his needs."'

'But who would decide the limits of people's abilities, and who would judge the level of their needs?' Mother wondered.

Daniel laughed. 'Imagination is a great handicap in a social revolution. It is better suited to a cinema star or a saint.'

Whatever about Mr Marx's views, this answer pleased me and I forgave Daniel his knitting. When Mother went off to do the hoovering I whispered: 'Ruth said your family was murdered by the Germans.'

'Ah! Yes.'

'How did you get away?'

'I was sent to school in England as a boy to study English. I think my father knew there was danger and wanted me to be safe. I was the only boy in the family. I suppose he thought the girls would be spared.'

'Why don't you go back and murder them?'

'The people who did such things, they have murdered themselves. I want to work for a better society, but I also feel it is my duty to try and live a happy life, for those who once gave me a happy life.'

'Was Ruth's family murdered too? Is that why she is angry?'

'No. Ruth is English. Poor Ruth never had a family. She was brought up in an orphanage. Because she loves me she feels it is necessary to avenge the death of the people I loved. That is why she is angry. She does not understand the warmth of love, only its demands.'

I could see Ruth's point of view. I too expected the people I loved to be heroic. 'Daniel's family was killed by Germans,' I told Mother. 'The Germans killed Jews who had done nothing.'

'That's true,' she said.

'You knew? Why didn't you do something?'

She seemed stricken now, as if the thought had only just occurred to her. 'We didn't know at the time. Ireland was a neutral country. We knew nothing until after the War had ended.'

Clare Boylan

I ran from the kitchen and shut myself in my room. While Daniel's family was murdered, she and Father had been dancing, in the golden era before the children were born. I had a strange, bitter sensation of hardening off, like a shrub after the first autumn frost. I couldn't forgive my mother for not being able to save the world.

Chapter Twenty-Eight

~

Ruth hadn't forgiven Daniel either. There were tense voices from the room upstairs, and once we heard her threatening to leave. When she went out, her footsteps on the stairs sounded both weary and threatening. Then one day we eavesdropped on Daniel anxiously in pursuit. 'Wait! Where are you going?'

'I'm leaving home.'

'Don't do that,' Daniel begged. 'What is the matter?'

'None of your business!'

'All right,' he said gently. 'Don't talk to me. We'll speak with the family.'

The answer was the merest grumble. 'I've done all the talking I want to do with them.'

After the front door banged, Daniel hurried downstairs. 'Quickly! She has gone on her bicycle. We must go after her.'

'Ruth has left?' Mother tried to sound surprised.

'Ruth? Oh, no! It is the young girl – Bridie!'

Mother rose like a blind swiftly drawn. 'Bridie!'

'She's probably gone to the shops,' Kitty said.

'Yes, the shops. She is fifteen,' Mother reminded herself.

'She had a suitcase! She said she was leaving home!'

'Oh!' She put a hand to her mouth. 'Go after her, Daniel. Take Eugene's bike.'

'She won't listen to me. I tried to stop her already.'

'Can you ride a bike?' Mother said hopefully to Kitty.

'No. You wouldn't let me. I've only ridden crossbar.'

'Shall I go to a telephone box and call the police?' Daniel offered. 'It is dangerous for a young girl to be out alone.'

'Oh, no!' Mother reacted with dismay. 'My husband would not like that. I am sure there is no need. My daughter is given to dramatic gestures. She will be back when she gets hungry.'

We didn't know what to do. We didn't know if Bridie had friends at school. She had been growing apart from us for almost a year and we hadn't done anything about it. None of us had gone with her to Miss Cornelia's funeral. Smoke and steam swamped the kitchen as Mother smoked endless cigarettes and we made endless pots of tea. At nine o'clock there was a knock. 'Thank God. She is back.' Mother smiled with relief. 'Don't anyone say anything. I'll make her black pudding on toast.'

A shrivelled young woman stood on the doorstep. She pulled her thin clothing around her. 'Would you have clothes for a poor boy in hospital?' she begged. 'I'll say a rosary for you in return.'

'I have no boys,' Mother said, and tears ran down her face.

There was another knock at eleven. 'I'll kill her! Such selfishness, putting the whole household in an uproar.' Mother ran to the door. 'Bridie!' Her voice broke as she grappled with the catch. It fell open and she threw herself on the shabby figure of Miss Taylor.

Kitty and I could not sleep. The empty bed between us was like a coffin. 'What do you remember best about her?' I said to Kitty.

'How she could play the piano and draw and ride a bicycle without ever learning,' Kitty said. 'We don't even know if she's ten times

cleverer than we are or if she tries ten times harder to impress. What
do you remember?'

My memory was so strong it sucked me back to a time before
memory. I am two and I am in the garden. As in a dream, the small
back yard with its twin apple trees has grown to a vast expanse
that stretches off into the distance. I am learning to walk. I have
undertaken this humiliating task alone with the aid of a seaside
spade and lurch along with splayed feet and trembling knees, my
eyes fixed on the endless stretch of crab grass, dappled with sun,
furred with honeysuckle. I am like an old person, knowing that what
I attempt is beyond me and that only pain and failure lie ahead, but
it must be done. Then I see feet, big feet in sandals with a little roll
of snow-white sock. I look up and there is Bridie. For once she is
smiling at me, holding out her hands. ''Mon, Rosie.' The whole
garden seems to light up with love as with sunshine. At once I drop
my spade and stagger towards her, laughing.

'Are you asleep?' Kitty said.

I tried to make heavy breaths to feign drowsing, but they came
out snuffled with loss.

Neither Mother nor Miss Taylor went to bed at all. Their whispers
reached us like draughts under the door. We heard the broken bits of
their conversation, richly mysterious as silk remnants in a scrap bag.
Miss Taylor had run away from home again. She had no money and
had spent several nights sleeping on the streets of Dublin.

'Mr Carson is looking for you. He still loves you,' Mother
said.

'Oh, please don't mention Mr Carson!' Selena started to cry.

Mother talked afterwards of the effort of making her voice stern,
for she felt desperately sorry for the other woman, grimy and cold,
with not a penny in the world. 'You are being selfish. You must stop
thinking of yourself and think instead of Mr Carson. You treated him

badly, running off without a word. Whatever the outcome, it is only fair and decent that you stay and face him.'

'I'd die of shame,' she whispered. 'No matter. I must stop thinking of myself. How about poor Bridie? Will she look for some place to stay?'

Mother gave a long sigh. She had welcomed the distraction from her family crisis. 'Bridie hates being dependent. I imagine the first thing she will do is look for work. But she is very young and doesn't make herself presentable.'

'What then? What if she doesn't find work? Would she end up like me on O'Connell Bridge?'

'Oh, don't say such a thing! She's only a little girl.'

'Never fret! We'll go together and look for her tomorrow. I know all the haunts now. We'll bring her back safe and sound.'

Kitty and I couldn't sleep much, and when a thin skin of grey pearl diluted the dark, we crept down to the cold, ash-smelling kitchen to find the two women, grey-faced, asleep at the table. Kitty shook Mother awake. 'Put on the kettle and we'll face the day.' She tried to smile. 'We'll all have baths and a big fry and then we will go out together to look for Bridie. Ruth or Daniel will be here in case she comes back. We will have coffee in Bewley's to keep ourselves awake. And pineapple tarts,' she coaxed, knowing that these little cream pastries were a great favourite with me. I went into her hug. I couldn't stay angry with her. Even if she had done nothing to save the Jews, I was sure that if they had come to her door she would have taken them in.

'Do you know,' Mother said to Miss Taylor as we shivered at a bus stop, 'that the famous artist, Mr Sean O'Sullivan, has been in court for refusing to pay for two heaters in his studio. He said they gave off insufficient heat for a woman sitter who might be *décolletée* and she would have to keep on her overcoat. The judge agreed that that would be unpleasant for a lady and the artist was released without obligation to pay. It is because the weather has stayed so cold.'

'You don't say!' Miss Taylor showed respectful surprise, although she had spent several nights out of doors in the cold.

When we reached the city Kitty and I could not help a surge of excitement, as we saw the big new neon sign on O'Connell Bridge, showing Don and Nelly, tossing Donnelly's sausages to one another in a lighted arc, but Miss Taylor was now acquainted with the hiding places of the homeless and she moved purposefully to the shabbier parts of the city, behind O'Connell Street and along the quays. Among the derelicts we met that day were respectable people who had had bad luck and had nowhere to turn; widows with large numbers of children; men who had lost their jobs and could not pay their bills. They loitered in alleys, in cheap cafés, in auction rooms, in churches – places from which they would not be thrown out. Mother was silent and distraught, handing out coins everywhere she went until there was no money left for our coffee. I could tell from her face what she was thinking. Imagine if this should happen to Bridie! Imagine, we thought we were poor! No wonder Ruth regarded us with scorn.

We went to the hostels and showed pictures of Bridie. No one had seen her. On the bus on the way home Mother clutched my hand and Kitty's. 'Now you see why I want to shelter you girls,' she said. 'It is because you are so precious to me. I could not bear to see you come to harm. I would swap all the comfort in the world to have Bridie back safe and sound.'

Daniel was waiting for us in the hall.

'Has Bridie come back?' Mother said.

'No, but there is word of her.'

'My God!' She looked as if she was going to faint. She could only imagine the worst.

'She is safe,' he added quickly.

'Where is she?'

'She is with Mrs Mankievitz.'

'Minnie! Did Minnie come here?'

'A maid brought the message.' He held out a note.

'"Bridie is with me",' I read out. '"She does not want to go home. You can come here, but only to talk. Minnie."'

'It sounds as if she is holding my daughter to ransom.' Mother gave a shaky laugh that quickly turned into a sob. 'I think the whole world is going mad.'

Chapter Twenty-Nine

~

After all we had been through that day, Minnie's little villa had so much the look of a gingerbread house that for a moment we just stood and gazed with longing. Smoke curled from the chimney, and inside there was soft lighting and the warm glow of a fire.

'It looks inviting, but her note was odd and not very friendly.' Mother sounded wistful. 'I suppose unhappiness has made her hard. Oh, Minnie,' she sighed, as if she longed for the old Minnie to side with her against the new one.

'Come on. We'll freeze.' I banged on the door. And there was Minnie, small and round and warm. Without a thought, she and Mother hugged each other. 'Where is Bridie?' Mother cried. 'Is she all right?'

'Of course she is all right. And so! You do not come rushing into my house like some rescue party. We've got to negotiate.'

'What's going on?' Mother shivered.

'About time you ask yourself.' Minnie stepped aside. 'Come on in, Edie. You look half froze. I've a nice fire and a nice supper.'

In the living room, Mo was watching television. He seemed completely mesmerised by the grainy figures on the screen. When the ads came on, he sang along softly with the jingle: 'Real-Brook

269

Toplin, the shirts you don't iron.' Kitty and I loved television and we quickly sat down beside him, but Minnie turned down the sound. 'The drinks, Mo! He missed the cinema. I bought him his own little cinema.' She smiled at him fondly as he handed a glass to Mother. 'Give the girls a little thimbleful,' she instructed. 'Sometime he spills some, but it doesn't matter.'

The room was so warm and the chairs so soft and we could have slept while Minnie went to make the tea. She returned with a tall young girl who carried the hot-water pot. 'Bridie!' Kitty and I screamed joyfully and we ran to greet her. Mother also rose but she stood back and watched with a puzzled frown. Bridie, our Bridie, wore a twin set and a slim skirt. Her hair was softly curled. The clothes showed a pretty figure.

Minnie stood back proudly to show her off. 'As you can see, I have already done my negotiations with Miss Bridie. I tell her, if she wants to be grown up, she's got to look like a grown-up.'

'Bridie!' Mother's anxiety gave way to anger. 'You are a very foolish girl and have caused us all a great deal of worry.'

Minnie stood in front of Bridie as if Mother might attack her. 'She is a sensible girl. Better she should try to sort her life at fifteen than make a mess of it at forty.'

'Do you realise that we have not slept since you walked out of the house, that we spent the entire day trawling the lowest parts of the city, mixing with drunks and beggars, while you have been here toasting yourself by the fire and . . . having your hair done?'

'Sit down and behave like a visitor,' Minnie commanded. She poured tea and passed around sandwiches. 'Now that you know the lowest parts of the city, you might as well know also that is where your daughter spent last night.'

'Bridie . . . !'

'Be quiet, Edie. She came to me this morning. No harm was done to her, except some teddy boys tormented her and she was frozen to the bone. I put her to bed and then we had a long chat. After that we went shopping for some clothes.'

'This morning? Why didn't you let me know?'

'Bridie would not stay unless I promised not to tell you. It was only after our chat that she agreed to see you.'

'She is my child.'

'She's not a child. She is a young lady.'

'But, Minnie . . . !'

'A gifted and ambitious girl. She needs musical training and drawing instruction.'

'I have always encouraged my girls to be creative. We are not rich. I can't pay for special tuition.'

'I'll pay.'

'We don't want charity. I will pay for my own children and bring them up as I see fit. Come home now, Bridie.'

'I won't go home, Mother,' Bridie said. 'I'm staying here.'

'She will stay with me,' Minnie said, 'at least until she can have her own room. Bridie will earn her keep. I will pay for her lessons and she will help me with the baby.' All pretence of sternness dropped from Minnie at the mention of the baby. Mo looked up eagerly and Minnie's face dimpled with sentiment. 'My little Betty! You want to see her?'

'What happened to Dora?'

'I told you. She ran off with Stefan.'

'And Stefan stole your money. Didn't you tell the police?'

Minnie flapped a hand to dismiss this idea. 'I got a bit hot under the togs. Really, it's just a loan. All he wanted was a little cash to make a fresh start. He's got too much talent for a small place like this. I told him, go to America. They like big talents in America. And Dora! She will love America.'

271

'You let them walk off with your money and leave you with the child?'

'That's right, Edie. What more could we want?'

Mother and Bridie watched each other across the room while Minnie went to get the baby. 'You were my baby,' Mother said to her. 'You were my first child. I love you more than you will ever know.'

'I know, Mother,' Bridie said, 'but you don't know me.'

Mother had tears in her eyes. 'Everything will be different now that your father is in a good job again.'

Bridie sighed and raised her eyes to the ceiling. 'Everything will be different because I'm not going to listen to that sort of thing any more. Please, Mother, I mean to stay here.'

Mother went to her. She put out a hand and touched her hair. 'You look so nice. Why would you never dress nicely for me?' At the touch, Bridie's chin shook and her arms went around Mother. 'Because unless I set myself against you completely, I would have done anything in the world for you. Say I can stay.'

'In the end,' Mother stroked her, 'no matter what I think, whatever is right for you will be all right with me. But it's hard to start losing my girls so soon.'

'You won't be losing me.' Bridie's voice was choked too. 'We'll be women together.'

'I know,' Mother said, 'but I can't help it, I prefer children.'

'Here she is! My pretty angel!' Minnie brought in the tiny girl. She had Dora's pink and pointy chin but otherwise she was a lovely baby, all smiles and tousled curls.

'You've grown fond of her, haven't you?' Mother said.

'You're a mother!' Minnie rocked the child. 'I don't have to tell you!'

'What about Dora? What if she comes back?'

'She won't come back. The police could get the wrong idea about her and Stefan – start asking where they got all that money. I warn her. It's only fair.'

'Minnie, you are a remarkable woman. After all you have been through.'

'Every family has its ups and downs.' She probed amid the frills to tickle the baby's chin. 'It's what makes people close in the end. That right, Mo?'

Mo had furtively turned up the television set again and was watching *Life with the Lyons*. 'That's right, Ma.'

'Yes, well she certainly is a lovely little girl,' Mother said.

Minnie laughed delightedly. 'Who'd have thought a pair of plain eggs like me and Mo would get such a beautiful child?'

~

When we got home Father was listening to a forlorn piece of opera on the gramophone. 'Where is Miss Taylor?' Mother said.

'Gone.' He gave her a brief, accusing look and pursed his mouth around his pipe.

'Gone where?' She cast a worried glance towards the window, which shut out a blizzardy night.

'With her paramour. All very proper, I daresay. He said he would lodge her with a lady until preparations for their wedding were complete.'

'Mr Carson!' Mother gasped. 'She has gone with Mr Carson. Oh, thank God.'

Had she not been so concerned about Miss Taylor she would have noticed at once that he was in a very bad mood. 'I came home expecting to find my tea and my family. And what do I find? A strange woman and a melodrama which was straight from a penny

273

romance. I begin to suspect that the fellow has not much sense. The woman is clearly touched and he is deluded.'

'How did Miss Taylor react to Mr Carson? She said she would die of shame.'

'Do you know, the woman damn near did die of shame. I could not sit down to eat my tea. She said he could not love her if he knew about her. He told her he knew everything.'

'Oh, poor Selena.' Mother shook her head. 'For such things to happen to such a modest person! What did she say?'

'She said she was grateful for his pity but he must understand that what had happened had made her unfit for marriage. She begged him to let her go.'

'How did he answer that?'

'He said, "Allow me as a man, and an older one, to know a little more than you, my dear. I can promise you absolutely that the sacred union of matrimony will wipe out all that has gone before. When you marry me, you will be a new bride."' You could tell that Father had admired this speech, for he performed it with his pipe held aloft, and Mother smiled, knowing that Selena would believe anything a man told her. Father frowned then, thinking she was not taking him seriously. 'After that they fell into each other's arms. I was ashamed of the man, showing off his feelings. I could not stay and watch.'

'Eugene, be happy for them,' Mother begged. 'I'm so happy. They were both lonely and now they have each other.'

'They are welcome to each other,' Father said irately. 'I suspect that neither one of them has an ounce of sense.'

'You are speaking of your employer,' Mother reminded him.

There was an uneasy moment when he took out his pipe and laid it across his lap like a little dead shrew. 'Not any more.'

'Oh, Eugene! You didn't argue with him?'

'There was no argument, merely the plain fact.'

274

'What . . . ?' Mother sat down in a defeated way.

'That my faith would be endangered by such a position. It was on my mind so I asked a priest. "Undoubtedly!" he said. "Undoubtedly your religion would suffer from exposure to alien rites." I have told Mr Carson that I cannot work for him.'

'Just when life was beginning to look hopeful again.' Already Mother had forgotten the bargain she had made, that she would be ready to give up anything so long as Bridie was safe. 'Where did you get such a notion?'

'It was Bridie! She put a doubt in my head the day of Miss Cornelia's funeral.'

'Bridie,' Mother breathed despairingly.

'And where is that young lady?' Father demanded.

Chapter Thirty

~

That spring a motorcyclist in Salthill ran into a pedestrian while scanning the sky for the Russian sputnik which was due to return to earth with the body of the dog, Laika. The first strawberries of the year appeared on the market at a shilling apiece, and our pocket money was restored. It was still only sixpence but after four years this avalanche of cash fell so heavily on Kitty and me that we found it impossible to spend it all at once. You could buy two packs of new Twinkles in ten heavenly fruit flavours. Midway through the week a consumer urge seized me and I raced to the Honeybee to place an order on the things I would buy when payday came. 'I place an order on a bar of Urney's Café au Lait,' I would say. By Friday the Café au Lait bar was old in my mind, as if already consumed. 'I cancel the order,' I would grandly declare.

Kitty piled her sixpences on the windowsill until there were four of them, and then she went into the Blackrock Stores in Chatham Street and bought a whirlpool bra for one and elevenpence. The brittle, circle-stitched cones clung to her flat chest like sea shells. With her long blonde hair combed out, she looked so exactly like a mermaid that I thought the one that sang inside her had come out and taken her over for good and all.

277

Why had we got pocket money? At first we thought it was to comfort us for the loss of Bridie, but it wasn't the only difference. Mother made lemon drops in a saucepan on the stove. The front door was open because the spring had brought lovely weather, and the sweet acid smell brought children from up and down the road. They watched as the gluey yellow syrup was poured in blobs on to the oilcloth-covered kitchen table. We had to wait while they hardened, and then Mother prised them off with a knife. They were eaten like that, not quite cold and not quite hard. I can still remember the tartness and toughness and a slightly yielding texture that made them pull deliciously on the teeth.

Like animals creeping out to sniff the air after the first thaw, Kitty and I inspected new shoes that had appeared in Mother's wardrobe, the amber bottles in the drawing room that spelled prosperity. We touched the tinsel-feeling new perm that moulded Mother's soft hair. The adults seemed to have noticed nothing. There was a more relaxed feeling in the house, but that might have been the change in the weather. Even the Fines were more at ease. Daniel had been right about motherhood changing Ruth. As she grew larger, she got a sleepy air. As if in sympathy, Daniel was putting on weight. On fine evenings he persuaded her to take a stroll around the streets of red-brick houses. He said it was important for her health, but we knew he wanted to show her off. He wore his pride in his family life like a gold watch.

'What will we wear to Selena's?' Mother leafed through the pages of a women's magazine. 'We have been invited to tea on Easter Sunday.'

'Why would we dress up for Miss Taylor?' we wondered.

'She is Mrs Carson now,' Mother reminded us. 'She is living in Blackrock.'

'We'll wear our New Zealand clothes,' we said delightedly. Since we bought them, they had hardly been worn. They had been chosen for a different climate and a distant place. Blackrock seemed a suitably long way away.

'You've grown up since then,' she said regretfully. 'They wouldn't fit.'

'Clothes cost money,' Kitty said pointedly.

She bit her lip and looked us over, considering. 'I'm not supposed to tell you. Don't say anything yet, but your father has been offered a new job.'

Kitty and I exchanged worried looks. Sometimes Mother made us feel a hundred. Nothing in our house would ever really change. The whole household would hang on Father's moods, borrow on his expectations and crash in a heap when his dreams turned to dust. And Mother would always go along with him and Kitty and I would be bumped in their wake.

'I'll make dresses for Rose and me.' Kitty sounded middle-aged and discouraging. 'We'll get Butterick patterns in Cassidy's.'

'I want you to have new dresses!' Mother noted our wary response. 'This time it's different, it really is. Do you remember when Father was at home after his car accident? He spent a lot of time doing the crossword in the *Radio Review* and he also applied for a lot of jobs. At the time there was no response but now he has been offered a very good management job. He is to choose his own car. He is being taken to lunch in Jammet's.'

'We'll go and *see* the dresses now.' Kitty attempted diplomacy. 'We could pick them out. I could put my pocket money down as a deposit.'

Mother looked downcast, as if we had rejected her instead of the new clothes. 'You don't believe me. You don't trust your father. You think he's to blame for not having work. It's not his fault. It's not anything. It's just the way the world was. Jobs and money have been scarce everywhere. Times are changing. There are more jobs on offer. They say everyone will have money and work in the sixties. You girls will be growing up in fortunate times.'

In our room, Kitty and I stared disconsolately at our reflection in the dressing table mirror. There wasn't a bump, a curve, a rosy cheek, anything to suggest that we would ever grow up. We looked grey and slope-shouldered and we had taken to wearing the dullest and most shapeless clothes we could find so that no one would notice that they didn't fit. 'I think she feels let down by us,' Kitty said. 'Now that she has had her hair done, she wants to have smart, pretty children.'

'What will we do?'

'Bridie!' Kitty said. 'We'll go and ask Bridie.'

Bridie had grown used to good clothes and food and had a sophisticated air. We adored her but she seemed years older than us now, and more like an aunt than a sister. Minnie was teaching her how to cook and she poured us delicious little doll's house cups of coffee while she thought. 'Mother and Father are never going to change and you two aren't going to stand up to them. There is only one thing to do. Take anything that's on offer. Let them figure out how to pay for it.'

'Well, maybe if they didn't cost too much,' Kitty said in a worried way.

'The most expensive you can find!' Bridie instructed. 'They're the grown-ups. If they made the offer they have to keep the promise.'

Kitty chose a shirtwaister in Swiss cotton, primrose-coloured, embroidered with tiny pink flowers and spear-like green leaves, with a wide, tight belt to give her a figure. My dress was scarlet corduroy with a broderie anglaise collar and puffed sleeves. Neither Mother nor Father seemed to notice the cost. We even got new underwear, white panties edged with lace. 'We can stand on our heads without disgracing Mother now that we have new knickers!' I whispered to Kitty. Kitty seemed not to hear. She had gone pale and she trembled. Her fingers nervously stroked the outside of her bag. 'I have to have a Cutex lipstick,' she whispered to me. 'Ice Pink. That's a month's pocket money. I need a stiff slip with layers of blue and pink net.'

'If you save up, you'll have them by summer,' I said.

'I have to have them now,' she said through clenched teeth.

'You could do some sewing!' I got a brainwave. 'Hems and zips. Put a notice in the Honeybee.'

'I need shoes,' she said in urgent tones. 'Black patent slingbacks.'

The dress, which seemed to have satisfied my needs for a lifetime, set up a hunger in prudent Kitty.

'Mother'll lend you her lipstick,' I said.

'Red lipstick!' she snapped. 'That's women's lipstick! I don't want to look like a woman. I want to look like a girl!'

As soon as we saw the house we knew that there was another reason why Mother wanted us to look smart. It was large and handsome, with leaded window panes and a tree-lined drive and a garden. Mother must have guessed from the address that Selena had gone up in the world, but even she was taken aback. 'She may have servants,' she warned.

'The woman had neither looks nor luck until you took up her cause,' Father said reproachfully to Mother.

It was the first time we three sisters had been in the car together in months. It was a strained journey because we were a bit awed by Bridie and Kitty was sulking. Mother had actually bought us new shoes, but they were Clarks sandals. After all the money that had been spent, we still looked like children, although very respectable ones, with bows in our plaits to match our frocks, and new white socks.

'All the girls in my class wear nylons,' Kitty complained. 'I am the only one still in short socks. You are determined to keep me a child.'

'Nylons won't make you look like a woman,' Mother replied, 'and when you look like a woman, short socks won't make you look like a child.'

We were shy on the doorstep, thinking a prim Protestant maid would step out and ask us for our hats and coats, but when the door opened, it was only Miss Taylor. 'Lovely yevening,' she said, and we laughed delightedly and ran around her. In spite of the big grand house, she had not changed at all. When she reached out to gather us up, there were still the thin arms like bent metal pipes in a brown suit. But she wasn't the same. She smelled different. A faint perfume of ferns and flowers came from behind ears which, we now saw, were tipped by softly waved hair. And the brown suit was a downy tweed. There was a row of small, glistening amber beads around her throat, like butterscotch or barley sugar, and they had the same way of holding the light as her hazel eyes. She examined us and exclaimed over us one by one and then she led us into the house, taking Kitty and me by the hand. 'Ye must come and meet my children.'

We were brought into a big drawing room and introduced to Peter and Nina, the two dull-looking children we had seen in Mr Carson's photograph. 'You children run off and play,' Selena said. We children watched each other with suspicion. 'We don't play,' Nina said.

'Spoilt miss!' Selena stroked the dark head and she smiled with conspiratorial pleasure at her husband, who was in an armchair at the fire with a rug over his knee.

Bridie stayed behind with the adults and Nina took Kitty and me to her room. 'Do you have horses?' She showed us the rosettes pinned over her mantelpiece.

'We're not from the country,' Kitty said scornfully.

'We're not the milkman,' I added.

282

'I've been riding since I was four,' she said. 'I won these rosettes at gymkhanas.'

Nina was about my age, but I thought she was the most boring girl I had ever met. I wondered how we were to fill in the afternoon and was about to ask if I could read her *School Friend* annual when Peter spoke. 'Are those real?' He was staring at Kitty, who flung her hands over her chest.

'You shouldn't ask,' she said. 'It's rude. Besides, you're too young.'

'I'm not too young,' he said. 'I'm fourteen. You look young – except for those.'

'I'm almost fourteen,' she said. 'I only look young because Mother makes me wear plaits and kids' shoes.'

'Let your hair loose,' he said.

'No!' She sounded nervous.

'Let me, then.'

'No!'

'You can have a pair of grown-up shoes. We have all Mother's shoes. Father wanted to get rid of them when he married Miss Taylor, so Nina kept them in her wardrobe. You can pick any ones you want.'

'Let's see!' Kitty and I said in unison.

Nina opened her great big wardrobe. One side had her frocks and skirts neatly hung up and pushed to an edge. The rest was occupied by women's suits and dresses and the floor was neatly stacked with women's shoes. Kitty fell to her knees and delved. She came out with two pairs – black slingbacks and gold mules. She rammed them on in a fever. The shoes were wider than her feet and a bit long, but she tightened the straps to the last hole and then walked around in them, clamping them with willpower to her heels. She would not take them off. 'All right,' she said to Peter. 'Do what you want.'

283

He told Kitty to sit on the bed. 'You kids go and play,' he said to me and Nina in a world-weary voice.

'No,' Nina said. 'If I'm giving away Mother's shoes, I'm going to stay and watch.'

He sat beside Kitty, carelessly pulling off her ribbons and then the elastic bands that secured the ends of her plaits, while Nina and I squatted on the floor. Very slowly he untwisted her hair, raking it loose with his fingers every few twists. He watched her closely and she stared straight ahead. The plaits had left her hair crimped and electrified. When it was free, he combed it loose around her face with his fingers. 'You're not a bad bit of stuff,' he said, and then he kissed her. He did this in a methodical way, as if leaving a print for the police. Kitty's eyes widened. 'I'll tell Selena,' she whispered.

'Selena does everything for us and she lets us do anything we like,' Peter said.

'Except we're not used to it, so we don't yet know what we like,' Nina added.

'Then we'd better go and ask her,' I said.

'Yes!' They got up at once. 'Let's go and ask Selena.'

I didn't know if I should follow them, for Kitty was still motionless on the bed. 'Wait!' she whispered.

I heard them chasing each other down the stairs. Kitty rose from the bed as if in a trance and went to stare at herself in the wardrobe mirror. 'They work,' she said, still in a whisper.

'What work?' I whispered back.

For a reply, her two fingers went to either side of her chest. She poked the points of her whirlpool bra, making dents in her new figure. I had a sudden memory of Sissy Sullivan pushing her falsies into her bra, asserting that reality was immemorial to men. 'It's like having wings,' Kitty said. 'Mother can't keep me back. I know how to fly.'

Selena said we should explore the house and then go mad in the garden. 'Mind you have a good poke around the garden,' she said. 'You never know what you might find.' It was a wonderful house, with an attic you could walk into and several pantries and a cellar, and the garden was almost as good as our grandparents' garden, except that it had run wild.

Peter climbed a tree and I showed Nina how I could stand on my head, and then I remembered what Selena had said and I began searching the garden, peering behind hedges and into flower pots.

'What are you looking for?' Nina said.

'I don't know. Selena said we should look. That must mean she has hidden something.'

We all joined in the hunt then, and Nina let out a cry. 'Look!' She had found an egg, dyed pale pink and patterned with flowers and with an initial on the side. 'Oh,' she said in disappointment then. 'It not my initial. It's a "K".'

'That's for Kitty,' I said. 'She's made us country Easter eggs. She must have left eggs for all of us.'

We began a frantic hunt, stopping at nothing until I began to claw away at a strange arrangement of moss and twigs at the base of a tree.

'Don't!' Nina cried in distress. 'You'll disturb them.'

'Disturb what?' I said.

'The little people.' Her voice dropped to a whisper, in case we would laugh. 'Selena says that's a fairy bower.' But Kitty and I grinned delightedly at one another.

There were dyed eggs for each of us. They were the four most beautiful eggs in the world – the colour of pink wine, with a delicate tracery of flowers and on each our own individual initial. 'I'll keep mine forever,' I vowed. But Selena came out and showed us how to roll them down the garden in a game, and we were soon caught up in the excitement of trying to smash one another's eggs. Afterwards we went in to a huge tea which Selena had prepared. At each of our places was a chocolate egg from Bewley's.

'What a lot of trouble you've gone to,' Mother said. 'Haven't you any help in this big house?'

She shook her head and smiled. 'Boris is always after me to get a maid, but why would I pay anyone to deprive me of the pleasure of doing for my own family?'

Mr Carson watched her fondly. 'She is a dear, unselfish girl. As long as I live, I can never get over my good fortune in finding a girl so sweet and good.'

Mother linked Selena's arm as we walked back to the car. 'I don't have to ask how you are getting on. I have rarely seen two people more happy, and you look quite the lady of the manor.'

'I am the happiest woman alive,' Selena said, 'but I'm not the lady of the manor type. Having a little family of my own is riches enough for me.'

As she said this, she foraged in our hands and we felt the sharp edges of folded paper on our palms. She closed our fingers over it in a gesture of intimacy and secrecy. We did not open our hands until we were in the car, and then Kitty almost jumped out of her skin. Selena had given each of us girls a pound note.

Chapter Thirty-One

~

Like spells they lay scattered on the bed; the Pink Ice lipstick, a stiff slip, Bear Brand stockings, a suspender belt and eight pink hair rollers, three large and five small. The slip was best. It was a fairy skirt, with its layers of coloured net crisp as an ice cream wafer. These weren't just dressing-up clothes. Each item was for Kitty alone. They were the right size and they were new. Somewhere, it was an accepted fact that someone like Kitty had a right to them. It had taken a whole day to find everything, for she had to rummage in bargain bins and trawl the bargain basements to find prices cheap enough to buy everything for a pound. When they were taken out of their packages, we gazed in silence at our unfolding future. Without a doubt, it was the best-spent pound in the history of the world.

'Try them on,' I beseeched.

'No, wait. Get me the scissors.'

When I brought them back she was at the dressing table with her plaits undone and a section of hair combed over her face. She took the scissors. Calmly and carefully, as if she was cutting fabric for a dress, she sliced through the hanging section. She looked quite different without her forehead.

'It's not bad,' I said doubtfully.

'It's not finished.' She damped her new fringe with a wet comb and twisted it in sections around the small rollers. The large rollers were made into bouncy anchors at the bottom of her hair. While it was drying, she got dressed, hooking up the suspender belt, twisting back her arms to snap the catch of her bra. She rolled each stocking into an accordion and pulled it slowly over her legs. This long performance made me uneasy. We always just jumped into our clothes in the morning and ran down to breakfast. She looped the belt of her new shirtwaister into the tightest hole. The skirt billowed over the layers of net, making her waist and legs look dainty. The Pink Ice lipstick took the last trace of colour from her pale face and she stepped into the dead Mrs Carson's sling-backed shoes. When she combed out her hair there was a froth of curls at her forehead. The wavy length she snapped into a pony tail.

'Do I look like Debbie Reynolds?' She turned to me excitedly. 'I copied her hair.'

I gazed at her glumly.

'Am I a fright?' she demanded anxiously. 'It's my mouse's eyes. I need mascara.'

'You look fab,' I sighed. Our Kitty was gone. My sister, who was also my independence. To make up for Bridie's departure, I was allowed to go out with Kitty. Now I would lose her too.

'Good!' She jumped up. 'Let's go and try it out.'

'Where?'

'I don't know.' We were not allowed to go to Cafolla's Soda Fountain in O'Connell Street, because my mother said that teddy boys went there. 'The pictures, I suppose. But I haven't any money left.'

'I'll pay.' I was humbly delighted that she meant to include me in the excursion. 'I'll buy you mascara if you like.' So far, I had only spent five shillings, on Tommy Steele's new record of 'Little

White Bull'. I was considering The Smoker's Selection Box, which was the most stylish thing I could think of. It had sweet cigarettes, chocolate cigars, a liquorice pipe, tobacco made of cocoa-dusted coconut strands and a box of edible matches.

We went to *Rooney* at the Savoy. As we passed the pillar on our way from the bus stop, we saw how the loitering youths eyed Kitty, and when the cinema usher showed us to our seats, he winked at her. She did not look at them, but after we were safely past she did a little shimmy of success and her icy cheeks tinged with pink. Each time someone admired her I would say, 'Did you like him?' and she would give a pretend shudder and say, 'Creep!'

'Didn't you like any of them?'

She shook her head. 'I don't like boys. I only want them to like me.'

I almost cried with relief. I wasn't going to lose her after all.

On week days Kitty still put on short socks for school, but when Saturday came, we set off to collect a new set of admirers. I watched from the bed as she re-created herself with bra, suspender belt, stockings, stiff slip, slingbacks and lipstick. It took hours. I just pulled on my clothes when she was finally satisfied. My parents seemed not to notice or to mind. Father was eagerly awaiting his new job. He had been offered his own choice of car and was planning to get a red MG. Mother was painting again, this time a large oil painting, which she worked on in secret in the drawing room. We had spent all Selena's money, so we used our pocket money for bus fare and simply wandered around town, she looking haughty and me giggling when there were looks or whistles. Sometimes we walked to the city and used our bus fare for chips in Woolworth's or ice cream cones. Now that Kitty had broken out of childhood, there wasn't any hurry about growing up. I was completely happy, for I had developed a crush on the new, glamorous Kitty and would have paid money to spend time in her company. She required nothing from boys except admiration and she didn't mind me tagging along. I was no challenge and no competition either.

The ritual of dressing up belonged so much to my sister that it was a surprise when a morning was given over to bedecking Father. The iron smouldered on the stove. He buffed his shoes and clipped his nails and trimmed the neat edges of his moustache as if it was a very small hedge. His hair gleamed with Vaseline Tonic. No one could get near the bathroom, which exhaled pink clouds from the crystals scattered on the tub's scuffed bottom. It was the day of his lunch in Jammet's.

It should have been a festive occasion, but he set off as if heading into battle, with the parting warning that the balance of our future hung on this meal. While he dined in the city's most exclusive restaurant we waited tensely for the portion of guilt that would be ours if he did not get the job.

'How was your meal?' Mother asked anxiously when he returned.

'Peas at five shillings a portion!' he uttered through gritted teeth.

'Oh, dear. He has had a fight with someone,' she sighed as he went to remove his hat and overcoat. 'He hasn't got the job.'

But when he came back down he demanded in belligerent tones: 'Aren't you going to congratulate me?'

'Of course!' Mother sounded almost faint with relief. 'I made a cake.'

'Can I have more pocket money?' Kitty said at once.

'Is that all you can think of?' He rounded on her. 'After all I have been through and all your mother has been through!'

'Now what is the matter?' Mother wondered. 'All that is in the past.' But in fact she knew. In taking a secure job, he was falling to earth. There would be no more great gambles, no prospect of extraordinary fortune. He would have to settle for a normal life. Mother had no such reservations. She let out a long, slow breath as if she had been holding it for years. 'From now on everything will be all right.'

On Saturday morning, as Kitty was putting the finishing touches to her make-up, the milkman knocked. Mother was in the bathroom and called to us to pay him with the money on the hall table. It must have been a luxury to her to be able to put out the coins without having to think about it, but Kitty and I had now forgotten that money had been short and we frequently grumbled about the meanness of Father. Kitty clacked downstairs in her slingbacks. Ages later, when I came down for breakfast, she was still in the doorway. The sad-faced milkman stared at her. He looked as if he was doing some sort of deal. A cigarette went in and out of his mouth and he tapped ash on the porch. Kitty was quite motionless, one knee bent, like a horse. I couldn't see her face. I went downstairs and poured cornflakes for us both.

When she finally appeared she planted two bottles of milk on the table. 'He knows poetry,' she said.

'Who?'

'Jer Cuddy. The milkman.'

'Why isn't he just Milkie? Our last milkman was always Milkie.'

She shrugged and sat down to her breakfast. 'He said I looked like the Lady of Shalott.'

'Dirty old eejit,' I laughed. 'He's about a hundred.'

'No, he's twenty-seven.' A spoonful of cornflakes went to her mouth and stayed there, wilting in milk.

'Come on. Let's go into town.' I tugged at her springy pony tail.

'Not today. I don't feel like it.'

'Oh, I understand,' I said slyly.

'No you don't! You don't understand anything!' she snapped, and she went back upstairs to rustle at the grown-up package in her drawer.

She was odd all week. When the milk van sighed down the street she ran to the window and watched like a cat. What had the new milkman said to upset her? By the weekend she seemed to have recovered and sat at her dressing table spitting in the box of mascara to make her fine lashes dark and lumpy. 'I'll pay,' she said, when the milkman knocked. I waited anxiously but she was back almost immediately. 'Quick,' she said. 'Breakfast! We're going into town.'

For an hour we strolled happily around the shops on George's Street, and then Kitty suggested that we should go to McCullough's music shop in Suffolk Street, where they sold the song sheets of the latest hit records. 'There's a new booth. You can listen to the music.'

We glanced at song sheets while the husky, anguished tones of Connie Stevens filled the shop and Kitty basked in unacknowledged admiration. When the record booth was free we squeezed inside. 'You put these earphones over your ears,' she said. 'What would you like to hear? What about "April Love"?'

'I'd like "Oh, My Papa",' I said.

'I'll go out and ask. You just stay here. Wait for me and don't move.'

The music came right into my ears. I waved to Kitty. She waved back as she walked out of the shop. 'Kitty!' I cried. I thumped on the glass door. It must have been sound proof, for she seemed to hear nothing. By the time I had freed myself from the headphones and run through the door, she was out of sight. Which way had she gone? If I ran after her she might come back and find me missing. She had told me not to move. I stayed in the doorway, peering anxiously up and down the street. Within five minutes I was swamped in despair. It wasn't just the fact that she had the money for our bus fare. She had dumped me. She had run off without telling me where. An hour passed. Several people stopped to ask was I all right? It was only when they did that I realised that tears streamed down my face. By the time Kitty got back I had abandoned hope so completely that I didn't even see her.

'Hey! What's the matter with you?' She looked nervous and excited, as if she could barely keep her feet on the ground.

'Kitty! Kitty! Where were you?'

'Calm down. What's the big deal? You're not afraid to be left alone for a few minutes, are you?'

'You ran off on me,' I whined. 'You never told me.'

'I *did* tell you. I saw a friend through the window and went out to say hello. We just had a cup of coffee.'

'Where did you get the money for coffee?'

'I didn't pay.'

'I'm telling Mother,' I said feebly.

'No, don't tell Mother.' She turned and shook me fiercely. 'If you do I'll never, ever take you out again.'

After that she was never the same. She spent hours staring out of the bedroom window, twirling the end of her pony tail around her fingers. She reminded me of a caged bird that tolerates its captivity but is always on the lookout for escape. She took no notice of me. She didn't even seem to see me. 'Take me out,' I begged, completely denuded of pride.

'I can't go anywhere,' she snapped. 'My nylons are in tatters.' But an hour later, she slipped out of the door.

'Where did you go?'

'The library.'

'You didn't take me!'

'I went to the grown-up section. You're too young.'

I didn't want anyone to see me in tears, so I hid in the wardrobe.

293

I took the paper with me to read 'About Dogs'. There were fewer stray dogs than there used to be. Mother was right. The world was changing. It was getting richer.

When she made the beds, Mother was surprised to hear gulps coming from the wardrobe. 'It's me,' I sobbed. 'Kitty doesn't like me any more. She won't take me anywhere.'

'You must remember that Kitty is a teenager now.' As she drew me out she glanced into the wardrobe with a frown, as if puzzled to find it still filled with children's clothes. 'All teenagers are difficult and moody.'

'You don't take me anywhere any more either!'

'You are all old enough to look after yourselves now,' she said regretfully. There was no use my pointing out that I was still young. She saw me as part of the conspiracy of growing up. If the older girls were turning their backs on her then some day I would do the same, and the sooner she got used to it, the better.

'Have a sweet,' she coaxed, 'There are chocolate marshmallows in my bag.'

Mother's bag was open on the kitchen table. I could see the sweets, her cigarettes, her lipstick, her purse. Just one twist and the purse gaped, showing a mouthful of silver change. Mother wasn't very interested in money and if there was less than she thought, she would assume she had spent it. I took the price of a pair of nylons.

When Kitty came home from school she saw the stockings on her bed. 'Where did they come from?'

'I bought them for you.'

'Where did you get the money?'

'I saved up. Now can we go into town?'

She considered this very carefully. 'All right. So long as you don't pester me or expect me to stay with you all the time. If I ask you to wait for me, you just have to wait. You will understand some day.'

294

We went to Grafton Street. After we had looked into all the windows we paid a visit to Clarendon Street church to light a candle. While I was kneeling, she ducked out and left me there. I knew she would be a long time so I went to confession and told about my theft. 'To steal from your mother is the worst sin in the world,' the priest said. 'If you died this day, your hand would stick up above the grave.'

'Worse than incest?' I asked him, and he said it would be better if I was dead than to be as degenerate as I was, and I should recite twelve Hail Marys. I knelt beside a very pious woman to say my penance. Her eyes were closed and she mouthed prayers with a sucking hiss, as if she siphoned holiness from the air. There was a glove balanced on her head, for women were not allowed to enter church without a covering on their head. Out of interest I slid my hand into the big maroon bag that rested at her side, and a flimsy ten-shilling note, with its tea-coloured engravings, drifted into my hand.

'If you had money, what would you like best?' I asked Kitty when she came back, breathless and edgy.

She glanced around at the dowdy people in church. 'A black lace mantilla,' she said.

Shrouded in the glamorous mantilla she began going to half-seven Mass in the morning before school. She said a nun had asked this of the girls in her class for a special intention. The clack of slingbacks barely grazed my sleep, but one day I woke early and thought I would surprise her. I jumped out of bed and pulled on my clothes in moments. There was no sign of her on the street so I decided to ask the milkman. As the milk van made its rolling progress, he kept just one hand on the wheel. The other embraced a girl in a mantilla and the awful old ape was kissing her. The shock was worse than the time I thought I had seen a body hanging from a tree. I wanted to cry out, 'Kitty!' but her eyes were closed. I knew then I must never say anything, not to her or to anyone else, but when she came home I couldn't help myself. 'I saw you!'

'Saw me where?' She eyed me sharply.

'You were with Jer Cuddy. You were kissing him. He's your boyfriend, isn't he?'

She paused to consider this. 'You shouldn't have been spying on me.'

'I wasn't. I only wanted to surprise you.'

'There is no point in discussing it with you because you wouldn't understand.'

'I would, Kitty. If you told me things I'd understand them.'

She seemed to be wondering whether to trust me. 'All right. I love him.' She said it in an oddly detached way.

The notion was so outlandish that it was a while before I could even speak. 'How can you love him? He's not even good-looking.'

'He's different. He looks right into my eyes.'

'But you don't like boys.'

'He's not a boy,' she said coldly. 'He's a man.'

'We were going to have fun!' I shrilly accused. 'We were going to go out with men who would buy us things and take us to parties. That's what we have been waiting for.'

'When you grow up, you don't want the same things. Now you know why I don't go everywhere with you any more. The things that interest me don't interest you.'

'They do,' I said in a shaky voice. 'They will. I'll prove it to you. You can go on meeting him and I'll say nothing to Mother and Father, and whatever you want, I'll get it for you.'

Kitty's requirements were very particular. She knew the size and the colour and the brand and the price, as if these items had been queuing for a place in her life in all the years of patience and self-effacement. Sometimes it was harder to get exactly the thing she wanted than to steal the money. Occasionally I took an item directly from the shelf without finding the money first. It was easy to explore the shelves of the chemist shop and slip a powder compact or a shampoo in my pocket while holding a sixpenny roll of sticking plaster, which I paid for with my pocket money. Each time I brought her something I begged to be taken out. Now and again she agreed. In the end I did not know if I stole in order to have a role in Kitty's life or for the slight sensation of danger which lessened the pain of being without her. There was only one thing I knew for sure. It was a part of growing up. Sooner or later everyone stole. Sooner or later everybody fell in love.

I always had an excuse ready when I gave Kitty something. A woman in church gave me five shillings. A girl brought it to school for a swap because her mother didn't like the colour. And I practised on ordinary things the deft movement needed to remove money from bags or pockets. When I went to visit Bridie, a swift dip into her biscuit jar to see if I could remove a chocolate whirl without even Mo seeing, and then when I took some dishes down to the kitchen, I picked up the tea towel to cover my hand before making the stomach-churning dive into Minnie's handbag.

'So! A swindler!' Minnie came up softly behind me.

'I was only . . . !' I jumped back.

'I know what you was only. I've seen enough of that kind of only in my lifetime.'

'It's not for me,' I said. 'Please don't tell Mother and Father.'

I could tell she was angry, but after a little while she seemed to relent. 'Please, Minnie,' I begged. 'I'm sorry. I'll never do it again.'

She leaned down on an indignant sigh. 'All right. I don't want to get them upset.' I breathed out a gasp of relief, relief at getting caught so that I would not go on doing it, and relief at getting away with it, and then Minnie let out a yell: 'Bridie!'

Chapter Thirty-Two

~

Until that moment I would have thought the worst thing that could happen would be for Father to find out, but when I saw Bridie's look of disappointment I just hung my head in shame and misery. 'How could you do such a thing?' she said faintly. 'And from Minnie?'

'I saw Kitty kissing the milkman,' I whispered, and she laughed. It sounded so funny I wanted to laugh too but instead I burst into tears.

'Where? Which milkman?' Her voice sharpened then.

'The new one. The one who looks like Norman Wisdom.'

'You mean he tried to kiss her?'

'They meet in secret. Kitty won't take any notice of me any more unless I buy her things. That's why I took money.'

'I could have given you money.' She patted me stiffly on the shoulder for comfort. We had never got used to physical contact. 'Don't worry about Kitty. It's probably just a joke as far as she's concerned. She has always been sensible.'

'No!' I protested on a piercing note. The heartbreak of Kitty's desertion, added to the small luxury of Bridie's touch, broke down the last of my defences. 'She loves him.'

This gave Bridie such a start that she backed away from me, as if

I was the one who had kissed the milkman. 'He's old! He's creepy,' she said in distaste.

'I know,' I cried despairingly. 'He's twenty-seven.'

'He's married!' she recalled in alarm. 'I've seen him at Sunday Mass with his family. And he's more than twenty-seven. He has a daughter your age. Do Mother and Father know?'

I shook my head. 'She made me promise not to tell.' The disloyalty of betraying her to Bridie made me feel worse than stealing the money.

Bridie thought hard. 'I'll have to come home.'

'Please!' I said. 'The Fines are still in the room but Father has work and there's enough money. Oh, Bridie, please come home.'

'No!' Minnie said.

'I have to.' Bridie had tears in her eyes.

'Your sisters are not your concern. They are your parents' concern. Stay here until your studies are finished. Go home for the summer holidays. As for you, Rose!' She put a hand on my shoulder. I was almost as tall as her now. 'With or without this milkman your sister is going to grow up. Stealing won't make a difference. Maybe you can come help me with Betty while Bridie's studying. I'll give you pocket money.'

As always, Minnie was kind and fair, but I was still lonely. 'Bridie, come home,' I pleaded, and Bridie looked torn.

'If you go back now, the money I spent on you will be wasted,' Minnie said. 'I do not like to waste my money.'

'I'll come home this weekend,' Bridie said.

'Hurray,' I breathed.

'Just for the weekend,' she went on. 'Then I must come back here and study. I'll be home for the summer holidays.'

At first I was disappointed by Bridie's proposal, but by the following day it didn't seem so bad. I liked babies and looking after

Betty would be something to do. I felt better now that Bridie knew. I had decided to make a jam tart and was rolling pastry when I heard the shouts. I ran up to the drawing room, where Father was yelling and Kitty was cowering. His arm was raised and I thought he was going to hit her. If he did, I decided, I would belt him with the rolling pin.

'You little trollop! A daughter of mine, cavorting with a married man!'

Kitty's panic-stricken eye made contact with mine and she ducked.

'I didn't tell him,' I said.

'I did.' Sitting in a corner, very subdued and unhappy, was Minnie.

'Minnie, how could you?' I gasped, and Father turned around.

'You knew about this too!'

Minnie stood up. 'I had to tell. I know what misery follows when girls get caught up with married men. I didn't tell for the children to get into trouble. They don't know no more than a bird. Myself I blame the parents, don't even know what's going on under their eyes.'

He calmed down a bit, although he swept over us a look of menace. 'I have always taught my children the difference between right and wrong.'

'That's good,' she agreed. 'Only sometimes it's hard to make right look as right as wrong.'

'I love my children,' he said. 'I think I know what is best for them.'

'I know you love them,' she said sadly. 'Don't do much good me knowing it. Where's Mrs Rafferty?'

'She is out visiting her sick mother. I am grateful for that at least. My wife doesn't like unpleasant scenes.'

'No, Edie doesn't like unpleasantness. Well, at least I got Bridie.'

301

I suppose I should have been grateful that Minnie said nothing about me stealing, but I knew that no matter what she said and no matter what Father said to her, this would be the end of everything for me and my sister. When she left he sent us to our room.

'Did you cavort with him?' I asked Kitty.

'None of you understand.' She shook her head sadly.

'But you kissed him. What was that like?'

'It was a profound experience.'

After that we sat in silence on the bed, awaiting our fate. Nothing happened until Mother got home, when we heard Father telling her it was all her fault and would not have happened if she had paid attention to her family instead of spending her time doodling.

'It's not doodling.' Mother tried to defend her work. 'It's art and it's worth something to me.'

'Is it worth it to you,' he demanded, 'to have one daughter run away from home and the other two harlots before they are in their teens?'

'I'm fourteen,' Kitty said furiously.

'Give me the blasted thing. Hand it here,' he insisted.

'My sketch book? What are you going to do?'

'I am going to throw it on the fire.'

He thundered up the stairs and we slumped on the bed like corpses, knowing our submission would make him worse. He did not even look at us, but ransacked the room, pulling out drawers, throwing the contents on the floor. All Kitty's make-up was taken, her rollers, the sling-backed shoes, each of her dainty pieces of underwear. When he came on the suspender belt he growled. As he left the room with his arms filled with Kitty's accoutrements of allure, he turned and glared at her. 'Why is your hair like that? What happened to your plaits? You look frightful.'

'She only looks frightful because she's crying,' I said.

Mother came up, meekly obeying his order. She brushed out Kitty's hair and wound it into tight plaits. When they were secured she took a handful of hair clips and, combing back the frothy fringe, nailed it flatly against her head.

'Don't!' Kitty's hands flew to her forehead. To have hair grips on show was worse than teeth braces.

Mother let her hands drop. She seemed completely detached from us. 'What became of my little girls?' she murmured in a soft voice.

Over tea, Father outlined our future. Kitty and I were to go nowhere except to school unless accompanied by Mother or Bridie. He even forbade me to babysit for Minnie. Outside of school, we were to stay at home, preferably in our room as he could not abide the sight of us. Mother looked bereft and we could not tell if it was because of what had happened to her drawings or what had become of us.

Kitty wouldn't talk about what had happened. She didn't even cry any more. For a long time she gazed out of the window. She was still there when I went to bed. When I woke I saw her grey shadow shuffling around the room.

'What are you looking for?'

'Anything,' she said in a thin voice. 'I thought there might be a pair of laddered nylons left.'

'What are you doing?'

'I was going to pack a bag, but there's nothing to put in it.'

I struggled against sleep to make sense of what she said. 'A bag . . . ?'

'I'm going away. When the milk van comes, I'll go with Jer.'

'Oh, no, Kitty!'

'Shh!' she warned. 'You don't think I'd stay here, do you? After what I have experienced I can't continue to be treated like a child. I'm sorry, Rose, but after this morning you may never see me again.'

'What about school?'

She looked dismayed and then irritated. I don't think school had even occurred to her. 'We'll move to some other place and I'll go to school there,' she said impatiently.

'What if he doesn't want to move? What if he doesn't want to go with you? What about his wife and children?'

'That's a black lie,' she said. 'There is no wife and children. He would have told me.'

At the faint banshee moan of the milk van, Kitty grabbed her small bag and made for the door.

'Don't forget your schoolbag,' I said, and she gave me a look of contempt. I thought I should tell her that her eyes were puffed from crying and her fringe had a flat and spiky look from the hair clips, but I didn't dare, so I hunched in my blanket saying hysterical Hail Marys.

''Bye, Rose,' she said then in a quaky voice. I heard her light, nervous footsteps on the stairs and wondered if they would wake Father.

Father had got there first. He too had been waiting for the milkman. The van soughed to a stop at our gate and the next thing I heard was the crash of breaking glass as Father launched himself on Jer Cuddy and our two pints exploded in a white lake on the concrete path. Mother and I hurried downstairs. One hand clutched at the front of her dressing gown and the other reached for my hand.

'You cur! You philandering guttersnipe!' In spite of his temper, Father never used physical violence and his fists now went around in a harmless, clockwork way. 'I'll see you in hell! I'll see you in jail! This is the last day you will ever deliver milk to respectable people!'

The surprise was Jer Cuddy. He did not fight back, or even try to defend himself. He just put out his hands to soothe Father, to smooth him down so that Father was forced to back along the path and the two men were soon crowded into the porch. 'Easy now, sir,' he said, as if Father was the troublemaker.

'You have been consorting with my daughter – a minor! That is a criminal offence, apart altogether from the fact that you are a married man!'

'I am indeed a married man, sir,' the milkman said. 'Young ladies, minor or major, are off the agenda, I fear.'

'I have it on the best of authority.'

'Have you a witness?' the milkman asked calmly.

'My own daughter has admitted it,' Father said.

'What daughter would that be?'

'Jer! Jer!' Kitty ran to him. 'I don't care that they know. I don't even care if you're married.' She collided with him so hard that I thought it must hurt her, but he did not even try to catch her. He just looked her up and down as if he'd never seen her before. I couldn't believe it. 'You must be joking, sir,' he coolly remarked. 'She's only a chiseller.'

'Jer!' Kitty cried bleakly. She tried to put her arms around him and he shrugged her off. 'Ugly little thing, ain't she?'

Father now looked doubtfully at Kitty. She wrapped her arms around herself and sobbed so desolately that her lower teeth stuck up, like a baby's.

'You don't want to believe everything kids say.' Cuddy was smiling. 'Housewives, now, that's another matter. I'll say nothing in front of the lady, but I could tell you tales.'

I wanted to defend Kitty, to tell them that she wasn't lying, because I had seen it, but suddenly I wasn't sure. All I had really seen was a black mantilla. Mantillas were all the rage. A lot of women wore them.

'I have no wish to hear your tales,' Father said. 'If you care for

305

your hide or your job you will ask for a transfer. Don't ever show your face here again.'

When the milkman went back to his van, Mother had to hold Kitty back, but he had not left. He returned with two fresh bottles of milk and presented them to Mother. Then he threw his cigarette away on the path.

'Someone clear up that mess.' Father gestured angrily at the spilt milk and broken glass, and then he turned on Kitty. 'Get up to your room, you wretched liar.'

'He called you a liar. Maybe that's not as bad as a trollop. Maybe that means we won't be locked up forever.' I was just saying anything I could to make her feel better. But Kitty had retreated into some private place. The colour was gone from her face and she seemed quite composed. She didn't look grown up but she didn't look like a child either. She was like someone with all the life gone out of them, who just goes on breathing because they have to. 'You believe me, don't you?' she said in a sleepwalking voice.

'Sure. I saw him kissing you.' I was beginning to feel some doubts.

'Because if you don't, no one will ever believe me.' She spoke in the same flat tone. 'I could see from Mother's and Father's faces. They didn't even believe that anyone could love me.'

'They just think you're too young. Everyone liked you in your stiff slip. In the summer we'll go to see Miss Taylor and she'll give us more money and then you can buy the things you need to look like a lady again.'

She shook her head. 'It doesn't matter. I'll never love anyone else.'

Bridie got a shock when she came home for the weekend. She had not known about Minnie's visit. She did her best to talk to Kitty. 'I do understand, Kit, or at least I can sympathise. You felt as if you knew him, or he knew you. Everyone's a stranger in their own family. As soon as you start to grow up you feel separate and lonely. But you've still got Rose and me.'

Kitty did not argue or respond. She wore her plaits and short socks painfully, but dutifully, as if she had used up a whole lifetime's spirit in her brief burst of glamour and romance, and now she was accepting an extended sentence of childhood.

'I'll give you my bike,' Bridie bribed.

'It's all right,' Kitty said. 'I'm not allowed to go anywhere anyway.'

'I'll stay home. Now that Father has some money I'll get him to buy me another bike. You'll be allowed out if you're with me.'

Kitty became a fourteen-year-old spinster. She dragged Mother's old sewing machine up to her room from the cupboard under the stairs, and passed her time in a frenzy of sewing. She didn't care what she made, or from what. Old dresses were cut down into cushion covers, cushion covers into dolls' dresses. The things she produced were neat and spare and finished to perfection. With each hand-sewn hem, she would furiously bite off the thread, throw it on a pile and start on something fresh. It was as if she imagined that if she completed sufficient garments she would earn her freedom.

It seemed to seal our fate when the summer ended halfway through July and it began to rain, heaving, slooshing downpours that gobbled over choked gutters and then crept into people's houses. Motorists entering the Phoenix Park were met by a cascade of muddy water, antlered with branches and brandishing debris. Cars were photographed floating in the streets and the potato crops rotted. Cookery writers suggested apples as an alternative staple to the potato.

Chapter Thirty-Three

~

Bridie was becoming an accomplished pianist. At weekends, when she came home, she practised in the drawing room and Father listened as if waiting for a flaw. After a faultless performance, he gave a grudging nod of approval. She was wearing a grey sweater and a row of pearls. Her hair, which had been drawn back from her face, sprang in small waves around her forehead. I watched with interest as his expression shifted from frowning to puzzlement and then settled into content. His face was quite sweet when he looked contented. I studied Bridie to see what he saw. She was becoming a very good-looking girl, not flighty or sexy, but straight-backed and pure. She was turning into an Ingrid Bergman sort of woman.

As she began another piece, Father left his chair to stand beside her. With one hand, he toyed with an accompaniment. 'If you ever decide to come back for good . . .' he pretended to concentrate on the keys, 'there'd be your own room for you.'

They played well together, and when the piece was ended they smiled at one another in relief. 'I'll fix up the room for you when the Fines leave.'

She beamed and started to thump out 'Chopsticks', but her fingers sank on to the keys as another sound seeped through the house, a moan as thick as blood. Then there was a series of sharp, gasping cries.

'Kitty!' Bridie called as she hurled herself out of the door.

Kitty was on the landing, leaning over the banister, pale as parchment. She motioned to the Fines' room, where there was the choking sound of a cry through clenched teeth. Daniel came out looking distraught, almost demented. He ran halfway downstairs, then stopped. 'Get someone!' He turned to us helplessly.

'What's happening?' Bridie said in a shocked whisper.

'It's the baby.'

'But it's too early,' Kitty stupidly argued.

'I know.' Helplessness and pain and sorrow wound themselves around him. 'Get a doctor.' He lunged back into the room like a drunk.

Bridie ran straight out of the door. 'Get Mother,' she instructed Kitty.

The noises went on for hours. In the end, Mother came down from the room looking worn-out and said that a tiny, perfect baby boy had been born but he had not lived. I was dying to see the miniature dead baby that came out of Ruth, but Mother said that I should go away and pray for it. There seemed to be a great deal of scuffling and tidying before an ambulance came. Daniel was like a ghost. 'She lost so much blood,' he said to Mother. 'What if she does not come back to me?'

Mother brooded unhappily. 'Ruth will be all right but she will need to be looked after. It's time you two set up a proper home.'

He looked utterly bewildered, as if ordinary words were hard to take in. 'This is a proper home,' he said. 'I don't know if Ruth and I would know how to set up a proper home.'

Everyone felt sorry for Daniel, but no one realised how much it would affect Ruth. When she returned from hospital she was strange and sullen. Although she still sat over her books for hours, her eyes were rarely on the page, but stared into nothing in a vague and belligerent way. Sometimes she did not bother to comb her hair.

'That poor young woman,' Mother said. 'She has no idea of the depths of her own passion. She has tried to convert it into ideals, but her heart is crushed in such a rigid cage.'

For a few weeks the whole house was affected by the sorrow that came from the spare room, but then our lives went on and Ruth and Daniel were left to deal with the empty space between them. One day I met Daniel in the hall. He was going shopping and had a string bag on his arm, but he seemed to have forgotten this and stood, staring into space. Loneliness surrounded him and isolated him but it wasn't a dark sort of loneliness. It was bright and cold, like a spotlight on a stage. 'I'm sorry about the baby,' I said.

'We never knew him, but we loved him,' he said. 'That is not much, but it is better than nothing. I think . . .' he began again, in an energetic way, as if about to embark on a more hopeful topic; but his voice trailed off and he fixed his gaze on the yellow bowl that was on the hall table, full of rusty and abandoned keys, as if we lived in a castle. 'I think,' he murmured softly, 'perhaps, I was born to be alone.'

It was agreed that Bridie would return to Minnie until the summer, when she could have her own room. Father threw himself into the task of preparing for her return, whistling as he looked at paint charts and rolls of wallpaper. The pleasant turn that his life had taken meant that he forgave Kitty. In spite of this, we remained shut up in our room.

'Will we run away?' I said. She shook her head.

'Let's go and find ourselves some new husbands, honey.' I dug out our old négligés and offered her a sweet cigarette. She picked up the slinky cast-off warily and began snipping with the scissors she had used to cut her hair. 'What are you doing?' I asked, but the clackety whirr of the Singer was all I got for conversation. The glamorous négligé was chopped and stitched into a chaste nightie with long sleeves.

When she let down her hair at night she looked like the peaky princesses in *Grimm's Fairy Tales*. By day, she wound her plaits around her head and scraped her hair back from her forehead, giving the impression of having made herself into a blade for cutting through the hard surfaces of life. At first I felt sorry for her but I soon found out that she was not to be pitied. She developed a superior air, like someone suffering a fatal illness. What had seemed to everyone else like a shameful and humiliating escapade became her stature. 'I have known what few people have known,' she declared. 'I have been in love.'

'I love Daniel,' I said.

'That's just a kid's crush. To love someone means that you would be willing to die for them.'

It was hard to believe that anyone would die for Jer Cuddy, but I was impressed by her loyalty. In spite of the way he denied her, she refused ever to say a word against him. And she was right about Daniel. Ruth got thin after her baby's death but Daniel stayed round and placid. Ruth grew angrier and more eccentric, and then one day she packed her bag of books and left. She left a note for Daniel to say that she had gone to Paris to join the demonstrations on the Left Bank protesting against the torture of Algerian prisoners. She did not mean to return as she needed to be with true comrades.

Mother told us to leave him alone, but after a couple of weeks I knocked on his door. 'Come in,' he greeted. 'I am glad to see you. I want to show you something.' He led me to the window, and showed off his view. The apple trees were in blossom and little feathery spring clouds were scattered like petals on a blue sky.

'It's just scenery.' I echoed my mother's old contempt. 'How can you care about scenery after all that's happened? Doesn't it annoy you that the world goes on?'

He remained silent for a while, and I thought I had hurt his feelings. When he spoke, it was almost to himself. 'The world goes on. That is the real miracle. Perhaps it is only when one has known affliction, when all comfort is stripped away, that the true beauty of the earth is revealed.'

It's just scenery, I thought crossly. I left him looking out of the window and went back to Kitty. In the end I was drawn by a tide of boredom and curiosity to the centre of her obsession. 'How would you know?' I begged her. 'If you fell in love, how would you know?'

'You will know when you fall in love because it is a feeling utterly unlike anything else in life.' She said this with the harsh authority of a spinster school teacher, condemned to stuffing facts into worthless heads.

Daniel completed his studies and left us to go in search of Ruth. When Bridie came home the whole house changed. She moved into the room and at last it got the perfect lodger. Her presence brought music and serenity and the sense of a grown-up authority that released everyone else from anxiety. Father got his new MG. It was red and sharp and shiny and we were all excited by it and wanted to be taken for a drive, but it was a two-seater, declaring an end to family outings. He took Bridie for a ride. Her red hair and his red car set them apart. They were a team now. Mother did not mind. She was pleased to have peace to get on with her painting. Bridie persuaded Father to let us have the gramophone in our room, and she brought us records and cosmetics, but she didn't rescue us. No one did. I suppose everyone was too busy. They just forgot about us. We never thought of asking for ourselves.

Mother finished her new painting. It was called *The Wedding*, and showed a thin girl with no clothes on, wearing a wedding veil and clutching a bunch of wild flowers. She was plain, but her radiant expression and bright hazel eyes made her beautiful. 'I think it's the best thing I've done. I'm hoping it may be accepted for an exhibition,' she told us excitedly. 'I am waiting for the right moment to tell your father.' Father was absorbed in his new, important job, and at weekends he polished his car, and swept Bridie off in it, proudly lecturing her on its mechanics.

Kitty and I settled into a humid trance. To make the time pass we tried the Pond's Seven-Day Beauty Plan, which promised a radiant complexion in a week, but we rubbed our faces with Pond's Cold Cream for a whole month and the mirror showed no change of heart. Kitty summoned me to the window one evening to point out a visitor at our gate. She had puffed-out blonde hair and a tailored green beret to match her green linen costume.

'Isn't she beautiful? I wonder who it is?' We admired her plumpish legs in glossy tan nylons, elevated on pinnacled shoes. Her face had the same unlikely burnish as her stockings. 'I love her costume.'

'It's Sissy!' I said excitedly. 'Sissy Sullivan! It isn't a costume. She's wearing an air hostess's uniform!'

We ran downstairs, but Father had answered the door. 'I came to see the girls.' Sissy's familiar lethargic tone delighted us.

'You will not set foot inside this house,' Father barked at her.

'Gawny mackerel, could you send them out to me so?' She sounded indifferent and slightly amused.

'Those girls have seen enough bad examples.' He shut the door and we raced back to the window. Sissy looked up and waved to us, but it wasn't just a wave. Her left hand made a gracious curve, like a royal person acknowledging their courtiers, and a shower of icicles flew out from it as the sun glanced off the diamond ring on her finger.

'She's engaged!'

'And an air hostess!' Kitty breathed.

We did not know it then, but signs of the future were already stacked up like presents under a Christmas tree. Already our fingers were scratching at the wrappings. In August, the Americans launched a rocket to the moon, although it exploded after seventy-seven seconds. Germany passed a new law which ruled that half a man's earnings and property belonged to his wife, and Father declared that that nation had been enfeebled by defeat in the War. A small package came for me and Kitty. There was no message, just a crushed green fabric flower and an old green comb. They were Sissy's. She had worn them years before, the night the man came. Kitty clamped the green flower to her hair, just above her ear. I held out my hands like a beggar until she tossed me the comb. What had happened to the baby? I was about to ask Kitty, but then I remembered that only I knew Sissy's secret, and anyway I wasn't really interested in the baby. It was Sissy who concerned me. In spite of her disgrace she had survived. For the first time in months, Kitty smiled at me.

When we wore out 'Green Door' and 'Rock Around the Clock' and the few other pop singles Bridie had brought us, we turned to Father's recordings. It was while listening to the duet from *The Pearl Fishers* that Kitty developed a love of opera and began to sing in her mermaid's voice that would later take her to the stages of Europe. Father inspected Mother's new painting and declared it lewd and vulgar and forbade her to show it. In September, when Bridie went back to her last year of school, Father bought her a brand-new bicycle and she gave Kitty her old cycle.

'It's mine too, isn't it?' I said anxiously. 'You'll give me a carry?' But Kitty reminded me that she was now at secondary school and she and Bridie pedalled away importantly in their uniforms while I trudged off to my old school alone.

315

Walking home one day, I was followed by a dog. I worded an advertisement for 'About Dogs': '*Found. Low-sized dog. Pink around mouth. Very short tail.*' At home, no one seemed to notice him, and outside, no one seemed to want him. I told him everything and he looked at me with great intelligence. It probably only meant that he was itchy, but he kept me going until I was in my teens.

In due course Daniel wrote to say that he had caught up with Ruth in France. He sent me a present of a fountain pen and red espadrilles. Later on came an announcement that he and Ruth had a little girl. He kept in touch over the years until there was a postcard sent from an American university, which mentioned that he and Ruth had split up and that she had custody of their daughter, Edie.

The earliest of these events were blurred and shadowed by the fact that Father bought a television set and we entered and were overtaken by the mesmerising, grainy worlds of *Dragnet* and *Whack-O* and *Life with the Lyons*. That summer when nothing happened seemed the end of time intensely lived. Now and again the rain stopped and the sun made a cellophane sparkle that slowly shimmered into mist. On these hot evenings Kitty and I let down our plaits. We bought dried camomile flowers in the chemist and boiled them into a swirling, fragrant brew in which we steeped our hair. We brushed it dry, stroking downwards with bent heads until the long strands flew around us in a crackling cascade which disturbed dust motes floating in the shadowed pink light. Kitty would put the green flower in her hair, and I twirled the green comb in mine. Afterwards, Kitty was tamed and went back to sewing or reading but I needed something to still me. I stood over the end of the bed, letting the wooden knob of the bedstead rest between my legs, and gazed out at the sky, listening to the tinkling notes of the ice cream van. I never found out where it was, but the music seemed to be getting closer.